RUTHLESS

A NOVEL SET IN GOTHIC VERONA

C. DE MELO

Note from the Author

Italian medieval politics consisted of two factions: *Ghibellines*, who supported the Holy Roman Emperor, and *Guelphs*, who supported the Pope.

The power struggle between the Holy Roman Empire and the Papacy began in 1075 and ended with a mutual agreement in 1122. In Italy, Guelphs and Ghibellines continued fighting well into the fourteenth century.

Francesco I della Scala, commonly known as "Cangrande" or "Big Dog," was born in Verona on March 9, 1291. A fiercely loyal Ghibelline, he was a friend and patron of Dante Alighieri, and is mentioned with affection in Boccaccio's *Decameron*. His relentless military campaigns expanded his territories to include Vicenza and Padua.

After many failed attempts to conquer Treviso, the Veronese warlord finally succeeded in taking control of the city. On July 18, 1329 he rode into Treviso a victorious conqueror, only to die a few days later on July 22, 1329. The diarrhea and fever he suffered prior to his death was documented as the result of consuming water from a polluted spring. Rumors of poison began circulating shortly afterward.

In an attempt to solve the mystery of Cangrande's sudden death, his mummified body was exhumed from its tomb in Santa Maria Antiqua in 2004. Researchers from the University of Pisa studied the toxicology of his remains and found traces of chamomile, black mulberry, and pollen grains from the foxglove flower.

Cangrande's relationship with his wife, Giovanna di Svevia, is open to speculation. The couple failed to produce children, but the warlord sired eight bastards. The children's names were recorded, but little is known about them—or their mothers, for that matter. The following is a list of Cangrande's illegitimate children (in order of birth from oldest to youngest):

Gilberto
Bartolomeo
Francesco
Margherita
Franceschina
Lucia Cagnola
Giustina
Alboino

Most of the events and battles described in this novel are the result of historical research, but this is a work of *fiction*. Many artistic liberties were taken based on Italian medieval traditions, speculation, and a few rumors.

DEDICATION

Thank you, D.

"The Devil is not as black as he is painted."

—Dante Alighieri

My beloved son,

I will be dead by the time you read this letter. There is so much I want to tell you, but I have little time left in this world. You will hear stories about me...Many will be true.

Forgive me.

Your devoted mother,
Agata, Countess Visconti

PROLOGUE
NOVEMBER 1311
VERONA

Cangrande sank to his knees before the magnificent gilded altarpiece. Staring at the intricate gold patterning on the Madonna's midnight cloak, the twenty-year-old warlord contemplated the burden that would soon be placed upon his shoulders.

A liveried page quietly crept into the Palazzo Scaligero's private chapel. "My lord, the physicians have done everything possible."

"Is my brother any better?"

"The barber-surgeon has been summoned."

Meeting Mary's benevolent gaze, Cangrande rose to his feet and crossed himself before exiting the small chapel with a heavy heart.

A cluster of nobles loitered outside the bedchamber where the current Lord of Verona, Alboino della Scala, lay dying. At the sight of Cangrande, the people fell silent and stepped aside to allow him access to the door.

Mastino detached himself from the crowd and intercepted his uncle. "Is Papa going to die?" the boy asked, his innocent brown eyes begging for a lie.

In that instant, the powerful warrior felt as helpless as a child. "I hope not, but we must accept God's will."

The boy sniffed and ran toward his mother, whose glistening eyes betrayed her fear of widowhood.

Cangrande felt the heat of several stares as he gripped the door latch. Taking a deep breath, he entered Alboino's bedchamber ready to face his destiny.

CHAPTER 1
JANUARY 1320
VERONA

Cangrande's stomach growled as he got out of bed. Twice a week, he sacrificed daily sustenance in honor of the Virgin Mary. Having lost his own mother at a young age, he drew maternal comfort from the Queen of Heaven. Rubbing his lower back, he shuffled to the window. Icy air cooled his face as he threw open the shutters and peered down at the courtyard. A scullery maid was on her knees, her wet hands redder than the terracotta tiles she scrubbed. A nostalgic smile touched his lips as he recalled how Alboino used to love reading beneath the potted fruit trees.

Since his brother's death nearly a decade ago, he had done little else but fight for the Ghibelline cause. So far, his efforts had earned him the western region of Lombardy, an excommunication from the pope, and several failed attempts to conquer Treviso.

Ah, Treviso—the thorn in his side.

He closed the shutters and sat on the edge of the bed before massaging the upper part of his leg. His thigh had been pierced by an arrow last summer during the battle against Padua. To prevent stiffness, the physician had instructed him to rub the damaged muscles every day. Such a wound would have barely made an impact during his youth. Now, with his thirtieth birthday fast approaching, the aches and pains were daily reminders of the inevitability of old age.

His valet entered the bedchamber with a bowl of scented water and a cotton cloth. "Good day, my lord."

"What news, Ercolano?"

"Signore Ottavio awaits downstairs."

The warlord ran the dampened cloth on his face and chest,

11

both of which bore battle scars. "Ah, yes. This morning's discourse should be interesting."

"I'm certain it will be." Ercolano helped his master don a wool tunic dyed the color of blood. "Shall I have the servants prepare fruit and bread, or would you prefer pottage?"

Scooping a handful of dried figs from a silver bowl, Cangrande replied, "I'll break my fast along the way."

The Lord of Verona exited the imposing Palazzo Scaligero and crossed the busy Piazza dei Signori with his most trusted advisor at his heels. "Make haste, Ottavio. I don't want to be late."

Eager vendors and dignified magistrates buzzed around the stalls that were set up along the edge of the piazza. Veronese silk merchants tried to entice potential customers by holding up bolts of fine cloth. One even approached Cangrande with a length of ermine.

The Lord of Verona shook his head. "Not now."

The vendor bowed and retreated.

Shivering with cold, Ottavio did his best to keep up with his overlord's brisk pace. The damp winter fog seeped through his wool cloak, settling into the marrow of his bones. "I'm looking forward to hearing the discourse."

"As am I."

"My lord, you *are* aware that Artemisio has already been promised the position of chair."

"So I've been told."

"Signore Dante will be disappointed."

"Of that, I am sure."

Teaching at the Studio di Verona would no doubt have pleased the aging poet. A man of his intellect and literary fame deserved a position of prestige and comfort in his final years.

Ottavio frowned. "So why allow him to—"

"Dante Alighieri is dear to the Scaligeri. He is always welcome in Verona. We will listen to his words today, and treat him with the utmost of respect."

"Of course, my lord, but—"

"*Basta*, Ottavio." Enough.

The arcaded façade of Santa Elena loomed into view as they rounded a corner. Cangrande acknowledged the noblemen and scholars loitering outside the humble church with a polite nod, then entered to take his seat.

Dante Alighieri struck an imposing figure in a long black robe with his silver hair neatly combed beneath a leather cap. The Tuscan studied his audience with an appraising eye before addressing the congregated men. "Good day, my lords. Today I will be discussing the *quaestio de aqua et terra* in the hope of securing your consideration."

Having already read the treatise, Cangrande allowed his mind to wander while the divine poet articulated his cosmic theories. Veronese scholars engaged the guest speaker in a lively debate afterward. Artemisio, famous for his teachings on logic, challenged the Tuscan on many issues. Dante never raised his voice and maintained the stoic demeanor for which he was known.

Cangrande eventually approached his old friend. "An excellent talk, Signore Dante."

"Thank you, my lord, but your stubborn scholars are not convinced by my arguments. It would have been pleasant to stay here for a while."

"And create another literary work in my honor?"

Everyone knew that *Paradiso* was dedicated to the Scaligeri—specifically, Cangrande.

Dante smiled. "Perhaps."

"My cooks are preparing a special meal in your honor."

"Then I shall summon my appetite in their honor." Casting a glance at Artemisio, Dante added, "After that debate, I would relish a walk along the river to clear my head."

"A fine suggestion."

Ottavio remained with the scholars as the poet and the warlord discreetly exited the church. A dirty sky dominated the landscape, transforming the Adige into liquid lead. A few vessels floated down the river, and a spattering of peasants huddled by a fire on the bank.

"Your nephews are doing well, I hope," Dante said while

13

maintaining the relaxed pace of his companion.

"Mastino never ceases to amaze me. Two years younger than his brother, Alberto, and he's already a fierce warrior. The lad if fearless."

"Scaligero blood courses through his veins, so I'm not surprised. They are lucky to have you as a mentor."

"Although I'm a warrior at heart, I do strive to be like my older brothers when it comes to matters of diplomacy."

"You display prudence, my lord, for Bartolomeo and Alboino were fine rulers. They would both be proud of your accomplishments."

"Would they?"

Startled by the Lord of Verona's self-doubt, Dante replied, "Yes, my lord. You are continuing their legacy."

"You flatter me, Signore Dante."

"I may be many things, but a false flatterer is not one of them. Your military conquests are known throughout most of the European continent, thus making you a legend within your own lifetime. That alone must bring you a measure of satisfaction."

Cangrande nodded. "I've been victorious in many battles, it's true, but Treviso is always there to remind me of my failure. You cannot imagine how this troubles me."

"It is only *one* city, after all."

"One city that *challenges* me, *mocks* me."

Aware of the warlord's obsession, Dante concluded, "I dare say to the point of consuming you."

"I am indeed a man consumed."

"There are other cities worth conquering, my lord."

"You are correct, but *heat cannot be separated from fire*. Those are your words, my friend, and they are an apt description of my relationship with Treviso. Our destinies are intertwined, and I will not stop until I have succeeded in my goal."

"One cannot help but admire your determination."

"I appreciate that."

They continued along the river in thoughtful silence. Sooty clouds gathered in anticipation of rain, prompting Cangrande to

14

head toward home. Palazzo Scaligero's impressive Ghibelline crenellations could be seen in the distance.

Dante cleared his throat. "My lord, as far as Treviso is concerned…"

"Yes?"

"Have you ever considered that, *perhaps*, Fate is urging you to focus your efforts elsewhere?"

Cangrande smiled without mirth. "Fate be damned."

Chapter 2
March 1320
Verona

A lone swallow glided across the milky expanse above Verona's rooftops, its forked tail quivering in the wind. My favorite bird signaled the coming of spring; a time of sunshine, blue sky, and flowers. I watched the bird's frenzied flight with a grin.

"Come away from the window," Mother said, placing a meager bunch of kale on the scarred wooden table. "Throw these into the pot. Hurry."

The pathetically thin baby in her arms regarded me with dull eyes as I chopped the coarse leaves. My younger sister recently died, and we were amazed that he didn't follow her to the grave. Despite my sadness over her death, I didn't dare question God's will. I loved Him above all things—even more than I loved Verona or Aunt Serafina. My aunt once told me that God had a plan for everyone, including me. I hoped His plan included wings so that I could fly with the happy swallows. The silly thought almost made me laugh aloud as I tossed a handful of chopped kale into the simmering lentil stew. Unfortunately, some of the pieces missed the target.

Sighing, Mother bent to retrieve them. "Daydreaming again, Agata? Stir the embers lest the fire goes out."

I grasped the poker by the hearth and coaxed the embers to life. Our drafty cottage was in a sad state of disrepair—the thatched roof sported holes, and wood rot had consumed the window shutters.

Mother placed the baby on the straw pallet in the corner. "I'm going to the market. Mind your brother while I'm gone."

"Did Father give you enough money for a new frock?"

Eying my threadbare garment, she shook her head. "You can

easily patch that tear in your sleeve and let down the hem."

"Pina hasn't outgrown anything in years. This dress is getting too tight for me."

"Nonsense, it fits you fine."

Father sauntered into the room. "You'll be married soon enough, Agata. Your husband can buy new clothes for you."

Mother glared at him. "You promised me that she would remain here until she turned fourteen. I need help with this one and, in case you've forgotten, there's another one on the way."

Father glanced at her protruding belly. "Stop whining, woman. Ernestina can help you once the baby is born."

Father often referred to the mute spinster living across the road as an "idiot" but I liked Ernestina. She taught me how to weave dandelion crowns so that I could wear them on my head like a princess.

Mother pursed her lips. "How will Ernestina be paid?"

He waved away her question with a flick of his wrist before helping himself to more ale.

She continued, "So, who is it?" Father's blank look made her frown. "You said Agata would be married soon."

"Don't be meddling in the affairs of menfolk."

"I have a right to know."

"The blacksmith's son—"

Horrified, I whipped around. "Father, please—"

"Shut your mouth, girl. Alvino and his son are respectable men. What's more, they've got coin."

I knew better than to defy my father, whose temper easily ignited at the slightest provocation. My feisty mother, on the other hand, often sported a blackened eye or a bruised lip.

"The boy has a clubfoot," she pointed out, regardless of the risk to her face. "He's practically lame."

Father slammed his fist on the table. "He won't be fucking our daughter with his foot, will he?"

She scowled at his vulgarity. "You're drunk."

Mumbling incoherently, he strayed into the tiny garden behind our cottage to finish his drink in peace.

Mother hastily hid the pitcher in a cupboard, then plucked a basket from the shelf. "I won't be long, Agata."

No sooner had she left than I felt Father's eyes burning into my back from the open doorway. I reluctantly turned around and met his insistent stare.

"Start showing some gratitude. A decent husband, a roof over your head, and food in your belly—that's more than anyone can ask for, don't you agree?"

I nodded and kept my mouth shut. I had no desire to marry, but the thought of staying at home with my parents held even less appeal. Pina, my older sister, wedded the butcher's son last summer. The city's prettiest girls had competed for his affection, but Pina had outshone them all. She reminded us of her "God-given beauty and charm" whenever she gifted us a greasy lump of bacon or a meaty bone. Father enjoyed claiming the latter from the soup and sucking the marrow—when he did this, I hated the sight and sound of it.

"Well, I'm off to find some work," he said before swigging the last of his ale and practically stumbling out the door.

I glanced at my drooling brother. Poor runt. It was only a matter of time before the Angel of Death swooped down upon our household—*again*. The misery trapped within these moldy walls seeped into our words, our food, our clothes...

Obviously, God was testing our faith. Like Job, we would someday be rewarded for our loyalty and devotion to Him.

God has a plan for me.

I wandered to the window and spotted the carefree swallow circling high in the sky. Overcome by envy, I turned away and returned to my chores.

CHAPTER 3
EASTER 1320
VERONA

The Lord of Verona frowned while studying his reflection. Ercolano's head poked out from behind the polished looking glass, which he held upright in his hands.

Cangrande sighed. "Well?"

"You are the epitome of elegance, my lord. The violet silk suits you."

"I feel more comfortable in a hauberk."

The valet hid his amusement.

A mouthwatering aroma from the kitchen prompted Cangrande to sniff the air with satisfaction. "Smell that, Ercolano? We shall feast today."

"You host the finest banquets in Verona."

The valet spoke the truth. His nobles expected good food, fine wine, and decent entertainment during Easter, and he had no intention of disappointing them.

The Veronese nobility and their overlord attended Holy Mass at the Duomo of Santa Maria Matricolare. At the service's conclusion, Cangrande slipped into a brightly frescoed chapel. A magnificent altarpiece depicting the Coronation of Christ dominated the space. He lit a candle while uttering a brief prayer of forgiveness for the sin of gluttony he intended to commit later that day.

Exiting the chapel, he veered toward the rear of the cathedral where an old Norman vestibule still stood. Consecrated in 1187, Santa Maria Matricolare had been built on the site of two much older churches, both of which were devastated seventy years ago during a great earthquake. Cangrande looked forward to visiting the sacred space after the Sunday service, and people knew better than to follow him. His breathing slowed as he entered the cool, dim interior.

The sound of a light footstep drew his gaze. To his surprise, a pretty girl stood amid the columns studying the carved capitals. She wore a tight-fitting frock of homespun wool that accentuated her budding breasts and shapely hips. Obviously, she had outgrown the garment and her family couldn't afford a new one. No father in his right mind would deliberately allow his blossoming daughter to exit the house in such provocative attire. Approaching the girl with silent steps, he took in the flowers strewn into her haphazard braid. A surprised gasp escaped her sensuous lips when she turned her head and noticed him.

Cangrande frowned. "What are you doing here?"

"The same as you, my lord. Enjoying a bit of solitude."

Such impertinence! "Do you know who I am?"

She nodded, her eyes lingering on the sword at his side. "You are the Lord of Verona, the most loyal Ghibelline on Earth, sanctioned by God and favored by the Madonna."

Silver-tongued, too. To his surprise, she didn't flinch when he closed the gap between them. In fact, she pinned him with a steady stare, her eyes glittering in the dimness like gemstones.

He pointed to one of the columns. "You were admiring the capitals when I walked in."

"I like them and so does God."

"We must not presume to know God's thoughts."

"Well, these columns *are* survivors."

"Survivors?"

"God preserved them during the great quake, so..."

"Who told you all of this?"

"My Aunt Serafina. She is a nun at the Convento di Santa Agnes."

"I see…"

"She taught me to read. Father believes it's useless to teach a girl to read. Do you agree with him, my lord?"

Cangrande stared at the precocious girl, baffled. Not even his trusted advisors spoke to him so candidly!

"Well, do you?" she pressed.

"Learning is a privilege afforded to very few," he replied, his tone stern.

"That's exactly what my aunt said, too! She says I'm clever, and that a fertile mind should not be wasted."

"What's your name, clever girl?"

"Agata."

"Your parents must be wondering where you are, Agata. It's not prudent for unchaperoned girls to linger in deserted places." He deliberately eyed her as a wolf would a lamb, then added, "I urge you to be more careful in the future."

This time, he'd succeeded in frightening the girl. She offered him a clumsy curtsey and ran off.

Stopping at the vestibule's exit, she turned around and said, "A blessed Easter to you and yours, my lord."

Resisting the urge to smile, Cangrande inclined his head at the girl. He waited until she was gone before running his hand along the cool, hard surface of a "survivor." Closing his eyes, he inhaled deeply and exhaled until there was no air left in his lungs. He repeated this exercise a few more times, savoring the stillness and silence. After a long moment, he rejoined his entourage.

The Veronese nobles followed their overlord to the Palazzo Scaligero. Everyone congregated in the main hall for the midday meal, and their host raised his chalice to the numerous guests in a toast of good health. Fresh spring greens adorned trestle tables groaning beneath the weight of platters piled with roasted lamb. Dancing and games followed the bountiful feast, but the guests tempered their revelry with moderation for Easter was one of the holiest days of the year. The merriment lasted well into the evening, long after the sun had set.

Somnolent and satiated, Cangrande watched the dancers with detached interest as a pair of oversized mastiffs foraged for scraps at his feet. It was late, and he desired the comfort of his bed—preferably with a partner. He winked at a pretty servant and caught his wife glaring at him over the rim of her chalice.

Arrayed in a gown of samite trimmed with mink, what

Giovanna lacked in charm she made up for with elegant clothing. Once an attractive woman with a shy smile and a pleasant demeanor, the passing of years had transformed his wife into a corpulent shrew. Childless and resentful, she went out of her way to make his life—and the life of his mistresses— as unpleasant as possible.

Fortunately, his sons and nephews held the power to lift his mood whenever Giovanna irritated him, which was often these days. His eldest son, Gilberto, had been entrusted to the care of his best knight and currently served as a young squire. Mastino, the younger of his two nephews, got on well with Gilberto. Both boys were warriors in the making, which pleased Cangrande, who had been knighted by his own father at the age of ten due to his love of the sword.

His second son, Bartolomeo, was like his oldest nephew, Alberto. Pensive and quiet, the studious boys preferred to stay indoors. Someday, they would become political strategists trained in the art of diplomacy.

At one point in the evening, Gilberto approached his father with a falcon on his forearm. "Look, my lord! Do you see how she obeys me?"

"You handle her well, my son. Remember—only offer her a reward *after* she has done your bidding, never beforehand."

"Once she catches the prey."

"Correct." The warlord's eyes shifted to Bartolomeo, who sat beside his mother, Grazia. The sensuous young woman accompanied her aunt and uncle to the Palazzo Scaligero on a regular basis. "What of your brother? Does he enjoy the sport?"

Gilberto shook his head. "He's afraid of the birds."

"Which is why *you* are my favorite. Don't tell your brother I said that." Cangrande ruffled the boy's dark hair while noticing Grazia's low-cut gown. The sight of her ample bosom caused a stirring in his loins. "It's late. You and your brother should be in bed. Go, tell your mother I'll be along shortly."

A servant came forth to take the falcon back to the aviary where the rest of the carnivorous birds were housed.

"Is it true that Bartolomeo is afraid of the birds?" Cangrande demanded once Gilberto was out of earshot.

"Yes, my lord—to the point of fainting if I force him to handle them."

"Let the boy faint. I'll beat the fear out of him, if needed."

The servant nodded, then backed away.

Cangrande saw Gilberto whisper in his mother's ear. Grazia met her lover's hungry eyes and, taking both of her sons by the hand, exited the main hall. The chilly wind outside compelled her to hurry across the piazza to her uncle's palazzo.

Once she had put her sons to bed in the cozy antechamber adjacent to her room, Grazia prepared for her lover's visit. She wiped the perspiration from her brow, chest, and armpits with a dampened cloth before dipping a point of the fabric into a small container of crushed sage and salt crystals. Running the cloth along her teeth, she carefully removed traces of food, then rinsed her mouth with a combination of vinegar, water, and ground mint. Hearing footsteps in the hallway, she hastily let down her long black hair and doused herself with rosewater.

The knock served only as a perfunctory courtesy, for Cangrande possessed the keys to the palazzo's side entrance. He entered quietly and locked the door behind him. Poking his head into the antechamber, he smiled at the sight of his sleeping sons.

Grazia stood beside the bed with open arms. "My love."

The Lord of Verona kissed her lips before burying his face in her big breasts.

CHAPTER 4
VERONA

Many women were forced into godly service out of poverty or after a marriage annulment. Such was not the case with Aunt Serafina. In fact, she had spurned two suitors before joining the convent. My mother's older sister was my favorite person in the world—a true blessing from God.

Serafina visited me often, usually after dispensing bread and comfort to the sick at a hospital near our home. She came over shortly after Easter, so I greeted her at the door and ushered her inside.

Extracting a tiny prayer book from the inner pocket of her gray nun's habit, she said, "I have something for you."

I accepted the book with reverence.

She continued, "You must be careful, for it's worth a tidy sum. If you return it to me unharmed, I'll let you borrow another one."

"Thank you, Aunt Serafina."

"Go on, read the title."

I stumbled over the words written on the cover, sounding them out slowly. Father entered the room and scowled at me.

Narrowing his eyes at Serafina, he demanded, "Why do you teach my daughter such nonsense?"

She regarded him coolly. "I would hardly call reading the word of God *nonsense*."

"Agata will be married soon. She needs to know how to cook, clean, and rear children—nothing more."

Disappointment was clearly etched on Serafina's face as she stared at me in shock. "Is this true, Agata?"

Father took it upon himself to reply on my behalf. "Yes, and it's a good match, too!"

I added sheepishly, "Father has arranged for me to marry Nunzio, the son of Alvino the blacksmith."

Before my aunt could utter any protest, my father pointed his finger at her. "Don't try to talk her out of it, Serafina. Your job is to pray and be an example to Christian women. Marriage is a sacrament, not that *you* would know."

Serafina bristled. "True, but not every woman is suited for matrimony. Mother Anastasia has been praised by the bishop many times for her piety and chaste conduct. She encourages all of us to read and study, so that we may contemplate spiritual matters."

"Oh, I'm sure the bishop doesn't know *everything* about that abbess of yours, does he?"

That my father would refer to a holy woman in such a disrespectful manner shocked me, but I was even more disturbed by Serafina's reaction. Rather than defend her superior, she hung her head in defeat.

"Regardless of what you think of me or the abbess, the sisters at Santa Agnes adhere to the philosophy of the Cluniac monks. Prayer is important, but so is wisdom and understanding of the Holy Scriptures."

Father crossed his arms. "I still don't see the point."

Indicating an empty chair at the table, she said, "You're more than welcome to sit with us and learn. That way, you might see the point."

He grunted and made a comment about women not knowing their place, then stormed out the front door.

Mother, who had witnessed the entire exchange, shook her head in disdain. "He's right, Serafina. There is no need for Agata to be as educated as you are."

"That's where you're wrong," she countered.

"It's not your place to decide what is best for my daughter."

"Women should know more than only dull domestic things."

"You say this because you've never been married."

Serafina crossed herself. "Praise God for *that*!"

"You've always been rebellious. Even now, as you hide behind that nun's habit, you try to corrupt your own niece."

"How can you say such a thing to me? I'm your sister! I want the best for Agata."

"Maybe you don't remember how much you made our parents suffer, but the memories are quite vivid in my head."

"Our parents were fools."

"Serafina!"

There was a moment of tense silence before my aunt said, "How I wish you had chosen the same path as me. Right now, we could be serving God together instead of you being…"

Mother lowered her eyes when her sister trailed off. "You knew my situation...I had no choice but to marry."

Serafina shook her head sadly. "You traded a moment of pleasure for a lifetime of pain. You could have married that well to do—"

"*But I didn't!* What's done is done! Leave it be."

"Forgive me," Serafina offered contritely.

Mother's eyes glistened with unshed tears. Pressing her lips tightly together, she returned to her chores.

I looked from one woman to the other, intrigued. Was my older sister conceived out of wedlock? I didn't dare ask. In that moment, I felt a surge of pity for my mother. She must have had hopes and dreams when she was my age. Had she also fostered the desire to fly away like the carefree swallow? Gracefully swoop into a better life with better prospects?

Serafina leaned close to me and whispered, "Marriage can be a prison sentence if you wed the wrong man. Being a common wife is a terrible waste of a fertile mind. Is this what you want in life—to be miserable like your mother?"

"No, but what can I do?"

Serafina's brow creased in thought as she folded her hands on the table top. "You can claim sanctuary at the convent and declare your desire to marry Christ instead of an ordinary blacksmith."

"Is that what you did when your parents tried to force you into wedlock?"

She smiled wryly. "I scared the first suitor away with my sharp tongue, but the second one had managed to strike an advantageous bargain with my parents. My father beat me when I refused to marry the man, so I ran away."

I pondered her words, then asked, "Why do you hate marriage?"

"I don't hate marriage....Let me explain. The majority of people in this world are poor, dull-witted fools destined for mediocrity. You are neither male nor noble, which lessens your options in life. Becoming a nun is by far the best solution for an intelligent girl like you—trust me."

Mother returned to the room and we both fell silent.

"I need to get some things at the market," she announced, refusing to meet our eyes. "Agata, watch your brother."

I waited until my mother was gone, then said, "I don't want to marry Nunzio, but the Bible commands children to obey their parents."

"You would be disobeying them in favor of serving the Lord—a forgivable sin. Imagine if Hildegard of Bingen chose marriage over God. What a loss to the world!"

The famous German nun had achieved greatness and fame within her lifetime. An artist, a scholar, a musician, and a poet, she had even garnered the respect of famed holy men like Bernard of Clairvaux.

I stood and announced, "I want to claim sanctuary at the convent. Neither of my parents are home, so let us make haste."

"You wish to go there *now*? Are you certain?"

"Yes."

"What about your brother?"

I glanced at the silent child watching us with wide eyes. "I'll leave him in the neighbor's care. Mother won't be long."

I convinced Ernestina to stay with my brother, then left with my aunt. My steps were light as we crossed the city. We arrived at the Convento di Santa Agnes and Serafina produced a key to unlock the iron gate. Once inside, I marveled at the cleanliness and orderliness of my future home. I offered a silent prayer of thanksgiving to God as my aunt led me to the abbess. I was surprised by Mother Anastasia's youthful appearance.

She offered me a warm greeting, then took Serafina's hand into her own. "I've heard so much about you, Agata. I'm happy that your aunt has managed to convince you."

Serafina tossed me an indulgent smile. "My niece will make a fine addition to our convent."

The abbess stroked my aunt's hand in a manner that was oddly intimate. "I have no doubt of that, Sister Serafina. Tell me, Agata, did your parents offer you their blessing?"

I cast a nervous glance at Serafina. "Actually, no."

My aunt added, "My brother-in-law may try to claim his daughter now that he's negotiated a marriage."

The abbess eyed me steadily. "I see."

"Please don't send me home, Mother Anastasia."

"Rest assured, child," she said soothingly. "You are free to live among us as a novice. Later, when the time is right, you will have the opportunity to take the vows. It's a shame you didn't come to this decision before your father promised you to a man. Hopefully, we'll convince him to accept your choice."

My body sagged with relief. *Thank you, God.*

Serafina placed an arm around my shoulder. "Come on, let's get you settled in."

My aunt and the abbess exchanged a lingering look before I was offered a tour of the convent. I was delighted by the pretty cloister garden and the extensive library. I imagined myself researching interesting topics and reading about the lives of various saints. There was also a room dedicated to the mixing of medicines and curatives. Mortars and pestles dominated the surface of a long table laden with various herbs. I liked the art of flower lore and already knew a little bit about it.

"Well? What do you think?" Serafina inquired at the tour's conclusion.

"I am so happy."

She embraced me. "So am I."

I spent my first few hours at Santa Agnes in the library trying to read the titles of books and scrolls. At one point, I smiled and sighed contentedly. Aunt Serafina, seated beside me, offered me a heartfelt smile.

My happiness was cut short when my father showed up at the convent later that day. Banging on the gate, he demanded to see me. Mother Anastasia went outside to deal with him while

Serafina and I lingered in the background.

Father pointed at me through the iron bars. "Insolent girl! I am going to beat you senseless! Do you think you can run away and make me look like a fool?"

The abbess remained silent as my father ranted and raved like a lunatic. He was drunk, of course. People with nothing better to do began to gather around to watch the scandalous scene unfolding outside the convent gate.

When he calmed down a bit, I said, "Father, please, I want to serve Christ and devote myself to God's work."

"Marriage is a sacrament, created by God."

"Yes, Father, but I don't want to marry Nunzio."

"I've already given Alvino my word! You've been promised to his son and you'll do as you're told." Turning his attention to Serafina, he added, "And *you*! Putting her up to this—"

Mother Anastasia raised her hand to silence him. "No one is forced into service. Agata came here of her own accord."

Giving her a dark look, he said through clenched teeth, "Open this gate and give me my daughter."

The abbess peered down her nose at him. "I cannot do that. Santa Agnes is an extension of the church, which is God's house. Anyone can claim sanctuary here, including Agata."

Father leered at her, shocking the three of us. "Is that what you call it in this place? *Sanctuary?* I know all about you..."

His implication prompted the abbess to cast a wary glance at my aunt. "I don't know what you mean."

Lowering his voice so that only she could hear, he said, "I know all about Serafina. My wife told me the stories…Caught her in the act, too. You would know all about those acts, wouldn't you, *Mother* Anastasia?"

The abbess blanched. "How dare you—"

Lowering his voice, he said, "As God is my witness, I will make your relationship public if you don't hand over my daughter. Do you understand?"

To my astonishment, she nodded. I could see from her shocked expression that she didn't anticipate his ruthlessness.

Father glared angrily at me as my aunt and the abbess retreated into the corner. Both were visibly shaken as they spoke in hushed tones. I tried to eavesdrop, but I couldn't make out the words.

Serafina broke away from the abbess and walked toward me, her face a mask of pity and regret. "I'm so sorry, Agata."

"Aunt Serafina, what's happening?"

"It's complicated…"

"What was my father talking about?"

Mother Anastasia rushed over to us, grabbed my wrist, and pushed me toward the gate.

"No," I begged.

"You can't stay here."

I struggled to release myself from her grip, but she was too strong. "Why? Please, don't!"

She unlocked the gate and thrust me toward my father.

***

The twenty-first of May drew many people to Verona from the neighboring villages. The Festival of San Zeno inspired the finest noble households to display colorful tapestries outside their windows. Most of these costly and elaborate fabrics boasted the family's coat of arms or holy images. A solemn procession, which wound its way through sunlit streets, was headed by six priests carrying a statue of the city's patron saint. The Lord of Verona followed the bishop, then came the nobility, wealthy merchants, and, finally, the Veronese citizens.

Serafina accompanied me and my family as we followed the great multitude of people. My parents had accepted her sincere apology—and mine, for that matter—but we were no longer allowed to be alone together. True to his word, my father had administered a sound beating for my disobedience. The entire incident came to be seen as a folly of my inexperienced youth.

I was disappointed with my aunt for not standing up to my father, but I accepted my fate with as much dignity as possible. God's plan for me obviously included the blacksmith's son, and who was I to question His will?

We entered the Basilica of San Zeno and I tilted my head

back to admire the large whale bone suspended from the vaulted ceiling. To my left, a chapel boasted a crocodile bone. Aunt Serafina once told me that it was from the Holy Land. A brave crusader had slain the ferocious crocodile beast—a creature she described as a giant reptile. I imagined it being similar in appearance to St. George's fearsome dragon. Whale and elephant bones hung in other basilicas throughout the city, each one brought to Verona by Christian men. It was widely believed that these exotic bones served as talismans against evil and protected the congregation from the machinations of Satan.

The procession concluded in the crypt. Forty five columns supported the ceiling, each boasting a different design. My favorite capitals depicted expressive faces. The bishop stopped before the wrought iron gate protecting the relic containing Saint Zeno's sacred remains. Mass was sung, communion was offered to all, and confessions were heard after the service.

From where I stood, I could clearly see the Lord of Verona and his entourage. The fur adorning the cuffs of his brocaded tunic appeared enticingly soft and I longed to touch it. He stood beside his fat wife, who wore an expression of disapproval on her doughy face. Perhaps her annoyance had to do with the fact that her husband's gaze kept wandering toward a voluptuous woman standing in attendance with the other nobles.

If the Veronese warlord's eyes looked my way, would he even remember my face after our recent encounter in the vestibule? I doubted it. After all, he was the most powerful man in the Veneto. I was nothing.

After the service, I wandered toward the old marble statue of Saint Zeno. Depicted smiling with a silver fish in his hand, the talented sculptor had rendered the saint's face in such a pleasing manner that worshippers often found themselves grinning back at the effigy. I was no exception.

My aunt paused beside me to study the statue. "You must be terribly angry with me, Agata."

"I'm not angry, Aunt Serafina. Only disappointed."

"Your father's threat frightened Mother Anastasia."

"You as well," I gently reminded her.

She blushed, nodding. "I'm so sorry…How can I correct the wrong I've committed?"

"Continue to teach me and be my steadfast companion."

Tears welled up in her eyes. "Always."

I caught a glimpse of a large, robust young man in a dark wool tunic exiting the church. One hand held a walking stick, the other was placed on his father's shoulder.

My aunt inquired, "Isn't that Nunzio?"

"Yes," I replied, relieved that he didn't hobble like a beggar.

"I hear he's a hard worker and a good son to his widowed father. Hopefully, he'll treat you well."

"Hopefully," I repeated.

Alvino and his son visited our household the following day. Under the watchful eyes of our fathers and my mother, Nunzio and I exchanged pleasantries for the first time.

He carried an iron pot, which he set upon the kitchen table with great pride. "I made this for you myself. A new pot for you to cook in once we are wed."

Most men offered their betrothed a sweetmeat or a posy. Instead, I got a pot—heavy, plain, and practical like my future husband.

Mother declared, "A fine pot, indeed."

I forced myself to appear grateful. "Thank you."

Father suggested we retreat to the garden to get acquainted with each other while he and Alvino discussed the details of our marriage. Mother gave me a warning look as I led Nunzio to the tiny patch of land outside the kitchen door. Three sets of eyes watched our every awkward move from the open doorway.

Nunzio stood with his back to our parents, his eyes glued to the swell of my breasts. "Father says we can marry before the harvest. You're nearly fourteen, yes?"

"I'll be fourteen in August."

"I turn eighteen in December." He studied me with an appraising eye. "You're very pretty, Agata. I would marry you tomorrow. I'm honored to have been chosen by your father."

Lowering my head for the sake of modesty, I saw that his left foot was misshapen and clumsy, turning inward. His clubfoot required a bigger shoe than the one on his right foot.

Out of the corner of my eye, I caught Mother exiting the doorway with two ceramic cups. She handed one to Nunzio and offered me one as well. Father rarely shared his ale with us.

I waited for her to retreat into the house. "Where will we live after we are wed?"

"In my father's house. He's a widower, as you know."

Would I be required to cook and clean for two men? "Do you have a servant?"

"My father pays the baker's widow to cook. Sometimes she tidies up the house and does our laundry."

Relief washed over me. "Donna Giulia?"

"Yes. We won't need her once you become my wife."

He smiled so guilelessly that I didn't know whether to laugh or to be angry. *Oh, how I wish I could join the convent!*

As the silence stretched, his smile faded. "Have I said something to upset you?"

"No..."

My face must have revealed my dishonesty because Nunzio balled his meaty hands into fists and cursed under his breath. "I wanted to bring the ring, but my father said it was best to meet you first. Now, I regret heeding his advice."

"What ring?"

"A wedding band fashioned from gold."

Gold? No one I knew could afford gold—even the parish priest only sported silver. Gold was for high-ranking clergy and members of the nobility.

Nuns didn't wear gold.

He continued, "It was my grandmother's ring and she passed it to my mother. Because I'm an only child, I must pass it on to my wife."

"Where did your grandmother obtain such a treasure?"

"She was a capable midwife who saved the wife and child of a wealthy goldsmith."

A gold ring! I preened at the thought of owning something so fine. Perhaps being married wouldn't be so bad after all.

Noticing my smile, he ventured, "You are pleased, then?"

I nodded. Glancing downward, I smoothed the skirt of my threadbare frock. "I hope to marry you in something better than *this*. It wouldn't do to wear rags on my wedding day with a gold ring on my finger, would it? I say this only to please you, of course, and bring honor to your household."

"I'll see if I can arrange something." His eyes were glued to my breasts again. "I do wish we could marry sooner."

The sound of chair legs scraping across the floor startled us.

Mother appeared in the doorway. "Agata, come inside."

Nunzio followed, his hungry eyes no doubt glued to my backside. Alvino, who hadn't addressed me once, inclined his head in my direction before ushering his son out the door.

Father said, "The wedding will take place in two weeks."

Mother crossed her arms. "I still think it would be better to wait until after the harvest."

"You heard Alvino. Nunzio is eager to marry, and rightly so! He's a healthy young man despite his defective foot." Looking at me, he added, "Alvino's smithy provides most of the weapons for the Lord of Verona's knights. Did you know that, Agata? You'll be living in a house that's bigger and better than Pina's."

While my father's words might be true, my brother-in-law wasn't lame, and my older sister didn't have to care for two men. Naturally, I kept these observations to myself.

"Your father has done well by you," Mother chimed.

"Indeed I have," he agreed. "Smile, and show some gratitude for your good fortune."

CHAPTER 5
VERONA

Everyone suspected Grazia of carrying another boy, some even placing secret bets on the baby's sex. Three sons in a row would greatly please the Lord of Verona—his virility would no doubt be extolled in the city—but he didn't pray for another male in order not to appear greedy or ungrateful to the saints.

Giovanna's foul mood at the onset of Grazia's pregnancy became unbearable as the young woman neared the final month. She and her loyal ladies went out of their way to make the young widow's life difficult, oftentimes insulting her in public.

The third Scaligero bastard, Francesco, entered the world on a sweltering summer night. The healthy boy cried lustfully, but the birth proved fatal to his mother.

Cangrande wept in the privacy of his bedchamber when Ercolano informed him of the tragic news. His beloved Grazia had been his favorite mistress thus far, and the thought of her bleeding to death distressed him.

Grazia's death was mourned by many since she had always displayed an agreeable disposition toward all. Unsurprisingly, Giovanna was not among the mourners. On the day of Grazia's burial, the Lady of Verona lit candles of gratitude to Saint Joseph, the patron saint of cuckolds.

***

Giovanna stormed into her husband's bedchamber two weeks after Grazia's death. "I want them out!"

Ercolano, who was in the process of shaving his master's face, managed to keep a steady hand despite being startled.

Cangrande sighed tiredly. *Not again.*

She continued, "Your motherless bastards must go."

"The children live across the way with their great uncle. What's it to you?"

"They may as well live here! They sit at our table, play in

the courtyard, and they've been sleeping under this roof."

"Be reasonable, Giovanna. I said they could stay here for a few days. The boys are in mourning—they've lost their mother."

Giovanna gritted her teeth. "*Your* boys, not mine. I turn a blind eye to your adultery, but to raise your illegitimate brood in our home as if they are your heirs—"

Cangrande slammed his fist on the nearby table, toppling the water bowl that Ercolano was using to rinse the blade. "Provide me with sons, woman!"

The valet cleaned up the mess with quick efficiency in the ensuing silence.

Glaring at him with unmasked contempt, she said icily, "I don't see how that's possible, husband, when you display such repugnance for our marriage bed."

"That's enough…"

"You seem to have no trouble siring male bastards on your lowborn whores!"

Cangrande grunted in annoyance, but she raised a valid point. When was the last time they copulated? "Leave the children alone. They are no concern of yours."

"They most certainly are my concern."

"I'll instruct the servants to keep them out of your sight."

"That's not good enough." Drawing herself up to her full height, she proclaimed, "Either they go or I go."

Goddamn the woman! Giovanna's father, Conrad of Antioch, was the nephew of Emperor Frederick II. For this reason, he kept a cool head.

"Well?" she prompted, tapping her foot impatiently.

"I will send the boys back to Grazia's uncle."

"No! I want them out of my sight, not living a stone's throw from my home. I don't want them coming and going as they well please."

"Giovanna—"

"Make your choice."

Cangrande heaved a tired sigh. "I will respect your wishes, my lady, for your happiness is my *only* concern in life."

36

Seething in the face of his sarcasm, she bit back an unkind retort and stormed out of the room.

Cangrande met his valet's eyes in the polished looking glass. "Find me a wet nurse and a suitable family."

"At once, my lord."

Two bastard children, a fat wet nurse, and a generous annual stipend were entrusted to the care of a distant relation who lived in the outskirts of the city. His sons would be close enough for him to see them, yet far enough from the palazzo to appease his coldhearted wife.

Gilberto currently lived with the knight in whose service he had been entrusted. Cangrande felt no need to send the boy to live with his two brothers. When Giovanna's temper cooled, he would summon his eldest to train him in the art of warfare.

Driven by obligation, Cangrande visited Giovanna's bedchamber with a love token—a confection of sweetmeats. She was fond of honey and hazelnuts, and these particular treats were shaped like tiny flowers. His duty was to produce heirs, but he disliked the perfunctory acts of copulation almost as much as she did. Although his wife expressed thanks for his gift and begrudgingly received him, she failed to conceive.

CHAPTER 6
VERONA

Donna Giulia showed up on our doorstep with a parcel bound in burlap. "I was told to deliver this to the bride."

Father took the gift from her hands and opened it with clumsy fingers. "What's this?"

I gasped in delight when he held up a dress. Mother pushed him aside and studied the garment at arm's length. Dyed yellow ochre, it boasted a bit of black embroidery on the cuffs and along the rounded neckline.

Remembering my manners, I said, "Donna Giulia, please convey my gratitude to Don Alvino and his son."

The widow nodded before taking her leave.

Mother smiled wryly. "Already spoiling you, I see. A new husband's attention lasts a short time. Enjoy it while you can."

I immediately washed up and donned the dress. Made of decent quality linen, it felt soft against my skin. Spinning in a circle, I almost laughed aloud from the joy of owning something that wasn't handed down to me by my sister.

Pina arrived at the house and her eyes widened in surprise at the sight of me. "Where did you get that dress?"

Father replied on my behalf. "A gift from Nunzio."

Pina's expression soured. "That color is wrong for her."

I shrugged in response to the criticism. The gown was new, clean, and not threadbare—I didn't care about its color.

She eyed my hair. "Well, let's see if I can tame that tangled mane of yours into something dignified."

I sat on a stool as she fished a wooden comb from my mother's rickety cupboard. I winced in pain as she forced it through my long wavy locks.

"It's a shame you weren't born with smooth hair like me," she said, working through a knot.

"Ow!"

38

"Be still!"

I bit my tongue. When she began braiding my hair, I ventured, "Pina, tell me what to expect tonight."

"What do you mean?"

"You *know* what I'm referring to."

"Blood and pain," she replied, pulling so hard against my scalp that I almost cried out again.

Mother flitted across the room and I waited until she was gone. "Is there no pleasure in the act whatsoever?"

Pina peered down her nose at me. "Only whores delight in carnal acts. Decent, godly women do not."

I said nothing more.

Mother entered the room again and placed a wreath of wildflowers upon my head. "We have to hurry."

Flanked by my parents, I walked to the church with anxious steps. I was leaving behind all that was familiar and the future loomed dark and uncertain before me. At least I would be free.

This is God's will…

We were followed by Pina and her husband, Biaggio, who always smelled faintly of offal.

Biaggio commented, "Such a pretty bride."

Pina elbowed him in the ribs and told him to keep quiet.

I turned around and smiled at him. "Thank you, Biaggio."

"Don't become vain, Agata," Pina chided.

I cocked an eyebrow at her. "Like you?"

Pina's nostrils flared. "Mother—"

Father frowned. "Quiet, both of you."

The thick-walled church dated back to the days of Charlemagne. Tiny windows allowed for little light to penetrate the dim interior. Alvino and his son stood at the front end of the nave, while curious onlookers gathered at the back. Father accompanied me to the altar, then handed me over to Nunzio with the grace of a farmer selling a cow.

The priest's expression remained stoic throughout the ceremony. I felt giddy when Nunzio extracted the gold band from his tunic. Taking my hand, he placed it on my third finger.

Mother whispered the word "gold" and Pina let out a soft

gasp. I hadn't told either one of them about the ring.

Serafina, who sat behind my family, caught my eye and offered me a sad smile. I was now what she once termed as a *common wife*. Would marriage really be such a terrible waste of my fertile mind? Only time would tell, I suppose.

Alvino hosted the wedding feast at his home, which was now my new home. True to Father's words, it was spacious and well-appointed. Pina and my mother whispered to each other as their eyes darted throughout the main room of the cottage. The envy I glimpsed in their gazes unsettled me.

Donna Giulia had prepared a wonderful meal consisting of spelt soup, skewers of roasted pigeons, goat stew, hard cheese, fresh bread, liver sausages, and fruit pastries. I had never seen a table laden with so much food!

My family and I ate to our fill, washing the food down with watered ale. By sunset, Father was thoroughly drunk and insisted that we dance to the tune of his bawdy songs. Alvino's face expressed mild displeasure, but he said nothing as I was spun from one man to the next in a merry jig.

Serafina eventually pulled me aside and hugged me. "God bless your union, Agata. Nunzio seems like a good man. You could have done much worse, my dear."

I glanced at my husband, who watched me the same way a child would stare a plate of sweet buns.

She extracted something from the pocket of her habit and placed it in my hand. It was the same prayer book she had let me borrow weeks ago. "I want you to have something special on this day, a book that can be passed on to your children."

"I can't accept this, Aunt Serafina."

"You must. With a little more practice, you'll be able to read all the words written in it."

I turned the pages with the utmost care and admired the colorful illustrations. An overwhelming sadness swept over me. "I'll treasure it forever."

"Remember, I'm here if you need me. You can visit the convent whenever you wish."

I fought back an onslaught of tears. "Thank you."

At the evening's end, the guests dispersed to their respective homes in order to rest for the night. No sooner had Nunzio and I retired to our bedchamber, than he began fondling my breasts and planting wet kisses on my mouth. Limping toward the bed, he practically dragged me along with him.

"Nunzio, please," I cried, almost stumbling to the floor.

He stopped. "Do you like your new frock?"

"I do, but—"

"And the gold ring on your finger?"

I glanced down at my hand for the hundredth time that day and nodded in response.

"More gifts will come your way if you're a good and obedient wife."

I allowed him to pull my new frock over my head. Too poor to afford an under tunic, I had nothing on beneath my wedding dress. Crossing my arms over my bare breasts for modesty's sake, I waited for him to do his business so that I could get some sleep. He didn't move, however.

"You're like a statue," he whispered, his eyes dilating as they roamed over my body. "Your skin is...*perfect*. No scars, no pustules..." He touched my shoulder and ran his hand down my arm. "Smooth as freshly churned butter."

I did my best not to stare at his deformed foot.

Catching one of my furtive glances, he asked, "Does my foot offend you?"

"No," I lied.

Sensing my dishonesty, he admitted, "I hate it, too. I wanted my father to cut it off when I was a boy. Sometimes, I even wanted to die because of it."

His confession moved me to pity. Nunzio wasn't handsome, but he wasn't ugly, either. Big and burly, yes, but not ungainly. Serafina was right, I could have done much worse—even with the clubfoot.

I've heard my parents grunting behind closed doors, but I had never witnessed them in the act. Would I have to get down on all fours like a dog?

"Get in bed," he said.

I obeyed and pulled the coverlet up to my chin.

He got into bed after me. "Have you ever done this with anyone else?"

"Never."

Satisfied, he stretched out onto his back and slid his hand under the covers. I saw his hand going up and down in the vicinity of his manhood until his breathing grew shallow. Suddenly, he rolled over and kissed me. Pinning me under his bulk, he forced my legs apart and pierced my maidenhead.

"Ow!"

Covering my mouth with his hand, he whispered, "Hush, you'll wake my father."

"It hurts!"

"It'll be over soon."

After the initial pain, the act itself was quick.

Father's vulgar words popped into my head. *He won't be fucking our daughter with his foot, will he?* I thought of Pina's words, too. I was gladdened by the fact that I was a decent, godly woman. How could anyone enjoy *this*?

Nunzio rolled off me and fell asleep almost immediately. I shifted away from him and grimaced. My hand crept toward the joining of my thighs and I cringed at the warm wetness upon my fingertips. I was a virgin no more and burdened with the weight of carnal knowledge. Would I conceive?

Did I want a child?

Mother conceived Pina at the age of fourteen…

Startled by my husband's loud snore, I stared at the timbered ceiling until my eyes grew heavy.

The bluish light of dawn filled the small bedchamber when I opened my eyes. I dressed hurriedly and braided my unruly hair before tucking it into a kerchief.

Nunzio sat in the kitchen, waiting to be fed.

"Good morning, *wife*. I allowed you to sleep late since I thought you'd be tired from yesterday's festivities."

Alvino entered the kitchen and took a seat beside his son. "I'll inspect the bed sheets after breaking our fast."

"I already saw the blood," Nunzio whispered, making me

blush in the process.

Alvino stared at me. "I need to see it with my own eyes."

Rolling up my sleeves, I looked around the unfamiliar kitchen. It took a moment to find everything I needed to prepare the morning meal.

The men silently watched as I poked the embers in the hearth to life and fanned the flames. Their stares made me feel self-conscious as I sliced yesterday's bread and placed it on the metal rack by the fire. There was a bowl of apples on the shelf, and a thick shard of cheese beside it. I set both on the table. When the bread was warmed, I presented it to them on a wooden trencher with a smile.

"What's this?" Alvino demanded.

I stole a nervous glance at Nunzio. "The morning meal, sir."

"Do you think us poor peasants, girl? We like hot pottage in the morning with sausage. My son usually eats a boiled egg."

Sausage? Boiled eggs? Despite my embarrassment, I was happy to have married into such a rich household. My family and I were lucky to eat sausage and eggs a couple of times a month, let alone every morning. God be praised!

Alvino continued, "We are successful blacksmiths. Our work requires demanding physical labor. We need to eat well."

I lowered my head. "Please, sir, have patience with me, for I'm still a child in many ways and have much to learn."

My humility seemed to soften my father-in-law, who allowed the faintest smile to touch his lips. My husband, on the other hand, beamed proudly as I set about making pottage, boiling eggs, and frying sausages. I noticed mint growing in the kitchen garden, so I ran out to tear off a few leaves. I boiled some goat's milk and added the mint.

Alvino accepted the cup and sniffed it. "What's this?"

"Boiled goat's milk with mint for stamina. My mother often makes this for my father, so I thought you might like it, too."

He took a sip. "Hmm. Make haste. We have work to do."

Alvino ate to his fill, then entered the bedchamber to examine the sheets. Satisfied that his son had married a chaste virgin, he returned to the kitchen and offered me his blessing before walking down the road to the smithy.

Nunzio lagged behind to kiss my lips. "My father approves of you and so do I. Do we have time for a quick…?"

I pushed him away. "Your father is waiting for you."

Nunzio looked out the window. The apprentices were fanning the fires and the sound of hammers on steel filled the air. Sighing, he patted my bottom before limping out the door.

I consumed a bit of pottage, then scoured the kitchen table, washed the sheets, and fed the chickens and goats outside in the pen. I collected the eggs from the hens, cleaned out the henhouse, and fed the rabbits. To my delight, one of the females had recently birthed a litter. I couldn't resist cuddling a soft little ball of fur before going inside to continue my chores.

I would never starve in this house.

At midday, I walked to the smithy with bread, cheese, and a jug of watered ale. A few of the shirtless apprentices were covered in soot and sweat. My eyes traced the sinuous lines of their lean, muscled bodies. Their chiseled arms and shoulders were strong from hammering steel, and I wondered if their flesh felt as firm as it appeared. I caught Alvino watching me intently, and blushed to the roots of my hair.

By supper time, I could barely keep my eyes open. With no one to help me, I was forced to do everything by myself. Too exhausted to eat, I picked at my food and listened as the men exchanged ideas on how to craft a better sword. My ears perked when they mentioned Cangrande's latest military endeavor. Since the smithy provided many of the weapons for our ruler, soldiers came and went with frequency, exchanging tidbits of gossip and current news.

Cangrande had no legitimate heirs, yet he had already sired three bastard sons—I wondered how the Lady of Verona felt about that…

"Agata!"

I jumped. "Yes, Nunzio?"

"I'd like some more of that tasty stew."

"I'm glad you like it." My eyes shifted to Alvino and I waited for him to compliment my cooking, but he said nothing.

After supper, I washed the plates, cleaned the kitchen, and went to bed. I was practically asleep under Nunzio's weight as he grunted and bucked between my thighs. I invented stories in my head to keep myself entertained as he did his business. Sometimes, I imagined myself as a wealthy lord upon a fine horse. Where would I go if I had all the money in the world?

The next day was the same as the first, and so on throughout the week. I couldn't tell the difference between one day and the next because they all bled into one another. It didn't take me long to realize that marriage didn't offer the freedom I had naïvely envisioned. I didn't question God's will, but I did wonder how being wed to Nunzio could be my reward for being a good and loyal Christian. I comforted myself with the fact that God revealed things in His own time. All I needed was faith.

The monotony of married life was broken only on Sundays. Holy Mass served as a weekly respite from my endless chores. During the sermon, I contemplated the frescoed walls, admiring the luminous colors. Sometimes, I imagined myself as an angel flying above the congregation in a billowing robe the color of fire. My wings were never white in these fantasies, but deep blue—like those of a swallow. I could almost feel myself gliding on the wind's current without a care in the world.

***

My sister, Bettina, was born in late July. Weakened by the difficult birth, my mother needed a few days of rest to heal from the ordeal. Pina arranged for Ernestina to help with the housework and cooking, while she and I took turns caring for the baby.

Nunzio noticed me getting ready and demanded, "Where are you going?"

"I'm spending a few nights at my father's house to watch over my mother. You said it was all right, remember?"

"Must you go?"

"I told you, my mother needs me."

"We need you, too."

I gave him a level look. "Neither you nor your father have ever undergone birth. It's a messy, painful business. My mother isn't as young as she used to be, and she barely escaped death this time. The house is clean and there's plenty of food in the larder. I made some rabbit stew for your supper—it's being kept warm on the hearth."

"Fine, you can go."

"While I'm gone, I'm sure Donna Giulia wouldn't object to taking over my chores for a coin or two."

He waved his hand. "Don't worry about that."

I assumed this meant that he and his father would care for themselves in my absence. Satisfied, I headed for the door.

Nunzio grabbed my arm. "No goodbye kiss for me?"

I dutifully pecked him on the lips and made to go, but he pulled me closer for a proper kiss.

"I'll miss you," he said, nuzzling my neck.

I tried to wriggle out of his embrace. "I should go."

"What's your hurry, Agata? You wouldn't deny me your wifely dues before abandoning our home, would you?"

Abandoning? I rolled my eyes, which made him frown. Not wishing to argue, I gave in to his lust and then hastily exited the cottage.

I froze at the sight of my mother when I entered her bedchamber. The violet shadows beneath her eyes and the paleness of her skin were the result of blood loss. Thankfully, Pina had left some beef broth in the cauldron, so I heated it up and made sure to pick all the bits of meat off the bones.

"Your father will be upset if I eat all the meat," Mother protested as I spoon-fed her the broth.

"I left him the bones so he can suck out the marrow."

"You know how he gets when he's angry…"

"Don't worry, Mother, I've brought some aged cheese and liver sausages. I left a bit out for Father and hid the rest for your midday meal tomorrow."

She smiled weakly. "Be sure to thank Alvino."

I said nothing. In truth, I had smuggled the food without anyone's knowledge.

I remained with my mother until Pina came to take my place two days later. I returned to my home, opened the door, and

46

almost fainted at the filthy mess before my eyes. Obviously, neither Alvino nor Nunzio had cleaned up after themselves, nor had they bothered to summon Donna Giulia while I was gone.

"Agata!"

Nunzio waved from the smithy while his father stared at me. Ignoring both of them, I marched into the house and set myself to the task of cleaning it.

I was unusually quiet when the men came home that evening. I placed their supper before them, then ground some herbs with a mortar and pestle as they ate their meal.

"Aren't you eating?" Nunzio inquired.

"I'm not hungry," I replied without looking at him.

Alvino's stare was so intense that it almost burned my skin.

"You should eat," Nunzio pressed. "Caring for your mother has taken its toll on you. I swear, you're thinner."

The silence grew heavy and I sensed that my foul mood unsettled the men. Nunzio shifted in his seat several times while casting furtive glances in my direction.

Alvino finally said, "Donna Giulia is sick. That's why she didn't come."

"Oh," I said, surprised by his comment.

"How is your mother?"

I stopped working and looked at my father-in-law. "Better, but far from well. I'm praying for her recovery."

"I'm sure God will hear you."

My eyes lingered on Alvino for only a moment before turning to my husband. "I'd like to see her again soon—perhaps in a few days, if that's all right with you."

Nunzio nodded. "You may go as often as needed."

I went to check on my mother the following week. To my dismay, I found my father in the kitchen laughing and pinching Ernestina's bottom as she kneaded dough for bread. I could see from the poor girl's pained expression that she didn't appreciate this unwelcomed act of lewdness. I cleared my throat loudly.

Father stepped back and regarded me sheepishly. "Your mother is asleep," he muttered before swiping his cup of ale from the table and wandering into the garden.

I entered the room and placed my hand on Ernestina's arm. "My father does terrible things when he drinks. I'm sorry for his bad behavior."

Ernestina nodded in understanding.

I walked to the hearth and held up the poker. "Next time, hit him with *this*."

Ernestina grunted hysterically—her own unique laughter.

It took me a moment to calm the mute down before I went in to see my mother. A bit of color had returned to her cheeks, which meant that she was regaining strength. I held my infant sister, whose rosy complexion belied good health.

"Thank you, God," I whispered in gratitude.

Mother ate some liver sausage and beef broth, then fed the baby. "Alvino is such a generous man. I'll be sure to thank him when I see him."

"No!"

"What?"

"I mean, there's no need. I've already thanked him on your behalf." It was a blatant lie, but I couldn't risk Alvino discovering my thievery.

She yawned. "Here, take the baby and put her to sleep. I need to rest a bit."

I put Bettina in the crib and sang softly to her until she fell asleep. Surprisingly, my little brother still clung to life with tenacity. Sickly and pale, he sat in the corner watching us with a crust of bread in his thin hands. I fed him some of the liver sausage, then played with him for a bit. He soon tired and fell asleep on the straw pallet.

To my immense delight, Serafina came by later in the day. Her cheery face glowed within the pristine white wimple. We embraced and exchanged pleasantries, happy to see each other. After cooing over the baby and sitting with my mother, Serafina pulled me aside to speak with me privately.

"I miss you, Agata," she confessed.

"I miss you, too, Aunt Serafina."

"I hope married life isn't too disappointing."

I sighed. "I knew that marriage would be tedious, but being

a wife to two men is sapping all of my energy."

Alarmed, she demanded, "What do you mean by that?"

"I do everything! I cook, clean, and launder the clothes for Nunzio *and* his father. I'm exhausted by the end of the day. I'm grateful they don't own any fields, otherwise they would harness me to a yoke!"

Serafina chuckled. "Does your husband ever mistreat you?"

"Nunzio is a bit careless in word and deed at times, but he's never cruel or unkind."

"I'm relieved to hear it. What of his father?"

"Alvino treats me well enough."

"Would you describe him as a godly man?"

I shrugged. "Yes, I suppose so. He reads the Bible and attends church regularly."

"What of his character?"

"He's not the frivolous type, and he certainly doesn't drink the way father does. Why do you ask?"

She smiled without mirth. "No reason, my dear. I overheard Donna Giulia speaking with another woman after Holy Mass this past Sunday…"

"What did she say?"

Serafina hesitated. "She's a lonely widow who likes to tell stories, so I'm not going to repeat gossip. Just know that I'm here for you should the need ever arise."

CHAPTER 7
VERONA

Cangrande strode across the main hall with purpose, his footsteps echoing throughout the vast space.

Ottavio hurried toward him with eager steps. "My lord, I have urgent news!"

"It will have to wait, Ottavio. I need to piss."

Undeterred, the man followed his overlord. "We have an opportunity to expand our territories with little military effort."

Cangrande slipped into the privy and peered out the tiny window. His nephews were sparring with swords in the courtyard. Mastino overtook Alberto with hardly any effort. The warlord chuckled as he urinated with the door open.

"My lord?"

"I heard you, Ottavio. Should we attack Serravalle?"

"Yes, and possibly Belluno, but we must act soon."

The Lord of Verona wished that they could attack Treviso as he readjusted his garments and exited the privy. Ottavio followed his master to an alcove where a pair of noblemen stood.

Cangrande demanded, "What news?"

One of the men replied, "Two of our spies arrived in Verona this morning. According to them, the Guelph citadels have been weakened by disease."

The other man added, "Ripe for the picking, my lord. The time to strike is now."

Cangrande eyed both men thoughtfully before calling out for his scribe. Clad in a brown monk's robe, a black-fingered man emerged from an antechamber.

"I wish to send a message to Passerino."

Taking a seat at the oak desk by the window, the scribe produced a piece of vellum and a stylus. After dipping the tip in charcoal based ink, he looked intently at his master.

The Lord of Verona dictated a letter to his old acquaintance, whose real name was Rinaldo dei Bonacolsi. The Mantuan nobleman had helped him in the past, and he hoped to rekindle their alliance for the sake of future military endeavors.

Ottavio suggested, "Perhaps we should offer him money or land to entice him into joining our cause."

Cangrande stared at his advisor in disbelief. "Perhaps we should suck Bonacolsi's cock, too, eh?"

Accustomed to his overlord's unpredictable moods, Ottavio frowned. "My lord?"

"Passerino will get a share of the spoils, the same as last time—no more, no less."

Ottavio's cheeks burned. "Forgive me if I spoke out of turn."

Cangrande waved away the apology. "Leave me, all of you. I need to think right now." When all but the busy scribe retreated, he mused aloud, "It probably wouldn't hurt to inventory the spoils at stake."

Nodding, the scribe added an itemized list of the enemy's lands and castles.

Frenzied barking drew Cangrande to the window. His mastiffs had cornered a wild hare in the courtyard. Desperate to escape, the doomed creature attempted to run past the dogs. His nephews stood by the fountain watching the scene, no doubt placing bets. When the bigger of the two hounds caught the frightened hare in its powerful jaws, Cangrande and Mastino smiled simultaneously. Alberto's face paled.

A soft step made him turn his head. One of his wife's ladies stood in the doorway staring at him. If his memory served him well, the unassuming girl was a recent acquisition to his household.

Cangrande failed to hide his irritation as he demanded, "What does my wife want now?"

"Her ladyship is in want of nothing, my lord."

"Thank God for small miracles," he muttered. "Why are you here?"

"I've come to offer you my services."

"Speak plainly, girl. I have no time for games."

She faltered, her eyes shifting to the scribe seated at the desk. "I was in the corridor earlier and overheard you mention something about *sucking cock*…"

The scribe stopped writing.

Cangrande's eyebrows shot up in surprise. The girl was neither a peasant nor a whore, but rather born and raised in a respectable household. Tiny and slim with a pale complexion and sharp features, she looked like a twelve year old boy. Her eyes, however, twinkled with mischief and the promise of forbidden carnal knowledge.

He was instantly intrigued. "I see. I'm assuming you are well-trained in this art."

"So I've been told…"

"How old are you?"

"Almost seventeen, my lord."

"And your name?"

"Bianca."

Grasping a pitcher from a nearby table, he poured wine into a pair of copper vessels. "Join me."

Hearing this, the scribe hastily spilled sand on the vellum sheets, shook it off, and silently retreated.

CHAPTER 8
VERONA

The Feast of the Assumption of the Virgin Mary took place in mid-August, which happened to be the same day as my birthday. A procession in honor of the Madonna wound its way from the Palazzo Scaligero to the cathedral.

The citizens of Verona were well aware of the devotion Cangrande held for the Virgin Mary. For this reason, the entire city celebrated the holy day with feasting, singing, and games. Vendors flooded the piazzas with stalls full of trinkets depicting the image of the Madonna. Some even sold precious vials of Virgin's milk. Acrobats and dancers delighted children as the smell of roasted meat and tasty pies filled the air.

The heat made me dizzy, whereas Alvino and my husband—accustomed to working closely with fire in the smithy—were immune to the scalding temperature. Wiping the perspiration from my brow, I placed my hand on a nearby wall to steady myself as I watched the colorful spectacle.

Alvino approached me with a solicitous expression on his face. "Are you all right? You look flushed."

"My head is spinning from the heat." I ran my finger along the inside rim of my garment's neckline to let in some fresh air.

His eyes traced the line of my clavicle before clasping my hand. "Come, before you faint."

We ducked into a narrow street engulfed in shadow.

I sagged against the cool brick wall of a building. "This is much better, thank you."

Alvino smiled at me for the first time. "Am I to be a grandfather soon?"

"What? I don't think so…I mean, I don't know."

"So innocent…"

He took a step forward, closing the gap between us. My stomach clenched. Something didn't feel right.

Nunzio ran toward me. "What ails you, Agata?"

Alvino stepped back at the sound of his son's voice.

"The heat, but I'm fine now." I straightened and smoothed the creases from my linen frock.

"Come on, then," my husband said, limping ahead of us. "We'll miss the procession if we stay here."

I accompanied Alvino and Nunzio, craning my neck to get a better view. Lords and ladies followed the priests who trailed behind the bishop. Eight priests carried a painted ceramic statue of the Virgin Mary draped in jewels and late summer blossoms.

"There is Cangrande," Nunzio said, pointing.

Built like a bull, he strode past me in a dark tunic with his head held high. I could easily picture him in a hauberk with sword in hand, slashing through enemy flesh. Surely, he struck an imposing figure on the battlefield. I had told no one of my encounter with him in the ancient vestibule this past spring. It was my own special secret, and I didn't wish to share it with anyone.

The Lady of Verona kept pace beside her husband in a pale red gown. Several nobles followed them, their noses high in the air as they passed us in their finery. Patterned velvets, dyed silks in shades of soft green and pink, gold thread and jewels adorning hems and capes—such staggering wealth!

"That's Cangrande's official mistress," Nunzio said, indicating a young woman who walked alone in the entourage.

Her pretentious cloak caught my eye. Made of finely woven silk, one half was red with silver rosettes, the other blue with gold griffins. Only high-ranking nobles could *dimezzare* their garments. The term referred to costly fabrics being halved or sewn into a herringbone pattern down the front. Protected by law, this particular style distinguished the elite class from everyone else.

"Isn't she violating sumptuary laws?" I asked.

Alvino smirked. "That cloak was a gift from her lover, no doubt, thus the leniency. Also, she's rumored to be pregnant."

Nunzio stared at his father in disbelief. "Already?"

My husband's eyes inevitably dropped to my midsection and

I read the silent question in his eyes: *why isn't Agata pregnant?*

"Who is she?" I asked.

Alvino replied, "Her name is Bianca. Daughter of Pietro della Passione, the illegitimate son of a wealthy nobleman. She was born of a bastard and now carries one in her own womb."

"Still no Scaligero heir." Nunzio pointed out. "His lordship has chosen an ugly one this time. She looks like a boy."

I couldn't disagree with my husband's unkind assessment. Bianca's plain features lacked femininity and her breasts were pathetically flat.

The procession stopped due to an unruly horse blocking the road, so I focused my attention on the Lord of Verona. He exuded confidence and virility. What was it like to bed a powerful man like him? He was bigger and stronger than Nunzio, yet Bianca was smaller than me. Did he cause her considerable discomfort? Cangrande's glittering dark eyes caught mine as these wicked thoughts flitted through my head. To my chagrin, there was a flicker of recognition in his gaze. Could such an important man recall a chance meeting with an insignificant peasant girl?

"What are you doing?" Nunzio whispered.

"Nothing," I replied, lowering my eyes.

"Trust me, you don't want him noticing you." Grabbing my wrist, he added, "I'm hungry and they're selling meat pies across the way. Maybe I'll purchase a sweet bun for you, in honor of your fourteenth birthday."

"I'd like that."

Later that night, after Nunzio had done his business, he inquired, "Agata, why aren't you with child?"

The question caught me off guard. He was usually snoring by now. "I don't know."

"You aren't taking any herbs to prevent—"

"No!" I exclaimed, crossing myself. "Wipe the evil thought from your head. I would never do such a vile thing."

"I didn't mean to suggest...I want a son."

"You'll have a son if God wills it."

"Am I not doing it right?"

"How would I know? You're the only man I've ever been with, Nunzio."

"Your mother is so fertile. I thought that you'd be, too."

"Pina hasn't conceived yet either."

"Maybe it takes time."

"Maybe."

"I'm glad that you're mine."

I leaned on my elbow to study his face in the moonlight. "Do you love me?"

"Yes," he replied without hesitation.

"Would you do anything for me?"

"Anything."

"Would you allow my aunt to visit me?"

"The nun?"

"Yes, she used to tutor me when I lived with my parents. I enjoy learning new things, and she knows so much. Please say yes."

"What does she teach you?"

"Well, remember that prayer book she gave me as a wedding gift? She was teaching me how to read it. She also knows about the lives of the saints and the history of our great city."

"I don't see the harm in her coming here, so, yes."

I kissed his cheek. "Thank you!"

I rose earlier than usual the next day in order to get all of my chores done ahead of time. With a light step, I made my way to the convent to visit my aunt. Serafina was thrilled at the prospect of tutoring me again.

To my relief, Alvino didn't mind my aunt's visits. As long as supper was on the table and the chores were done by the time they returned home in the evening, neither man objected to my weekly lessons. Now, I had Sundays and Serafina to break up the monotony of my life.

***

Things were going rather well until Mother paid me a visit in early November. To my dismay, her clothing hung loosely on her thin frame. She bore Bettina in her arms wrapped in nothing more than a scrap of fabric. I ushered them both inside and fetched a wool shawl for the baby.

"You haven't been by in a long time, Agata."

"Forgive me, Mother, but I have been so preoccupied these days…"

"Serafina visited me recently and mentioned that she is tutoring you twice a week now."

I nodded. "It began with weekly morning visits. Now she comes twice a week, the second visit being in the late afternoon because Nunzio sits with us sometimes. He likes learning as much as I do."

"I see."

I reached for my sister, taking in her pink cheeks. "Bettina is healthy, God be praised."

"Unfortunately, your brother wasn't."

Wasn't. I crossed myself. "When did he die?"

"Last night."

"He is in Heaven and no longer suffering, at least."

Mother's sly gaze swept over me. "I thought for certain you'd be pregnant by now."

Given my husband's insatiable sexual appetite, I thought I'd be pregnant, too. "I suppose when God deems me ready, He'll fill my womb."

"God isn't the one who fills your womb." She looked around the cottage. "Your father-in-law treats you well?"

"Yes."

"I'm surprised he hasn't remarried. He's a strong man with plenty of work left in him. Not unpleasant to look at, either."

"He's a pious man."

"Do they give you enough to eat?"

"Yes, why do you ask?"

"You're as thin as a reed."

I thought her comment ironic given her emaciated appearance. "Remember those liver sausages I brought you? We eat those regularly, along with fresh eggs and grain, and whatever vegetables I can forage from the garden."

Her eyes widened in surprise. "I underestimated the wealth of this household and, apparently, so did your father. You should be thankful to him for negotiating this marriage."

"I *am* grateful, Mother. You know that."

"Perhaps you can spare a few eggs to show your gratitude? We have nothing in our larder at the moment."

"What about the garden?"

"Your father failed to tend to it while I was ill, and the weeds overgrew…I barely salvaged an armful of kale."

I hesitated before furtively gathering a half dozen eggs from the basket on the shelf. "Here, take these."

Mother tucked them into the deep pockets of her frock without bothering to thank me. "Give me some sausage and cheese, too."

"Our supply is low and Alvino will notice."

"He didn't notice all the other times you've stolen from him. What does it matter, anyway?"

"How did you know that I stole the food?"

"The man treats your father and I like insects."

"That's not true," I countered.

"Oh no? Why did you have to steal the food, then?" My lack of reply prompted her to add, "Can you at least give me some bread?"

"Mother—"

"Do you have flour? I'll take whatever you can spare."

"What if he whips me for stealing?"

"Feeding your family is not stealing. Unless Alvino's snobbery has rubbed off on you. Do think yourself too high and mighty to help your own kinfolk?"

"It's not that. I don't—"

The door opened abruptly, ending our conversation.

The baby in my arms began to wail. "Hush, Bettina."

Alvino stood in the doorway, his expression disdainful. "We weren't expecting visitors today."

Mother smiled a bit too sweetly at him. "Good day, Don Alvino. I was on my way out. It was good to see you, Agata. Please come and visit us soon."

I transferred the baby to my mother. "I will."

"Pina is coming next week. I'll save you some bacon. You

58

can use it to make a nice bean soup for your father-in-law."

Mother left and, rather than return to the smithy, Alvino stared at me. "Agata, pour me some wine."

Unaccustomed to the sound of my Christian name coming from his lips, I stared at him.

"Don't stand there gawking at me. Do as you're told."

"Yes, sir."

He pulled out a chair and sat down. "You're no doubt wondering what I'm doing here in the middle of the day."

I handed him a cup of wine and kept silent.

He took a sip. "I saw your mother enter my house."

"She came to inform me of my brother's death."

"What did you give her?" I gaped at him silently, and he added, "Her sole purpose in coming here was to beg."

"That's not true. My brother—"

"Died three days ago."

"What?"

"Poor, naïve creature. No one in your family cared enough to tell you—not even your aunt."

"Aunt Serafina would have told me had she known."

He waved his hand dismissively. "I ask again, what did you give your mother?"

"Only six eggs."

"Only?"

"She'll give me bacon in exchange for them."

"I don't need bacon."

"Forgive me. I didn't think you'd mind."

He took another sip then regarded me thoughtfully. "Your father was sent home from work today."

"Why? Is he hurt?"

"Oh, your mother didn't tell you?" I shook my head and he continued, "Too drunk to handle his tools, he fell down several times and made a spectacle of himself in public. I'm sure we'll be seeing more of your mother now that she and your father are destitute with an extra mouth to feed."

My face burned with humiliation. "Pina provides them with meat almost every week."

59

"Your sister tosses table scraps at them because she pities your poor mother. Everyone in the city knows your father is a worthless drunkard who beats his wife." I lowered my head in shame, compelling him to add, "You must overlook my bluntness, child. I only speak the truth. I also know about all the food you pilfered from my house when you were looking after your mother."

Mortified, I said, "You deserve to know the truth. I took the food because my mother desperately needed it. The birth left her weak and she needed to fortify her blood. You're a good man, Alvino. I know you won't allow my parents and the baby to starve over the winter."

"What did you call me?"

"I meant no disrespect, sir."

"You took what didn't belong to you."

"God will repay you for your Christian charity."

Alvino drained his cup and stood. "Christian charity?"

His eyes swept over my body as he sauntered toward me. Stunned, I backed away until my back hit the wall. "I think I should start making supper."

Stopping inches before my face, he stared at my mouth with longing. "My charity comes at a price."

"I don't know what you mean."

"I think you do," he countered, his hand hovering at the base of my throat. "Say my name again."

"Alvino," I whispered.

"When your father came here seeking a husband for his second daughter, I had no idea…"

"What do you mean?"

He dipped his head toward mine.

I shoved him and ran to the other side of the room. "Stay away from me!"

"Agata, please—"

"Don't!"

Muttering a curse under his breath, he stormed out of the cottage. I set about doing my chores with racing thoughts and trembling hands. My heart hammered within my chest as I

60

recalled the lust in Alvino's eyes. My aunt would surely know what to do in this situation.

I sat down and covered my face with my hands. I couldn't bring myself to tell Serafina. It was simply too humiliating. I thought of confiding in Nunzio, then decided against that, too.

In the end, I told myself that Alvino had fallen in a moment of weakness—he was lonely, after all. The biblical book of Matthew states that the spirit is willing, but the flesh is weak. As a Christian, I pitied Alvino. He was probably feeling remorse and shame for propositioning me. Like Mother said, he was still a strong and virile man. I came to the conclusion that what he needed was a wife.

In the days following the incident, Alvino's behavior toward me was courteous yet subdued. I remained cool and distant, allowing him ample time to reflect upon his folly. I also visited churches and markets in search of suitable widows or spinsters who'd be willing to wed my father-in-law.

During my tutoring session with Serafina, I enlisted her help in this endeavor. "I'm searching for a suitable spouse for Alvino. Do you know of anyone?"

Puzzled, she replied, "Why are you doing this? If he wishes to marry, he should see the matchmaker."

She referred to an old woman in our city who possessed the knack for arranging successful unions.

I replied, "Alvino is a lonely man. It would be good for him to remarry. At least I would have another woman to talk to and she could help me around the house."

"Is that the only reason?"

"Yes," I lied.

"If I find a suitable candidate, I will tell you." Her brow creased with concern before she added, "I have to be honest. I've noticed a change in you, Agata, and it troubles me. You've grown too thin, and I rarely see you smile these days."

The truth sizzled on my tongue but I swallowed it down. "As I've told you before, caring for two men is exhausting."

"Surely, they can afford to hire a servant to help you? If you continue at this pace, you'll become ill."

"You're right. I'll speak to Nunzio."

I broached the subject with my husband during supper later that day. "Could you please hire someone to help me with the housework?"

Alvino and Nunzio stared blankly at me.

I continued, "I am cooking and cleaning for two men instead of one, and I must tend to all the animals."

"The sooner you start bearing children, the sooner you'll have the help you need," Alvino pointed out.

I glared at him. "Well, Nunzio? Are you going to let your father speak for you?"

Alvino stood. "You forget your place, girl."

Nunzio touched his father's arm. "What if we ask Donna Giulia to come here once a week? Agata does work very hard, and she's a good wife."

Swallowing my pride, I arranged my facial features to resemble an expression akin to humility. "Forgive me, Don Alvino, I meant no disrespect."

Alvino accepted my apology. "Fine. Donna Giulia can help you once a week."

"Thank you," I said, smiling at each of them in turn.

True to their word, Donna Giulia arrived at the house two days later. She helped me with the heavier chores like cleaning and moving the henhouse, baking bread for the week, and laundry. It was wonderful to have a lighter workload as well as a pleasant companion. I tried to determine if Donna Giulia knew of any unattached women. I couldn't risk asking her outright for fear of angering Alvino.

Luckily, I eventually encountered a comely widow at the market. She stood beside me holding her small son by the hand. I made friendly overtures and she seemed inclined to chat, so casually I mentioned that I lived with my husband and *widowed* father-in-law. The mention of the latter made the woman's eyes widen with interest. Encouraged by this, I proceeded to list Alvino's good traits: *hard worker, devout man, runs a successful smithy…*

Donna Costanza and her son came over the following day

on the pretense of teaching me how to make a poultice for inflammation. Alvino must have seen them enter the cottage because he burst into the kitchen a moment later.

"Who is this?" he demanded, staring at the woman seated at the table.

Embarrassed by his rudeness, I turned to my guest and said, "Donna Costanza, this is my father-in-law, Don Alvino. Oh, and this is Daniele, her son."

The woman smiled while demurely lowering her gaze. Her son stared at the blacksmith with hope in his eyes.

Alvino's mouth hardened. "A word, Agata."

I followed him outside.

Grabbing my arm, he demanded, "Why did you bring strangers into my home?"

"I met Donna Costanza at the market. She is teaching me to make a poultice."

"I've watched you make poultices and draughts. Who is she? Don't lie to me or I swear—"

"Calm yourself, please. She is widowed like you and I thought that perhaps…She is pretty, don't you think so?"

Realization dawned on him and his face twisted into a mask of fury. "How dare you?"

"Shhh, she'll hear you."

"You've taken it upon yourself to play the matchmaker, have you? I should beat you for your impertinence!"

Costanza exited the cottage with her son in tow. "It's late and I should get going," she said, clearly mortified at having overheard our exchange. "Perhaps we'll run into each other at the market again soon."

I waved goodbye to them, then marched into the kitchen with Alvino at my heels. "There, now you've done it. She overhead you."

"I don't care."

"She was looking forward to meeting you. She lost her husband three years—"

Alvino slapped me hard across the face. "Don't you *ever* humiliate me like that again, do you understand?"

63

Touching my stinging cheek, I gasped. *"Humiliate you?* I was trying to help you! It's obvious you're lonely."

He shook me so hard that I thought my teeth would shatter. "Shut your mouth, you insolent girl. I don't need your help."

I was dumbfounded in the wake of his fury as he stormed outside and returned to the smithy.

Supper that evening was a tense and silent affair. I deliberately avoided Alvino's eyes and said little to him. I doubt that Nunzio noticed my comportment since his head remained buried in his plate for most of the evening.

I went to bed seething that night. After tossing and turning, I finally fell asleep at dawn only to be yanked from slumber by the sound of someone pounding on the door. Nunzio, who could sleep through a tempest, continued to snore beside me. I got out of bed and threw my cloak over my linen shift to see who was making a ruckus at such an ungodly hour. I opened the door a crack only to have it hit me in the face when my father rushed into the room.

"Agata, you ungrateful daughter!"

I pressed my palm to my nose. "Father!"

"Wicked girl!"

"Calm yourself," I said, closing the door.

"You haven't bothered to visit or bring us any food."

"I'm sorry…"

Tears formed in his bloodshot eyes. He stank of stale ale, too. "I have no money. God forgive me."

"What happened?"

"Your mother's breasts dried up days ago. The baby got sick and grew weak. It's been so cold at night…"

"Oh, no! Bettina—"

"The Lord took her this morning."

"Santo Cristo!"

"Your mother has lost her wits—I don't know what to do with her."

"What about Pina? Isn't she providing you with meat?"

"Her mother-in-law has taken ill and the curatives are costly. There's been no meat for a long time."

"Why didn't you come sooner?"

Father's eyes shifted from me to a spot behind my shoulder. "Because of *him*!"

I turned around and saw Alvino staring at us from the doorway of his bedchamber.

Father sneered. "He came by our house after your mother's visit, and warned us to stay away." Pointing at Alvino, he added, "Heartless bastard!"

"Worthless drunkard," Alvino shot back.

My father staggered. "My daughter is dead because of your selfishness!"

Alvino stared coldly at him. "She and all of your other children are dead because you have failed to provide for your family. You spend every cent you make on drink instead of food, then expect me to feed you?"

"Go to Hell," my father muttered.

Alvino's eyes narrowed. "Agata, hand this beggar a loaf of stale bread and send him on his way."

"I'll give him more than bread," I retorted defiantly before packing bread, cheese, eggs, and sausages into a large basket.

My father accepted the food with eager hands. Alvino strode across the room, pushed him out onto the stoop, and slammed the door on his face.

I frowned at my father-in-law. "What kind of Christian turns away a man in need?"

"You should thank me for saving you from that vile family of yours."

Furious, I pushed him away from me. He regained his balance, cupped my shoulders, and slammed my back against the wall. I lifted my hand to strike him and he grabbed my wrist in an iron grip.

"My sister is dead because of you!"

"She would have died sooner or later."

My vision blurred with tears. "Thanks to you it was sooner. I don't want my parents to suffer any more than they already have. My father can't help himself, he's tried to stop drinking many times. Please, help them."

"I told you before that my charity comes at a price."

"No…"

Placing his hand on my breast, he whispered, "Let me have you, and your parents won't starve over the winter."

I slapped his hand away, ran into my bedchamber, and locked the door. Nunzio still snored away in bed. I donned my frock and braided my hair with the guilt of little Bettina's death upon my shoulders. Mother was already starving when she came to see me—no wonder her breasts stopped producing milk. Placing my head in my hands, I wept.

"Agata, what ails you?" Nunzio asked sleepily. When I didn't respond he sat up in bed and rubbed his eyes. "Tell me what happened."

"My baby sister died. My father came here to tell me."

He yawned, then scratched his head. "Don't fret, her tender soul is with God." Then, as an afterthought, he asked, "She *was* baptized, wasn't she?"

"Not yet."

"Oh..."

I went to the door. "I need to start the morning meal."

Neither man spoke to me as I set out pottage, sausage, and boiled eggs. I went to see my mother afterward. She stared straight ahead and barely said two words to me. This was the third child she had lost in one year. I tried to comfort her as best I could, then returned home to do my chores.

During supper that night, Alvino announced, "I paid for a mass to be sung on behalf of your sister's soul."

I stared down at my plate and said nothing.

"I think it's best if you visit your family once a week and bring them some food. At least until your father finds decent work."

Did he just proposition me right under Nunzio's nose?

Meeting Alvino's gaze, I nodded. I lowered my eyes, but not before I caught the look of triumph on his face. As usual, Nunzio was too busy eating to notice anything out of the ordinary.

The next afternoon, Alvino crept into the cottage while I was preparing supper.

"Where is Nunzio?" I inquired nervously.

"He's supervising the making of two swords."

Taking the wooden spoon from my hand, he set it down on the table and cornered me.

I shook my head. "Please…"

His fingertips brushed against my neck before he rested the palm of his hand on the center of my chest. "Your heart is racing."

"That's because I know God is watching us."

His eyes dropped to my mouth. "My son told me, you know."

"What did he tell you?"

"You're flawless…Nunzio said that your skin is as smooth and sweet as freshly churned butter."

"Why would he tell you such things?"

Rather than respond, he kissed me. I tried to wriggle out of his embrace but he tightened his grip. His mouth tasted slightly salty, and he smelled of smoke and iron. When he urged me toward his bedchamber, I cried out in protest. Muffling my screams with his hand, he threw me onto the bed and fell on top of me. I tried to resist by fighting him, but Alvino's strength prevailed.

"Lord forgive me," he mumbled into my hair when he released his sinful seed into me.

Hot tears streamed down my cheeks. "My God, what have you done?"

Alvino got up and adjusted his clothing. "Our sin will be forgiven if we repent."

"*Your* sin."

I received a sharp look for my bold comment. "If you speak of this to anyone, you'll regret it."

CHAPTER 9
VERONA

I visited my parents every Sunday and gave them enough food to last the week. Gradually, they began putting on weight. In exchange for Alvino's charity, I conceded the use of my body. Overwrought with guilt and shame, I feared for my immortal soul. I prayed to God daily with renewed fervor, but I knew it was useless. Venial sins could be forgiven through prayer, but mortal sins—like adultery and fornication— required confession and the sacrament of penance.

I didn't tell Aunt Serafina. I *couldn't* tell her. How does one confess to having made a deal with the Devil? I would risk losing the respect of the only person who really mattered in my life. Too ashamed to confess my sin to our local parish priest, I invented an excuse to cross the river. I explained to Nunzio that my mother needed herbs from an apothecary located beside a remote church on the hillside.

The morning service had reached its conclusion by the time I arrived at the ancient little church. I stood at the back, carefully eyeing the parishioners to make sure that nobody knew me. People lined up to confess, and I waited along with them. Part of me wanted to bolt out the door, but the priest's kind face gave me courage. When it was finally my turn, I quietly confessed my sin to him. My mortification was so great that I couldn't meet the man's eyes. The priest listened in silence, his expression placid.

"The sin of adultery is grave," he said at length. "If you fell in a moment of weakness, God will forgive you, but only if you truly repent and do penance for your sin."

I crossed myself. "I do repent, Father. I love God with my whole heart and it pains me that I've offended Him."

"You must not commit this abhorrent act again."

Despite my shame, I hesitated. "My family will suffer if I

stop giving in to this man's lust."

"Your soul will suffer eternal damnation if you continue to willfully disobey God's commandments," he countered in an authoritative tone. "You *must* avoid this man at all costs."

"He is my husband's father and he lives with us. How can I possibly avoid him?"

The priest slowly searched my face before his eyes roamed over my body. "I see…"

To my horror, he looked at me the same way Alvino did! Glancing over my shoulder, I noticed a few people waiting for their turn to confess. I felt a sudden rush of gratitude that I wasn't alone in the church.

He continued, "In that case, you are not blameless."

I frowned, perplexed. "Father?"

"Unfortunately, you are burdened with the curse of beauty and youth. As a daughter of Eve, Satan can easily set you upon the path of godly men as a stumbling block. It's your duty to be chaste and modest in your dress and demeanor so as not to tempt men into sin." He paused to allow this information to sink in. "Even a smile from you could be interpreted as an invitation to indulge in immorality. Your father-in-law is suffering daily in his attempt to resist your womanly charms, which you obviously possess in abundance."

Too shocked to speak, I merely gaped at the priest. I felt utterly humiliated and defeated.

Pointing at me, he added, "Remember, vanity and arrogance lead to corruption. You must pray to God for humility and forgiveness—one hundred Paternosters and a week-long fast to cleanse your body of mortal sin."

He raised his hand to make the sign of the cross over me, but I turned my back on him and hastily exited the church.

I walked home in a daze of disillusionment. Why did God forsake me in such a harsh manner? Would He have preferred that I let my family starve to death? Why did He allow my parents to suffer and my siblings to die?

I pondered these questions for days. My brooding silence did not go unnoticed by Alvino and Nunzio. Both men avoided me at all costs except when it came to satisfying their lust. At least they were quick about their business. I awoke one morning to the startling realization that I was nothing more than an empty vessel for them to fill at whim. Devastated, I finally decided to tell my aunt.

That very Sunday, I approached her after the service. "Aunt Serafina, I…"

When I trailed off, she placed a hand on my shoulder. "What's wrong, Agata?"

Rather than reply, I embraced her tightly and refused to let go. At first she stiffened in my arms and then she hugged me back.

When I finally pulled away, she studied my face with concern. "Oh, my sweet girl. You've lost your joy."

It took all my resolve to not break down and cry.

She continued, "Is everything all right between you and your husband?"

Unable to bear the burden any longer, I replied, "I have something to tell you."

Serafina gave my hand a squeeze and cast a sidelong glance at Alvino and Nunzio as they approached us.

"Come, Agata. We're leaving," Nunzio announced.

I desperately held my aunt's hand. "Can you come see me tomorrow?"

Her worried eyes searched my face. "I can't tomorrow, but I'll come the day afterward, I promise."

I stared at her as Nunzio led me toward the exit.

I spent the next day preparing for my aunt's visit, mentally rehearsing my words. Sleep eluded me that night as I braced myself for Serafina's reaction to my sinful relationship with a father and son. To my surprise, she failed to come on the appointed day. It wasn't like her to break a promise, especially after seeing how upset I had been on Sunday. When the next day passed with no sign of my aunt, I decided to visit the convent. Although my mind tried to find plausible excuses for her unexplained absence, my gut instinct insisted that something was terribly wrong. A piece of wood barred the convent gate and someone had nailed a sign above it. The crudely painted letters read: QUARANTINE.

My heart instantly sank. I glimpsed a matronly nun walking beneath the portico and called out to her. She came toward me but didn't get too close.

"Stay away, child," the nun warned. "The Devil has brought the sweating sickness to this holy place. Go now, lest you catch the fever, too."

Dismissing her warning, I put my face between the iron bars. "Would you please tell Sister Serafina that her niece, Agata, is here?"

The nun's face fell as she crossed herself. "Sister Serafina passed this morning, I'm afraid."

My head swam. *No, no, no…* "But I…I spoke to her the other day…this past Sunday."

"We've lost three nuns and our dear abbess."

"Mother Anastasia is dead, too?"

The nun regarded me levelly. "Sister Serafina and Mother Anastasia died on the same day, in each other's arms…"

My knees wobbled so I held fast to the bars of the gate to steady myself.

"I'm sorry, child," she added. "God bless you."

She hurried indoors, leaving me staring after her in disbelief. Sinking to my knees, I wept. God had failed me.

Again.

I cried all the way home and shut myself inside of my bedchamber. The men arrived home that night to find me listless on the bed and no food on the table.

At the sight of my pale face and red eyes, Alvino demanded, "What happened?"

"Serafina is dead," I heard myself say before succumbing to another fit of weeping.

"She'll make herself sick if she continues like this," Nunzio said, sitting beside me and holding my hand. "Her pulse is weak. She probably hasn't had anything to eat or drink all day."

Alvino went into the kitchen to heat up some leftover broth that was in the cauldron. Nunzio fed me the broth, and I fell

71

asleep from sheer exhaustion shortly afterward.

Donna Giulia was in my kitchen the next morning. The men had already broken their fasts and left for work. The kind widow helped me with my chores and tried to comfort me in my time of grief as best she could. I appreciated her presence, for I was in no mood to be alone.

I went to visit my mother a few days later and we both cried over our mutual loss. I attended Serafina's funeral with my family, and begged God to give my aunt a good place in Heaven.

***

The first two weeks of December were as bleak as my mood. Alvino came home one day and informed me that he had invited two merchants and their wives for Christmas dinner. He described them as "godly people," which made me instantly dubious since I was angry with God at the moment.

Aunt Serafina was godly, I reminded myself. She was also funny, intelligent, wise, kind, loyal, trustworthy…

I missed her so much that it physically hurt.

"I thought it would cheer you to have something festive to look forward to," Alvino explained.

"Festive," I repeated dully.

"I'll expect you to cook a fine meal for my guests."

"I'll do my best."

I quickly ascertained that hard work served as a distraction from pain. In the days leading to the event, I made panforte and scrubbed the kitchen until it was spotless. I polished the brass plate on the shelf and made sure the painted ceramic vase was strategically placed in order to be noticed by the guests. I also decorated the room with evergreen, which emitted a fresh scent throughout the cottage.

The men came home from work early on Christmas Eve. I stood by the hearth stirring the bean soup for our evening meal when Nunzio handed me a parcel.

"What's this?" I asked, surprised

"Father and I thought you should wear something suitable while entertaining our guests tomorrow."

Two new dresses in one year?

"Open it," Nunzio prompted.

I set aside the wooden spoon and did as he instructed. It was a blue wool gown, finer than the yellow one I already owned, with decorative white stitching around the neckline. Holding it against my body, I muttered my thanks for the gift.

"You were correct, Father," Nunzio said while admiring me. "The color suits her well."

Alvino said nothing, his eyes glittering in the dimness of the candlelit cottage.

I carefully folded the gown and placed it on a nearby stool. "You two must be hungry."

"Famished," Alvino murmured, his gaze full of lust.

I kept my head lowered as I ladled the soup into two bowls and set them before the men.

"I smelled bread baking earlier," Nunzio said.

I placed the fresh loaf on the table and he tore it in half with his sooty hands. After filling their cups with watered wine, I served myself a bit of soup and sat down with them. We abated our hunger in silence.

At length, Alvino said, "Agata, are you certain that you purchased enough food for tomorrow's feast?"

"Yes."

"Did you buy a fat goose?"

"My brother-in-law gave me the best bird in the butcher shop along with some lard. I also bought parsnips and kale, as you instructed."

"You'll have to wake up early—"

"I know," I snapped irritably. "The bird is already dressed and marinating in vinegar."

I had paid a visit to Donna Giulia's cottage earlier in the week at Alvino's insistence in order to learn how to prepare the dishes exactly how he liked them. She couldn't help me tomorrow since she would be spending the holy day with her children and their spouses.

Alvino cleared his throat. "Do not disappoint me."

"I won't."

73

Nunzio set down his spoon, bewildered by our verbal exchange. Alvino and I spoke to each other in a familiar manner, the way married couples do. I was struck afresh by my husband's total lack of perception.

I cleaned the kitchen as the men rested by the fire. When I was done, I removed my apron. "I'm going to bed."

Nunzio moved to follow me, but Alvino said, "Let Agata rest tonight, my son. She has a busy day ahead."

At dawn, I crept out of bed so as not to awaken my husband. I dressed quickly, then immediately set the kale to boil since it took a long time to make the tough leaves tender. The goose slowly roasted while I prepared mashed parsnips.

My mind wandered as I busily peeled and chopped, which is why I didn't hear Alvino's stealthy footsteps. He stood behind me and grabbed my wrist, compelling me to drop the knife. His other hand snaked around my waist, pulling me back against his body. I felt his desire through my clothing.

"Do you like your new dress?" he whispered in my ear.

"Yes, now let me go."

I felt the skin on my neck prickle at the touch of his lips.

"Agata…"

The sound of Nunzio's cough made me stiffen. "Your son will be up soon."

He lifted my skirt from the back. "I'll be quick. Please, I need you…"

I gripped the edge of the table and endured the assault with my eyes glued to my bedroom door.

"Oh, Agata."

I adjusted my clothing and walked to the opposite side of the table to continue my work. His seed slid down the inside of my thigh and left a cold slimy trail. Tears welled up in my eyes, blurring my vision.

"Tell me you care for me," he whispered.

"No."

"You should be *my* wife."

"Alas, I am not. Leave me be. I have work to do."

Nunzio walked into the kitchen a moment later. Sporting a

74

grin, he said, "Happy Christmas to you both."

"Happy Christmas, my son," Alvino replied flatly.

I quietly wiped my hands on my apron before serving the men their morning meal. Nunzio ate with gusto, oblivious to the treachery taking place beneath the roof under which he resided. When they had finished, I scrubbed the table clean and placed a new candle in its center. I basted the goose one last time before walking out into the cold morning air to attend Holy Mass at the cathedral with my fellow Veronese.

The merchants and their wives accompanied us home after the service. The aroma from the perfectly cooked goose filled the room, making everyone salivate. I invited the guests to sit, then sliced the raisin spice bread I had baked the previous day. Meanwhile, Alvino plied them with watered wine. As I served the women, I noticed that their clothing was fashioned from finely woven wool. They wore silver jewelry, too. I did everything possible to show off my gold ring in the hope that it would offset my inferior garment.

Donna Maria was talkative, which suited me fine since it allowed me to listen and eat in peace. She was considerably younger than her husband, and livelier than him, too. With a ready smile and kind words, she went out of her way to be friendly toward me. The other woman, a dour-faced matron, barely spoke to me—or Maria, for that matter. Both of their husbands paid little heed to any of the women as they discussed politics with Alvino. As for Nunzio, his head remained buried in his plate for most of the afternoon. My husband's capacity for consuming vast amounts of food was nothing short of incredible. Unfortunately, I had to bear that stifling weight upon my slim frame almost every night.

"This goose is so tender, Donna Agata," Maria commented, cutting into my thoughts. "Quite tasty, too."

"Thank you. It's Donna Giulia's recipe."

"The baker's widow?"

I nodded. "She is a good cook."

"So are you, my dear."

Maria changed the topic to markets and told me where I

could find the best deals. I doubted I could afford to buy anything at the places she mentioned, but I enjoyed listening to her describe various foodstuffs and wares.

My panforte received many compliments. This pleased Alvino, who offered me a smile and inclined his head ever so slightly in approval. Maria's husband had brought some sweet wine, so I poured a bit for everyone. The little I consumed went straight to my head, making me dizzy. The men drank far more than the women did. As a result, by the time the meal was over, they were drunk. That didn't prevent them from consuming ale by the fire as the women helped me clean up the kitchen.

At one point in the evening, Alvino took hold of my wrist as I passed his chair. The feel of his hot fingers on my skin made me flinch. Nunzio failed to notice the intimate gesture, but Maria narrowed her eyes at my father-in-law.

"Bring us more ale, Agata," Alvino said before releasing his grip on me.

My cheeks burned as I refilled their cups. Four sets of male eyes silently roamed up and down my body, making me feel uncomfortably self-conscious. Once again, my oblivious husband paid no mind to the men's lustful stares.

The merriment continued into the late afternoon with the men gathered around the hearth and the wives seated at the table. The older woman eventually nodded off, affording Maria and I the opportunity to enjoy each other's company. When her husband stood to take his leave, she stood, too. They thanked us as Alvino walked them to the door. Maria, who was about to follow her husband outside, stopped and kissed my cheek.

In my ear, she whispered, "My door is always open if you ever need me."

I watched her slip her hand into the crook of her husband's elbow as they walked down the road in companionable silence. The other couple left immediately afterward, and I saw them out.

"Close the door, Agata. You're letting the cold inside!"

I obeyed Nunzio's command.

Alvino looked at me and said, "The food was good and you

were a fine hostess. Well done."

"I'm glad that you're pleased."

I cleaned up the remainder of the dirty cups and swept the kitchen floor. By the time I went to bed, I was completely spent. Thankfully, Nunzio was too full and too drunk to do anything else but sleep.

I stretched out on the bed and stared at the ceiling. Was this to be my life from now on—an adulterous wife bound for Hell?

CHAPTER 10
JANUARY 1321
VERONA

The day after Advent dawned cold and gray. I allowed my mind to wander as I lay in bed, reveling in the warmth afforded by a sheepskin coverlet. Nunzio stirred beside me and placed his beefy arm across my chest. I pushed off the fleshy dead weight and crept out of bed. Shivering from cold, I hastily donned a linen shift over my naked body.

"Agata."

"Go back to sleep."

"It's early…come to bed."

"I'm going to make pottage and some hot tea to ward off the chill. I'll wake you when the food is ready."

He mumbled something before returning to his slumber. I went into the kitchen and poked the embers, then fanned the fragile flame. As I reached for a bowl, Alvino exited his room and froze at the sight of me.

"Agata," he whispered. "What are you doing up?"

I set the bowl on the table. "I can ask the same of you."

"I can't sleep."

I set about making the pottage and said nothing.

He took a step toward me. "Come here."

Ignoring his request, I turned my back on him. He seized my arm, spun me around, and kissed my mouth. To our mutual surprise, I slapped his face. Furious, he gripped my throat and forced me toward his room. Unable to breathe, I panicked. My eyes darted to the closed door of the bedchamber that I shared with Nunzio.

Following my gaze, he whispered, "He's never overheard us before, why would he now?"

Despite my resistance, he succeeded in pushing me inside of

his room. He bolted the door, then fell upon me. I submitted to the act in the hope that he would hurry up and let me make my pottage in peace. I emerged from the bedchamber and froze when I caught sight of Nunzio.

Alvino exited the bedroom after me. "My son—"

"Don't!" Nunzio cried, balling his hands into fists.

I took a tentative step forward. "Nunzio, please—"

"I know what you two were doing in there! *I heard you*...How long has this wickedness been going on?!"

Alvino spread out his hands and replied, "This was the first time. I fell in a moment of weakness."

The lie had escaped his lips so smoothly that I didn't flinch.

Nunzio turned to me. "Is this true, Agata?"

Before I could reply, Alvino interjected, "Like you, I'm a man with needs...I don't know what came over me. Surely, you can understand that. I've been a widower far too long."

Nunzio frowned. "So rather than find yourself a wife, you use mine as one would a whore?"

Alvino winced and lowered his head.

My husband turned to me, his eyes shiny. "Agata, how could you do this to me? With my own father?"

Placing his head in his hands, he began to cry like a child. My heart twitched with pity. Despite being clumsy and dull-witted, Nunzio was a good man and didn't deserve the pain of such an enormous betrayal.

Suddenly, Alvino pointed at me, his eyes wild. "She made me do it!"

I recoiled. *"What?"*

Nunzio looked up and sniffed. "What?"

"Look at her! You said yourself that she's as lovely and as unblemished as the finest noble ladies. How do you think she manages this *divine beauty* coming from a poor family? God's teeth, she was sired by good-for-nothing drunkard! Yet there she stands, as powerful as any mythical siren."

Nunzio studied me with a puzzled expression. "Speak plainly, Father."

"Isn't it obvious, Nunzio? Her beauty and charms are the

result of an enchantment—*a spell*."

"Are you saying…?"

"Agata is a witch."

My knees went weak and I staggered against the wall for support. An accusation of witchcraft carried a heavy penalty under the law. I couldn't believe Alvino would stoop to such a low level in order to avoid blame.

"A witch…?" Nunzio repeated, dumbfounded.

Alvino appeared outraged. "I am a godly man, my son. You know that!"

"Yes, but—"

"When your mother lay dying, I made a vow before God that I would never love another woman. I have managed to keep that promise for years. Agata lured me with her charms and her lustful gazes. I am only flesh and blood!"

An icy chill settled in the pit of my stomach when Nunzio stared at me with suspicion in his eyes.

Alvino continued his tirade with the zeal of young priest delivering his first sermon. "She is a temptress who seduces men and sends their souls to Hell. To think that I chose Satan's instrument as a bride for my own son!"

"Father, calm yourself," Nunzio said, patting his back. "This excitement isn't good for your health!"

Alvino's face went from crimson to purple, and I expected him to start foaming at the mouth at any moment. Sinking to his knees, he cried, "God, forgive me!"

Nunzio's face morphed into a mask of fury.

Terrified, I darted into Alvino's bedchamber and bolted the door. My heart thudded against my ribcage as I paced the floor and debated my next move. Nunzio pounded on the door, demanding that I come out and face him. Rather than obey, I shrugged into one of Alvino's heavy wool tunics and escaped through the window.

I ran down the road as fast and as silently as I could in my bare feet, grateful for the thick winter fog. My first impulse was to seek out my aunt, then I remembered with a painful jab that she was dead. I could go to Mother, but given Father's unpredictable nature, I thought it best not to take that risk. For all I knew he would take Alvino's side in the matter and deliver me to the magistrates in exchange for a reward. That left Pina, my envious sister who disliked me and would probably gloat over my fall from grace.

Luckily, I recalled Maria's parting words at Christmas. Although I barely knew her, she seemed more trustworthy than any of my family members. Huddling against the cold, I ran toward her home while uttering a silent prayer.

Maria opened the door and almost recoiled at the sight of me. Taking in the male tunic and my bare muddied feet, she asked, "Agata, what happened?"

I glimpsed her husband drowsily smoking a pipe by the fire and my mind raced. "Please forgive the intrusion, Donna Maria, but I'm in desperate need of advice. It's of a *womanly* nature."

Maria's husband cleared his throat in irritation and waved us out of the room. Thankfully, he didn't spare a glance in my direction.

Maria led me into the bedchamber and closed the door.

"I'm sorry," I whispered. "I have nowhere else to go."

Noticing the bruises on my throat, she demanded, "Did your husband discover your secret?"

"What?"

"I *know* what's going on between you and Alvino."

My stomach instantly fell to the floor. "How?"

Taking me to the farthest corner of the room, she whispered, "The baker's widow *and* the cleaning woman Alvino hired before her..."

"He's done this to other women?"

She nodded. "The moment I laid eyes on you, I knew he wouldn't leave you in peace. Young, beautiful—Alvino is a man with a voracious appetite from what I've heard."

I stared at her, speechless. I couldn't picture the matronly Donna Giulia and Alvino in an intimate embrace.

Pointing to my neck again, she repeated her question. "Did Nunzio do that?"

"No, Alvino did it before he ravaged me."

81

Maria's eyes reflected empathy. "How long?"

"Since November. I gave my family some food and he made it clear that his charity came at a price."

"God curse him and his eager pecker."

Such vulgarity coming from Maria's lips surprised me. A knock on the door made us both jump. Her husband poked his head into the room and she ran to him. I heard her whisper the word "miscarriage" before tossing a look of pity in my direction. The man frowned and left us alone.

She came back to me and asked, "So, what happened?"

"Alvino convinced Nunzio that I am a witch who cast a spell on him—and my oafish husband believed him!"

"Naturally."

Unable to contain my roiling emotions, I wept.

"Shhh," she admonished, her eyes darting to the door.

"I have nowhere to go, no money…"

"If Alvino makes an official accusation against you, you'll have to answer to the magistrates. If Nunzio supports the claim, it will be your word against theirs."

"Two respected men of the community against one girl from a poor family with a drunkard father. Oh, Maria, what am I going to do?"

"First, let's get you cleaned up," she said while extracting a black wool frock and a pair of leather shoes from a cupboard. "You seem to be about my size."

She fetched water and a cloth so that I could wash up. There was a cut on my foot and she applied an ointment to it before handing me a pair of knitted wool stockings. I exchanged Alvino's tunic for the black frock, then slipped my stockinged feet into the shoes.

Maria extracted a coin purse from a drawer and handed me a few coins. I shook my head but she curled my fingers around the money. "You need this to get out of the city."

"I can't…I don't know anyone outside of—"

My panic prompted her to grip my shoulders. "Look at me, Agata. You must leave *now*, do you understand?"

Hot tears streamed down my cheeks. "Can't I stay here with

you for a little while?"

"Nowhere in Verona will be safe once the magistrates begin searching for you." Glancing at my hand, she added, "You have enough money there to get to Venice."

Venice? The thought of leaving my beloved Verona filled me with sadness. "What will I do there?"

"I don't know, my dear, but it will better than staying here to face the charge of witchcraft. I'm sure you'll find work. You're young and strong."

"I hope you're right."

"I know I am. God watch over you, Agata."

Her blessing sounded more like a curse.

CHAPTER 11
VENICE

True to Maria's words, the money she had given me got me as far as Venice, but it wasn't enough to sustain me. The dazzling marble palazzos and grandiose churches had initially impressed me, but the beauty of the city soon wore off as hunger gnawed at my insides.

To make matters worse, I was forced to contend with January's cruelty while seeking employment. Endless rain, biting winds, and bone-piercing dampness plagued the vacant streets. I knocked on countless doors, only to have them slammed in my face. Fortunately, an elderly couple allowed me to take refuge in their goat pen. I shared the stinky space with two ornery goats, one of which enjoyed chewing on the hem of my frock.

I wandered the streets by day in search of honest work, but no one wanted to hire a lone foreign woman. By nighttime my hunger was so great that I stole the vile table scraps and moldy bread meant for the goats. The foul vittles made me sick, but I didn't care. My belly wasn't empty, thus temporarily relieving the pain of starvation.

After several days of living in this pathetic manner, I began to stink as much as the goats. My matted hair and soiled frock caused people to wrinkle their noses in disgust as they passed me on the street. I continued to look for work but my efforts failed to produce results. No wonder! Who would hire me in such a deplorable state?

On a gray Sunday morning, I spied a group of well-dressed people entering a church. Their kind faces gave me the courage to approach them. Shivering and wet from an icy drizzle, I extended my hand in the hope that someone would feel pity for me. One woman reached into the pouch at her waist and extracted a coin of small value. She was about to place it in my palm, then stopped.

"Anyone who can afford a gold ring shouldn't be begging," she stated coldly before retracting the coin.

Those accompanying her tutted in disapproval and shook their heads as they hurried into the church for Holy Mass. I stared after them with tears in my eyes.

I sold my gold wedding ring the next day. It pained me to part with the only thing of value that I owned, but I couldn't eat the precious metal. The money allowed me to rent a shabby room and buy some decent food. Sleeping in a flea-infested bed proved better than damp straw crawling with mites and rats. At least I could breathe without inhaling the stench of goat dung. Also, I was able to wash my frock and bathe.

Unfortunately, I was back on the streets within a fortnight. I desperately pleaded with the elderly couple to let me sleep with their goats again, but they branded me a thief and cursed me.

I grew more desperate with each passing day while longing for my beloved Verona. Having exhausted the possibilities within the city center, I began expanding my search to the outskirts. Hopefully, someone would hire me as a laundress or a scullery maid. Of all the doors I knocked upon, only one opened for me. An old servant woman looked me up and down as I begged for post in the spacious villa.

Shaking her head, she said, "You're far too pretty, child."

She was about to close the door but I placed my foot in the crack. "I can work hard despite my appearance."

"My mistress isn't daft. She knows her husband all too well. Sorry, but I can't risk her anger by hiring you."

"Please," I said, fighting back tears. "I'll stay out of sight. Please..."

"Good luck and God bless you."

The door closed and I cursed under my breath. I wanted to slice off my face and make myself ugly.

Back in the city center, I tried again in vain to find work. When my blistered feet and frozen limbs could take no more, I offered sex to a random man in exchange for bread. He regarded me with disgust and refused, pelting me with harsh insults for good measure.

Sagging against a nearby wall, I glanced upward and spied a lone swallow in the sky. It glided and swooped with the kind of gracefulness that only birds possess. Wasn't it too cold for him? Maybe he was like me—too weak to fly to a warmer climate. I wanted to be up in the sky, too. Perhaps when I died— which would certainly be soon—my soul would float toward Heaven…

Lack of food and exhaustion caused my head to throb. I took a few steps forward and staggered from weakness. The world around me grew dark at the corners and the blackness eventually engulfed the light until it became a tiny pinpoint. A gasp escaped my lips as my knees buckled, and then there was nothing.

I woke up in a soft bed with two men leaning over me. Neither of them could tear their eyes from my naked malnourished body. The younger man poked and prodded me as only a physician would. When he nodded his head, someone came forth with a bowl of bread soaked in fish broth and a cup of diluted wine. I hastily stuffed the food into my mouth, swallowing it down before they retracted the offer.

"Wait, not so fast," the man warned.

My greediness resulted in a torrent of vomit. Groaning in dismay, I let myself fall back against the pillow.

"You must eat slowly at first. What's your name?"

I wiped my mouth with the back of my hand. "Agata."

"Where are you…"

Overcome by a wave of dizziness, I blacked out and never heard the end of the sentence.

My head ached as I squinted against the sunlight spilling into the room. I woke up in the same bed, but there was no sign of the vomit. Someone had washed my body and dressed me in a clean cotton shift.

"You had us worried, Agata," the young man said, coming to stand beside the bed.

"Who are you?"

"I am Messer Ubaldo Donini's personal physician, and you

are in his home."

"How did I get here?"

"You swooned in front of his horse and Christian duty compelled him to stop, just like the Good Samaritan in the Bible. You are a fortunate girl."

"Thank you for taking care of me."

The physician offered me a hesitant smile. He left curatives and instructions with the servants, then bade me farewell.

Thanks to my host's generosity, my vitality returned within days. A lovely embroidered frock was laid out for me one morning. I washed and dressed, then went in search of my savior to thank him. The lonely old man made it perfectly clear that he expected something in return for his hospitality—I didn't recall that part in the biblical tale of the Good Samaritan.

My charity comes at a price.

This is how I became Ubaldo's mistress. Naturally, he inquired about my family and my reason for being in Venice. Rather than tell him the truth about me or my past, I pretended to be an orphan.

In the months that followed, I rarely spoke and did my best to mimic the Venetian accent. Winter melted into spring. By summertime, I spoke like a local. Being an old man's lover was certainly better than starving and freezing on the streets—better than facing a witchcraft charge, too. I had every intention of eventually finding honest work. In the meantime, I enjoyed decent food and slept in a comfortable bed—*his bed*.

***

"Agata!"

I rolled my eyes and released a heavy sigh. How many times a day did he call my name?

Remember, he saved your life.

Putting on my sweetest smile, I made my way to his bedchamber. "Coming, Ubaldo!"

My lover was propped up on silk pillows beneath the magnificent embroidered canopy of his bed—the same bed I have shared with him almost every night since he rescued me. I often stared at the designs stitched onto the lush velvet while his gnarled hands greedily groped my young flesh. Sometimes, the lecherous old man forced me to do things that neither Nunzio nor Alvino had ever demanded of me.

"Agata, fetch the physician," he said the moment I appeared in the doorway.

"He came only yesterday. Don't you remember? Why don't you take some of the—"

"Fetch him again!"

I bit my tongue.

You are alive thanks to him…

Ubaldo fell sick last week and was diagnosed with an advance stage of gout.

"Agata! More wine!"

I went to the sideboard and poured wine into a chalice. Handing it to him, I said, "Shall I have Cook prepare some broth for you?"

Ignoring my question, he took a deep sip of the wine then licked his lips. "I think I'll die before the month is done, my dear."

"Don't say that."

He lifted a veined hand to caress my cheek. "Sweet Agata. God works in mysterious ways, does He not? Setting you in my path…I never thought I could feel such passion in my old age. You make me feel young again! Oh, how I miss the golden days of my youth. Tell me you love me, my girl."

"I love you, Ubaldo." The lie felt bitter upon my tongue, but my instinct for survival had long overshadowed my Christian conscience.

"My son won't tolerate your presence here once he arrives."

I hid my panic. "I didn't know you had children."

"That's because I never told you. News of my illness has surely reached Pietro by now. I'm expecting him and his pesky wife any day."

The thought of returning to the streets with no money or prospects made me sick to my stomach. "I have nowhere to go, Ubaldo. Please speak with your son on my behalf. I could serve as maid to his wife."

"I wouldn't let my enemy serve that ugly cow."

"I don't care. I'm a hard worker who knows how to cook, clean, and mend—*please*."

"I'll give it some thought, although I doubt she'll go for the idea. You're far too attractive, my dear. No prudent wife wants someone like you around. She'd be forced to keep an eye on her husband at all times. Besides, she already has a maid."

I had heard the same thing from the old servant woman. "Will you at least give me some money so that I may find a room in the city until I figure out what to do?"

"I'll do better than that. I'll introduce you to an old friend of mine who can provide you with some work."

I sagged with relief. "Thank you, Ubaldo."

His eyes glittered wickedly as he turned down the coverlet. "Why don't you come here and show me your appreciation?"

***

An elegant woman with a curvaceous figure arrived at the palazzo the following evening. Sporting a red silk cape, she seemed like a proper lady. On closer inspection, I noticed that her face bore an exaggerated amount of rouge and lip paint. Also, she arrived unaccompanied despite the late hour, and no woman of good repute would do such a thing.

Cocking an eyebrow, she said coldly, "It's impolite to stare."

I lowered my gaze. "Forgive me."

Turning to Ubaldo, she said, "Greetings, old fried. I was both surprised and pleased to receive your message."

Ubaldo opened his arms. "Carmen, it's always a pleasure to see you. Come and give me a kiss."

She kissed his cheek, careful not to leave a red lip print on his skin. "You look well."

"And you're as beautiful as a summer rose."

"You, sir, are a flatterer." Pointing at me, she added, "Is this the girl?"

"Yes."

Carmen's eyes ran up and down my body, causing me to shift uncomfortably under her scrutiny. When she finally met my gaze, she smiled at me with her mouth but not with her eyes.

"She is exactly as you described, Ubaldo. Aren't you going to introduce us?"

Ubaldo grinned. "Carmen, this is Agata. She is seeking work in Venice."

I offered the woman a curtsey and she smirked. "How old are you, girl?"

"Fourteen, my lady."

"And your parents?

"She's an orphan," Ubaldo replied on my behalf.

"Convenient. Any illnesses?"

Ubaldo took it upon himself to reply for me again. "My physician examined her recently. I can assure you that she's as healthy as a mare in her prime."

Carmen slowly circled me, her gaze lingering on my hips and breasts. Suddenly, she cupped my buttocks with both of her hands. I cried out, alarmed.

"Good, firm," she said, paying no heed to my reaction.

I stepped back and stared at her with mouth agape.

"Close your mouth, it's unbecoming." She waited for me to comply before asking, "Are you disfigured in any way?"

"What?"

She rephrased the question in a tone normally reserved for children. "Do you have any scars?" I shook my head and she said, "Excellent. Raise your skirt to the level of your thighs so I can see your legs." I did as I was told and she nodded in satisfaction. "Good. Now, turn around *slowly*."

I spun in a circle.

Carmen looked at Ubaldo and nodded. "We have a deal. Pack your things, Agata."

Ubaldo beamed. "Splendid. The girl owns nothing in this world but the clothes on her back—and even that was a gift from me."

"Where am I going?" I asked.

Carmen ignored my question as she retreated to the far corner of the room with Ubaldo. I watched as they engaged in discussion, each one casting a brief glance in my direction. I stood perfectly still, gazing out the window. Two fat pigeons were perched on the roof of the palazzo across the street. I would have happily traded places with either of them.

After much whispered negotiation, Carmen handed Ubaldo money. I contemplated darting out the door when I realized that I was being sold like a slab of beef at the butcher shop.

Ubaldo came up to me after conducting his business, and kissed my mouth. He pulled away and held me at arm's length. "Farewell, my sweet girl. You have pleased me more than you know. God bless you, Agata."

Too shocked to speak, I merely stared at him before Carmen pushed me toward the door. "Come along."

We stepped outside and I almost stumbled down the stairs in a daze of confusion. My new mistress walked briskly, forcing me to move fast in order to keep pace.

Carmen turned a corner, then darted down a dark alley. "Make haste, girl."

I caught up with her and asked, "Am I to be your maid?"

"No."

"Where are we going?"

"To the sestiere of Rialto. Hurry! It's late and we cannot be out after curfew."

I knew the neighborhood she referred to and the kind of people who lurked there. The authorities enforced curfew in an attempt to keep the area free of crime. The sun had already set, and the feeble light of dusk was quickly fading into night. Torches burned along the Grand Canal, and I glimpsed the silhouettes of vessels gliding upon the water. Being a merchant city, foreign and domestic ships brimming with cargo were a common sight. We crossed a sturdy wooden bridge boasting two inclined ramps that met at a central section. The ramps could be raised and lowered as needed to allow the passage of tall ships.

Carmen rounded a corner and I remained at her heels, struggling to keep pace. "What sort of work will I be doing, Signora Carmen?"

She tossed a sly look over her shoulder. "The sort that you're already familiar with, my girl."

CHAPTER 12
JUNE 1322
VERONA

To Bianca's relief, Cangrande displayed pleasure and affection for his fourth child. Having sired three healthy boys in a row, the nobleman could afford to indulge in happiness over a daughter. After all, he had already proven his male prowess to everyone.

On the day of her christening, he dedicated little Margherita to the Virgin Mary. The girl would eventually be sent to a convent as a gift to God, securing her father's place in Heaven. What better purpose in life could there be for a daughter?

Despite the favorable reaction on Cangrande's part toward Margherita, Bianca did everything possible to conceive again immediately, which she did. Determined to provide her lover with a son, she ingested costly potions and followed a strict diet believed to produce males. A son would secure her future when she was older and no longer desired by men. Men could easily obtain gainful employment and provide for their mothers—especially the sons of powerful noblemen.

"There, there little one," Bianca said to her colicky daughter. Turning to her maid, she added, "I think she's hungry. Take Margherita to the wet nurse. Hurry, my lord will be here soon."

The servant plucked the fussy baby from her mother's arms and vacated the bedchamber. Bianca stood before the looking glass and pinched her cheeks to give them some color. Next, she applied rosewater to her throat and wrists, then rinsed her mouth with it.

Cangrande arrived a moment later in high spirits, which was rare these days. The tragic news of Dante Alighieri's death last autumn had taken a toll on his mood. The divine poet had suffered a high fever prior to his death. He was interred at San

Pier Maggiore in Ravenna.

Bianca kissed Cangrande's lips, then said, "You seem to be in a jovial mood, my love."

"I've just received word that Enrico di Gorizia is dead."

She knew that Enrico had caused many problems for the Scaligeri family. "A dead enemy is always cause for rejoicing."

"Indeed! Castelfranco is now mine for the taking."

"This is good news."

He grinned. "Yes."

"Why don't you sit down, my lord? Shall we celebrate with some wine?"

Cangrande took a seat and watched as she poured the ruby liquid into a chalice. The sunlight seeping through the open window caused the highlights in her hair to gleam like copper. Bianca was no great beauty, and her body was far from what he considered the feminine ideal, but in that moment she appeared ethereal—like a petite Madonna. There was nothing saintly about the girl in bed, however. In addition to being as flexible as an acrobat, her lust was insatiable. Most men found no fault in these traits, yet he craved a woman who wasn't so…so…

"I have some sweetmeats, too, if it pleases you," she said, cutting into his thoughts.

Cangrande shook his head in response. Placing a hand on Bianca's belly, he caressed the subtle swell of flesh. She was young, fertile, and eager to please—what every man craved in a woman.

Every man except him.

"The child grows stronger with each passing day, my love." She kissed his cheek then whispered seductively, "I am no longer with the daily sickness."

"I'm glad to hear it," he said, hating the period of vomiting that women endured at the beginning of pregnancy. He usually avoided his mistresses during the first three months, opting instead to satisfy his lust elsewhere.

She smiled. "I know it will be a boy this time."

"We will name him Alboino, after my brother."

"A fine name," she said, toying with his hair. "You have not

93

visited my bed in quite some time."

"I didn't wish to disturb you during your difficult months. I knew you weren't feeling well."

In truth, he found Bianca's company tiresome. He longed for a woman who possessed wit and intelligence. A woman with a sense of humor whose spirit matched his own. Someone who could provide a mental challenge as well as ignite the fire in his loins.

Did such a woman even exist?

Bianca waited for him to take another sip of wine before placing the chalice on a nearby tabletop. Straddling him, she whispered, "I feel perfectly fine now, my lord."

To her chagrin, her sensual gyrations failed to stoke his passion. Taking the rejection in stride, she slid off of his lap and sank to her knees. She licked her lips in a suggestive manner then smiled at him. Cangrande returned the gesture, but not before she glimpsed the boredom in his eyes.

CHAPTER 13
AUGUST 1322
VENICE

Carmen's palazzo overlooked the courtyard of an old church. A total of six women lived within its faded walls. My new mistress ran her household with the help of two matronly servants, Anna and Lucia—two large women who seldom spoke and never smiled.

Next in command was eighteen-year-old Gisella, who had been with Carmen the longest. A willowy young woman with curly dark hair, her face did not merit her vanity. What's more, she was missing several back teeth from the upper row. Whenever she laughed, I was instantly reminded of a donkey. Gisella ensured that the rest of us upheld the strict rules and regulations set forth by our mistress.

Rosina, at seventeen years of age, emulated her older peer by bossing around sixteen-year-old Miriam. Although both of them sported fashionable golden locks and light eyes, their features were plain. Aside from that, the two girls had nothing in common. Rosina emulated Gisella's meanness of spirit, whereas Miriam, although friendlier, leaned toward shyness.

I was the newest and youngest addition to the household, having recently turned fifteen. I spoke as little as possible and kept my own counsel.

On the night of my arrival, Miriam led me to the tiny room in which she slept. Only one small window allowed light and air into the dismal space.

Indicating the narrow cot by the door, she said, "We'll be sharing this room and that's your bed. Gisella and Rosina share the bigger chamber across the hall, whereas Carmen sleeps on the top floor. Her chamber is the grandest of all."

"Lucky Carmen," I muttered.

Miriam pulled one of the wool coverlets off the bed and handed it to me. "Take this, in case you get cold at night. I imagine it will be warmer now that there are two bodies in this room instead of only one."

"Thank you, Miriam. You're very kind."

"Hopefully, we'll become friends."

"I'd like that."

My new home, although somewhat dilapidated, boasted glazed terracotta floors with vivid patterns and soaring ceilings with peeling frescoes. A shabby Oriental carpet dominated the main salon, and a pair of threadbare tapestries adorned the walls.

Carmen had inherited the palazzo from her former mistress, a successful woman who had taught her many things. Carmen still lived according to the deceased woman's rules and insisted that we all do the same. For example, Carmen carefully monitored everything we ate in order to keep our skin clear and our bodies lithe. Our diet consisted mainly of fruits, vegetables, and grains, and we weren't allowed to indulge in wine unless it was heavily diluted with water. We were obliged to respect a curfew, and all of us were expected to engage in charity work. Carmen, a devout Catholic, regularly fasted and took Communion every morning. Such devotion was not a requirement for the rest of us, but she insisted that we attend church on Sundays and holy days. Finally, we were urged to dress modestly. Our diet, combined with our seemingly chaste lifestyle, gave us the appearance and demeanor of healthy young women and—with a bit of stretch from the imagination—virgins.

Women like us were confined within the *Castelletto*, a group of houses near the sestiere of Rialto in the parish of San Matteo. In the evening, after the third bell tolled from the bell tower of San Marco, we were forced to confine ourselves within the house under penalty of a steep fine. Six custodians guarded the Castelletto to enforce the city ordinance. Ferries connecting the two banks of the canal were used by the Venetians to reach Castelletto, but the boaters were forbidden to transfer men to our sestiere during Easter and other religious festivals.

Three days after my arrival at the palazzo, Carmen had taken me to the top floor and thrust me into one of the bedchambers. The old man she expected me to "service" flaunted fine clothing, but his rotting teeth repulsed me. He motioned for me to sit on his lap. Reluctantly, I crossed the room and obliged him. When he grabbed my breast, I slapped his face and fled the room.

Carmen caught up with me at the end of the hallway and seized a fistful of my hair. "You will go back in there and do your job."

"No!"

Narrowing her eyes at me, she demanded, "Do you think you can simply eat and live here for free? Everyone works around here, including me."

"I'll find a way to pay you back…I'll earn my keep another way. I can find work as a servant or a laundress, perhaps—"

I was instantly silenced by a sharp slap across my face.

"You stupid, ungrateful wretch."

Tears stung my eyes. "Please, don't make me do this…"

Carmen stared at me for a long moment, then dragged me downstairs to the kitchen were Anna and Lucia were quietly mending clothes.

Shoving me toward the two big women, she said, "This one needs to be taught a lesson. Careful with her face and teeth—it's a miracle she has all of them and none are rotten. This filly will rake in a good profit."

Carmen departed, leaving me alone with the two menacing women. Anna and Lucia set down their mending and walked over to where I stood. They stared at me with vapid expressions, then began pummeling my body with their beefy fists. I attempted to defend myself, but they were too strong. Falling to the floor, I begged them to stop their violent onslaught. Anna kicked me a few times, but she left my face and teeth intact. Lucia carried me to my room and put me to bed with surprising tenderness.

Carmen checked on me a little while later to assess the

damage. At length, she said, "The sooner you face what you are, the easier your life will be."

Fighting back tears of rage and humiliation, I said nothing. I hated her and I hated Venice. Oh, how I missed Verona!

She continued, "Well, do you have anything to say for yourself?"

Pressing my lips tightly together, I shook my head. She gave me a long look, then left me alone. Miriam crept into the dark room after having finished her "work" and I pretended to be asleep. She got into bed and was soon snoring softly. Only then did I allow the hot, silent tears to dampen my pillow.

I could barely move the next morning.

Miriam approached my cot. "Do you need some help?"

I shook my head. "I can manage, thank you. Go on. I would hate for you to get in trouble because of me."

It took me twice as long to get dressed and comb my hair. I made my way downstairs and took my seat at the table to break my fast with the other girls. Rosina snickered at the sight of me.

Gisella eyed me with loathing. "Serves you right."

"Leave her alone, Gisella," Miriam said in my defense while handing me a piece of bread.

Carmen entered the room and everyone fell silent. She cast a glance in my direction, then walked out.

I ate slowly, then rose to go. Gisella followed me.

Grabbing hold of my arm, she demanded, "Do you believe yourself to be above us? Too good for the likes of our clients?"

"No…I only—"

"You *only* ran away, which meant that I had to do your job last night. That old man's breath was as foul as the Grand Canal in the peak of summer."

"I'm sorry, Gisella."

"Don't let it happen again," she warned with a hard shove that made me almost fall to the floor.

I continued resisting my fate despite the threat. I pretended to be sick for two days, claiming that I was most likely contagious. Everyone avoided me the first day, but by the second day they saw through my ploy. My lie earned me a hard pinch from Gisella and a sharp kick to the shin from Rosina.

Carmen instructed Anna and Lucia to deny me food until I relented and agreed to the house rules. I fasted for three whole days. On the fourth day, Carmen sent Anna into my room with a tray of food.

"I thought Carmen meant to starve me," I said.

The woman looked at me dully, pointed to the food, and then pointed to my mouth. I shook my head and crossed my arms. Anna shrugged, left the room, and returned with Carmen.

My mistress glared at me and said, "Eat."

"I would rather die."

"Not until I make a profit."

"I'm not eating!"

Carmen's eyebrow shot upward. "Very well."

I should have known by the tone of her voice that I would regret my belligerence. Carmen left and returned a while later with Anna and Lucia in tow. One carried a giant bowl of pottage and the other a crude funnel with a leather hose attached to it.

Carmen said, "I paid Ubaldo a lot of money for you, and I will not have my investment ruined by your stubbornness and stupidity."

Horrified at the prospect of being force-fed by two the brutes, I submitted to Carmen's wishes—cursing my life and cursing God, too, for abandoning me in my time of need. For the first time in my life, I had no faith.

I was promptly handed a spoon and the three of them watched as I ate the pottage. I hated Venice and the Venetians with a vehemence that surprised me, but I swallowed my bitter resentment along with the gray mush for the sake of my survival.

After swallowing several mouthfuls, Carmen took the bowl away. "Too much will make you sick and I don't want you vomiting all over the coverlet."

Anna and Lucia took the spoon and the bowl, then retreated to the kitchen.

Crossing her arms in satisfaction, Carmen declared, "I've finally broken you."

"I'm going to Hell."

"Most of us are, my dear. Now that you have accepted your fate, you must learn to do your job properly."

I shrugged. "I don't know what you mean."

"Well, you can't just lie there!"

In truth, that's exactly what I thought she wanted me to do. "Am I supposed to sing or recite poetry as a man does his nasty business?"

To my surprise, the corners of her mouth lifted a tiny bit. "I see I have my work cut out for me."

For the rest of that day and throughout the next, Carmen taught me the movements and sounds expected of me when "entertaining" a patron. In short, I had to "perform" in order to convince men that I actually enjoyed fornicating with them. To make matters worse, Carmen demonstrated several vile acts with phallic fruits and vegetables, then insisted that I do the same under her watchful eye. I found these lessons both humiliating and tedious, and cried when I was alone.

God had completely forsaken me.

"It's not so bad," Miriam whispered in the darkness one night.

"Did you also have a difficult time at first?"

"Oh, yes—as bad as you if not worse."

"How did you end up here, anyway?"

"I lost both of my parents. They were drowning in debt, you see. Solicitors seized our home and all of our belongings. Having no brothers or uncles, and no money left for a dowry, I had few prospects. Carmen found me in this desperate state. I was given a choice—either work for her or starve to death."

"I'm sorry, Miriam."

"It's all right, Agata. I've been here almost a year now. You'll get used to it. Just wiggle around and moan as if a man's prick is the best thing in the world. Most of these poor louts have frigid wives at home and only want to feel loved for a little bit. It gets easier with time, believe me."

I took Miriam's words to heart and faced my fate with courage. I also consumed the required herbal concoctions to prevent pregnancy with no argument. All the girls took them. My soul was already bound for Hell, so one more sin wouldn't make a difference.

The first man I serviced was old enough to be my father. I imagined his wife at home, matronly and cold. I repeated the movements Carmen had taught me—gyrating and moaning in the process. The man seemed pleased with my performance and promised to return the following week.

Months passed before I could face my reflection in the looking glass without feeling deep humiliation and shame. I extracted some measure of comfort in the fact that we were different from the other women plying the oldest profession in history. Carmen insisted that we service no more than three men per night, and all business was conducted within the walls of the palazzo—never in some filthy street corner. I once glimpsed a prostitute rutting with a patron against the wall of a house in broad daylight. Carmen would have us whipped for committing such an act in public. Since she offered a higher quality product at a greater cost, our clients consisted mainly of foreign traders and merchants passing through Venice. Ruffians and drunkards were promptly turned away at the door.

Rival prostitutes regarded us with envy and contempt, but Carmen didn't care. She paraded around the city with her head held high and a wicked *misericordia* hidden in the cleft between her breasts. Originally designed to offer a quick death to wounded knights, for it could easily pierce through the spaces in armor, the French dagger could also be used in close combat. The needle-like blade would pierce through an assailant's eye or throat without hindrance.

Carmen openly referred to us her "investments" and insisted that we also carry daggers for our own protection. Since I had never used such a weapon, she taught me how to defend myself. I had to admit, carrying something sharp and dangerous made me feel much safer whenever I went out alone.

In time, I accepted my fate with complacency instead of vitriolic resentment. I couldn't return to my beloved Verona anytime soon, so I made do with the cards that life had dealt me.

The most positive aspect of being a prostitute was the information I gleaned from my patrons. Carmen instructed us to listen rather than speak, which is exactly what I did when the men talked of politics, business, and world events. I kept abreast of current affairs simply by paying attention to their words.

I learned to admire Carmen, too. Clever and practical, the woman shaped her own destiny. It soon became obvious that—like me—she came from nothing, yet she had managed to make *something* of her life. She singlehandedly maintained a roof over her head and food in her belly, which is more than I could say for most women who suddenly found themselves destitute—myself included. To achieve this kind of success, one needed to be ruthless. Once I arrived at this conclusion, I made an earnest attempt to emulate my mistress, paying close attention to everything she said and did. I also vowed that if things didn't work out for me here, I would be like Carmen and find another way to survive. Of one thing I was certain: I would never again starve in the cold, cruel streets of Venice.

***

Carmen knew how to speak and behave like a proper lady thanks to her distant cousin, Nina, who served in a noble household near our home. Fortunately for me, Carmen passed this valuable knowledge to the rest of us so that we, too, could mimic the speech and mannerisms of ladies. I committed these rules of etiquette to memory, and practiced whenever I was alone. Naturally, putting on these airs rendered us more attractive to male clients, thus allowing our mistress to sell us at a higher price.

Nina visited Carmen frequently and, being a notorious gossip, she repeated various tidbits of fascinating information regarding the city's most important nobles. I usually remained out of sight during these visits, but always within earshot in order to make mental notes and memorize names. Apparently, the lords of Venice were as ambitious and cunning as those of Verona. To them, keeping secrets and betraying friends were small prices to pay for social and economic advancement. It became evident that in order to truly thrive in the world, one had to be shrewd and—most importantly—*patient*.

From the moment I woke up in the morning until it was time to go to bed, I spoke, walked, ate, and behaved in the manner Carmen had taught me. The other girls only acted like ladies in the presence of patrons or in public, whereas I completely abandoned my old ways for new ones. *Better ones.* For some reason, the change in my comportment annoyed Gisella, who often went out of her way to mock me.

I had washed my shift and was setting it out to dry in the courtyard one day when Gisella asked, "What's the matter, Agata? Has your maid abandoned you, *my lady*?"

Rosina, whom I mentally referred to as "the sycophant," snickered. "You'll ruin your fine white hands if you continue doing menial work—won't she, Gisella?"

The two of them giggled as I went about my task.

Gisella said, "In case you didn't know, pretending to be a lady doesn't actually make you one."

"I know," I agreed.

"Then why do you try to act high and mighty?"

Rosina added, "Do you think you're better than us?"

I finished my task and faced them squarely. "I'm no better than either of you. Thanks to Carmen, however, we've been given a chance to improve ourselves. Why not take advantage of a free gift?"

Gisella eyed me scornfully. "Improve yourself? You're a prostitute, remember? We're *whores*."

"Yes, so what's your point?" When neither of them answered my question, I continued, "You're free to do as you please, so allow me to do the same. Now, if you'll excuse me, I need to clean my shoes because I'm a poor prostitute who doesn't own a lady's maid."

Rosina laughed, which earned her a sharp slap from Gisella. I didn't stick around to see or hear what happened next because my shoes were indeed caked with mud.

I saw Carmen hovering near one of the doorways as I stepped into the hallway. The way she smiled at me suggested that she had overheard the entire exchange.

Later that night, I woke up with a start. I couldn't breathe! I opened my eyes to see the shadowy forms of Gisella and Rosina in the moonlight. They stood on either side of my cot and Rosina's hand was clamped tightly over my mouth. I screamed into the flesh of her moist palm and struggled to free myself.

"Hopefully, this will serve to humble you," Gisella whispered, raising her arm.

To my horror, there was a leather strap in her hand and she brought it down on me with considerable force. Oblivious to my muffled screams, she hit me again and again. By the time they retreated, I felt broken inside.

Another silhouette loomed by my bed a moment later. "Are you all right?"

I whimpered. "Miriam."

Miriam struck a piece of flint and lit a candle. "Santa Madonna, look what they've done to you!"

"Quick…fetch me a clove of garlic and some linseed oil from the kitchen."

"Maybe I should awaken Carmen…"

"No! Do as I tell you. *Please.*"

Miriam left the room and I winced in pain as I tried to sit up. Divesting of my shift, I glanced down at myself. The skin on some of the welts had broken and were bleeding, but they weren't deep enough to leave scars.

Miriam returned and I bit the garlic clove in half before rubbing its pungent flesh over each of my wounds. Next, I applied a liberal amount of linseed oil.

"Carmen will punish them," Miriam assured me.

"Carmen will never know. Neither you nor I will mention this, do you understand?"

"But—"

"If you tell Carmen about this, I'll whip you with the same leather strap that Gisella used on me."

Miriam stared at me with wide eyes over the flickering candlelight, then went to bed without saying another word.

The next day, I glimpsed a hint of regret in the eyes of Gisella and Rosina as I sat down with them to break my fast. I remained silent when Carmen joined us at the table, which prompted them to smile sheepishly at me. Their eyes pleaded with me to be silent, so I didn't say a word.

From that moment onward, my enemies and I silently agreed to leave each other alone.

I kept to myself and continued to do whatever Carmen expected of me without complaint. I eventually became so proficient in the art of lovemaking that a few of the patrons came to the door requesting me by name. Once, a richly dressed woman wearing a mask arrived at the palazzo with a proposition for my mistress. The mysterious woman wished to "borrow" me for a week in exchange for a handsome sum. To my surprise, Carmen refused the offer, rudely slamming the door on the woman's face.

Noticing my shocked expression, she explained, "Do you have any idea what they would do to you had I agreed?"

"No."

"Let's just say you'd be of no use to me afterward."

"Why?"

Carmen's eyes grew hard. "Because you probably wouldn't survive the week. I know her lover—a perverted, sadistic man with more money than good sense. He's known for his *peculiar* tastes, most of which verge on extreme violence. One must always be wary, Agata. Trust no one. Let that be a lesson."

I shivered. "Thank you."

She placed a hand on my shoulder. "I know you and I have had our differences in the past, but you've become exemplary in your work and conduct. That deserves reward, not a punishment. Now, ready yourself because Messer Narino is expected tonight."

The successful poet had been Gisella's regular patron until one night she couldn't entertain him due to the onset of her monthly. Carmen forbade us from engaging in sexual intercourse during menstruation—unless a patron specifically requested it, then she would charge extra.

Messer Narino prided himself on being a fastidious man, so anything "messy" was out of the question. I had been presented to him as a substitute for Gisella, and now he requested me all the time. I didn't mind. Always polite and meticulously groomed, the poet performed in noble palazzos throughout the city.

Three of the upstairs rooms were utilized as bedchambers for servicing clients. Each boasted tasteful décor. I entered one of them and positioned myself on the stool before the looking glass. He liked to see me at my toilette, so I began combing my hair. My client arrived a moment later.

Capturing his gaze in the reflection, I smiled and titled my head to the side. "Messer Narino."

He threw his cloak over a chair with dramatic flourish and came to stand behind me. Before kissing my neck, he said, "*Basta, amore mio*…call me by my Christian name."

I stood and faced him. "Sandro."

He claimed my lips while placing my hand upon his cock. When he pulled away, he said, "I composed a poem in your honor. Would you like to hear it?"

I tried to appear excited at the prospect of yet another evening of Sandro's bad poetry. I thought of all the times that Aunt Serafina and I had read Hildegard of Bingen's exquisite poems.

Groaning inwardly, I said, "I would be delighted."

It wasn't long before we were both naked on the bed. The jaunty poet enjoyed matching the rhythm of his verses to his thrusts, which rendered his lovemaking rather amusing. I couldn't resist giggling, which angered him because it made him spill his seed too quickly.

He pouted. "Now look what you've made me do."

"Don't be cross, dearest. Read me another one of your fascinating poems while I pleasure you."

"Very well."

The mediocre verses soon became punctuated with "ahs" and "ohs" as my deft fingers went to work. Rather than allow him to mount me again when he was ready, I slid off the bed and sank to my knees. He abandoned the poem altogether in favor of delirious moaning.

A short while later, he cried, "Cristo Santo!"

I stood, then wiped my mouth with the back of my hand. I sat before the looking glass and waited as he dressed.

"I have something for you, Agata. I hope you like it." He reached into his pocket and extracted a strand of green glass beads flaunting an amethyst pendant. Fastening it around my neck, he added, "Until we meet again, my sweet."

I kissed his hand. "Thank you for the lovely gift."

Carmen escorted him to the door, then confiscated my necklace. Anything we received from the men we serviced was considered payment and belonged to our mistress. Honestly, I didn't mind. She clothed us, fed us, and kept a roof over our heads. Besides, what use did a whore have for a necklace? It wasn't as if I had any social engagements. I was naked most of the time, anyway.

I made my way to my humble bedchamber with Sandro's sweat still drying on my skin.

"Agata?" Miriam whispered.

"Still awake, my friend?"

"I have so much to tell you!"

She had accompanied Anna and Lucia to the market earlier, so I knew that she was eager to gossip. I contributed little to these conversations since I rarely ventured out and, when I did, I never paid attention to the cackling old crones in the piazzas. Who cares what they had to say? Their lives reflected a string of bad choices and a tremendous lack of ambition.

I, on the other hand, possessed an overwhelming desire to better my situation in life. Aunt Serafina—God rest her soul— had always admired my cleverness and my aptitude for learning new things. She had called it a gift. Well, it was time to put my "gift" to good use.

CHAPTER 14
VENICE

One morning, while we were gathered around the dining table breaking our fast with bread and fruit, Carmen announced, "I am officially betrothed."

Stunned, I stared at her. What respectable man would marry such a woman?

Gisella inquired, "Do we know him?"

Carmen smiled mischievously. "Oh, yes."

Miriam's face lit up. "Is it the baker? It's obvious he's in love with you."

Carmen laughed scornfully, prompting Gisella and Rosina to frown at Miriam.

"Do you honestly think our beautiful mistress would settle for a mere baker?" Gisella demanded. "Honestly, Miriam, sometimes I wonder if you're daft."

"Perhaps she *is* daft," Rosina added with a giggle.

Sycophant.

I glanced at Miriam's red face with pity. I loathed the fact that Gisella and Rosina bullied her.

"Who is it?" Gisella demanded.

Carmen's eyes slid my way. "You don't seem excited or happy for me, Agata."

"On the contrary, Signora Carmen," I countered smoothly. "I'm eager to discover the lucky man's identity."

Satisfied, she said, "Geraldo Santino."

Everyone gasped in surprise except for me. I didn't dare ask who he was for fear that Gisella and Rosina would pounce on me for being ignorant.

"His jealous wife is known to have a bad temper," Gisella pointed out.

Rosina inquired, "Wasn't she the one who pushed her husband's last lover into the Grand Canal?"

Carmen nodded. "The very one."

I said, "You're betrothed to a married man? Forgive my ignorance, but, how is this possible?"

"The fat old sow is on her deathbed," Carmen replied. "Can you believe it, girls? The owner of the city's most prosperous inn has chosen *me* to warm his bed and be his next bride."

Rosina squealed in delight. "A wedding!"

While Gisella and Rosina clapped their hands with glee, Miriam and I exchanged worried looks. Surely, Geraldo would not allow his wife to continue her current way of life, which meant that we would need to find another means of supporting ourselves.

Miriam mustered the courage to speak. "Signora Carmen, I'm very happy for you, but what is to become of us?"

"You will all continue providing services to the patrons who stay at the inn, of course."

"Don Geraldo will allow this?"

Her eyebrow shot upward. "He suggested it."

***

Geraldo's wife died within a fortnight. Carmen wasted no time setting her affairs in order. She found a buyer willing to pay a fair price for her palazzo, then married the wealthy innkeeper without further ado.

Gisella, Rosina, Miriam, and I were instructed to pack our few belongings and accompany our mistress to church. Carmen then told us to pray to Saint Nicholas, patron saint of merchants, for the success of her future business endeavor.

"My success is your success," she reminded us before kneeling down to pray.

After Holy Mass, Carmen led us from the Castelletto to the sestiere of San Marco. I lagged behind the others, relishing the late morning sun while admiring the Basilica of San Marco. We crossed the piazza and entered a maze of narrow, muddy streets that reeked of human waste and horse manure. I tried to keep up with Carmen's brisk pace, but a rooster darted out in front of me along with several chickens. Shooing them out of the way, I ran to catch up with the others. We arrived at the well-appointed inn in time for the midday meal.

Carmen had struck a brilliant bargain with Geraldo. The cost to keep us housed in one of the inn's storage rooms and feed us leftovers from the kitchen was considerably lower than what she had been paying up until now to maintain us in her palazzo—not to mention the extra money the innkeeper would gain from our services. What husband didn't appreciate a frugal wife with good business sense? Furthermore, the money from the sale of Carmen's home was now safely hidden away—a guarantee against starvation in her old age should Geraldo ever leave her for a younger woman.

A neatly dressed servant led us to a large room on the ground floor of the well-kept inn. The entrance was in the middle of the wall, and a straw pallet had been placed in each of the four corners. Carmen found a piece of chalk and drew a cross in the center of the floor, dividing the space into four equal parts.

Pointing to the lines, she said, "You will share this room and get along with one another. I don't want any of you to make trouble for my new husband."

"Don't worry, Signora Carmen, we're very grateful," Gisella said, taking it upon herself to speak for everyone.

Miriam inquired, "Will we have to sleep with men in front of one another?"

Carmen sighed. "No, you will go to *their* rooms."

This had been obvious to me from the beginning, and it was rather shocking that Miriam couldn't figure this out for herself.

The same servant who had led us to the room returned with an armful of colorful garments.

Carmen said, "My generous husband wants you to feel welcome. New frocks, compliments of your new master."

"I want the red one," Gisella cried.

"No, I want it," Rosina countered, trying to grab it out of Gisella's hands.

Miriam stood off to the side watching them.

I walked up to Carmen and said, "Please convey my thanks to Don Geraldo. This is very kind of him."

Carmen smiled at me, then turned to the servant. "Bring me

110

all of the frocks."

The woman collected all of the garments and brought them to Carmen. She then doled one out to each of us. As luck would have it, I received the red one, earning vicious stares from the two older girls.

Not wanting any trouble, I turned to Carmen and said, "I don't need the red one. All the frocks are lovely, so I'll be happy with any color."

Carmen looked pointedly at Gisella and Rosina. "But *I* want you to have the red one, Agata."

I lowered my head and said nothing more.

The moment our mistress left the room, Gisella turned on me. "You've been plotting against me behind my back."

I backed away from her. "No, I haven't."

Gisella shoved me. "Why would she give you the dress that I wanted? I've always been her favorite."

"I didn't ask for the red one. You heard me tell her that I would be happy with any color."

Ignoring my valid point, she demanded, "What vile things have you been whispering in her ear?"

Planting my legs firmly against another assault, I replied, "I haven't said anything about you."

Gisella pressed her lips together tightly, chose a rectangle, then proceeded to unpack her belongings. Rosina followed suit. Every once in a while, the two of them threw hateful glances in my direction.

I quietly unpacked my things, glad that I now owned a total of three frocks, two shifts, a pair of wool stockings, a wooden comb, a pair of leather shoes, and a yellow ribbon for my hair.

Carmen purchased a pot of rouge and a bottle of rose water for our communal use. These items were kept in a box under Gisella's cot. Each day, before servicing our patrons, we were expected to redden our cheeks with a bit of rouge and sweeten our skin and breadth with the floral scented water. Carmen insisted that our cosmetics be applied in a way that enhanced our appearance rather than garishly announce our profession. According to her, we should appear as innocent as "blushing brides."

The inn's patrons congregated in the dining hall after sunset to eat and drink. Our job was to serve the food and engage male patrons in flirtatious banter. Carmen and Geraldo lurked in the shadows, ready to negotiate our price should any man wish to take us upstairs.

One man cupped my bottom as I passed his table. "Stay and keep me company," he said in a gruff voice.

Aside from being the largest man in the room, his cold eyes scared me. When I moved away from him, his hand darted out like a snake and clamped down on my wrist.

"My mistress is waiting for me," I said, discreetly trying to wriggle out of his grasp.

The man stood, pulling me close to his chest. I had to crane my neck because he was so tall.

Carmen was beside me at once. Seeing the terror in my eyes and the violent determination on the man's face, she quickly invented an excuse to get me away from him. "I'm afraid this young lady is needed elsewhere."

"My money is as good as anyone else's," the man bellowed. "I want this one."

Carmen's eyes narrowed. "I *said* she is not for you. Now, let go of her or there will be trouble."

My mistress placed her hand on her chest, ready to whip out the dagger with lightning speed.

Geraldo arrived at the table in the nick of time with a ceramic pitcher of complimentary ale. "Let me refill your tankard, good sir!" Cocking his head at me, he added, "You don't want this scrawny one, trust me."

The man eyed me warily, then let go of my wrist and sat down.

Carmen ushered me into the kitchen at once. "Take a deep breath, Agata. You're safe. I'll have Geraldo keep an eye on that one. We'll serve him plenty of ale, which will render him useless. He's leaving in the morning, anyway."

"Thank you."

Carmen touched my cheek. "I'm an orphan, too. The world

can be a cruel place for girls like us."

I made no reply to her startling admission.

Gisella stormed into the kitchen. "What's going on here? Why aren't you out there with the rest of us, Agata?"

Carmen frowned. "I needed to have a word with her. Any offers yet?"

Gisella made a sour face. "The fat leather merchant seated by the fire said he wanted to tan my hide."

Despite being shaken, I found her comment amusing. Carmen and I both giggled, prompting Gisella to join us.

I peeked at the red-faced leather merchant. "I bet he hasn't lain with a woman in a long time. At least it would be quick."

Gisella chuckled and, to my surprise, placed a hand on my shoulder. "Come on, let's go back out there."

Carmen crossed her arms in satisfaction. "It's good to see you two finally getting along. You girls should think of each other as sisters."

Gisella grinned. "You're right. What say you, Agata?"

"I like that idea."

Carmen nodded in satisfaction. "Good. Now, back to work, the both of you!"

The camaraderie between Gisella and I ended the moment we were out of our mistress's sight. She pinched my arm and shoved me in the direction of the leather merchant. Predictably, the fat man beckoned for me to come to his table.

CHAPTER 15
CHRISTMAS 1322
VERONA

Bianca's second child was christened Franceschina. Cangrande, who had been so delighted with his first daughter, remained indifferent toward the second girl. The puny infant barely ate and she cried incessantly, adding to her mother's anxiety.

Bianca desperately wanted another chance at pleasing her lover with a son, but Cangrande had not visited her bed in months, making it obvious that his disappointment matched her own. Although she lived only a stone's throw from the nobleman's palazzo, his visits had ceased long ago.

Christmas Day dawned sunny and clear, and Bianca's spirits were high for she had received an invitation to partake in the celebrations at the Palazzo Scaligero. One of her noble friends had no doubt interceded on her behalf, and she would not waste the precious opportunity. If she couldn't win back Cangrande's love by the end of tonight, then she would have to put another plan into action.

"The day is fine, my lady," Bianca's maid said as she opened the window shutters. "It's almost as warm as a spring day!"

Bianca eyed the winter sky from the comfort of her bed. Sunshine in winter was rare enough in Verona, but warmth, too? Suddenly, she had an idea. "Fetch me some horse urine."

The servant turned away from the window with a quizzical expression. "My lady?"

"Do as you're told. Go on!"

The girl scurried out of the room. Bianca got out of bed and padded to the looking glass in order to examine her face and body. In the last few weeks, she had spent a small fortune in beauty tonics and elixirs to summon her appetite. She couldn't

114

gain weight no matter how much she ate, and it frustrated her to no end. Oh, how she longed for a voluptuous body with luscious curves!

The maid returned a moment later with a wooden bucket brimming with stinky horse urine.

The pungent odor summoned the bile to Bianca's throat, making her instantly irritable. "It took you long enough!"

"Forgive me, my lady. I had to beg some from—"

"I don't care where you got it. Hurry, you must comb it evenly throughout my hair." Seeing the girl's shocked expression, Bianca explained, "Don't you know that horse urine lightens the hair?"

The maid shrugged. "No."

"Every lady's maid knows this trick, you stupid girl."

"I never trained as a—"

"Silence!"

Bianca cursed her father. Burdened with too many debts, he couldn't afford to hire a properly trained lady's maid. At least the twit possessed all of her teeth, which made it appear as though she was well-fed.

Bianca spent the entire morning reclined on a straw palette on the floor. Her hair was carefully fanned around her head like a halo, each strand exposed to the sunlight. Her face and body remained in shadow, protected by a linen cloth in order for the sun not to burn her delicate white skin. Hopefully, the smelly process would significantly lighten her hair. Ideally, it would turn it blonde.

The maid asked, "Which gown shall I set out for you?"

"The rose silk with mink collar."

"Paired with the gold and pearl girdle?"

"What other girdle do I possess, you fool?"

Bianca rose from the floor several hours later. Stiff and sore, she endured a series of herbal rinses to rid her hair of the noxious smell. She dressed with the help of her maid, then admired herself in the reflection of the looking glass. The blonde highlights in her hair glistened in the afternoon sunlight, and her eyes were bright and dilated, thanks to a few drops of belladonna.

Bianca and her maid made their way to the Palazzo Scaligero, then followed the music to the main hall where nobles were already gathered with chalices of mulled wine in their hands.

Bianca took hold of her maid's arm and instructed, "Make yourself invisible and keep your eyes and ears open. I'll want a full account afterward."

"Yes, my lady."

Bianca's gaze settled on the Lady of Verona. The two women had barely spoken in the last year. Unsurprisingly, Giovanna had become angry when she discovered that her husband had impregnated her former lady's maid—twice.

To Bianca's surprise, Giovanna went out of her way to catch her eye and smiled triumphantly. The gesture sickened her, for it could only mean one thing…

Caterina.

The Lord of Verona headed toward his noblemen without glancing in Bianca's direction, instantly causing her heart to sink. The expensive tonics, the lavish creams, the constant consumption of fatty foods to gain weight—it was all for naught. She had even endured an afternoon of nasty horse urine to mimic her rival's fair locks, and he didn't even notice.

Hiding her dismay, she approached him cautiously. "I bid you a most happy and blessed Christmas, my lord."

"Bianca…Happy Christmas to you as well. How are my daughters?"

"They are well, my lord. I take it you are in good health?"

"I am, and so are you, I see. I hope you enjoy the festivities."

He tossed her a half smile, then proceeded to speak to his men. It was a dismissal. Bianca's heart sank as she walked away, for she knew that Giovanna had witnessed the entire exchange.

Caterina glided across the main hall in a gown of flowing silk. Cangrande's eyes were instantly drawn to her meaty haunches. Blessed with an ample bosom and hips that swayed provocatively with each dainty step, the voluptuous blonde

116

attracted the eyes of several men. Childhood fat still clung to Caterina's cheeks, and her innocent expression made her irresistible to the hungry wolves who wished to devour the girl.

Bianca saw her rival smile shyly at Cangrande and deduced that the girl couldn't possibly be over fifteen years of age. He returned the gesture, only it seemed more like a lecherous leer than a smile. Feeling suddenly ill, she slipped into a dimly lit corridor and leaned against the wall.

No matter how hard she tried or how fervently she prayed, she could never compete with a woman like Caterina. The time had come to accept defeat and cut her losses. She reminded herself that Margherita was the apple of her father's eye, so perhaps there was still hope. As if on cue, Cangrande's raucous laughter drifted in from the main hall, mocking her.

Bianca poked her head through the doorway and saw him talking to Caterina. His hand was on the girl's waist, his eyes on her ample breasts.

Thanks to another lady—one of the few allies she still had left in the Veronese court—Bianca discovered that Caterina's mother was a distant cousin to Cangrande. The girl had been sent to the Palazzo Scaligero to serve the Lady of Verona and find a good husband.

There was no doubt in Bianca's mind that Cangrande would claim Caterina's maidenhead for himself before arranging a marriage for the girl.

I must act quickly before the opportunity is lost.

Putting on her best smile, Bianca rejoined the celebration with firm resolve. She ate little and drank even less, all the while monitoring her former lover's every word and deed. When his florid face signaled that he had consumed a copious amount of wine, she casually stood beside him.

"This is such a fine celebration, my lord."

"You should be dancing," he said, playfully chucking her under the chin.

"I will dance until I drop if it pleases you. But, first, I must speak with you about an urgent matter."

"Now? Really, Bianca—"

117

"Please, my lord. It's of utmost importance to me and it will only take a moment of your time."

He sighed. "Go on."

"I think it's time for me to marry—if you find such an arrangement agreeable, of course."

"You're no fool, woman."

She looked pointedly at Caterina. "No, I am not."

"There is no use denying the truth anymore, is there?"

"No."

"You pleased me well, so take comfort in that fact. I know my wife won't accept you back in her service, so I'm prepared to make arrangements for your future."

She grasped his hand and kissed it in gratitude. "You are a generous man. Thank you."

"Rest assured, I will find a suitable husband for you," he said in a tone that implied her dismissal.

"Please know that I will devote my life to making sure your daughters honor you and your family name."

He turned his face away. "Of that, I am sure."

Bianca walked away from him with a light step and a lighter heart.

CHAPTER 16
SPRING 1323
VENICE

The twenty-fifth of April was the holy day dedicated to St. Mark, the patron saint of Venice. People from neighboring towns and villages poured into the city to partake of the festivities. The innkeepers of Venice eagerly anticipated a spike in business, including Geraldo and Carmen.

I took extra care with my toilette since the holy day also meant the arrival of a certain merchant named Stefano. The middle-aged Genoese man traveled to Venice every month to sell exotic merchandise from the East. A regular guest at the inn, Stefano requested my company every time he was in the city. He paid for me to stay with him all night, for the duration of his trip.

Carmen happened to be passing along the outside corridor of the room that I shared with the other girls. I happened to glance up while applying rosemary-scented oil to my hands and caught her staring at me.

"You're as pretty as a spring blossom, Agata," she said from the open doorway.

"Thank you. I'm readying myself for Stefano, who should be here at any moment."

"Does he treat you well?"

She had never asked me such a question before, so I found it odd. "Well enough."

"I'm glad to hear it. You're my best girl—and I say this truthfully. If only the rest of them were more like you."

No sooner had Carmen walked away than Gisella materialized. "Making yourself pretty for your admirer?"

To my surprise, the question lacked the usual sarcasm. "I'm expecting Stefano today."

"The weather is fine so he may arrive early."

Her comment prompted me to throw back the window shutters and allow the balmy sunshine to warm my face. "Such a lovely day."

"Take care, lest the sun darken your skin."

She was right, of course. Current fashion dictated an alabaster complexion, compelling some noblewomen to rub lead-based cosmetics into their skin. Since we couldn't afford such costly products, we kept ourselves pale by religiously avoiding the sun.

Gisella said, "It's a shame that we can't slip out after the midday meal. I would love to partake of the festivities in the city."

"I would like that, too."

The inn's barn, located directly across the way, housed the horses and carts of overnight guests. I couldn't keep the shutters open for very long because of the revolting stench of horse manure.

Miriam rushed into the room. "Stefano is here!"

Gisella said, "I told you he'd be here early."

I pinched my cheeks. "How do I look?"

"Charming," Miriam replied.

Gisella added, "Don't keep the man waiting."

I took a deep breath before going upstairs to Stefano's room. I found him eagerly anticipating my arrival.

Offering him a dazzling smile, I said, "Welcome back to Venice, Don Stefano."

Seated on the edge of the bed, he demanded, "Ah, Agata. Where's my kiss?"

I sauntered over to him and kissed his cheek.

He grabbed me by the waist and forced me onto his lap. "I've missed you."

"I trust you had a good journey."

"Yes," he replied before plying my neck with rough kisses. "Did you miss me?"

I straddled him. "I did."

He extracted a red ribbon sporting a round silver charm. "I

120

have a gift for you. I hope you like it."

I studied the strange marking stamped into the silver. "It's lovely, but what does it mean?"

"That came all the way from Cathay, and the symbol represents the word *resilient*."

"Cathay?" I repeated, awestruck.

Marco Polo, the famous Venetian merchant, died this past January. Carmen had pointed out the old man to me and told me of his incredible travels. Now, I owned something from that magical land in the East.

"I heard that Marco Polo once purchased a similar charm with the same symbol," Stefano said, cutting into my thoughts.

"Really?"

"I wouldn't lie to you."

"Thank you, Stefano. I'll treasure it forever."

He tied the ribbon around my neck, then fondled my breasts. I knew his preferences, what stoked his passion and what cooled it. I proceeded to service him with the expertise of a well-trained prostitute.

The difference between Stefano and the other men at the inn was his desire to hold me in his arms and engage in conversation after the act. I had been instructed by Carmen to indulge his every whim. After all, he paid dearly for my company.

"How long will you stay in Venice?" I inquired while toying with the graying hair on his chest.

"Two days."

"Why such a short stay?"

"My wife is with child and I'm anxious to return home. The midwife is convinced it's a boy this time. Maybe God will finally answer my prayers."

Stefano had four daughters and desperately wanted a son. "I shall pray for your wife's safe delivery of a son."

He kissed the top of my head. "You're a good girl, Agata. If I didn't already have a wife, I would marry you."

I said nothing in response. Although his words were an attempt at kindness, I knew full well that women like me rarely married. Few were as lucky as Carmen.

He put on his tunic, hose, and boots, then kissed my mouth. "I'll see you tonight when I return."

I stood at the window and watched him ride off in his cart. Laden with goods, the ungainly vehicle barely made it down the narrow street due to its width. Metallic items with exotic etchings on their surfaces gleamed in the sunshine. Since they were half hidden by an oil tarp, I couldn't tell if they were vases or chalices. I imagined myself drinking sweet wine out of a fine silver chalice, then chastised myself for being silly. My lips would probably never touch anything as costly as glass, let alone silver.

I took my time going downstairs, daydreaming as I did so. As I made my way down the corridor, I heard the unmistakable sound of weeping. I tiptoed to my room and found Gisella crying on her bed. I hesitated, not knowing what to do.

She glanced up at me and scowled, prompting me to walk past her in silence and sit down on my own bed. Obviously, the rare moment of friendliness we shared earlier was already forgotten. I took out my mending and began to stitch a fragment of hem that had come undone on my undergarment. She continued to weep and the pitiful sound eventually compelled me to set aside my sewing.

I went over and touched her shoulder. "Gisella—"

"Leave me alone!"

I sighed in frustration. "Are you hurt?"

"What do you care?"

"I thought we were becoming friends."

"Well, you thought wrong."

I sat on the edge of her bed. "Shall I get Carmen?"

"No!"

"Why not?"

Sniffing, she placed both of her hands on her lower abdomen and gently caressed the area. "She can't know."

Gisella eyed me strangely in the ensuing silence.

Realization hit me. "You're with child."

Tears welled up in her eyes. "Oh, God…"

"Are you certain?"

"One of the city's midwives confirmed it."

"When?"

"This morning. I snuck off while you were upstairs with Stefano. Carmen was at church."

I stared at her. "What will you do?"

"I have every intention of keeping this child."

"Carmen won't allow it."

"Carmen can go to Hell!"

I tossed a nervous glance at the open door. "You don't know what you're saying."

"He's already promised to care for me and the baby."

"You know who the father is?"

"Of course, I do! Why do you think I want to keep it?"

She averted her eyes and I knew in that moment that she'd broken the cardinal law of prostitutes. "You're in love with this man, aren't you?"

Her eyes revealed the tragic truth, making a verbal reply unnecessary.

I shook my head. "Gisella…"

"His wife is barren and he's so happy that I'm carrying his baby. Please don't tell Carmen."

I hesitated. "She should know about this…"

"*Please*. She'll have the baby cut out of me!"

I recoiled in shock. "Carmen wouldn't do that."

"You think you know our mistress, but you do not."

"She goes to church and takes Communion daily. Wipe the heinous thought from your mind. It's a mortal sin!"

Gisella snorted. "Agata, we are all drowning in sin."

"Yes, but this—"

"There was a girl about your age who came to the house two years before you did. The poor wretch wasn't very smart, and she conceived after a few weeks. She wanted to keep her baby. Carmen drugged the girl and had a barber-surgeon cut the infant out of her womb."

"Oh, no!"

"The girl bled to death during the night."

Horrified, I covered my mouth.

123

Gisella continued, "I have no choice but to run away."

"Where will you go?"

"My lover lives in Genoa."

"You mentioned that he has a wife."

"He'll choose me over her, I know it. I must go to Genoa as soon as possible. If only I could figure out how to get there."

"We'll think of something," I assured her with far more conviction than what I felt.

"We?" she repeated, blinking away her tears.

I took her hand. "I know you and I haven't been friends, but I can't allow you to suffer in your condition. I certainly won't stand idly by while someone cuts you open."

To my surprise, she hugged me. "I'm sorry for the way I've treated you in the past, Agata. I can see now how badly I've misjudged you. I hope you can forgive me."

I offered her a smile. "Don't worry."

Gisella wiped away her tears and got off the bed. "I need to get to work. Thank you, *friend*."

I watched her go, then stretched out on my bed and stared at the ceiling. How could I help Gisella? I pondered her plight throughout the remainder of the afternoon.

Later that night, in Stefano's arms, I decided to enlist his help. He listened as I described the dire predicament in which my new friend found herself.

"She wants to run away," I concluded.

"I would, too, in her place."

Caressing his cheek, I said, "You must swear not to reveal what I've told you to anyone."

"I promise."

"Will you help me smuggle Gisella out of Venice? Her lover is also from Genoa. You may even know him."

"I don't think—"

"Please?" When he hesitated, I planted soft kisses on his face as my hand stroked his manhood.

"Dio," he sighed before pushing my hand away.

"What's wrong?"

"I'm afraid your tricks won't work this time, my little

124

temptress. I have a good relationship with Geraldo."

"Gisella is desperate!"

He shook his head. "I feel bad for your friend, but it's none of my—"

"Carmen will make her kill the baby!"

Stefano sobered instantly. "She wouldn't do that. Carmen is a decent woman."

"She's done it before to another girl. The poor thing died along with the baby…She bled to death."

"Agata—"

"Think of your pregnant wife. Try to imagine Gisella's terror at the prospect of having an infant cut out of her womb. That is a mortal sin, Stefano!"

He cursed under his breath as he debated what to do. Finally, he said, "Very well. She can ride with me to Genoa when I depart."

I hugged him. "Thank you. God is smiling down on you for doing the right thing."

"I have only one question: what happens if your friend gets caught?"

"It can't be worse than what will happen if she stays."

***

"He's willing to help you," I whispered to Gisella the next morning while we were in the kitchen.

She swallowed a bite from the apple in her hand. "What did you say?"

"Stefano. You can ride with him to Genoa."

One of the servants passed us and we both fell silent until she was out of earshot.

Gisella set the apple on the table. "Wait here." She ran down the corridor, peeked into a room, then returned to where I stood. Clasping my hand, she led me out of the kitchen. "Let's go into our room where it's private."

We crept into the chamber we shared, then Gisella closed the door. "You told Stefano that I was pregnant?"

I nodded in response. "I also convinced him to smuggle you out of Venice when he leaves tomorrow."

125

"How will he do that?"

I reached for her hand and smiled. "You can ride with him to Genoa."

"I see."

"Everything will work out, don't worry."

A mocking smile touched her lips. "I'm not worried. *Not anymore.*"

"I wish you didn't have to go, Gisella. I'll miss you."

"I'm not the one who's leaving."

"What do you mean?"

"Farewell, Agata," Gisella said before opening the door. Carmen stood in corridor.

I walked straight into Gisella's trap like a gullible buffoon. I remained silent as Carmen chastised my lack of gratitude and loyalty. Gisella smiled smugly when our mistress cursed me and pointed to the door. At least I was allowed to collect my meager belongings before being tossed into the street like a stray dog.

I slept in a doorway that night, then loitered near the inn the next day. Miriam crept outside at one point to offer me some bread and cheese.

Placing an arm around my shoulders for comfort, she inquired, "What will you do now?"

"I don't know, but I'll think of something. I bet Gisella is gloating right now, isn't she?"

Miriam nodded. "Carmen is in a foul mood."

"Gisella is a treacherous bitch," I muttered, balling my hands into fists. "I risked so much to help her, too!"

"I'm sorry for you, my friend. If there's anything I can do…"

"I appreciate that, Miriam."

"I had better go inside now."

I thanked her and waited for Stefano to emerge from the inn. The moment he exited the door, I pounced on him.

Startled, he took a step backward. "Agata! I heard what happened. I'm sorry for your troubles."

I walked behind him as he entered the barn. "I have nowhere to go, Stefano. No money, either."

Hitching his horse to his cart, he muttered, "I wish I could help you."

"You can!"

Sparing me a brief glance, he asked, "How?"

I placed my hand on his chest. "What about an advance? Rather than pay Carmen for my services, you can pay me directly, *now*, upfront. The next time you're in Venice—"

"I don't think so."

I slid my hand down and grabbed his cock. *"Please."*

He slapped my hand away. "No."

Stunned by his callousness, I glared at him. "Very well. I'll go to Genoa and introduce myself to your wife. I'm sure she would love to meet me."

"Are you threatening me?"

"No."

"Good," he said before hoisting himself up into the cart.

Keeping pace with the horse as it exited the barn, I peered up at Stefano and squinted my eyes against the morning sun. "I'm *promising* you that I'm going to find your wife and let her know how we engaged in prick-play while she sat at home— heavy and miserable—carrying your child."

"You wouldn't dare."

"Oh, but I would." I raised my hand, palm up. "My secrecy comes at a price."

Cursing me to Hell, damnation, and every other unsavory place, he reached into his pouch and gave me some coins.

"Thank you, Stefano," I said sweetly.

He drove off in his cart without another word, leaving me behind in a cloud of dust. Casting a backward glance at the inn, I spit on the ground and walked away.

Stefano's money allowed me to rent a humble room in the poorest part of the city, so my situation wasn't as dire as when I had first arrived in Venice.

Alone—but certainly not without options after all I'd learned from Carmen—my mind raced with ideas of what I could do to do better my situation in life. I wanted nothing more than to leave Venice and all the ugliness behind me, but then what? Returning to my beloved Verona without guaranteeing my safety and securing my future was out of the question. I vowed that if I ever returned to my birth city, it would be with my head held high. How this lofty goal would be achieved, I had no idea—at least not yet.

My best option was marriage, of course. My former mistress lived comfortably thanks to her financially stable husband. Why couldn't I enjoy the same arrangement? Carmen was neither smarter nor prettier than me, so I set out to find a suitable mate.

Desirous of breaking completely with my past, I embellished the backstory I had originally invented when Ubaldo found me. If questioned, I would tell people that I was a runaway orphan from a convent in the countryside; the secret lovechild of a nobleman unbeknownst to me. My vivid imagination even went as far as creating the unkind nuns who had beaten me for years, thus prompting my daring escape.

Days of wandering the city in search of potential husbands resulted in blistered feet, despair, and frustration. Perhaps I had been naïve in believing that I could find a rich bachelor. I was on the verge of abandoning all hope when I spotted *him*—an impeccably dressed elderly gentleman accompanied by a liveried manservant. Jewels sparkled on his gnarled fingers and his rheumy eyes followed the swaying hips of every young girl in the market square.

Perfect.

Keeping my distance, I tracked my prey as stealthily as a cat would stalk a mouse. In a matter of days I discovered that his name was Count Armando Visconti. The old nobleman had recently buried his third wife and, in addition a Venetian palazzo, he owned a considerable amount of land in Treviso.

Treviso…

The Lord of Verona had not yet succeeded in conquering that city, and every Veronese knew that was his greatest desire. My desire to be the next Countess Visconti triggered an idea for a much grander plan—one that would allow me to return to Verona unscathed.

First, I had to conquer Armando Visconti's heart. I took

extra special care with my toilette the following morning and chose a spot in the piazza where I could discreetly observe the count's palazzo. Boats laden with cargo floated past me on the canal and, in an attempt to ease my boredom, I tried to guess the contents of each barrel or ceramic vessel that I glimpsed on board.

My patience was finally rewarded when Armando exited his home with his liveried manservant in tow. I tracked them across the bridge to a piazza featuring a special market. The weekly affair attracted the city's wealthier customers due to its fine wares—bolts of high quality fabric, scented oils, specialty foods, and rare spices.

Armando stopped to examine a pair of delicate glass goblets, then wandered to the furrier to purchase a measure of expensive ermine. I maintained a certain distance while monitoring his every move. A corpulent woman in plain garb hovered near him—obviously a servant sent on an errand. Edging closer, I discreetly pinched my cheeks and bit my lips to heighten their color. Extracting a coin from my purse, I "accidentally" shoved the fat servant into the old man, causing him to lose his balance and fall to the ground. Before the outraged woman had a chance to curse at me, I pressed the coin into the palm of her meaty hand while issuing a warning look. Taking the hint, she bit her thumb at me and stormed off toward a spice vendor.

I stepped in front of Armando's manservant before he had a chance to help his master. "Are you all right, sir?"

Not bothering to look at me, the old man impatiently waved away my question. "Where's my valet?"

I sank to my knees and reached for his veined hand. "Here, let me help you."

Glaring at the fat woman, he said, "Did you see that, Rino? The cow plowed right into me and ran off! I've a mind to report her to the authorities."

Rino made another attempt to help his master and I shooed him away. "People have lost their sense of propriety nowadays. Are you hurt, my lord?"

"I don't believe so. I think—" Armando stopped speaking

when he finally turned his head and looked at me. *"Oh."*

"What do you think?" I prompted, batting my eyelashes.

He smiled, his eyes slightly dilating when they rested on my bosom. "I think you're an angel."

I offered him my most provocative laugh—a practiced sound mimicking tinkling bells. "You are too kind, my lord."

"Oh, that I were your lord! Your husband is a fortunate man, indeed, to have such a comely and gracious wife."

His eyes held a wicked gleam as he leered at me, and I was instantly reminded of Ubaldo. *Lecherous old men.* I lowered my gaze in feigned modesty. "I'm unmarried, sir."

Armando looked at me in a way that I'd seen countless times. Rino helped him to his feet, but the old man kept his eyes on me.

He bowed. "I am Count Armando Visconti."

I curtsied. "It's an honor to meet you, my lord."

"May I have the pleasure of your name?"

"Agata."

"Agata..?"

I hadn't thought to give myself a fake surname. Panicked, I blurted the first word that came to my head. "Rondine."

"Like the bird?"

"Yes."

"How unusual. Well, the swallow is pretty and graceful, so I suppose the name suits you perfectly. I was about to partake of some wine to quench my thirst. It would please me greatly if you joined me."

"I'm afraid I have no maid to escort me, and I don't wish for my lack of chaperone to appear unseemly."

"Fear not, my dear, your chastity will remain intact. My valet, Rino, will accompany us."

I allowed him to lead me to a fine tavern where we drank good wine and chatted for the remainder of the morning.

Armando and I became inseparable after that day—I made sure of it. In the following weeks I repeatedly rejected his amorous advances while playing the role of the coy maiden who'd been raised in a convent. I eventually allowed him to

130

seduce me, of course, then announced my pregnancy two months later. My elderly lover became overjoyed and I insisted that we get married. Thrice widowed and nearing death, he didn't seem to care when I told him that I was a nobleman's bastard.

To my irritation, Rino eyed me with suspicion. Admittedly, I couldn't blame him. He knew as well as I did that Armando could barely lift his cock to urinate let alone impregnate a fertile young woman like myself. Despite this, he displayed prudence by remaining silent.

Naturally, I "lost" the baby shortly after our wedding day. It was easy enough to buy some pig's blood from the butcher across the canal and splatter it on the bedsheets to make it appear as if I'd suffered a miscarriage. If the servants suspected my deception, they said nothing about it. The fact that I often plied them with trinkets and coins no doubt encouraged their willful ignorance. As for Rino, he avoided me altogether, which suited me fine.

I pretended to be melancholic for days, shutting myself in my room to grieve over our lost child. Armando took pity on me and purchased lovely gifts to lift my spirits—sweetmeats, hair ribbons, and even a shiny gold bracelet! I gradually allowed myself to feel happiness again, being careful not to destroy the ruse by appearing too joyful too soon.

The best gift Armando gave me was Bea, my lady's maid. Recently widowed and older than me by almost a decade, her late husband's gambling debts forced her into service. Blessed with a sharp tongue—and an even sharper wit—she and I took to each other instantly. Practical and cunning, my maid's perception and resourcefulness would come in handy in my quest toward financial and social stability. We became inseparable companions and, for the first time since Serafina's death, I felt like I had a real friend.

CHAPTER 17
VERONA

Caterina eventually married a wealthy nobleman old enough to be her grandfather. Cangrande had enjoyed weeks of languid lovemaking with the nubile girl prior to her marriage. Once she was properly wed, he departed on another military campaign to secure more territory for the Ghibellines.

Caterina declared her pregnancy a mere month after her wedding night, prompting her husband to brag of his virility despite his advanced age. Unfortunately, the girl had lain with the Lord of Verona the night before her nuptials, so she had no idea whose baby grew inside of her womb.

By the time she was in the painful throes of childbirth, Cangrande's attention had already shifted to Teodora. The sophisticated lady had managed to curry his favor despite being married to one of the most arrogant nobles in the Veronese court. The torrid affair began as spontaneously as it ended, with Teodora allowing the lustful warlord to possess her in a shadowy corridor during a dinner feast. They were both drunk and repentant afterward, but that didn't stop them from continuing their clandestine relationship.

Teodora eventually became pregnant and gave birth to a female child. Her clueless husband insisted on naming the infant Lucia, after his mother. As Lucia got older, the uncanny resemblance she bore to Cangrande could no longer be ignored. Suspicious of his wife's infidelity, Teodora's husband beat her so badly that she didn't show her face in public for weeks. No words were ever exchanged between the cuckolded husband and his powerful overlord. The bastard came to be called Lucia *Cagnola* (bitch pup) by the nobles, and the child was sent to Bergamo to be raised by Teodora's family.

Military campaigns kept Cangrande busy throughout the summer and fall. He returned to Verona in the winter and met

Petronella. Widowed at a young age, she had accompanied her father to Verona to hunt for another husband. Tall and fair with a pleasant laugh and soulful eyes, he met her at the home of a mutual acquaintance. Within weeks, he lured the delightful woman into his arms. The affair, although discreet, ended in disgrace when the lady became pregnant.

Giustina, Cangrande's seventh child, was born months later. Disowned by her father, Petronella still managed to find joy in motherhood. She and her daughter took up residence in a nearby villa where her lover would frequently visit them. Giustina instantly won her father's favor thanks to her good looks and sweet disposition.

Petronella devoted herself wholeheartedly to the task of raising her daughter, and she didn't seem to mind when Cangrande's romantic interest in her faded away. In fact, she became his friend and confidant, offering wise counsel and easing his troubles with her merry company. It wasn't long before the nobility welcomed her back into their fold, including her father. Petronella was soon invited to many events at the Palazzo Scaligero, and even Giovanna was seen speaking to the young woman on a few occasions.

***

In July 1325 the Lord of Verona was on the battlefield in Modena, his dented shield a testament to the many gruesome fights he had endured in his lifetime. The new hauberk he had commissioned was sturdier than the last one and more resilient.

An enemy soldier came barreling toward him. Emitting a battle cry, Cangrande wielded his sword with such force that it partially severed the man's arm at the shoulder. He then jabbed the wounded man in the neck. Blood spurted violently from the severed artery, splattering the horse's sweaty coat with dark red spots.

He stared at the dying man's face. "Go to Hell, Guelph scum."

"My lord!"

Cangrande swiveled in his saddle. A soldier rode toward him at top speed. They were both engulfed in a cloud of dust when the sweaty horse came to an abrupt halt.

"My lord, a messenger has arrived at the camp! Vicenza is burning!"

"What?!"

"A fire has raged through the city!"

Cangrande turned his horse around and galloped toward the encampment where a messenger waited to ply him with more details. Leaving his troops under the command of his military captain, he departed for Vicenza with a select group of men that included Ottavio.

They spotted the smoke from miles away. Upon arriving in Vicenza, the men were dismayed to see that much of the city lay in charred ruins. Cangrande dismounted and paced the ground with angry steps, cursing as he did so. Noticing the ancient church across the road, he stopped.

"My lord, what's wrong?" Ottavio demanded.

Ignoring his advisor's question, Cangrande made a beeline for the church's entrance. The men followed their overlord into the ancient structure, then watched as he stormed into a chapel covered in Byzantine mosaics. A painted wooden statue of the Virgin Mary gazed down upon him with an expression of maternal compassion. A pair of candles flickered in the dim space, illuminating her placid face.

After glaring at the statue for a long moment, he demanded, "Santa Maria, why have you forsaken me—*me*, of all people, your most loyal and faithful devotee! Tell me, what have I done to deserve such disfavor, to provoke such anger?"

The men exchanged wary glances in the ensuing silence.

"Have I not fasted enough times for you? Prayed frequently and fervently? Honored you at every turn?"

Cangrande continued ranting and raving inside the chapel. Overhearing the angry one-sided exchange, the men cringed and huddled together in fear. One man hastily vacated the church, crossing himself in the process.

Ottavio poked his head into the chapel and cleared his throat. "My lord, perhaps we should—"

"I'm not finished!"

Cangrande's eyes were unusually bright, his face contorted into a mask of rage. Fearful of God's wrath, Ottavio joined the other men who waited outside.

The Lord of Verona eventually exited the church with a pale face. He walked straight to his advisor and confessed, "My anger and disillusionment are too heavy to bear, Ottavio."

"I can understand your frustration, my lord, but who are we to question the will of God?"

"I feel strange…"

"You don't look well."

Cangrande muttered under his breath as he heaved himself into the saddle. A film of sweat broke out on his brow, and his teeth chattered as chills raked through his body.

The men scoured the city for survivors and news before heading back to Modena. No sooner had they arrived at the encampment than Cangrande fell ill. His men carried him into his tent and summoned the physician. Draughts and elixirs were prescribed, but they failed to alleviate his condition.

Cangrande prayed to the Virgin Mary and, for the first time in his life, she wasn't there for him. Terrified, he squeezed his eyes shut and prayed harder, begging her forgiveness. His failure to get better forced his return to Verona in order for him to fully recuperate.

Speculations were made that perhaps the Queen of Heaven had decided to castigate Cangrande for his pride and the disrespectful manner in which he had addressed her in Vicenza.

The Lord of Verona was greatly troubled when these rumors reached his ears. Overwhelmed by guilt, he summoned his priest to his bedside and confessed his sin. As penance, he fasted for several days, praying frequently and fervently for the Virgin's forgiveness. He even swore to name his next female child Maria if she granted him mercy.

To everyone's amazement, and Cangrande's immense relief, his health improved considerably. He grew stronger by the day and was back to his old self by early autumn. To show his gratitude, he offered a sizeable donation to Santa Maria Matricolare.

By November, the Lord of Verona was out battling for the Ghibelline cause once again. With the help of Passerino, he enjoyed a great victory at Monteveglio over the Bolognese Guelphs. Meanwhile, his fellow Ghibelline, Castruccio Castracani, triumphed over the Florentine Guelphs at Altopascio. Despite these two devastating losses for the Guelphs, their stronghold remained unchallenged.

Treviso, still unconquered, continued to silently mock the Lord of Verona. He vowed to bring it under control within his lifetime, even if it killed him.

CHAPTER 18
JUNE 1326
VENICE

Located on the bank of the Grand Canal, Armando's palazzo afforded us a stunning view. Vessels of every shape and size passed outside our balconies. Passenger ships transported wealthy magistrates flaunting fur and expensive velvet garments. Cargo ships slid past, carrying wine, oil, and exotic foodstuffs from the East.

During the summer months the stench from the canal could summon the bile to one's throat. Bits of rotten food and human waste sometimes floated past on the water's surface. One time, I spied a bloated man bobbing face-down. Concerned for my "feminine well-being," Armando had pulled me away from the window when he spied the decaying corpse.

The dazzling palazzos across the canal boasted colorful banners. Noble families competed with each other to show off their wealth. Some even sewed gemstones to the vibrant fabrics, or had their coats of arms embroidered in costly silver thread. These expensive decorations were usually displayed from the highest windows, far from thieving hands. The Visconti banner, fashioned from green velvet, hung from a window high above our heads.

One June morning as I gazed out the window, I recalled the date. It was the fifth of June. Six years ago, I had married Nunzio. If only I had I been permitted to remain at the convent with my aunt. My life would have turned out so differently. The dark memories of Alvino and the cruelty of Venice cast a shadow on my current mood.

A swallow zipped past my line of vision, instantly lifting my spirit. The bird tried to catch a fish and failed. Two more attempts and the swallow succeeded. I smiled as it soared toward the riverbank to enjoy the fruit of its labor.

Armando shuffled into the room. "Agata, come away from the window lest you catch cold."

The cantankerous old goat shivered with cold in the middle of summer and assumed that everyone suffered the same plight. Not wishing to argue, I closed the shutters and crossed the room to where he stood.

Placing my arms around his neck, I smiled. "You're worried about tonight, aren't you?"

"I want the banquet to be perfect."

"It will be. I've already seen to the preparations."

"Go and see to them again," he ordered, patting my bottom and urging me toward the door.

Important people were visiting the city and my husband had invited them to sup with him. I wandered downstairs to the kitchen to oversee the preparations. The servants eyed me with resentment, but I didn't care.

I picked up a bowl containing beaten eggs and sniffed. "These aren't fresh. Toss them out and start over."

One of the servants took the bowl. "Yes, Contessa."

I preened inwardly whenever anyone addressed me by my noble title. I had earned this privilege.

The banquet ended up being a great success that night, which sweetened Armando's sour mood. So pleased was he by my handiwork that he suggested we try to make another child. I readily agreed, for there was nothing I wanted more than a son to secure my position.

He visited my bedchamber that night in high spirits with flushed cheeks, claiming to have consumed a virility tonic prescribed by one of the city's most trusted apothecaries. While it did help him get through the act with less difficulty than usual, it also made him curl up in pain afterward.

"Where did you get that concoction?" I demanded, alarmed.

"The apothecary said the mild herbs are—*Santo Cristo*!" He couldn't finish the sentence due to a spasm.

I hastily shrugged into my surcoat. "My God, he's poisoned you! What's in that tonic?"

138

"Roots from India? Or is it Africa?"

"I'm fetching the physician."

"Get Rino—oh, it hurts!"

Rino was fast asleep in the antechamber of my husband's room. "Wake up! The count is ill."

The valet barely hid his contempt and suspicion as he demanded, "What's wrong with him?"

"He drank a love potion."

Muttering vile curses, Rino ran past me. I followed him back to my chamber. We found Bea seated on the edge of the bed trying to comfort the count.

Seeing us, she explained, "I heard him cry out."

Armando's eyes watered at the sight of his valet. "Rino! I am dying! Why did I take that vile love potion?"

"Those were your exact words the last time something like this happened, my lord. The physician has warned you to abstain from exotic concoctions."

"This one is different. It's made from southernwood."

Rino sighed and pinched the bridge of his nose in irritation. "Southernwood is closely related to wormwood, which doesn't agree with you."

Bea and I exchanged wary glances. How many other times had the count consumed love potions?

Rino said to me, "We must make him vomit."

Armando groaned in protest as Rino urged his master to stick his finger down his throat.

Noticing our empty chamber pot, I said, "Wait!" I grabbed it and held it beneath my husband's chin as he dry heaved.

Rino took the chamber pot from me. "Here, I'll do that."

I went to stand by the door, unsure of what to do next.

Bea inquired, "Shall I dispatch a servant to fetch the physician?"

"Yes," Rino and I replied in unison.

By the time the physician arrived, Armando had already purged his body of the dubious love potion. Weak and tired from the harrowing ordeal, Armando fell asleep after ingesting a healing draught.

"Feed him beef broth and fortified wine when he wakes up," the physician instructed.

Wringing my hands, I inquired, "Is there anything else I should do?"

"Pray for him."

Rino escorted the physician downstairs.

Eying my snoring husband, I wondered if, *this time*, he'd managed to impregnate me.

As if reading my thoughts, Bea whispered, "Did he at least perform the deed?"

Rolling my eyes, I replied, "Barely."

"Hopefully, it was enough for you to conceive."

"From your lips to God's ear."

To my frustration, I did not conceive. Determined, I consulted with every physician, midwife, and apothecary in the city for fertility cures. Everyone seemed to agree that the problem rested with me. Only one person—a courageous wise woman—laid the blame at the count's feet. According to her, Armando's seed lacked the potency needed to create new life in my fertile womb. Simply put, he was too old.

"Will you write to him?" Bea asked me one evening while turning down the coverlet on my bed.

"I'll send the letter tomorrow."

I had hoped to conceive before putting my plan into action. Returning to Verona as the mother of a little count or countess would only increase my chances of success.

Bea said, "Time passes quickly and youth fades fast, so take advantage of your beauty and charm while you still have it. Also, given the current political climate, the time to strike is now. Goodnight, my lady."

Bea's words hung heavily in the air. She was right, of course. It was time to entice the Lord of Verona with a proposal that he could not refuse. If I continued to wait, I might lose the opportunity.

I wrote a brief letter by the light of a fading candle, then went to bed. Mustering my courage the next morning, I sent the secret message to Palazzo Scaligero.

"He's still alive?" Cangrande demanded in surprise before tearing into a haunch of roasted venison.

"Alive and well, it seems," Ottavio replied.

The warlord chuckled heartily as he chewed. "How old is he? One hundred? Two hundred?"

Ottavio laughed, as did several other nobles who sat around the dining table. "I believe he's well past seventy, my lord."

"A ripe old age, indeed. I must know Visconti's secret for longevity. I hear he's widowed two times over."

"Three times," Ottavio corrected. "And he's currently on his fourth wife—a bonny girl, no less."

Cangrande held out his chalice and a servant came forth to refill it with wine. "Who is she?"

"A nobleman's bastard, if the rumors are true."

"Whose?"

"No one seems to know. Not even the girl. The count is currently residing in Venice with his wife. Our spies have confirmed that he owns a considerable amount of land in Treviso."

The Lord of Verona sat back and took a long sip of wine, his mind racing with the possibilities this information represented. "Still no leads on who sent the letter?"

"No, but it's obviously one of your allies."

"*Or* it could be a trap."

"The script is neat, almost childlike. Your scribe suspects a female hand."

"Visconti's wife?"

Ottavio shrugged. "Perhaps."

Cangrande thoughtfully picked his teeth with the sharp tip of his knife. "Read it again to me."

Ottavio held up the vellum sheet, which bore no seal. *"To the most honorable Lord of Verona…That which you desire is now within your reach. A considerable amount of land in Treviso can be yours for a price. Count Armando Visconti is a reasonable man, but make no mention of this letter."* He paused. "That's it."

141

Cangrande nodded thoughtfully. "I believe we should pay the count a visit."

"We don't even know if what this letter says is true," Ottavio pointed out. "Remember, Count Visconti is the brother-in-law of the late Rizzardo da Camino. I doubt he'll be happy to see you."

The Camino family ruled Treviso, and they supported Padua's rebellion against Verona.

Cangrande made a face. "Guelph bastards. At least his son, Guecellone, had the good sense to change sides before he died at Serravalle."

At this, all the noblemen around the table raised their chalices in a toast.

Ottavio cleared his throat. "What exactly are you hoping to accomplish with this visit to Venice, my lord?"

"Isn't it obvious? Purchase Visconti's land, of course. Having a foothold in Treviso may serve us in the future. After all, the old count is on the verge of death and certainly doesn't need it."

"According to our spies, he's in considerable debt."

Cangrande grinned. "Even better. A pile of money to spend on his new young wife should appeal to him."

"And if he refuses to sell?"

"Leave that to me, Ottavio. Besides, I'm curious to meet Visconti's bride."

CHAPTER 19
JUNE 1326
VENICE

Armando broke the wax seal and read the letter while the messenger's eyes rested on the cleft between my breasts. I made no attempt to move or cover myself and, when the young man met my eyes, I didn't flinch. In fact, I fluttered my eyelashes at him. To my amusement, his cheeks grew red and he lowered his gaze.

Someone cried from atop a passing barge, drawing my gaze to the open window. The late June breeze carried the scent of rain, so the fishermen were steering their boats toward the bank. A storm brewed in a tumultuous sky, and the weather matched my state of mind.

My husband crumpled the vellum sheet in his hand, then nodded to the messenger, who spun on his heel and exited the palazzo. I watched as Armando paced the room, his expression a mixture of worry and resignation.

"All is well, I hope," I prompted.

He threw up his hands. "The Lord of Verona will be in Venice next week and wishes to come here."

"Here?" I repeated with feigned surprise. My letter had produced quick results! "Whatever for?"

"There's no mention of his intention in the letter aside from paying his respect while he's conducting business in the city, but I know his *true* reason."

I poured wine into a chalice, then held it out to him. "Oh? What would that be?"

Armando took the vessel from my hand and drank deeply. "Treviso is the one city he cannot overtake."

I had underestimated my husband's intelligence. "What does that have to do with you?"

143

"My family owned many properties in Treviso. My sister, Giovanna, was the wife of Rizzardo da Camino. My part is valuable—a huge expanse of fertile land on the city's outskirts."

Rizzardo da Camino, the sworn enemy of Verona. "I see," I said before taking a sip of wine.

"I've been a staunch Guelph my whole life, and Cangrande is the most ardent Ghibelline in Europe, as I'm sure you know."

"Do you think he's coming here to make you an offer on your property?"

"Why else? Owning the land would give him an edge."

I gave him a blank look. "An edge to what?"

"Is there nothing but air in that lovely little head of yours, Agata? An edge to conquer Treviso, of course! Everyone knows Cangrande lusts for it."

"I didn't know," I lied.

"I'm not surprised. Women are vain creatures. They only care about frivolous things like fashion and cosmetics. This is why God made men leaders."

My blood boiled in the face of his condescending words. "Would you sell to him?"

"Never!"

I hid my dismay. Obviously, this would not be as easy as I had hoped. "Why not, my love?"

"That Ghibelline scoundrel can go to Hell!"

I allowed him a bit of time to compose himself before pointing out, "But you once mentioned to me that your family switched sides…"

"We had no choice! Do you honestly believe that I would willingly accept the emperor after a lifetime of loyalty to the pope? My weak nephew betrayed his family name while he lay dying in Serravalle—people do stupid things under duress. Secretly, I'm still a Guelph at heart."

I placed my hands on his frail shoulders and massaged them. "I understand, but you *will* receive the Veronese nobleman regardless, won't you? It would be an honor to have such an illustrious guest under our roof."

144

"I have no choice but to receive him. To do otherwise would incite his anger and I'm too old for squabbles. We'll prepare a fine supper for his arrival and welcome him in a manner that befits his station. I'm counting on you."

"Worry not, Armando. I will do my best to impress the Lord of Verona."

***

Cangrande arrived at our palazzo accompanied by another man. I watched from my bedchamber window as our guests crossed the courtyard. Both men sported weft-patterned silk flaunting heavy gold thread and silver beading. The garments were deliberately chosen to show off their wealth and power—two things one should always bring to the bargaining table.

After a long afternoon of beauty treatments, I had opted to wear a low-cut red velvet gown that displayed my smooth décolletage to its fullest advantage. A single pearl suspended from a gold choker hovered in the hollow of my throat.

Bea came to stand beside me at the window. "You look stunning, my lady. Good luck tonight."

"Thank you, Bea. Don't wait up for me."

I entered the main hall where Cangrande and my husband were engaged in conversation. Keeping my eyes lowered, I respectfully curtsied before the men. The heat of their collective stares burned my skin.

Placing a possessive arm around my shoulders, Armando introduced me to our guests. Cangrande bent over my hand, his eyes lingering on my face. His advisor, Ottavio, followed suit.

I spoke little throughout the meal while adopting a modest demeanor. Cangrande's eyes sought mine a few times, but I doubted that he recognized me. In the six years since our encounter in the ancient vestibule, I had undergone a great transformation.

The men talked of Venice, then Cangrande mentioned new projects underway in Verona. I listened quietly, fighting the surge of emotion at the mention of my birth city. They gravitated from neutral topics to politics, which I knew tried my husband's patience due to the heightened color of his face. I

145

also noticed that Ottavio kept plying Armando with undiluted wine, refilling his chalice to the rim whenever it was empty.

At one point, Cangrande said, "You're an experienced man of the world, Count Visconti. You must suspect my reason for being here."

Armando set down his chalice. "You want my land."

If Cangrande was startled by my husband's lack of subtlety, he didn't show it.

"I'm willing to pay you more than what would be considered a fair price," he said smoothly.

Armando's face remained stoic. "That's my ancestral property, and I'm bound by duty to keep it in my family."

Cangrande smiled tightly. "You have two living daughters, but both of your grandsons are dead—killed simultaneously in a hunting accident, if my memory serves me well. Your surviving grandchild is a nun at the Convento di Santa Cecilia. There are no males in your family to inherit."

"You have obviously done your research."

"I wouldn't be here propositioning you otherwise, sir. I'm not the kind of man who wastes precious time."

Armando pointed at me and all eyes turned in my direction. "My wife is young and fertile, as you can see. For all we know she may be carrying my son in her womb as we speak."

I lifted my chin and risked a glance at the men.

Cangrande smiled at me. "Are you with child, my lady?"

The count stood, his face a florid mask of drunken outrage. "How dare you address my wife in such a manner?"

"I beg your pardon, Count Visconti." The Lord of Verona turned to me and added, "My apologies."

I lowered my head without comment.

Not wishing to argue with the volatile warlord, the count sat down. "I will consider your proposal, my lord."

"I respect your desire to contemplate the matter," Cangrande assured his host in a placating tone.

Ottavio refilled Armando's chalice. "You would benefit greatly from accepting my master's offer."

The count frowned. "Verona would also benefit greatly—

146

I'm certain that your master didn't come here out of the kindness of his heart to help a poor old man!"

My eyes slid to Cangrande to gauge his reaction. Although he maintained his composure in the face of Armando's harsh words, I could see that he wanted that land—*badly*.

"As an ally of Verona, this shouldn't be a problem for you," Cangrande pointed out in a deceptively soft tone.

Ottavio eventually led my inebriated husband to a chair by the fire on the far end of the room. Cangrande and I remained at the table. He glanced at the servants hovering in the background, then gave me a pointed look. Taking the hint, I immediately dismissed them with a wave of my hand.

When we were alone, he refilled my chalice before refilling his own. "Dinner was delicious, my lady. My advisor and I are grateful for your fine hospitality."

"You honor our home, my lord. You must excuse the count. He is an extremely stubborn man."

"While that may be true, he has impeccable taste in women."

I smiled slightly. "You flatter me."

"I'm certain that you're aware of your power over men, Countess Visconti. You can easily convince your husband to sell his land. After all, the sum I'm offering will cover his outstanding debts."

My stomach sank. *Debts?*

Cangrande studied my face closely. "I can see by your expression that you had no prior knowledge of your husband's financial dilemma."

"Armando never shared that information with me," I confessed in a shaky voice.

"I apologize for causing you distress."

"How bad is it?" When he hesitated, I prompted, "Should I be worried?"

"Most definitely."

Dropping my fake Venetian accent, I said, "Only a prideful old fool would reject a generous offer from the Lord of Verona, *the most loyal Ghibelline on Earth, sanctioned by God and favored by the Madonna*."

147

Recognition lit up his features. "Someone said those same words to me once. A clever, silver-tongued, Veronese girl—"

"Admiring the columns in the ancient vestibule behind Santa Maria Matricolare."

"*You* sent me the letter."

"I did."

"Why?"

"I thought I could convince my husband to sell his land, but I was wrong. He's far more belligerent and stubborn than I believed possible. I still want to help you, *especially* now that I know the count is in debt."

"You didn't know about his debt until now," he pointed out, his hand resting on the hilt of his sword. "Explain yourself."

"I hate Venice, my lord. I desire nothing more than to return to my beloved Verona. I hoped to enlist your help by proving my loyalty to you and the Ghibelline cause."

He glanced at Armando, fast asleep in a chair. "How do I know you're not a spy for the Guelphs?"

"If you suspected me of such treachery you would have already run me through with your sword."

"True," he conceded.

"Armando's land could be your foothold into Treviso. It's only a matter of time before you conquer that city."

His dark eyes roamed over my face and throat, then settled upon the jewels sparkling on my slender fingers. "Seated before me is a countess in all her finery, but I remember a poor girl in rags. You must have quite a story to tell. You're not really a nobleman's bastard, are you?"

"No, but as far as the count and all of Venice is concerned, I am. If I tell you the truth, will it remain between us?"

"You have my word."

"I was born and raised in Verona. My parents are very poor. I fled to Venice in search of a better life and succeeded in my goal." There was no reason for Cangrande to know about my marriage to Nunzio, the accusation of witchcraft hurled against me, or my former life as a prostitute.

"I admire your resilience. Not many women exhibit such

resourcefulness and courage."

"I appreciate that, my lord."

"I came to Venice with the intention of acquiring your husband's property legally and honorably. Given the political circumstances, however, I prepared myself for the possibility of the count's rejection."

"How so?"

"I had a bill of sale drawn up with his signature."

"A forgery," I concluded.

"My scribe is a man of many talents. All I need now is the Visconti seal to make it valid."

"Do you have the document with you?"

"No."

We both looked at Armando when a loud snore escaped his lips.

I stood. "I can sneak into his study right now."

"Wait—one of the servants might see you. You can take the seal once your household is asleep."

I sat down. "How will I get it to you?"

"Bring the seal to the Basilica di San Giacomo tomorrow after Holy Mass."

"I'll send my maid—"

"No. I want *you*."

I hesitated. "Very well, my lord."

"Your eyes harbor a question. Ask it."

"If you intend to use a forged bill of sale to obtain a piece of property, *something else* needs to be done in order to avoid any future complications."

He gave me a long, measured look. "Life in Venice has transformed you into a cunning woman."

"A *prudent* woman."

"I stand corrected, my lady. You're right about taking action, and I'm prepared to carry it out."

"You risk implication, my lord. Think of the dire consequences if something goes wrong." I paused for emphasis. "Allow me to prove my loyalty to you."

My words impressed and surprised him. "Are you certain

that you can go through with it?"

"Yes, but only on one condition…"

"I'm listening."

"An act of that magnitude deserves compensation. You were prepared to offer my husband a handsome sum for his land. I propose that you give it to me, instead."

Cangrande crossed his arms and stared at me.

I continued, "Do we have a deal, my lord?"

"We do, my lady."

***

I crept to the Basilica di San Giacomo while my husband slept off the effects of too much wine. Once inside, I slipped into a dim chapel. A man in a hooded cloak came to stand beside me. We were the only two people in the church at that hour.

Cangrande whispered, "Do you have the seal?"

I handed him the small iron seal bearing the Visconti coat of arms. He placed it in the leather pouch at his waist, then extracted a glass vial.

Handing it to me, he said, "I assume you know what this is."

My hands trembled as I raised the vial toward a colorful sunbeam pouring from a stained glass window. Its contents resembled liquid amber. "Yes."

Searching my face, he whispered, "The light of day turns to ash the promises made in the night."

"I haven't changed my mind."

"You haven't said a word, either."

I put on my most vulnerable face. "I'm frightened."

Once again, my words surprised him.

Taking a step closer, he said, "In the unlikelihood that you're caught, you'll be protected from any legal ramifications. Of that, you have my word."

"I'm afraid of other consequences…"

"I don't understand."

"I've never killed a man, my lord. What if his soul seeks revenge? What if I'm denied Heaven when I die?"

His eyes softened in the face of my youth and vulnerability. "I've slaughtered countless Guelphs on the battlefield and not a

150

single soul has come back to haunt me. Aiding the Ghibelline cause carries God's blessing."

I gently touched his arm. "I am relieved."

To my delight, he brought my hand to his lips. "You're a brave girl, Agata."

I smiled at his use of my Christian name. "My lord, if you tell me not to fear, then I shall not fear."

"I am almost twice your age and have seen many things in life. You can trust me."

"I do, with my whole heart."

"Good, now, listen carefully. You must wait at least a week after my departure before slipping the poison into your husband's wine."

"Will he suffer?"

"Death will come quickly."

I crossed myself. "How and when will I retrieve the seal from you?"

"Ottavio will be at the gate of your husband's palazzo tonight at midnight to return it. You must meet him there."

"Very well." I paused in thought. "What will happen after I bury my husband?"

"I will officially summon you to Verona. Isn't that what you want?"

"Yes, my lord." I ran my fingertips along my collarbone, drawing his eyes to my throat. "I'll be a helpless widow."

"What of your family in Verona?"

I shook my head. "I prefer to continue living my life as an orphan."

"As you wish, but take comfort in the fact that you'll be under my protection, so you won't be helpless."

I reached for his hand and kissed it, then pressed his palm to my cheek. "Thank you."

Cangrande's eyes dropped to my mouth. "Agata…"

Sensing that he was going to kiss me, I inclined my head and ran out of the chapel. He called after me, but I pretended not to hear as I exited the church then ducked into a maze of alleys.

I spent the day making plans for my departure from Venice.

Bea helped me inventory all the valuable items in the house that could be sold. We conducted our business with the utmost of discretion in order not to draw attention to ourselves. I also went through my personal belongings. Only the best jewels and garments would accompany me to Verona, the rest I would sell. By sunset, my mood was buoyant and hopeful. For the first time in my life, the future held the promise of good things.

Armando complained of Cangrande's arrogance during supper that evening. "That Ghibelline upstart assumed that he could barge in here and manipulate me. Well, he was wrong!"

"Perhaps you should reconsider his offer. The Lord of Verona was willing to pay you more than—"

"That's enough! I didn't marry you to hear your opinions on business, woman."

"I'm only trying to help."

He slammed his spoon on the table and growled, "This soup is cold!"

A servant scurried over to remove the bowl.

"Here, why not have some of the meat?" I suggested in my sweetest tone.

"It's overcooked and tough."

I sighed. "I'll make sure it doesn't happen again."

"You should be supervising those lazy servants, Agata. Making sure that your husband gets a decent meal is one of your duties as a wife!"

I stood and walked over to his chair. Sitting on his lap, I implored, "Don't be angry with me."

He smiled lecherously. "There's a good girl."

Snaking my arms around his neck, I whispered provocative things into his ear. Armando's body refused to cooperate with his mounting desire for me, causing him extreme frustration.

Finally, he snapped. "Enough! I'm tired!"

I hid my wicked amusement as I slid off his lap. "It's late, my love. You've been so stressed over Cangrande's visit and I understand why you're upset. You should get some sleep."

My words placated him. He nodded and kissed my cheek. I watched as he shuffled off toward his bedchamber. Once I heard

152

him close the door, I ran upstairs and locked myself inside of my room.

My maid exited the antechamber with a soft cloth and scented water. "Do you think he'll come?"

"I'm certain of it," I said, divesting of my garment.

"How can you be so sure?"

"I saw the look in his eyes this morning. Oh, Bea, I've risked everything for this moment…I cannot fail."

"You will not fail. I have the utmost faith in you. Besides, how can any man resist your charms?"

"I hope you're right."

I bathed and applied perfumed oil to every inch of my body. Bea helped me don a silken garment that felt wonderful to the touch, yet was easy to remove in the heat of passion.

My maid then held up a polished looking glass. "You look perfect for your midnight rendezvous, my lady."

I exhaled a deep breath. "Now, let's hope that I'm right about who will actually meet me tonight."

At the appointed time, I made my way downstairs and spied a shadowy figure outside the palazzo gate. Holding my breath in anticipation, I threw back the bolt. No sooner had he slipped into the courtyard than I wound my arms around his neck and claimed his lips. Stunned by my bold act, he gaped at me.

"The Feast of the Assumption of the Virgin Mary," I explained.

"What?"

"Six years ago. It was a very hot day. I was fascinated by the clothing and jewels of the nobility—I'd never seen such pageantry! The power and strength that you exuded left me breathless. I've often imagined what it would be like to touch a man like you…to kiss you. Now, I know."

After uttering those well-rehearsed words, I placed my hand on Cangrande's cheek. He gripped my wrist with considerable force.

I continued in a soft voice, "The fact that you remembered our encounter in the vestibule flatters me."

The whites of his eyes glimmered in the moonlight as he

153

debated what to do next. My appeal to his vanity produced the desired effect, for he bent his head and plundered my mouth. I responded to his kiss with passion tempered with sweetness—a combination most men found irresistible. His rough hands roamed over my silk garment, first fondling my breasts, then cupping my buttocks. When his need for me grew to the point that I feared he would ravage me against the brick wall, I squirmed out of his embrace.

Cangrande's ragged breathing and lustful gaze frightened me, for it was colored with anger. He reminded me of a bull about to charge, so I kept my distance.

"I don't know what game you're playing, girl, but I'm not a man to be toyed with."

"Forgive me, my lord, but I am no whore to be taken in such a manner—*here*, outside, like this. Every time I've fantasized about you…"

I trailed off, doing my best to appear embarrassed.

"You've thought of me all this time?"

"Yes," I whispered, lowering my head.

Lifting my chin with his fingertip, he said, "Indulge me."

I put my lips to his ear and whispered a list of passionate scenarios. When I finally pulled away, he stared at me in disbelief. I could see his dilated eyes in the flickering torchlight.

"Take me to your bed, Agata."

I smuggled him into my bedchamber, locking the door behind me. "I've dreamed of this moment…"

I used every whore's trick I knew to please him—twice, in fact, which was no small feat for a man his age. Wrapping my legs around him, I took his face into my hands while bearing his weight on top of me. I kissed his cheeks, eyelids, and lips with utmost tenderness before allowing him to rest his head against my bosom.

Carmen had once told me that to be loved by a man, a woman had to be half whore and half saint. It made perfect sense. I said nothing as he dressed afterward. Carmen had taught me that trick, too. The less you say to a man, the more intriguing you will become in his eyes. I stretched languidly, like a cat, showcasing my nubile body. This caused him to want me again—even though it was physically impossible at this point.

"I need to see you again," he said. "You must return to Verona immediately after your husband's funeral."

Need. Must. "As you wish, my lord."

I watched from the window as he crossed the courtyard and let himself out through the gate. By the time he melted into the inky night, I knew the Lord of Verona was mine.

CHAPTER 20
VENICE

Twelve days later, the body of Count Armando Visconti was interred in the Chiesa di San Cassiano. My husband's advanced age and declining health placed me outside the realm of suspicion, yet that didn't stop Rino from eyeing me warily after the funeral. I paid him the wages owed him, then I informed the pesky valet that his services were no longer required.

"Let me stay, my lady," Rino implored.

I glanced at Bea, who stood beside me, then said, "I have no need for a valet."

"I could stay and serve you in other ways."

Shaking my head, I replied, "I would prefer it if you collected your things and vacated my home."

Rino spread out his hands. "I beg you, *Contessa*, I'm too long in the tooth to find employment elsewhere."

"I don't plan on staying in this cursed city."

"Please," he said.

"Bea is the only servant coming with me, and my maid is worth two of you." I knew it was a cruel thing to say, but I despised the man.

His eyes narrowed into two slits. "You'll be sorry for treating me so treacherously—I'll make certain of it."

"How dare you?" I snapped.

"You are nothing but a fraud," he retorted.

Bea stepped forward and slapped the impertinent valet across the face. Rino raised his hand to retaliate, but I extracted my faithful dagger from its hiding place between the cleft in my breasts. Seeing the murderous intent in my eyes, the valet fled the room.

I sheathed the weapon. "Good riddance!"

It wasn't long before Cangrande sent one of his men to accompany me safely to Verona. The timing couldn't have been better since Armando's solicitors and debt collectors were swooping down on the palazzo like ravenous vultures picking over a carcass.

My escort, a knight named Paolo, arrived in Venice with the money from the purchase of Armando's land and a message from Cangrande. The letter informed me that I would be presented to the Veronese court as the orphaned cousin of Ottavio—born in Verona, raised in a remote convent, and then married off to an elderly count.

Paolo also brought an extra horse with him and explained, "This gentle mare is called Stella, and she's a gift from my master."

I was astonished and extremely flattered. "A gift from the Lord of Verona?"

"Yes, my lady."

"She's lovely, but I've never ridden a horse before."

"Stella is trained to follow my lead. Perhaps we can take a few turns around the courtyard before venturing into the street?"

Paolo demonstrated the proper way to handle the reins before helping me up into the saddle. True to the knight's word, the docile gray mare made no protest.

Bea and Paolo's squire would accompany us on mules laden with our belongings. I packed my gowns and jewels, along with all the money from the sales of the goods. Despite having enough wealth to last me for a long time, I still had to secure my future.

So far, my plan was working.

I bade Venice good riddance as Paolo led us through the city's winding maze of streets. It had rained throughout the night, so the ground was muddy and slick. I held on tightly to the reins as my horse gingerly picked its way through the puddles. A grubby hand tugged at the hem of my cloak and I looked down to see a slovenly dressed pregnant woman.

"Please, my lady. Spare a coin."

Matted hair framed her gaunt face, and the hem of her soiled garment was torn. On closer examination, I saw that the beggar was none other than Gisella!

"Halt Paolo," I called out, causing the knight, the squire, and my maid to stop.

Gisella's eyes widened in surprise. "Agata?"

"Countess," I corrected, peering down my nose at her.

"What…how?"

"I am the grieving widow of the late Count Armando Visconti. You will address me in a manner befitting my status. What happened to you, anyway?"

"I met a man a few months after you left the inn."

"I didn't leave by choice," I reminded her coolly.

"I know…"

"Carmen cast you out, didn't she?"

Tears welled up in her eyes. "My lover refused to marry me as promised, and I couldn't bring myself to…to…"

"Let me guess—rid yourself of the burden."

"Yes."

The irony was priceless.

Pinning her with an icy stare, I said, "This is God's punishment for what you did to me."

"Agata—*my lady*—please forgive me. What I did to you was wrong and I'm sorry. Take pity on me and my unborn child."

I withdrew a single gold coin from my purse and held it up. "I know how cruel life can be to young women like us—the streets of Venice are merciless."

Gisella's eyes lit up at the sight of the valuable coin. "Oh, thank you! Thank you!"

Rather than place the money in her outstretched hand, I deliberately threw the coin into a muddy puddle. Glaring at me, she got down on her knees and fished it out.

I urged my horse forward, then glanced over my shoulder. "God never sleeps, Gisella. Remember that."

CHAPTER 21
VERONA

My heart swelled with love the moment Verona loomed into view. I pulled on Stella's reins, causing the mare to come to an abrupt stop. I took in the bell towers and the bridges with a smile on my face. The city held painful memories, yes, but that didn't diminish my sense of civic pride. I was Veronese to the core, and happy to be home.

I had left Verona under dire circumstances with only the clothes on my back, without saying goodbye to anyone. My mother, my father, Pina...how had they reacted to my sudden disappearance? Have they missed me all these years? A sinister thought occurred to me—had my parents starved to death in my absence?

I glimpsed the black smoke from Alvino's smithy in the distance and my stomach clenched. Had Nunzio remarried? Was Alvino molesting his new daughter-in-law or had he remarried, too? I shuddered at the thought of those dark days.

Seeing Verona as a rich woman from atop a horse offered me a totally different perspective of my birth city. We were crossing Piazza dei Signori when two knights opened the Palazzo Scaligero's iron-studded gates. The moment we entered the spacious courtyard, liveried pages emerged to assist us.

The Lady of Verona stood beside her husband in the main hall dressed in yellow silk with silver embroidery. "Welcome, Countess Visconti."

I offered my hostess a curtsey. "Thank you, my lady."

"I want to personally express my gratitude for helping my husband."

"As a loyal Veronese, I only did my duty."

She smiled with her mouth but her eyes remained cold. I was suddenly reminded of Carmen. Thankfully, Ottavio approached us. He made it a point to greet me with feigned familiarity, thus adding authenticity to my fabricated backstory. I was led to where Cangrande stood, then offered him my best curtsey.

He kissed my hand and welcomed me with solicitous formality. "We have a fine supper and some merry entertainment planned for this evening. You will be our honored guest, *Contessa*."

"My lord is most kind and generous."

Bea and I were led to a modest bedchamber hung with tapestries and flaunting a frescoed ceiling. A short corridor led to the antechamber that would serve as Bea's room. My maid unpacked our belongings, then I readied myself for supper. I wore my best gown and jewels, knowing that I would be closely scrutinized by members of the nobility. I stood before the looking glass, pensive and distraught.

"What ails you, my lady?" Bea inquired.

"I can barely believe it…I'm really *here*."

"You deserve to be here more than anyone I know."

I waved my hand at the space around me. "This is the Palazzo Scaligero…"

"Yes, it is." Grinning, Bea added, "Enjoy this moment, my lady. You've earned it."

"I'm so nervous. What if they suspect that I'm a fraud?"

"No one will think that. You are the Countess Visconti."

Taking a deep breath, I nodded. "Thank you, Bea."

I went downstairs and did my best to emulate the behavior of the sophisticated court ladies. I listened to their chatter and answered their questions. Mindful not to say too much, I offered vague replies and prompted them to talk about themselves. Appealing to the egos of others was something that I had perfected into an art form during my days as a prostitute.

During a tasty meal of braised rabbit and roasted pheasant, I listened to the people around me. Two men vied for my attention and I pretended to be shy and coy. I felt the heat of Cangrande's stare as I allowed one of the noblemen to lead me in a merry jig after supper. I calculated every feminine movement, every smile and glance, all while avoiding his gaze.

Cangrande approached me and took hold of my hand. I risked a glance at Giovanna as her husband led me toward a group of dancers. Although her expression was placid, her eyes revealed contempt.

"You are smiling," Cangrande commented as he spun me around.

"I'm surprised that a fierce warrior such as yourself can move so gracefully."

He chuckled, drawing several glances. "Battle is a dance of sorts. Have you ever used a sword?"

"No, my lord."

"Someday, I will demonstrate for you."

"Nothing would bring me greater pleasure."

He cocked an eyebrow at me. *"Nothing?"*

I had the good sense to blush. Deliberately changing the subject, I said, "Tomorrow, I must set myself to the task of finding a place to live."

"You will remain here."

"My lord?"

"You are my guest. A young widow who has recently lost her husband. It's my Christian duty to help you."

"Thank you, but I insist on procuring my own lodging."

"And you shall, in time," he said in a tone that warned me not to broach the matter again. "*I want you here.*"

I resisted the urge to cry out in triumph! Instead, I inclined my head in acquiescence. After the guests had dispersed, I thanked my hosts and retreated to my bedchamber. Bea helped me undress and brushed my hair. Cangrande entered the room as I sat on the edge of the bed rubbing rosemary oil into my hands. His eyes traced the outline of my body beneath my flimsy silk shift, making his intention clear. Bea curtsied and disappeared into the antechamber.

Closing the gap between us, he devoured my mouth while his hands groped my breasts.

I returned the kiss, then pushed him away. "My lord, we will wake your wife."

Nuzzling my neck, he lifted the hem of my garment. "I need

161

you *now*."

He took me as hard as a stallion would a broodmare. I withstood the onslaught easily, for I'd known patrons in the past who were far more violent in their lovemaking.

Afterward, he confessed, "I've thought about you every night since I left Venice. Tell me you've missed me, too."

"I have missed you, my lord."

"I longed for more than your body, Agata. I craved your mind, your words…"

I smiled, tracing the curve of his cheek with my fingertips. "I am flattered."

"Now, you are *mine*," he said, crushing me to his chest.

"I cannot be your mistress under your wife's roof."

He frowned. "You would deny your overlord of your affection?"

Snaking my arms around his neck, I responded to his words with a soft kiss. "I don't wish to deny you anything, but I've only just arrived in Verona and have no desire to make enemies."

"Let me lay your fears to rest, dear girl. Giovanna and I have not shared a bed in years. Trust me, she will not be a problem."

"In that case, I am yours to command."

"That's better," he muttered before claiming my lips.

Cangrande sought my bed the following night and the night after that. During the day, Bea and I kept to our quarters unless invited by the Lady of Verona to sit in the garden or the solarium to read prayer books.

On my fourth day in Verona, Giovanna invited me to work on a large altar cloth that she was creating for the Duomo. Thankfully, I knew how to stitch fairly well and could contribute my skill to the project. Three other noble ladies sewed with us.

One of the women eventually inquired, "So, *Contessa*, is our city to your liking?"

"Very much so," I replied.

"Is it true that you were born here?"

"Yes, but I was sent to the convent as a baby."

An unsettling silence ensued.

Giovanna finally said, "I assume Signore Ottavio is helping you secure lodging." When I stared at her blankly, she added, "Your *cousin*…?"

"Ah, yes. He's been so helpful."

The three women regarded Giovanna expectantly.

The Lady of Verona cocked an eyebrow at me. "I'm happy to hear it. I'm sure you long for the comfort and privacy of your own residence. Let's hope you find something suitable soon."

Three sets of eyes slid my way. The message was clear: I was not welcome here. Did she suspect her husband of sleeping with me? I nodded in response to her words and bent my head over my sewing.

Later that night as the Lord of Verona lay in my bed, I said, "Your wife doesn't want me here."

"But I do," he said, kissing my temple.

"She knows about us."

"Given that she snores louder than any of my knights and sleeps in a separate chamber, I doubt it."

"Servants can have loose lips if coins cross their palms."

He peered closely at me. "You're truly worried about this."

"I am, my lord. I don't want to make enemies. Especially one as powerful as your wife."

"The only thing you should be worrying about is pleasing your master," he said, positioning himself over me. Entering me with a hard thrust, he added, "I can assure you that I am much more powerful than she is."

I closed my eyes and pretended to enjoy his rough lovemaking.

If Giovanna knew about us, she took the affair in stride and turned a blind eye to her husband's adultery. She avoided me at all costs, and made me feel unwelcomed in her home.

One day she and her ladies passed me in the corridor. Pausing to eye me with contempt, she asked in a sarcastic tone, "Still the grieving widow?"

Her ladies snickered as my face burned. I inclined my head at her nonetheless and scurried off to my room.

Despite the tension between me and the Lady of Verona, I reveled in my new role as mistress to her powerful husband. People treated me with reverence, and the servants went out of their way to please me. *Francesco*—I preferred to call Cangrande by his proper Christian name—was a generous man, too. Strands of pearls, jeweled brooches, and sweetmeats often found their way into my bedchamber with attached love notes.

***

A week after my arrival in Verona, I purchased a lovely gift for Maria and set off for her cottage accompanied by Bea. Arrayed in costly patterned silk and my best jewels, I attracted considerable attention as I crossed the city. A scruffy man eyed the gemstones at my throat a bit too closely and I stared him down. My lack of fear must have struck him as odd for he didn't dare come near me. If he had, we were ready. Bea and I carried daggers, the weapons tucked safely in our bodices.

Unpleasant memories surfaced as I neared Maria's cottage. The last time I had been there, I was cold, desperate, barefoot, and terrified…

"Are you all right, my lady?" Bea asked, searching my face. "You've grown pale. Shall we go back?"

I shook my head and knocked on the door. Maria eyes widened in surprise at the sight of a richly attired woman and her servant standing on her doorstep. At first, she didn't recognize me.

"Hello, Maria."

Narrowing her eyes, she said, "Agata?!"

"Forgive the intrusion. This is my lady's maid, Bea. May we come in?"

Maria's head bobbed up and down as she took in my expensive garment and glittering jewels. Remembering her manners, she opened the door wider. We walked into the neat cottage and, this time, I noticed details like the cross-stitched bible verse by the doorway and the painting of St. Mark over the hearth. Maria flitted back and forth like a dizzy moth, setting out cups and ale.

I stepped in front of her and took her hands into my own.

"Please stop fretting over me."

Flustered, she confessed, "It's not every day a *lady* visits my home. I'm simply overwhelmed...look at you!"

"I'm still the same Agata, only a little older and a lot wiser."

"And wealthier, obviously."

"That, too," I conceded. "I've recently returned to Verona and wanted to see you."

"Many prayers have been said on your behalf, my dear. I've often wondered what became of you. I can see that you've done well for yourself."

"My story is long and far from pleasant. Don't let my outward appearance fool you. I'm doing well *now*, but when I first arrived in Venice..." I trailed off, unable to speak.

Maria's brow creased. "I'm so sorry, Agata."

"I went through a difficult time, my friend."

"Still better than facing a witchcraft trial, I hope."

"Yes, but not by much."

"Sit, please," Maria urged, pulling out a chair for me. She also motioned for Bea to sit. "Here, let's celebrate our reunion with a bit of ale, shall we?"

Maria filled three cups with golden ale and we drank to our mutual health. I motioned to Bea, who presented our hostess with the gift.

"This is for you," I explained. "Six years ago, on a cold January morning, I showed up at your door in desperate need of help. Not only did you show me kindness, you gave me money, a frock, and a pair of shoes. I'm grateful to this day for all you did for me. Unfortunately, I can't return your frock because a pair of hungry goats chewed up the hem as I slept in their stall, so I've brought you something else."

She laughed, lightening the mood. "I was glad to help a fellow woman in need—especially one who had been treated as treacherously as you had been by Alvino."

I reached across the table and squeezed her hand. "Please accept this gift as a token of my appreciation."

Maria unwrapped the parcel and gasped. "This is too much. I can't possibly—"

"Yes, you can."

She lifted the costly velvet cloak flaunting silver thread and seed pearls. "It's beautiful!"

I smiled. "The green matches your eyes perfectly, Maria. Don't you agree, Bea?"

Bea smiled at Maria and replied, "Yes, my lady."

"I've also brought these," I said, placing a pair of silver and seed pearl earrings in her hand. "They go well with the cloak."

Maria eyed me incredulously, then hugged me. "Thank you, Agata. I've never owned anything so fine in my life."

"You deserve this and more. Were it not for you, I would have been condemned to hang in the gallows."

"Nunzio remarried, you know."

I raised an eyebrow. "Oh?"

"His new wife is a heifer—God forgive me. I doubt Alvino would dare lay a hand on this one. She'd pound him into the ground with her mannish fists!"

I laughed aloud. "She's a big woman?"

"Enormous. As for Alvino, he re-hired Donna Giulia and continues to bugger the poor woman."

"They should wed."

"I agree." Maria hesitated, then said, "Tell me about your life in Venice."

I shared a few details, omitting my dark days on the streets and my work as a prostitute. She listened with rapt attention and, thankfully, didn't ask too many questions. The pleasant visit came to an end with an embrace and the promise to see each other again in the near future.

"Your friend is a good woman," Bea commented when we were back on the road.

"Yes, she is. Now, I must see my mother. Six years is a long time to disappear and not send word."

"Why didn't you send her a message from Venice?"

"Shame," I confessed. "I left Verona an adulteress accused of witchcraft, then became a prostitute in Venice. How does one reconcile with that? Besides, no one in my family can read or write. I can barely do so myself, and that's only because of my

Aunt Serafina." The thought of my late aunt made me wince. I missed her so much.

"That vile blacksmith is to blame for all of your suffering in Venice. God curse his soul to Hell."

I rewarded her loyalty with a smile.

Bea's eyes reflected surprise at the sight of my father's dilapidated cottage. The dwelling was in worse disrepair than I remembered. While my maid knew of my humble origin, she wasn't aware of its extent.

To my surprise, Pina came to the door. Her eyes bulged from shock. *"Agata?"*

"Hello Pina," I said, instantly noticing her gaunt features and lusterless hair.

"What are you doing here? We all thought you were dead." She frowned in confusion at the sight of my clothing and jewelry. "We searched the city and the countryside for days after your disappearance."

"I've been in Venice all this time and returned only a couple of weeks ago."

"Venice?"

"May I come in? I'm here to see Mother and Father," I said, still standing in the doorway.

Pina stepped aside to let me enter. "Mother died in childbearing last spring. Father is gone."

I stared at her, stunned. "Mother is dead?"

Bea placed a comforting hand on my shoulder as she urged me to sit on a stool by the crumbling hearth.

Pina nodded. "She bled out."

"And the baby?"

"Stillborn."

My eyes drifted to the scarred kitchen table. Everything seemed familiar and foreign at the same time. For some reason, I couldn't summon any tears over the loss of my mother. Married to an abusive drunkard, her life had consisted of repetitive childbearing, starvation, and burying babies. For once, the Angel of Death had offered a welcomed respite to a member of my family.

167

I glanced at Pina. "What do you mean Father left?"

"He took up with a woman across the river after Mother died. I rarely see him. He drinks all day and makes his wife beg for money outside the churches."

I shook my head to clear it. "Father will drink himself to death eventually."

"Yes…"

Looking around, I asked, "What are you doing here?"

"My father-in-law died three months ago. Biaggio had to sell our home to pay off his debts, so we moved in here." A baby cried in the other room and she explained, "That's our son. Would you like to meet him?"

"Of course, I would."

Pina went into the back of the cottage and emerged with a brown-eyed baby in her arms. He was fat, which meant he was well-fed. My sister no doubt sacrificed sustenance for the baby's sake. The thought made me sad.

"This is Pietro," Pina said. "Say hello to your Aunt Agata."

I reached out for the little cherub and Pina let me have him. Like his father, the butcher, the baby smelled faintly of offal. "You are blessed to have such a healthy child."

"You're the one who appears to be blessed," she shot back, her eyes sliding to Bea. "Is this your servant?"

"Bea is my lady's maid," I replied. "She's also my friend."

Pina smiled to my maid then met my eyes. "How did you manage to get so wealthy?"

"I married a cantankerous count old enough to be my great-grandfather. He died several weeks ago."

"Does that mean you're a countess?"

"It does."

She stared at me in awe. "What is Venice like?"

I recounted the same choice bits that I had shared with Maria. My sister listened, then asked several questions.

Finally, she inquired, "Where are you living now?

I'm at the Palazzo Scaligero, fornicating with the Lord of Verona right under his wife's nose! "I've taken up lodging in the center, near the river."

168

"Well, I'm glad that you're back in Verona."

"Me too."

We embraced, putting our past differences behind us. Before taking my leave, I undid the fat coin purse at my waist and placed it on the table. "This is for you and Biaggio. I don't want your child to ever go hungry the way we did."

"This is a fortune!"

"Yes, it is."

Pina's eyes welled with tears. "God bless you, Agata."

The finest ring on my finger was fashioned from gold and sported a large ruby. I removed it and placed it in the palm of her hand. "Here. A gift from your younger sister."

She preened in delight as she slipped it on her finger. "It's the most gorgeous thing I've ever seen...thank you!"

"I'll send some clothing for all of you, too."

Pina hugged me tightly and wept with gratitude.

I felt satisfied as we made our way back to the Palazzo Scaligero.

Bea said, "You have a good soul, my lady."

***

The heat of summer did little to curb my lover's lust. Francesco continued to claim my body nightly, reveling in our sticky tumblings beneath the hazy moon. I envied him during these amorous encounters, for he truly enjoyed them whereas I did not. In fact, the act of copulation had never brought me pleasure.

One evening, as I gazed out the window pondering this matter, Bea entered the room to aid me in my nightly toilette. Holding an ivory comb in her hand, she eyed me expectantly.

I sat down on a stool with my back to her, then asked, "Bea, may I ask you an intimate question?"

Her eyes met mine in the polished looking glass. "Yes."

"When you were married...Did you *enjoy* the act of lovemaking?"

Bea's lips puckered and she shrugged. "I suppose it was pleasant enough, yes."

I turned around to face her. "But was it the same level of

169

pleasure that your husband experienced?"

She laughed disdainfully. "Of course not. Women don't enjoy carnal acts the way men do. We can derive pleasure from the secure feeling of having a man's arms around us. I admit, I sometimes miss that. My husband was a good man."

"I'm sure he was." I swiveled on the stool to face the looking glass again and she resumed her task. "I wish we could feel what they feel."

She sighed. "I'm afraid that's not possible."

"Why not?"

"Eve's act of rebellion cursed all of womankind. This is why we are deprived of pleasure and burdened with pain. We suffer pain as girls during menstruation, then pain in childbirth, and pain throughout our lives."

"There must be some women who enjoy the act of lovemaking."

Bea paused in her task. "Do you know of any?"

"No."

"Now it is my turn to ask an intimate question, my lady, if I may." At my nod, she asked, "Does he hurt you?"

I knew she referred to Francesco. After all, as my personal lady's maid, she had seen the bruises on my inner thighs, buttocks, and breasts. "He can be rough at times, but he's never violent or inconsiderate of my limitations."

She set down the comb. "I'm relieved to hear it."

I recalled our conversation as Francesco made love to me that night. I still wiggled and squirmed the way Carmen had taught me, punctuating the carnal act with soft moans and phrases of encouragement. He eventually cried out and his body shuddered with pleasure.

Despite the surge of envy and resentment, I inquired sweetly, "Do I please you?"

"I would venture to call that an understatement." Staring into my eyes, he inquired, "Are you pleased by me?"

"Yes," I lied, smiling.

CHAPTER 22
JULY 1326
VERONA

In an attempt to convince Cangrande to break his allegiance with Louis IV of Bavaria—the current Holy Roman Emperor—Robert of Anjou, King of Naples, sent his envoys to Verona. Commonly known as "Robert the Wise," he was also King of Jerusalem and widely respected under the common banner of Christianity.

Cangrande made it clear to his nobles that Robert's men were to be treated with the utmost of respect during their visit. Verona's power and wealth would be displayed in the forms of pageantry, feasting, and entertainment. Red Scaligeri banners were hung from the outer windows, each one depicting a ladder—the family's coat of arms. Vibrant tapestries hung from the windows of the inner courtyard, too.

The highest towers and noble homes throughout the city followed Cangrande's example in order to impress the foreign dignitaries. In a matter of days, Verona was draped in colorful banners, intricate tapestries, and floral wreaths. Even the peasants donned their best garments.

The Neapolitans arrived in Verona much later than expected due to unseasonably heavy rain. Bea and I stood at the window trying to get a glimpse of them in the courtyard below. The two richly dressed noblemen, a pair of servants, and several armed knights were ushered inside the palazzo by liveried pages.

Bea and I tiptoed to the door and opened it a crack. The soaking wet guests followed the servants past our room and up the stairs. The flickering torchlight in the wall sconces revealed a disparity in their ages, but no further details.

Bea stood over my shoulder trying to see. "Well?"

I closed the door. "I couldn't see their faces, but I could

171

discern that one is young, the other, old."

"How exciting. I've never met anyone outside the Veneto."

"Neither have I."

"They say Naples is hot year round. Perpetual summertime."

"Really? That would be splendid."

Verona's nobility flaunted their finery at the welcoming banquet held in the Palazzo Scaligero's impressive main hall. Vibrant frescoes adorned the walls, and the high beamed ceiling boasted intricate designs. All of the ground floor doors leading to the inner courtyard garden were open to allow fresh breezes to pass freely from one room to the next. Some guests sat outside amid the potted fruit trees and the marble fountain.

Bea and I stood beneath one of the archways, quietly observing the scene. A big birdcage hung from a ring in the center of the vaulted ceiling, and tiny birds delighted the guests with their songs.

"There they are," Bea said.

I followed her gaze and saw a distinguished man with silver hair speaking with Ottavio. Beside him stood the young man I had glimpsed on the stairs last night. Although he contributed nothing to the conversation, his intelligent blue eyes took in every detail of his surroundings. Tall and fit with a proud nose and regal bearing, I couldn't tear my eyes away from him.

Francesco studied my face as he came to stand beside me. "Handsome, is he not?"

"Whom?" I asked, noticing Bea's subtle retreat.

"Antonio, the royal bastard."

"Is he really the king's illegitimate son?"

"Born of a whore shortly after Robert's first wife died."

"Who is the older gentleman?"

"Mauro, Duke of Taranto. He is the king's cousin and a shrewd political strategist. Antonio's mother didn't survive the birth, so he was entrusted to Mauro's care."

"I see." The two men were like a father and son.

"You didn't answer my question, Agata." When I regarded him with a blank expression, he said, "Antonio's good looks?"

"He's rather plain," I lied, feigning disinterest in the

handsome newcomer. Bea must have overheard my reply from where she sat on a nearby bench because I saw her stifle a smile.

Mauro, Antonio, and Ottavio began walking toward us and, for some absurd reason, I felt the acceleration of my heartbeat. To my disappointment, Giovanna intercepted them. After a few words, Mauro excused himself while Antonio and Ottavio remained engaged in conversation with the Lady of Verona.

Mauro inclined his head at me in greeting, then said to Francesco, "My lord, I have a message from the king that is meant for your ears only."

Francesco led the duke away from the guests toward his private study, leaving me alone.

Giovanna's laughter drew my gaze and I noticed Antonio speaking to her in an animated fashion. Others joined the group and they listened to the young man's words with amused faces. I wanted to hear what was being said, too, but I knew Giovanna wouldn't appreciate my presence.

To my chagrin, Antonio caught my eye. When I failed to avert my gaze, he offered me a mischievous grin. The corners of my lips instinctively turned upward in response to the gesture. Taking it as an invitation, he excused himself from the group and came toward me.

Feeling self-conscious, I shifted from one foot to the other and discreetly patted my hair to make sure it was in place. Antonio's confident gait commanded respect and attracted attention—especially from females. I knew it was rude to stare, but I couldn't help myself. He bowed before me with the grace of a seasoned courtier. Modesty demanded that I lower my eyes, so I looked down at his well-shaped legs. A few people noticed the courtly display and began to whisper among themselves. I politely extended my hand to the Neapolitan, and he brought my knuckles to his lips.

"My lady, you stand out like a flower in a barren field."

Despite his deep voice, his words were spoken softly so that only I heard them. "You flatter me, sir."

"I speak the truth," he said, rising to his full height and forcing me to tilt my head back.

173

"Welcome to Verona, Signore Antonio."

"Ah, you already know my name. May I have the honor of knowing yours?"

"My name is Agata."

He appeared shocked. "*Agata*, you say?"

Alarmed, I nodded warily.

He undid the two top hooks of his tunic and extracted a circular pendant suspended from a silver chain around his neck. The disc, fashioned from smooth, highly polished agate stone, flaunted tan and red striations.

"A gypsy fortune-teller gave this to me many years ago," he explained. "It's a talisman against evil, but the old woman also predicted, '*L'agata ti porterà gioia.*'"

"The agate will bring you joy," I repeated, smirking.

"My magical stone is your namesake." Closing the gap between us, he added, "Does this mean that you will someday bring me joy?"

He waggled his eyebrows for effect, making me giggle. "You are quite amusing, Signore Antonio."

His eyes swept over me in a way that caused me to blush— *me*—a former prostitute! "And you are enchanting, Signorina."

"Signora," I corrected. "I am widowed."

He searched my face. "So young?" Appalled by his own lack of constraint, he amended, "Forgive me."

I dismissed his apology with a slight shake of my head. "My husband was the late Armando Visconti." Antonio blinked in surprise, prompting me to add, "You've heard of him?"

"Who hasn't?"

"As you know, there was a considerable age difference between us."

"Considerable, indeed. Something tells me that you are a woman with many interesting stories to tell, Signora Agata—or shall I address you as *Contessa*?"

I met the Neapolitan's azure gaze and experienced the delicious sensation of drowning in his soulful eyes. "I dislike formalities."

"In that case, you must call me Antonio and I will call you

Agata—with your permission, of course. After all, we are similar in age."

"That pleases me." Changing the subject, I said, "My maid tells me that Naples is quite warm year round. Is this true?"

"Our winters are mild," he replied with a hint of pride in his voice. "I live in a villa atop a hill facing the Naples Bay. The water is the most amazing shade of blue."

Like your eyes... "The view must be lovely."

"Vesuvius dominates the landscape in the distance."

"Aren't you frightened to live so close to a volcano?" I asked, remembering what Aunt Serafina had taught me about Pompeii.

"Ah, I see you know the story of Pompeii. The answer to your question is no. God calls us to Heaven when He sees fit. I don't waste my time worrying about death, for it comes to us all sooner or later." He shrugged and grinned. "I prefer to enjoy life to the fullest day by day."

The flush of warmth that spread throughout my body in that instant surprised me. There was something special about this man. Bea came to stand by my side and the spell was broken. I made a quick introduction, then noticed Ottavio hovering in the open doorway.

Antonio bent over my hand again, then said, "Duty calls. I am sure we will speak again, Agata."

I arranged my facial features to appear nonchalant and resisted watching his retreat. A passing servant with a tray of chalices served as the perfect distraction while I regained my composure, so I helped myself to a bit of sweet diluted wine.

Bea whispered, "In addition to flirting so openly with you, he dares to use your Christian name?" When I said nothing, she added, "It's not like you to be so..."

She trailed off and I prompted, "Speak plainly."

"Tread carefully, my lady. Royal courts are breeding grounds for charming couriers who can easily sweep a lady off her feet, destroy her reputation, and cause heartache."

"You speak as though you have experience in this matter."

She flushed. "I do not, but you wouldn't want to ruin what

175

you have with the Lord of Verona."

As usual, she was right. I clasped her hand. "I fell in a moment of weakness, Bea. Antonio is indeed charming."

"You're still a young woman and it's normal for you to be flattered," she said, speaking to me as a friend rather than a servant. "Enjoy Signore Antonio's company while he's here, but I advise you to construct a fortress around your heart."

"I shall heed your wise counsel."

Later, Francesco took his place at the high table beside his wife and high-ranking nobles. Mauro and Antonio sat among them. Servants paraded splendid platters containing all kinds of culinary delights—swans and peacocks roasted to perfection with feathers expertly replaced, haunches of venison and wild boar, smoked baby pigs, stewed goat and lamb.

I sat at one of three long trestle tables with a group of pleasant lords and ladies. Antonio stared at me throughout most of the meal. I did my best to be discreet, but I couldn't help meeting his gaze and returning a few of his smiles. Each time we looked at each other, a flurry of butterflies sprang to life in my stomach.

What was wrong with me?

Music followed the sumptuous meal, and the trestle tables were cleared away to make space for the couples who wished to dance. I stood tapping my feet to the music when Antonio approached me.

"Dance with me, Agata."

I accepted his proffered hand without a second thought, relishing the warmth and strength of it. We joined the other dancers and stepped in tune to the music. Every time he touched me or our eyes locked, I felt giddy. At one point, I caught Francesco staring at me.

Tread carefully, my lady.

The music stopped too soon. I eyed Antonio wistfully as the musicians began playing another melody.

"Would you like to continue?"

I shook my head. "Thank you, but I should retire."

"So soon?"

176

He could barely hide the disappointment in his voice and, for some reason, this pleased me.

He continued, "I look forward to seeing your lovely face tomorrow. May your dreams be as sweet as you are, Agata."

My face lit up in a smile. No man had ever spoken to me in such a tender manner.

***

The theatrical performances and concertos throughout the following days were delightful. More importantly, these events served as excuses for Antonio and I to spend time together. To our mutual delight, our conversations were animated and surprisingly candid. We talked of many things and seemed to agree with each other on important issues. Perhaps the amiable comfort between us was due to the fact that Antonio was only a couple of years my senior.

The novel concept of knowing a man without bedding him intrigued and delighted me. Aunt Serafina would have approved of my Neapolitan.

My Neapolitan...

Francesco still came to my bed almost every night, but his demeanor was cool toward me. I knew he felt jealous and perhaps a bit angry, but I simply couldn't help myself. Antonio evoked foreign emotions in me and I didn't know how to control them.

Antonio and I were laughing together one evening and I caught Francesco scowling at me. I sobered instantly and bade my handsome friend goodnight. The look Francesco gave me as I exited the main hall made me shudder with worry.

Later that night, my lover slipped into my bed and touched me until I gave in to his need. Spooning me from behind, he bit my shoulder. "You want him, don't you?"

Ignoring the pain from his bite, I replied, "Francesco, you're the only man I want."

He panted in my ear. "Are you sure about that?"

"Yes, my darling..."

The Lord of Verona said my name in his final thrust. To my horror and shame, I imagined Antonio in Francesco's place. I watched my lover dress in silence, mortified by my wicked thoughts.

Francesco touched my shoulder, his eyes lingering on the angry red bite mark. "Did I hurt you?"

"Not at all, my lord."

He pecked my lips and exited the chamber.

I stared up at the shadowy ceiling rafters as tears gathered in my eyes. The more I thought of Antonio, the more I felt like crying. A strange heaviness settled in the center of my chest, causing me to sigh. The image of his broad shoulders popped into my head. The man possessed a fine physique and strong, beautiful hands. I imagined those hands caressing me, holding me...

A foreign ache began to form deep within my core; an inexplicable desire to be filled.

Could this be *lust*?

My hand moved, as if of its own accord, and found the sticky wetness left behind by Francesco. Allowing my curious fingers to slide into the warm, wet opening, I imagined drowning in Antonio's blue gaze, his insistent knee prying my legs apart, his mouth on mine...

My breathless gasp pierced the silent night. What was *that*? The intense release simultaneously frightened and delighted me.

Is this what a man experiences during sex?

I heard Bea's sleepy voice from the other room. "My lady, are you all right?"

Trying to hide my shame and bewilderment, I replied, "I...ah, I had a nightmare. I'm fine, Bea. Go back to sleep."

I was confused, yet gloriously happy by my discovery. *I, too, can experience pleasure.*

How could I possibly resist Antonio knowing this? I would have to find a way. I couldn't risk losing Francesco for the sake of my own lust.

CHAPTER 23
VERONA

I did my best to protect my heart whenever Antonio and I were together. Try as I might to remain neutral toward him, the fortress around my heart crumbled with each smile, each kind word, each subtle touch…I felt like I was floating down a river with a strong current.

The first week of events ended with a splendid jousting match. Everyone made their way outside to admire the knights and horses. Francesco and I stood side by side, shading our eyes against the sun.

He suddenly grunted. "I hope he falls off his horse."

Following my lover's gaze, I saw that he referred to Antonio. "Don't you like him?"

"I don't like how he looks at you."

"You're being jealous, my darling."

"Am I?"

"Our Neapolitan guest has been nothing but respectful and kind toward me."

"While that may be true, I'm looking forward to their departure. Mauro hasn't yet succeeded in his mission, nor will he. My loyalty will always be to the emperor."

"What will Robert of Naples do if you refuse to bend your knee to the pope?"

"What can he do? Nothing. The king has his own troubles in the south. He can't spare the men or the time to fight me." He peered up at the sky. "Well, at least we can be thankful for good weather."

I risked a glance at Antonio. The mere thought of his departure caused a pang of distress. "I'm looking forward to the joust."

He looked at me. "Are you, now? Antonio will be pitted against one of my knights. Whom will you cheer on, my lady?"

Antonio. "My fellow Veronese, of course."

He chucked me under the chin. "Good girl."

Francesco sat beside his wife as the nobles took their seats to enjoy the jousting match. The Piazza dei Signori had been transformed into a tournament field complete with wooden stands for the richly dressed onlookers. Peasants crowded the edges of the piazza to catch a glimpse of the noble sport.

The knights paraded before the crowd in their gleaming armor and brightly colored tunics, then moved to the center of the piazza. Antonio stopped directly before me and requested my embroidered handkerchief as a favor. I glanced uneasily at my lover before reaching into the cuff of my sleeve and pulling out the dainty cloth. I was about to toss it at him when Antonio shook his head and pointed to his bicep. Blushing, I stood and descended the few steps. Leaning over the barricade, I tied the cloth around his upper arm, relishing the feel of his hard muscle beneath the hauberk. His eyes never left my face.

"I hope to bring you victory, my lady."

"God be with you." To my surprise, my voice trembled.

"Agata, are you worried about me?"

"Please be careful. Don't fall, Antonio."

His sensuous lips curved into a smile. "Do not fret, my sweet. I shall dance with you tonight."

My sweet. I reclaimed my seat in a daze. Sighing contentedly, I stole a glance at Francesco, who glared at me. Giovanna's expression, on the other hand, was a combination of humor and smugness.

My attention turned to the jousting match, which caused many cheers and cries from the crowd. I cringed every time a lance hit a shield and splintered with a loud cracking noise. One knight got hit in the head, causing him to fall from his horse in an unconscious heap. I sat on the edge of my seat when it was Antonio's turn. He seemed skilled at the sport, so I gradually relaxed. Suddenly, his horse reared upward, causing the shield to fall from his hand just as the lance hit his side. I almost cried aloud when he fell from his saddle. My body sagged in utter relief when he raised himself on his elbow.

180

Thank you, Santa Madonna, for sparing his life.

Two squires ran over to Antonio, then dragged him to the makeshift infirmary located within the Palazzo Scaligero. The Veronese knight who toppled him won the joust, and the crowd cheered on the next pair of men. My first instinct was to run into the palazzo and sit with Antonio in the infirmary, but doing so would risk Francesco's ire.

The joust held no interest for me after that, and I sat through the remainder of the event barely paying attention. Thankfully, there were no fatalities. Feasting commenced shortly afterward, and the minstrels played festive tunes for the pleasure of the lords and ladies in the main hall. My eyes scanned the large room for Antonio, but he was nowhere to be found. Lacking an appetite, I only ate a morsel for the sake of appearance. In truth, I felt physically ill.

Bea, who sat beside me, said, "I'm sure he's fine."

"Why isn't he here?"

"I don't know, but the lance didn't pierce him."

"I hope you're right, Bea."

She stared at me long and hard. "You didn't take my advice, did you?"

I met her eyes and slowly shook my head.

She bit her lip worriedly and said nothing more.

People mingled and danced at the meal's end. I stood near an open doorway scanning the scene while eagerly anticipating Antonio's appearance.

Someone grabbed my arm from behind and pulled me back into the corridor. "Flirting with him right under my nose."

"Francesco!"

"You can't deny it this time." Slamming me against the wall, he roughly devoured my mouth. "*Mine*," he said when he pulled away from me.

"I couldn't deny Antonio's request for my favor at the joust. You know it's customary for a knight to ask for a token of luck. It would have been rude of me to refuse, not to mention disrespectful to the King of Naples."

He knew I was right but wouldn't admit it. "Stay away from

181

that *bastardo*."

He stormed off, leaving me alone and trembling. I slipped back into the revelry of the main hall virtually unnoticed, and accepted a chalice of wine from a servant to soothe my frayed nerves. A few ladies came over to speak with me. I indulged in a bit of harmless gossip before wandering away from them.

Francesco sat alongside Mauro, whose company he seemed to enjoy even if he disagreed with the man's politics. Before long, both men became inebriated while exchanging war stories. I crept downstairs through the maze of corridors leading to the infirmary. Nobody was there so I retraced my steps. Halfway to the main hall, I spotted movement inside the shadowy library. Only one candle burned in the room. Pausing in the doorway, I saw a familiar silhouette.

"Antonio?" The relief in my voice was unmistakable.

He spun around to face me. "Agata."

"What are you doing?"

He waved his hand around the room. "I wanted to see the Lord of Verona's collection of manuscripts."

"You shouldn't be here."

He frowned. "Why not?"

"Forgive me, I don't mean to be rude, but Francesco doesn't like it when people—strangers—wander into his private chambers."

"Francesco?"

My face burned. "Yes, the Lord of Verona."

He promptly replaced the manuscript, but made no move to approach me.

"I've been so worried about you," I admitted. "Were you hurt badly in the joust?"

"No."

The curt reply puzzled me. "Why weren't you present at supper?"

"I remained in the infirmary to aid the barber-surgeon. The knight who was hit on the head needed to be stitched up, and another man's leg required a splint. Tending to the wounded left me in no mood to eat or dance." Seeing the look of astonishment

182

on my face, he added, "Mauro's wife was a healer, you see."

Antonio's cool tone mimicked his demeanor, which I found disconcerting. "You mentioned that you were raised by Mauro, but you never mentioned his wife."

"Lucrezia was like a mother to me. I was devastated when she died a few years ago."

"I'm sorry to hear it." An awkward silence followed. "Antonio, I can't help but notice that your comportment toward me has changed from when we last spoke."

He looked off to the side, debating whether or not to reply to my accusation. At length, he said, "One of the knights in the infirmary mentioned that you are Cangrande's mistress. Is it true?"

My heart sank as I nodded.

"Why didn't you tell me?" When I refused to answer, he demanded, "Do you love him?"

I hesitated. "I have to go…"

"Do you love him?"

"No," I whispered.

"I knew it," he said, finally coming toward me.

"I shouldn't be here alone with you."

His face lit up. "You feel it, too, don't you?"

I shook my head, but I *did* feel it. Although we had only known each other briefly, there was an inexplicable connection between us—and it terrified me.

"It's in your eyes, Agata," he said softly.

Hearing my name uttered from his lips filled me with joy. Was this the "love" troubadours sang of in their ballads? I've always enjoyed listening to their poetic verses, but I had never experienced that wondrous emotion—*until now*. My heart brimmed with tenderness toward this man.

My body burned for him.

Placing my hand on his chest, I whispered, "Antonio."

He looked at me in a way that thrilled me. It wasn't lust I saw in his eyes—it was something else. Something foreign and wonderful. Something that possessed the power to pierce my heart and wound me to the core.

183

I didn't move when he gathered me into his arms and bent his head as if to kiss me. I held my breath as his lips barely brushed mine. They felt smooth and hot. I wanted to lick and bite them…*Santo Cristo*.

It took all of my strength to push him away and run out of the room. I arrived in the main hall breathless and confused. Suddenly, everything seemed different to me. Could love be seen on one's face? The sobering thought made me retreat into the shadows.

Francesco sat engrossed in conversation with his men, so I was safe from his scrutiny. Antonio entered the main hall, his eyes scanning the room in search of me. I infiltrated myself into a group of people and focused on their words. To my relief and disappointment, Antonio did the same. Occasionally, he tossed a glance in my direction and I could see the confusion in his eyes.

The revelry continued until midnight. Too drunk to visit my bed, Francesco sought the comfort of his own bedchamber to sleep off the effects of the wine. I, too, left the party and readied myself for bed. Unsurprisingly, sleep evaded me. Bea offered to whip up a draught but I refused and sent her to bed. Tossing and turning, I imagined myself entwined in Antonio's arms.

Only whores delight in carnal acts. Pina's words were false, for I had never derived pleasure during my days as a prostitute.

Restless to the point of sleeplessness, I got dressed and stole downstairs. I squinted my eyes to see better in the dimness, for several candles and torches had already sputtered out, casting the main hall in darkness.

Someone came up behind me. "Agata."

I turned around and came face to face with Antonio. Smelling the wine on his breath, I recoiled, but he quickly grabbed me and plundered my mouth.

This time, I didn't run.

When we broke apart, I demanded breathlessly, "Why are you still up?"

"The more I thought of you in the arms of another man, the greater the need to obliterate the image with wine." He pulled me against him so that I could feel his desire. "I've never wanted anyone as much as I want you."

"Nor I," I confessed. "Someone will see us here."

He led me into a dark corner of an empty room. Trailing fiery kisses along my collarbone, his hands explored the curves of my body through the fabric of my garment. "Come upstairs with me, Agata."

"I shouldn't…"

I allowed him to kiss my lips, melting against him and responding eagerly to his touch. Finally, he lifted me in his arms and carried me to his bed. We were careful not to make a sound. I gave myself to this stranger with a passion and wantonness that frightened me. Overcome with mounting pleasure, I moaned deliriously, compelling him to cover my mouth for fear that I'd scream aloud with its release—which I eventually did.

"Oh my God," I whispered afterward, satiated. "Tell me, is this what men feel when they…?"

Antonio chuckled softly. "Yes, which is why we seek it out so often." When he saw that I wasn't laughing, he frowned, studying my face in the moonlight. "Why do you ask? Have you never…?"

I shook my head. "Never. I'm shocked by—"

Placing his finger on my lips to silence me, he shook his head. "Say no more or you'll ruin this perfect moment, my darling. Your innocence is endearing."

I took his finger into my mouth and gently suckled it, which aroused him. To our mutual astonishment, we made love once more. Euphoric and bewildered by the intensity of what had just transpired between us, we held each other.

"We depart for Naples next week," he reminded me.

"The thought of it fills me with angst."

"You must return with me."

I gazed up at his strong jaw, my eyes lingering on the planes of his pleasant face. "You barely know me."

He met my eyes and caressed my cheek with touching tenderness. "I know enough to say that I can't lose you now that I've found you."

***

Antonio and I invented all kinds of excuses to be alone during the next few days. We confessed our most intimate thoughts between countless passionate kisses, and our lovemaking—although furtive at times—never ceased to amaze me.

By the end of the second week, which flew by far too quickly, I realized that the handsome, charming, clever, kind, funny, blue-eyed Neapolitan possessed my heart.

The foreign envoys thanked their hosts and said farewell to everyone after enjoying their final supper in Verona. As usual, Francesco provided entertainment, and we enjoyed listening to a eunuch's clear voice as he sang Christian hymns.

Mauro approached me near the evening's conclusion. "May I have a word with you, my lady?"

In the last two weeks the sophisticated nobleman had barely spoken to me. Antonio must have informed him of our love, and my intention to leave Verona with them.

Smiling with pleasant anticipation of what he would say, I replied, "Yes, of course."

We retreated to the edge of the room and he regarded me with a serious expression. "I love Antonio like a son, and his happiness is paramount to my own."

"From what he's told me, he loves you, too, my lord."

"He has informed me of his tender sentiments toward you, and I can see by the way you look at him that you love him. Am I correct?"

My cheeks flushed. "I do, with my whole heart."

Mauro's tight smile and cold eyes filled me with foreboding. "But not with your whole body."

"My lord?"

"You are my host's mistress."

The way he said it made me feel like a worthless whore. "It's true, but—"

"Antonio told me that he invited you to accompany us to Naples."

"Yes…"

"This complicates matters. You see, the king and I have no issue with the Lord of Verona. We understand and respect his political stance. Stealing his current mistress may cause a problem, however."

It took all of my willpower to keep my tears at bay as my heart splintered into a thousand tiny fragments. My chest tightened to the point that I couldn't breathe.

Seeing the color suddenly drain from my face, his hand shot out to take hold of my elbow. "My lady?"

I flinched from his touch. "I'm all right."

"Do you understand the situation we are in?"

"Perfectly, my lord."

"Good." He turned to look at Antonio. "Please say nothing to him right now. The last thing anyone wants is a scandalous scene."

I took a moment to compose myself before joining the other guests. Despite feeling physically ill, I put on a brave face and did my best to appear cheerful. Antonio beamed at me from across the room, confident that I would be leaving Verona with him at dawn.

After the guests had dispersed and it was time to retire, Antonio plied me with kisses in the shadowy corridor.

"Goodnight, my love," he said. "Get some sleep, for we are leaving early in the morning."

I nodded, then went into my room and wept.

"His lordship may enter at any moment," Bea gently pointed out.

Wiping my eyes, I said, "He hasn't visited my bed in two days."

"If he decides to come today, it won't do for him to see you crying over another man." Dampening a cloth in rose water, she added, "Best to wash your face. Be sure to press the cloth against your eyelids, too."

I pressed my entire face into the fragrant cloth and took several deep breaths. At the sound of footsteps, I hastily threw the cloth aside as Bea slipped into the antechamber.

Francesco entered the bedchamber and eyed me

187

suspiciously. "What ails you?"

"Nothing, my lord."

"You're sad because he's leaving."

"I admit, I shall miss his witty humor. Nothing more. You haven't sought me out in days…I thought you had tired of me."

"Are you saying that I'm the source of your tears?"

"Who else?"

"My sweet girl…"

I opened my arms. "Come."

He entered the circle of my arms and consumed my body with the same selfish greed as always. In my mind, I imagined Antonio's thoughtful caresses. My true love considered my pleasure as well as his own, and did things to me that no man had ever done. I endured Francesco's clumsiness, all the while pretending to enjoy it, exactly how Carmen had taught me.

With Antonio, there was no need for pretense.

"Ah, Agata," Francesco growled in my ear as he collapsed on top of me.

My first instinct was to push him off and flee the room, but I prudently embraced him. My heart and mind engaged in a fierce battle in that moment. No sooner had Francesco left than I got dressed and tiptoed to the door.

Bea stood in the doorway of the antechamber shaking her head. "Are you sure you want to do that? It will only cause you more pain."

"I must see him…Just one more time."

"Be careful."

I crept into Antonio's bedchamber. Staring at his sleeping form, I mustered my courage. I got into bed and pressed myself against his broad back, kissing his fragrant neck until he opened his beautiful eyes.

"Agata…"

"Shhh," I said before kissing his lips.

"What are you doing here? You should be resting up for tomorrow."

A lump rose to my throat. "I had to see you." I snaked my arms around his neck. "Make love to me."

He happily fulfilled my request, leaving me breathless. I clung to him afterward, committing to memory the feel and scent of his body.

If I had the power to stop time, I would live in this moment forever.

We stared into each other's eyes in the silvery moonlight pouring in from the open window. The balmy breeze carried the sound of crickets as it gently caressed our naked skin.

Antonio's eyes crinkled at the corners whenever he smiled, which I found endearing. "You bring me joy, Agata."

I touched the agate pendant that he always wore around his neck. We held each other until a dull gray light filled the room. I suddenly hated the dawn and cursed that time of day with every ounce of resentment in my being.

"We need to go," he said, trying to untangle himself from my arms. I clung tightly to him, my tears dampening his skin. Realization made him stiffen within my embrace.

"No…Oh, no, Agata…Don't do this."

I held him tighter. "I love you, Antonio."

"You would love my city, too. Naples is sunny and warm, and full of vibrant colors…" The hitch in his throat was followed by a quiet sob.

"I'm sure I would." I hated myself for causing him pain.

He stared at me intently, his eyes pleading in the growing light of dawn. *"Please."*

I kissed his lips as tears streamed down my face. His eyes welled up, too. He knew as well as I did that the Lord of Verona would be furious with us both if we proceeded with our initial plan. Neither of us spoke of it. Instead, we only wept.

I dressed with haste, then helped him dress. I held him for a long moment, listening to the sound of his heartbeat.

"Agata—"

I shook my head to silence him, and he appeared stricken. Without another word, I fled the room.

For the second time in my young life, I felt the excruciating pain of loss. In the privacy of my bedchamber, I placed the pillow against my mouth and gave in to heart-wrenching sobs.

CHAPTER 24
OCTOBER 1326
VERONA

Eyeing the storm clouds gathering in the sky, I said to my maid, "Another downpour will soon be upon us."

It had been raining for several days and, during a brief respite of milky sunlight, I insisted on going to the market in order to get some much-needed fresh air.

Bea sidestepped one of the many puddles in the potholed street. "We should start heading back soon."

I glanced over my shoulder. "Do we have time to—Oh!"

I collided with what felt like a brick wall.

"Forgive me, my lady."

My entire body tensed. I knew that voice well, for I was still legally married to the man attached to it.

"Agata?" Nunzio eyed me, stunned. "Where have you been? What are you doing here?"

Bea placed herself between us and glared at him. "You are addressing the Countess Visconti. A bit of respect on your part would be quite fitting."

"Countess?" he repeated, perplexed.

Thank you, Bea. I raised myself to my full height and regarded him coolly. "That's right. I am the widow of the late Count Armando Visconti."

He stared at me incredulously. "You remarried? How could you when you were still married to me?"

"You have also remarried, from what I hear."

"Only because I thought you were dead. Why didn't you send word? I searched for you for days…"

"I had no choice but to flee Verona after your good-for-nothing father accused me of witchcraft. You have no idea what I've endured because of his treachery."

Nunzio removed the wool cap from his head and twisted it between his big sooty hands. "My father eventually confessed the truth to me. I was so angry with him! I made him confess to the priest and almost turned him in to the magistrates." He paused, remorseful. "I'm so sorry, Agata."

The sincerity in his eyes and in his voice dampened my anger. After all, Alvino had betrayed us both.

He continued, "Where did you go?"

"I went to Venice."

"Alone?"

"Alone, cold and hungry on the streets. It was horrible."

To my astonishment, tears welled up in his eyes. "I wish you had come home."

"How could I?"

"If it's any consolation, I still haven't forgiven my father for what he did to you—to us."

"Alvino is a liar and a rapist."

"You have every right to say that. I can't even defend his honor." He sniffed. "What can I do to rectify the past?"

"Nothing you can do will change the past, but you can help me in the present by pretending not to know me. I've had to construct an entirely new identity, you see. It's for my own protection."

"I understand."

"Do you, Nunzio?"

"I do, and you can count on me to keep your secret." He pointed to a corpulent woman with a swollen belly. "That's my wife with my son, Lapo."

Maria had called her a heifer, and it was an apt description. The woman held the little boy by the hand as she bartered with one of the vendors in the piazza. "Your wife is with child."

"Yes. We lost the last one."

"I will keep her in my prayers for a safe delivery."

Nunzio smiled. "Thank you, Aga—*Countess Visconti*."

***

"You've become wanton," Francesco commented in the pale morning light.

I stared askance at him. "My lord?"

"Which one of my knights have you bedded?" he teased, but his eyes revealed suspicion.

"That you would even ask such a thing is offensive to me."

"You're...*different*. In fact, you've been different for a while now." He peered closely at me. "Are you with child?"

"I've never conceived, so I wouldn't know."

"Let me look at you."

I got out of the bed and stood naked before him.

"Turn around," he instructed. "Slowly."

I did as I was told. "Well, am I?"

He sighed. "What you are is a goddess, which is why every man in Verona wants you."

"I don't want them...I want you, Francesco."

"My little minx is clever-tongued, too." Smacking my bare bottom, he added, "I'm going hunting with my men."

"I was wondering why you came to my bed at dawn instead of last night."

"I needed my sleep to ensure my stamina," he said after dressing hastily. "I bid you good day."

"Likewise, my lord. I hope you catch a fine stag."

"I'd prefer a fat boar," he shot back over his shoulder as he exited the room.

I walked to the looking glass and studied my naked body. I cupped my breasts, squeezing them slightly. They were sore and felt heavier than normal. Turning sideways, I noticed a slight swell below my navel. Almost three months had passed since Antonio and I...

Panicked, I cried, "Bea!"

My maid materialized. "My lady?"

"Fetch the midwife, and be discreet about it."

She gave me a measured look. "I've been waiting for you to tell me. You haven't bled in two months."

"That's nothing new. You know how my menstruation cycle fluctuates sometimes."

"True," she conceded.

"Hurry, I need to know before Francesco returns."

I was later examined by a woman with a face like a walnut. As her strong brown hands gently prodded me, she inquired, "Are you feeling ill? Vomiting?"

"No," I replied.

"Do you get dizzy or suffer fainting spells?"

"I feel perfectly fine."

"You should thank God for your good fortune, my lady. Most women in your condition suffer during this phase of their pregnancy." Turning to Bea, she added, "I'll give you a list of foods and herbs that will be beneficial to your mistress."

My maid listened to the midwife's advice before escorting her out. I went to stand by the window. I could see the Adige in the distance, and my thoughts ran as deeply as the river.

I risked everything for this.

Bea returned and inquired, "Shall I go out to get the items the midwife suggested?"

I met her gaze. "I need you to consult with the city's best apothecaries and wise women. This baby must be born male."

"You're agitated, my lady. Calm yourself, please."

"Armando's money won't last forever. Being the mother of Francesco's son may secure my future—and yours."

"I know that, which is why you need to be in good health and in high spirits." She hesitated. "You haven't been well since Anto—"

"Don't!"

"Forgive me," Bea offered contritely.

"Please don't say his name in my presence."

"I worry about you."

Swallowing the lump in my throat, I took a moment to compose myself. I withdrew money from my coin purse and placed them in her hand. "I'm willing to try any potion or special diet that guarantees male children. If anyone attempts to swindle you, tell them the child in question was sired by the Lord of Verona."

Bea ran off to do my bidding. Meanwhile, I paced the floor of my chamber feeling anxious and elated at the same time. My heart desired the baby to be Antonio's, but my head needed it to be Francesco's next male bastard. After siring four females in a row, my lover needed a son to prove his virility to everyone. I intended to provide him with that prize.

Francesco and his men returned late in the afternoon, unscathed from the hunt. Servants butchered the prize boar and the delicious aroma of roasting meat soon permeated the air. There would be feasting tonight.

Intent on whispering the happy news into my lover's ear after supper, I chose one of my finest gowns. My heart raced as I approached my lover. One of his former mistress's, Petronella, stood beside him. I wasn't surprised since she made an occasional appearance at the Palazzo Scaligero.

Francesco smiled at the sight of me. "Did you see the size of that boar, Agata?"

"I saw your arrival from the window," I replied. "Biggest boar I've ever seen."

"I believe the countess is correct," Petronella said. "I, too, have never seen such a big boar."

"You both flatter me," he accused playfully. Lowering his voice, he inquired of Petronella, "How is my sweet girl?"

"Giustina is doing well. You should come and visit her soon. She asks about you often."

"I shall bring her a new dress next time I see her."

Petronella flashed me a look that made me bristle. "You spoil her, my lord."

"She's my favorite girl child."

I watched the exchange with interest. Wasn't Margherita—the girl destined for the Church—his favorite daughter?

He continued, "When Giustina is older, I shall find her a rich husband."

"I have faith that you will make a fine choice," Petronella said, rubbing his arm affectionately. "You must excuse me now. Your wife has invited me to pray with her this evening."

"Then you mustn't keep her waiting."

Petronella inclined her head at us, then walked away.

"She is friends with your wife?" I whispered, surprised.

"It seems so," he replied distractedly. "Ottavio, there you

194

are. I need to speak with you. Would you excuse me, Agata?"

"Yes, of course."

I didn't particularly care for Petronella, but to hear Francesco speak fondly of their child and even promise to secure the girl's future through an advantageous marriage filled me with hope. A disturbing thought struck me: what if the infant in my womb came out looking nothing like Francesco? Worse still, what if he resembled Antonio? Overcome by fear, I decided to withhold the news of my pregnancy.

Later, in the privacy of my bedchamber, Bea inquired, "Well? How did he take the news?"

"I couldn't tell him."

"Why not?"

"What if the baby comes out looking like Antonio?"

Bea rubbed her chin in thought. "His lordship and the Neapolitan have the same hair and skin color."

"But their features and eye color are vastly different." Placing my face in my hands, I cried, "Bea, what am I going to do?"

"You're going to tell the Lord of Verona that you're carrying his son, and leave the rest in God's hands."

"How do you know it's a boy?"

"I don't," she admitted. "But neither does he."

"You make a valid point."

She smiled. "You should tell him tonight. Come, let me comb your hair before he arrives."

Francesco crept into my room later than usual, and a bit inebriated from the hunting celebration.

After enduring his clumsy lovemaking, I said, "I have something to tell you."

"You sound serious." Leaning up on his elbow to peer down at my face in the candlelight, he added, "You look serious, too. What troubles you?"

"Your son grows in my womb," I replied without preamble.

He grinned widely before planting a hearty, wine-infused kiss on my lips. "Agata, this is good news," he said, slurring slightly. "Wait! You said *son* instead of child. Are you certain

195

it's a boy?"

"Yes," I lied.

"How do you know?"

My mind raced to produce a convincing lie. "I dreamed of a male child."

"Oh? What else did you see in the dream?"

I blurted out the first thing that came to my head. "Feathers."

"Like an angel's wing?"

"I don't remember..."

"What else could feathers mean in a dream if not an angel?" He crossed himself and uttered a quick prayer of thanks to the Madonna before turning his attention back to me. "I've been praying for a son ever since my second daughter was born. God has finally deemed me worthy. Don't' you see? This is a sign!"

His joy was contagious, making me smile and play along with the charade. "I'm so happy, my lord."

Filled with wine and emotion, he gathered me in his arms. "The Virgin Mary has finally interceded on my behalf." Then, as an afterthought, he declared, "This son will be given a title in her honor!"

A title? Astonished, I said, "You are most gracious, my lord."

Pressing me to his chest, he whispered, "*Mia donna.*"

"I am indeed yours, Francesco—body, heart, and soul." Throwing caution to the wind, I whispered, "If only Giovanna weren't an impediment to our happiness."

My words sobered him instantly. Silence followed my bold comment and, as it stretched into an awkward moment, I searched my brain for something redeeming to say. I'd gone too far in my ambitious quest to secure my future in Verona.

"Never say such a thing again," he admonished in a deceptively calm tone. "My alliance with her family is a strong one, and I need as many friends as possible right now if I'm to further expand my territories."

"I meant no offense, my lord," I offered contritely. "My love for you blinds my practical nature at times. I can assure you that I hold the Lady of Verona in the highest esteem."

He nodded in satisfaction of my remorse, then tickled me to lighten the mood. His big rough hands were soon fondling my swollen breasts and he lifted my shift to take me again. This time, he tempered his lust with gentleness.

Francesco displayed more than the usual attention toward me now that I was carrying his son. The fact that I wasn't suffering any illness whatsoever only solidified his belief that my pregnancy was some sort of divine intervention. I caught Giovanna studying me closely on a few occasions, and knew that my days living in the Palazzo Scaligero were numbered.

One morning, Francesco invited me to walk with him in the courtyard garden. We watched a pair of turtledoves bathing in the fountain, then he led me to a shadowy corner beneath a portico to claim my lips. Suddenly, he stopped.

"What's wrong?" I inquired.

A group of knights were gathering around the main gate as he replied, "We're expecting a shipment of twenty swords and I want to see if they meet my standards."

Slipping my hand into the crook of his elbow, I said, "May I accompany you?"

"Certainly."

"Does weaponry interest you, my lady?"

"Everything that interests you, interests me, my lord."

We walked to the gate and the knights parted to allow us through. I lagged behind when I noticed Alvino and Nunzio. They both stood off to the side as the knights tested the weight and balance of the new swords. My first instinct was to run and hide inside the palazzo. Instead, I decided to stand my ground. Alvino tossed a quick glance at me, unaware of my identity until his son whispered in his ear. The second time he looked at me, realization lit up his features. I thought I glimpsed remorse in his eyes.

Turning to the knight standing nearest me, I inquired, "May I?"

At Francesco's nod, the bewildered man relinquished the weapon. I tightened my grip around the hilt and held the heavy sword straight out ahead of me, deliberately aiming the point at

Alvino's throat. If I lunged forward, he would be dead. He must have guessed my murderous thought, for his face paled. I stared Alvino down, which made the knights uneasy.

The tension grew until Francesco's hand covered mine, forcing me to lower the weapon. "It seems the Countess Visconti is trained in the art of battle," he said with deliberate levity, adding a chuckle for good measure.

The knights dutifully laughed and I smiled sweetly at Francesco. "This is a fine sword, my lord."

"Then perhaps I'll have one made for you."

Although the comment made the knights smile in amusement, I shot Alvino a triumphant look before replying, "You are most generous, but what would a helpless lady like me do with a sword?"

"Ah, my dear, but you are far from helpless. Come, let us go inside." To Alvino and Nunzio, he added, "We'll need another twenty swords before Christmas."

Francesco reached for my hand in public during a concerto later that evening. Petronella, who happened to be seated near me, noticed the gesture. After the concert, I saw her speaking with Giovanna. Her suspicion was now confirmed.

News of my pregnancy leaked and spread throughout the city faster than a brushfire in July. Before long, people were whispering about Cangrande's "live-in mistress" and bets were placed on the baby's sex.

Swept up in the excitement of the moment, I didn't give my dark past a second thought. My former life as a prostitute in Venice seemed like a childhood nightmare long forgotten. Alvino, who suffered an apoplexy days after seeing me, was relegated to the back of my mind.

Only Antonio haunted my thoughts on a daily basis.

In short, I reveled in my newfound glory. I was young, beautiful, and carrying the child of the most important man in Verona—in the Veneto, for that matter. I was untouchable, or so I thought. Like Icarus, I soon discovered that I'd flown too close to the sun.

CHAPTER 25
VERONA

"How much longer must I tolerate her presence in my home?" Giovanna demanded, her dark eyes flashing.

Cangrande sighed tiredly. "The Countess Visconti is a young widow with no family. How could I not open our home to her? It's my Christian duty! Remember, she aided me in acquiring the land in Treviso."

The Lady of Verona laughed mirthlessly, causing her jowls to quiver. "Do you honestly think I don't know you by now, dear husband—after all these years of marriage? You may have taken in the girl out of so-called *Christian duty*, but you bedded her out of lust."

"Giovanna—"

"I know she's pregnant," she snapped. "It's your bastard, isn't it?"

"God's teeth, woman. Will you listen to reason?"

Staring at him intently, she laughed again. "You're not even certain, are you? Ha! I'll wager that little trollop has been sleeping with other men—under our roof, no less!"

"How can you make such an accusation?"

"Are you blind? She practically threw herself at the Neapolitan bastard."

Cangrande shook his head in disgust. "You're a petty, jealous woman, Giovanna."

"Call me all the names you want, but that woman needs to go."

"I promised to house her until—"

"She's been eating at our expense for months! I don't care if she aided you or not, get her out of here!" Narrowing her eyes, she added, "Perhaps a letter to my family—or the emperor himself—would quickly resolve the problem."

"Don't you dare trouble them with such a frivolous matter,"

he warned in a menacing tone. "You'll be sorry if you do."

"Save your threats for the battlefield, my lord." She tilted her head back haughtily. "If you don't find alternate lodgings for your merry widow, then I will."

***

"I've secured a place for you to live," Francesco said to me after supper one evening.

I expected this, but pouted prettily for the sake of playing out the farce. "I'm so happy here with you."

Ignoring my comment, he continued, "It's a charming little palazzina by the river, where you can raise my son. There's a courtyard garden, too. You know you can't stay here indefinitely. My wife's patience has run thin and I don't want to create any problems."

"Of course. She's been so kind and accommodating. I'll purchase a gift of thanks before I go."

"I'm sure she will appreciate the gesture."

The lie hung heavy in the air between us. We both knew Giovanna wanted nothing from me.

In fact, the Lady of Verona didn't even come downstairs to bid me farewell on the morning of my departure.

Although my lodgings were not spacious, I liked my new home. The palazzina's frescoed interior, combined with the steady roar of the Adige, lifted my mood. Carrying a child agreed with me, for it rendered my complexion luminous and my hair lustrous. My lover found my new maternal beauty irresistible and his lust became insatiable. He explored my changing body with wonder, relishing my full breasts and ever-growing belly.

In time, Francesco's daily visits were replaced by frequent visits, then occasional visits. These lapses were accompanied by plausible excuses—meeting with other nobles, attending to matters of state, aiding the magistrates, and so on. I took comfort in the fact that he loved me enough to send notes attached to flowers or sweetmeats, explaining why he couldn't come to see me. I remained docile and understanding, secure in my role as his favorite lady and mother to his future child.

Several days passed with no word from my lover. Naturally, I grew worried. Was he poisoned or stabbed by an enemy? Had he gone off to battle without informing me because he feared that I would worry?

"I'm sure he's doing well, my lady," Bea said to me on a cold November night. I continued to pace the room silently, prompting her to add, "Perhaps he is overly occupied with matters of state."

"He has so many enemies…"

"If calamity were to befall the Lord of Verona, the entire city would know within the hour."

"You're right," I conceded.

"Rest assured that he is alive and well."

"Why hasn't he sent word? No flowers, no gifts, no love notes…I don't remember saying or doing anything to incur his disfavor."

"He'll come around eventually."

To my dismay, I detected a note of uncertainty in her tone.

Two more weeks passed with no word from Francesco, so my maid and I ventured to the Palazzo Scaligero. The first week of December proved bitterly cold, so Bea had fastened a fur around my shoulders for added warmth. The icy air transformed each breath into a vaporous cloud as we hastened across the Piazza dei Signori. To my mortification, I—who once held such a prominent position amid the Veronese nobility—was promptly turned away like a common peasant. As I crossed the piazza to return home, I looked over my shoulder and glimpsed Giovanna in the upper window glaring down at me with a smirk on her face. Something about her expression made me wary, and I experienced a strange foreboding.

***

December passed and I grew more despondent by the day. I tortured myself continuously, wondering what I could have said or done to offend Francesco. I thought for certain that I would be invited to the Christmas celebration hosted by the Lord of Verona, but no summons arrived at my door. My melancholic state sapped my beauty and stamina, compelling me to send Bea into town for curatives and tonics to restore my youthful vigor. Unfortunately, none of them worked.

God no longer played a role in my life, but I still attended Holy Mass for the sake of my reputation. Each Sunday, Bea and I were the last to arrive at the tiny church near my home and, since we socialized with no one, we were the first to leave. While exiting the church on a cold February morning, I overheard someone whisper her name: *Dalia*.

Turning to Bea, I whispered, "Who is this woman?"

"The girl is newly arrived to Verona and rumored to be quite a beauty."

"How do you know this?"

She shrugged. "Everyone in the market is talking about the daughter of Eugenio, Duke of Soave."

The passing of weeks led to more wagging tongues. I soon discovered that "Dalia" possessed long blonde hair, aquamarine eyes, the face of a goddess, and was seven years my junior. One troubadour sang of her being so enchanting that she could steal a man's heart from a distance of twenty paces. Aware that such lavish praises of beauty were often exaggerated by those wishing to be handsomely rewarded, I didn't pay much heed to them. The troubadours had also lauded my beauty and charm when I first arrived in Verona, and Francesco himself had once referred to me as a goddess.

When I overheard someone gush over Dalia's dancing skills during the Christmas banquet at the Palazzo Scaligero, I became ill.

"Bribe whomever you can," I said to Bea one day while handing her a heavy coin purse. "Market vendors, apothecaries, the Palazzo Scaligero's servants—I need to know why Francesco has stopped coming to see me."

"As you wish, my lady."

"Be discreet."

"I am *always* discreet."

Bea spent the next few days gathering as much information as she could. During this time, she was morose, pensive. I experienced the same foreboding I had felt when I saw

202

Giovanna smirking at me from the window.

"I know why his lordship has stopped seeing you," Bea said to me one night as she combed my hair. "I can no longer withhold the truth from you."

Gripping her wrist, I met her eyes in the reflection of the looking glass. "You must be honest with me, no matter what."

"Dalia is his mistress."

Tears of rage stung my eyes. "I see."

"Some are whispering—"

At the sight of me crying, she stopped.

"Tell me," I insisted.

"Forgive me, I shouldn't have broached the subject before bed. How inconsiderate of me. We can talk tomorrow. I don't want to upset you or the baby."

"I know the truth is sometimes cruel, and I can handle it. Trust me, I've been through worse."

She exhaled a long breath. "Cangrande is in love with the girl. He declares it openly. Some of the older servants are saying that he loves Dalia more than he loved Grazia."

"Grazia?"

"The mother of his first three sons and the only mistress he has ever loved—until now."

I rejected Antonio's love in favor of Francesco, and *this* was how he repaid me?

Bea continued, "I'm sorry to say, there's more. Dalia speaks ill of you to anyone who will listen."

I stared at her aghast. "She doesn't even know me!"

"On the contrary, my lady. Somehow, she knows many things about you."

"What is she saying?"

"I've said enough for now. Let me fix you a draught."

"Bea," I said in a warning tone.

I could see her distress and braced myself. "She mocks your lineage, my lady. She claims you're peasant in regal clothing who had the good fortune of marrying above her station. She's told people that you're not really Signore Ottavio's cousin, but rather, a bastard."

I groaned in dismay. "How does she know so much about me? My late husband certainly wouldn't have gossiped behind my back…"

Realization suddenly hit me. *Rino.*

Armando had lived his life in a perpetual haze of inebriation, and had spilled private details about me to his trusted valet. Rino must have spread my story throughout the Veneto in retaliation to my poor treatment of him. Being from Soave, Dalia may have heard rumors about me from her servants. I had no way of verifying my theory, but it was the only logical scenario I could piece together.

"This must be Rino's doing," I mused aloud.

"I arrived at the same conclusion, my lady."

Pain spread through my chest and I could barely breathe. Bea whipped up a potent calming draught so that I could get some sleep. I woke up the next morning with red, swollen eyes and a dull ache in the center of my chest. I got out of bed and stood by the window, pensive and silent.

Bea eyed me worriedly. "The sun is shining today. Why don't we take a nice walk?"

I shook my head.

"Would you like me to read to you in the courtyard?"

I continued to stare straight ahead. "I want to be alone."

"My lady—"

"Bea, please go."

Rather than obey my request, she hovered in the doorway. "I didn't have the heart to tell you last night…"

I met her insistent gaze and braced myself.

She continued, "When Dalia first arrived and learned of your existence, she bribed all of the Palazzo Scaligero's servants."

I frowned. "Why would she do that?"

"To collect as much information about you as possible. One of the pages claimed that he saw you in Antonio's arms on the night of the joust."

I felt the blood drain from my face. "Oh no…"

"Is it true?"

"Antonio made to kiss me in the library, but I ran away."

Bea wrung her hands. "The Lord of Verona was informed of it."

"How do you know this?"

"I befriended one of the scullery maids during our stay at the Palazzo Scaligero. I bribed her for information on a regular basis."

"You kept a spy behind my back?"

She shrugged. "I did what any loyal lady's maid would do. Besides, my future depends on your future."

I felt a surge of gratitude toward this savvy woman. No wonder Francesco stopped coming to see me! "What should I do now? What would *you* do?"

"I think you should set the matter straight at once. Be honest with him."

"I shall send Francesco a letter."

Bea nodded in agreement with my plan and left me alone. I leaned on the window sill and watched the people in the piazza below. Rich people, poor people, young and old people. Two nobles walked across the piazza engrossed in deep conversation. I wondered what they were talking about. War? Politics? Whores? *Me?*

An elderly couple caught my eye. Elegantly dressed, they sauntered arm in arm, heads bent toward each other. The woman smiled as the man kissed her cheek. Despite the wrinkled skin and silver hair, they behaved like young lovers.

That could have been me and Antonio someday.

I stood before the looking glass. Red, swollen eyes stared back at me. I no longer felt self-pity, but rather, anger. The bitter resentment I harbored toward Francesco overwhelmed me. How could he behave in such a manner after all I had done to help him? I killed my husband for this man!

I sacrificed Antonio for this man…

Dalia had cleverly planted the seed of doubt in Francesco's mind where me and Antonio were concerned, then squeezed herself into the distrustful gap his suspicion had created between us. I imagined her whispering horrible things about me in his ear, then availing herself to "comfort" him. *Seduce* him.

The Lord of Verona was a lustful man who could not resist the feminine wiles of a beautiful girl.

I paced the room, my anger escalating with each determined step. There were no more tears to shed. My mind raced with ways to get back at the little slut who stole my lover from me. First, I must convince the Lord of Verona that the baby in my womb was sired by him.

I sat down at my desk and wrote a letter to Francesco. I confessed to spurning Antonio's "inappropriate advances" in the library—at least, that much was true. I also restated my love and loyalty to him, adding that his son grew stronger daily within my womb. I ended the letter by reminding him of my "divine dream," and how this male child was the answer to his prayers.

Thanks to Dalia's devious scheme, I may not be able to salvage Francesco's affection, but I could at least appeal to his paternal side. He was fond of his children, especially the males. I dispatched the letter, then got down on my knees and begged the Madonna to grant me a son.

To my dismay, I never received a reply from him.

***

Bea went out of her way to protect me from the cruelness of Dalia and the Veronese nobles who supported Francesco's new favorite. The inevitable day came when I confronted Francesco face to face. I was in the process of walking—or rather waddling—into the Duomo on Easter Sunday with my maid at my side when I spotted him.

"That girl over there is Dalia," Bea whispered.

I followed her gaze. A few feet away from Francesco stood a stunning young woman accompanied by an impeccably dressed man, presumably the Duke of Soave.

"I see why Francesco left me," I confessed. "Dalia is exquisite."

"What good is outer beauty if her insides are rotten? I hear that she's a mean and petty creature."

I gave her hand a squeeze in appreciation of her words. "You are worth more to me than gold, Bea."

206

Francesco and Dalia stared at me as I approached them. Had I a dagger in my hand, I would have stabbed both of them through their hearts. Instead, I gave them my most dazzling smile. "Blessed Easter, my lord."

"Ah, Countess Visconti, how good to see you. How are you feeling these days?" he inquired, his eyes drawn to the huge bulge beneath my garment.

The fact that he addressed me formally made me want to spit in his face, yet I replied in a honeyed tone, "I am well, thank you. As you can see, I'm very close to my time. *Your son* should come any day now."

"Which is exactly why you should be home in confinement," he said sternly. To Bea, he added, "Your mistress should not be out and about this late in her pregnancy."

"Bea takes excellent care of me, I assure you. It's such a lovely morning, and I insisted on attending Holy Mass on this special day."

"I often pray to the Virgin Mary for your safe delivery," he confessed. "I've also arranged for a mass to be sung while you're in the act of childbirth. Does that please you?"

"Very much."

To my surprise, he took my hand and kissed it. Turning around, he said, "Signorina Dalia, the countess looks radiant, does she not?"

"Yes," the girl dutifully replied, her eyes as cold as ice.

Turning his attention back to me, he whispered, "I received your letter and you can put your mind at ease."

Relief washed over me. "Thank you, my lord."

I caressed the fleshy mound between us, my jeweled fingers sliding tantalizingly over the luscious velvet of my cloak. Unable to resist the covert invitation, Francesco placed his hand on my belly. To my immense pleasure, the child inside of me moved, making his eyes grow wide with wonderment. Dalia watched us with a mixture of anger and envy.

I boldly took hold of Francesco's wrist and guided his hand. "Here, my lord, feel your son's head."

Francesco smiled. "He moved again!"

207

I shot Dalia a triumphant look. "He's very strong."

"God is truly great." Remembering where he was, Francesco let his hands fall to his sides. "I shall see you soon, I promise."

"I await your visit with pleasure."

I smiled slightly at Dalia and the duke, then tilted my head back and strutted down the nave of the cathedral like a queen.

Bea kept pace beside me. "Well done, my lady."

***

Nothing prepares a woman for the pain of childbirth. Fortunately, I was assisted by a midwife with an excellent reputation. My labor pains began at dawn, and it was now nearing sunset—I was exhausted.

"Push!"

I held Bea's hand as I pushed with all of my might.

The midwife instructed, "Push harder."

"This child will rip me in half," I muttered.

"I see the head! Push as hard as you can, my lady!"

I screamed in agony with my final push.

The midwife's florid face broke into a grin. "A boy!"

His lusty cry pierced the room, making my eyes well up with relief and gratitude. "Bring him to me!"

I soon held a red-faced infant smeared with blood. I counted his fingers and toes, checked that he wasn't deformed in any way, and then fell back against the covers. The baby opened his eyes and, to my immense relief, they were dark like Francesco's instead of blue. My son's facial features mimicked my own.

A girl poked her head into the room and said to me, "I beg your pardon, my lady." To the midwife, she added, "What news?"

"Who are you?" I demanded.

"A servant from the Palazzo Scaligero," the girl replied.

It was a lie, of course, for she was far too well dressed to be anything but a lady's maid. I didn't know if she worked for Dalia or Giovanna, but I said, "God has granted the Lord of Verona a healthy son."

The girl ran off to carry my message. No sooner had she left, than a liveried page arrived from the Palazzo Scaligero. This time, I knew the servant was sent by Francesco.

"Tell your master the Madonna has answered his prayers," I instructed.

The boy nodded and left.

Summoning the last scrap of energy I possessed, I sat up in bed. "Bathe the infant and wrap him in clean linen." The midwife gaped at me, so I added, "Hurry."

She took the baby from me and did as I commanded.

"Bea," I cried, extending my hand. "You need to help me clean up and get dressed."

"My lady, you must rest."

"Francesco is coming," I said, eyeing the bloodied sheets. "We need to strip the bed. Make haste!"

"You have just given birth," the midwife pointed out with concern. "You should sleep."

"There's time for sleep later!"

The women moved swiftly, cleaning up the mess of birth. Bea combed my hair, applied rouge to my cheeks, and helped me don a blue surcoat that enhanced the color of my eyes. I barely had time to settle back into bed when Francesco arrived at my home. The late afternoon sunlight cast me and the bedchamber in burnished gold.

He paused to admire the ethereal scene. "Agata."

"Come meet your son, Francesco."

It was with pride and satisfaction that I presented the healthy male infant to the Lord of Verona. His eyes narrowed as he carefully studied the infant's face. I held my breath and didn't release it until I saw him smile.

"Alboino, my son," he said while gently stroking the downy hair on the infant's head. "May the Virgin Mary always watch over you and the Lord guide your steps."

After receiving the blessing from his father, the infant began to cry. Although the sound caused my nipples to leak, the wet nurse came forth to take him.

Francesco asked, "The birth was not too difficult, I hope."

"Not at all," I lied. "I'm strong and healthy. Are you happy?"

"You have provided me with a son, which is no small thing,"

he replied, extracting a string of pearls from the inside of his cloak. The necklace flaunted a decent-sized ruby at its center. "A token of my appreciation."

I accepted the gift with gratitude and motioned for Bea to fasten it around my neck. "It's lovely, Francesco, thank you. Your continued friendship is reward enough—as is the title you promised to bestow upon our son."

The smile vanished from his face and he averted his gaze. "You must be tired after such an ordeal..."

"I feel perfectly fine. Please, sit. I'll have Bea fetch you some sweet wine to celebrate."

"We'll celebrate another time, Agata. The shadows have grown long and you need to rest."

I studied his retreating form and continued to stare at the closed door long after he left the room. My maid came to stand beside the bed, but I kept staring straight ahead.

Finally, she prompted, "My lady, what troubles you?"

"Something doesn't feel right."

"You should rest."

"No..." I met her gaze. "Francesco is hiding something."

"Are you certain?"

"Dalia is pregnant." I don't know what made me say those words.

Bea eyed me dubiously. "Did his lordship tell you that?"

"No, but I can feel it in my bones."

"Be reasonable, my lady. We saw Dalia a couple of weeks ago in the cathedral. She didn't appear to be pregnant."

"I know, yet something about Francesco's demeanor..." I trailed off, my brow creasing in thought. "I need to know if my suspicion is justified. You know what to do, Bea."

"Yes, my lady."

I watched her go with a tight chest. The thought of Dalia carrying Francesco's child made me furious. He *loved* her, which would make their offspring special in his eyes. What if she bore him a son? I took a deep breath to calm myself.

Alboino's insistent cry cut into my thoughts and caused more milk to leak from my breasts, thus staining my surcoat.

"Bring me my son!"

The wet nurse trudged into the room with Alboino fussing in her arms. The woman's big breasts were heavy with milk, yet my son refused to latch on to either of her meaty nipples. I took the infant and put him to my breast. He immediately began suckling hungrily, making me wince in discomfort.

The buxom woman watched us while wringing her hands. "My lady, that's what I'm here for."

"Why is he crying?"

She shrugged and I shooed her away. "I'll feed him myself. You can try later."

If my son rejected her again, I'd find another wet nurse.

I fed Alboino until he was full, then watched him fall asleep. Despite the tenderness of that special moment, only one word repeated itself over and over in my head: *vendetta*.

CHAPTER 26
VERONA

Bea confirmed my suspicion a few days later. By the end of the month, all of Verona knew that Dalia carried Cangrande's love child. The ambitious Duke of Soave didn't seem to mind that his fourteen-year-old daughter had willingly given her maidenhead to a married man almost old enough to be her grandfather. Perhaps this had to do with the plot of land he received as compensation from the Lord of Verona.

Coddled and spoiled her entire life, Dalia barely tolerated the difficulties of pregnancy. To my immense delight, rumors of her argumentative nature and constant illness were rampant in the market and apothecaries where herbs and curatives were frequently purchased by the girl's lady's maid. For a coin or two, the vendors of these goods gladly divulged many details to Bea, who then passed them along to me.

Knowledge of Dalia's suffering not only made me smile, it gave me hope. Perhaps I could regain Francesco's favor—even his affection—now that his young mistress was indisposed. It wouldn't be long before he sought another woman's bed to satisfy his lust, and I planned on that bed being mine.

I sat mending some linens by the fire one afternoon when Bea came running into the room. Seeing the look on her face, I became alarmed. "What's wrong?"

"The Lord of Verona is here," she whispered.

Grinning, I set aside my sewing and stood. "I knew it was only a matter of time."

Bea's face beamed. "I've been praying on your behalf, my lady. Good luck!"

I pinched my cheeks and smoothed my silk gown as I went out to meet him. My maid followed me at a discreet distance.

He greeted me amicably, then said, "I'm here to see my son. Where is he?"

I motioned to Bea, who fetched the wet nurse. I stood quietly off to the side as the buxom woman transferred the infant to Francesco's arms.

His eyes softened and a smile touched his lips. "Alboino has grown since I last saw him. It gladdens my heart that he's thriving."

"He sleeps throughout the night and eats heartily during the day. He'll grow up to be strong like his father."

"And you."

I smiled at the compliment as he lifted the child in his arms and studied his face. Alboino stared at his father quizzically, compelling the warlord to chuckle. He eventually relinquished the baby to the wet nurse.

When we were alone, I said, "It's good to see you, Francesco. I've missed you."

"It's good to see you, too, Agata." Meeting my gaze, he added, "I know that I've hurt you."

"You are a man who cannot be tamed. I knew this fact from the start, yet walked willingly into your arms despite the risk."

"If you could go back, would you take that risk again?"

No, I would have run away with Antonio. "Without a second thought, my lord. You've given me the gift of Alboino. How can my heart not long for you?" I trailed my hand along the mink collar of his cape, adding provocatively, "I'm aware that Dalia is indisposed due to illness."

"How do you know this?"

"Everyone knows it, my lord. Servants talk and so do the vendors at the market."

He blew out a frustrated breath and confessed, "When she isn't sick, she's screaming and complaining. I had no prior knowledge of her foul temperament. The girl was all honey and smiles at first."

I pounced on the opportunity his candid admission presented by snaking my arms around his neck. "Let me give you what she cannot…" I kissed his cheek, then his earlobe. "I will be all honey and smiles for you, my lord."

"I confess that sometimes I do miss you, Agata. At least you

213

didn't complain or exhibit anger in my presence."

I took hold of his hand and placed it on my breast while my fingers undid the ties of his leggings. Slipping my hand inside the fabric, I grasped his cock. "Let me comfort you."

"Agata…"

"Why deny yourself of something you want, my lord?"

Taking him by the hand, I led him into my bedchamber. To my relief, I pleasured him as easily as I had in the past. I wanted to bring up Alboino's title and talk of my son's future, but thought it best to leave that discussion for another day. Right now, all I cared about was making the Lord of Verona mine again.

He sighed contentedly. "I needed this."

"Me, too. I have no one to warm my bed."

"No one? In all of these months?"

I shook my head. "I am yours, my lord."

This pleased him, for he kissed the top of my head.

"Stay for supper," I suggested while my fingers played with the hair on his chest. "Better yet, spend the night."

"I cannot. Ottavio is supping with me this evening and I am meeting with my military advisor early tomorrow." He moved to get off the bed. "I must go."

"Off to fight another battle?"

"I am," he replied while shrugging into his tunic.

"Treviso?"

"Not yet. I'm going on a campaign to aid the emperor."

Stretching lazily, I cupped my breasts in a provocative manner and smiled. "To expand the Ghibelline territories."

"Precisely, my little vixen," he said, eyeing my naked body with appreciation. "You're as lovely as ever, Agata. No, I take that back. I believe motherhood has made you even prettier."

"Come back to bed…"

"Alas, I cannot. Although I am tempted."

I leaned up on my elbow. "I anticipate our reunion, Francesco. I'll be praying for your glory and safe return. God bless and watch over you, my lord."

He bent to kiss my lips, then departed.

Humming a cheerful tune, I began getting dressed.

My maid poked her head into the room and grinned from ear to ear. "You've finally succeeded, my lady."

"It was like old times, Bea. He even kissed me before he left and promised to visit me when he returns to Verona."

We shared a moment of mutual glee before she said, "This is good news. Perhaps he'll tire of that childish brat and you'll be reinstated as his favorite mistress."

"That is my greatest hope."

Rather than waste my days away pining for Francesco's return, I decided to follow his example. I transformed my humble palazzina into a cultural center of art and music. I began hosting small gatherings where amateur singers and poets debuted their talents. My parties were a great success and quickly gained popularity. The people who came to my home were mostly well-to-do merchants, artisans, musicians, and writers. Occasionally, a Veronese noble would sneak in to enjoy a theatrical performance or listen to a concerto. The acoustics in my home paled in comparison to that of the Palazzo Scaligero, but I wasn't in competition with anyone. I was only offering a stage to lesser-known talents.

Snippets of juicy gossip always found their way into these events, and I soaked them up like a thirsty sponge. I soon discovered that several members of the Veronese elite despised Dalia for her harsh words and arrogant demeanor. I bit my tongue and listened in silence whenever anyone brought up her name. Knowing how abruptly societal tides can turn, I was careful never to speak ill of anyone. My prudence rendered me trustworthy, compelling people to confess intimate details about themselves and others.

Francesco returned to Verona after a month-long campaign where he managed to bring two Guelph nobles to heel. I wondered if and when he would ever tire of warfare, but I already knew the answer: *never*.

One night, while a flutist performed in my home, Francesco appeared on my doorstep. I hadn't seen him since his return to Verona and slipped away from my guests to greet him. The

215

moment he saw me, he gathered me into his arms and kissed my lips.

Pulling away, he said, "You have company, I see."

"A party, actually. The young flutist in the other room has never performed in public."

"Is he handsome?"

His jealousy lifted my spirits. "He's barely sixteen."

"A mere boy."

I giggled. "Yes, my jealous warlord."

Nuzzling my neck, he said breathlessly, "I've missed you, Agata. Take me to your bed."

Feeling him hardening against my thigh, I whispered, "I have a room full of guests. I'm the hostess…"

"And I'm the master of this entire city," he shot back, urging me upstairs toward my bedchamber.

The act was quick and urgent.

"This is the only moment of peace I've had since my return," he confessed in my arms. "Giovanna and Dalia will put me into an early grave, I swear."

"You're more than welcome to stay here."

He kissed my forehead. "The offer is tempting."

The applause from the guests downstairs reached our ears.

"I should go back to my guests," I said.

"Do you think the flutist would play for me?"

"The boy would be honored, Francesco."

Francesco's visits increased in frequency after that pleasant night. I wasn't his only mistress, but I didn't care. Remaining in his good graces secured my continued success and survival, so I didn't mind sharing him with other women. My heart belonged to another man anyway—a man that I could never have.

"Dalia is always indisposed," Francesco lamented to me one night after we had made love. "The girl is constantly sick and complains of swelling. Why can't she be more like you?"

"Not all women are the same. The midwife proclaimed that I was extremely blessed, and she was right. I felt wonderful during my pregnancy."

"Carrying my child was a joy?" he teased.

L'agata ti porterà gioia. The words crept unbidden into my thoughts, making the breath hitch in my throat. *Antonio...*

My lover continued, "Is there anything you can recommend for Dalia? I know you're somewhat versed in flower lore."

I knew of many herbs and soothing teas designed to curb nausea and ease the discomfort of swollen limbs. "No, my lord," I lied. "I truly wish I could help the poor girl."

"Me, too," he admitted.

My conscience prickled at my wickedness and I almost relented, then I remembered how she had turned some of the Veronese nobility against me for no other reason than malice.

Let her suffer.

***

Francesco began sharing my bed regularly as Dalia's pregnancy progressed. His lovemaking was often tempered with sweet words, making me believe that he cared for me. When I broached the subject of Alboino's future, he told me not to worry so I let the matter drop. Convinced that I had won back my lover completely, I basked in glory—and even grew a bit cocky.

I also arrived at an important conclusion: Dalia must never again be given the chance to steal Francesco away from me. A plan began to take shape in my head. I summoned Bea early one morning and informed her that I wished to take a walk. We donned our cloaks and strolled along the riverbank.

At one point, Bea studied my profile as she kept pace beside me. "Something has been troubling you."

"You know me too well."

"Dalia's pregnancy will eventually come to an end, and you don't want to lose your hard-earned lover."

"She cannot have this child."

Bea frowned. "My lady?"

"*We* are going to make sure that she loses it."

"How?"

"I don't know yet." Taking her arm, I glanced around. "You see how Francesco seeks my bed. Dalia has lost her hold on him—*for now*. We must get her out of the way completely so that I can be reinstated as his favorite."

Bea's brow creased in concern. "The girl's father is a duke."

"An *impoverished* duke."

"Still…"

"Eugenio is a weak man—a pimp who prostitutes his daughter like a common whore in exchange for material wealth. Believe me, I know the type." An idea suddenly struck me. "We'll poison her."

Bea eyed me warily. "Is that really the best solution? What if we get caught?"

"My father once fed hemlock to a pesky dog that kept digging up our garden. It paralyzed the animal's lungs…I still remember the mangy beast suffocating to death." I paused, pointing to the woods on the hills. "The hemlock plant grows everywhere, so it would be hard to trace its source."

"What if we cause Dalia to miscarry, instead—not to kill her, but to make her lose the child?"

"Would a miscarriage keep Francesco out of her bed? He could easily impregnate her again."

"You make a valid point." Bea bit her bottom lip in thought. "This is a dangerous endeavor."

"I'm willing to take the risk. Will you help me?"

"Of course I will. Our destinies are entwined." Her brow creased in thought. "There is one man in the city who makes poison, and he sells it for a high price."

"Money is not an issue."

"He runs a tiny apothecary shop across the river by day. At night, he services a different clientele. It would be safer if I bribed someone on the street to get it for me."

"Then that's what you'll do."

I gave Bea a substantial amount of money later that day. She disguised herself as best she could, then slipped out of the palazzina after supper to procure the poison. She returned hours later with a much lighter purse.

"Foxglove," she said, placing a tiny ceramic amphora in my hand. "A dose strong enough to kill a man."

I stared at the amphora, puzzled. "I told you to get hemlock."

"The apothecary didn't have any. Given the stealthy nature of my errand, I purchased what was readily available."

"Very well," I said, locking the poison in my jewelry chest. "Now, all we have to do is wait for the perfect time."

***

Francesco's visits tapered from nightly to weekly in a matter of months. I spotted Dalia in the market one morning and discovered the reason for this change. Clad in ivory silk, the girl resembled an exquisitely painted Madonna with gilded locks and an alabaster complexion. Apparently, the illness phase of her pregnancy was over.

Any man would easily fall under her spell, especially Francesco. I imagined him tenderly caressing her protruding belly and gently suckling her swollen breasts, chuckling playfully whenever he got a mouthful of milk...

Dalia turned her head and caught me staring at her. Rather than look away, which would have been the wise thing to do, I continued to glare at her. In retaliation, she eyed me as one would a loathsome insect. She said something to her lady's maid, prompting the girl to look at me and laugh aloud. It wasn't enough that the little shrew stole Francesco, she wanted to strip me of my dignity! I walked away from the incident feeling defeated and humiliated.

That night, after a long talk, Bea and I abandoned the idea of poisoning my enemy. There was no way to carry out the deed without risking implication. Neither of us wished to be executed, so we decided to accept whatever Fate tossed our way. Carmen often came to mind during those tumultuous days. If she could be resilient and resourceful, so could I.

***

To my surprise, an invitation written in Francesco's own hand arrived at the palazzina. He had planned a concerto for a pair of visiting allies, and thought I would enjoy the event. I dressed for the occasion with meticulous care, donning my best gown and jewels. Bea accompanied me to the Palazzo Scaligero to serve as my extra set of eyes and ears.

219

Francesco greeted me cordially when I arrived, and dutifully inquired after Alboino. To my disappointment, there was no flicker of desire for me in his gaze. We chatted for a bit about mundane things, then he went off to speak with other people.

"Did you see that, Bea?" I whispered.

"I did."

"I've lost him. *Again*."

Bea said nothing. She and I stuck close together, our eyes scanning the room. Some of my former acquaintances spoke with me, but the majority of the Veronese avoided me.

I spotted Dalia conversing with a few people on the opposite side of the room. Arrayed in patterned velvet, she looked radiant. Her hair glistened like pure gold in the candlelight, and her full lips resembled garnets. The acknowledgement of her unsurpassed beauty was accompanied by a sinking feeling in the pit of my stomach.

Hail to the victor.

"You're gaping at your rival, my lady," Bea observed.

I closed my mouth and averted my gaze. "She's an enchantress. Look around you. Everyone is staring at Dalia."

"Not everyone."

Following her gaze, I saw Giovanna glaring at me. I rolled my eyes at Bea and we both laughed.

During the concerto, I chose a seat toward the back of the room. From my vantage point, I could study everyone present. Dalia sat in the front row with her father. Despite her big belly, Francesco's eyes were drawn to his young lover several times during the evening. The clever girl had chosen a low-cut gown that displayed her ripe breasts to their fullest advantage. She would give birth soon enough, and the Lord of Verona would completely forget about me. Sadly, this meant that Alboino would suffer, too. The negative thoughts racing through my head were so loud that they prevented me from enjoying the music.

Servants offered food and wine at the performance's conclusion. A few friendly nobles sought me out, and I provided them with witty banter while casting furtive glances at my rival. Francesco openly displayed his affection for her, right under Giovanna's nose!

My fury bubbled over like soup left unattended in a cauldron. Had I the power to strike Dalia dead in that instant, I would have done so. A pang of guilt followed the evil thought.

The Lady of Verona eventually excused herself from the festivities, allowing Dalia to stick to Francesco's side. Naturally, my former lover and father of my child avoided me. Why did he invite me here in the first place? Did Dalia put him up to it so that she could gloat in my face?

Noticing my mounting irritation, Bea said, "Perhaps we should leave, my lady."

"He never treated me like this," I said, sickened by the sight of Francesco kissing Dalia's cheek in front of everyone. "He doesn't even attempt to be discreet!"

"Let's go home."

"No."

Dalia shot me a triumphant look, then excused herself and waddled toward the back stairwell. I knew exactly where she was going—the privy. The final stages of pregnancy placed a strain on the female bladder.

On impulse, I said, "I'll return shortly."

"Wait—"

I slipped out through the nearest side door. Having spent several weeks in the Palazzo Scaligero, I knew it well. I rushed to the privy via a different route and arrived there before my rival did. Crouching in the shadow of a deep doorway, I waited as silently as a cat. I soon heard Dalia's labored breathing as she slowly made her way down the corridor.

She paused for breath outside the privy door, which was beside a stairwell leading to the cantina. Located in the bowels of the palazzo, the cantina housed casks of wine, ale, and oil, along with a variety of foodstuffs. Two torches burned in iron sconces, casting eerie shadows on the walls. Their shifting light illuminated the first few steps of the stairwell, while the remainder faded into a yawning mouth of blackness.

It would be so easy…

221

Despite the temptation, my feet were cemented to the floor. Squeezing my eyes shut, I recalled to memory my life in Venice. The cold streets, the desperation, the hunger…

Alboino.

Before I knew it, I was behind Dalia.

God forgive me.

Clamping my hand over her mouth, I yanked her backward toward the stairwell. She resisted the assault with surprising strength. Suddenly, I froze. I couldn't do it. I was many vile things, but I wasn't a killer. Releasing her, I moved to face my enemy, leaving her standing with her back to the stairwell.

Her eyes bulged at the sight of me. *"You!"*

"I'm sorry, Dalia," I offered contritely.

"You attacked me! Your apology means nothing!"

"I can explain—"

Her eyes narrowed into slits. "I'm going to tell Francesco about this and insist that you be banished from Verona!"

Ignoring her threat, I demanded, "Why are you sullying my name and creating problems for me? I've never done anything to you. Can't you just leave me alone?"

"I'm only stating the truth," she replied with a sneer. "Everyone in the Veneto knows the Visconti widow is a bastard and an opportunist."

This information made me reel. "Who told you this?"

"Does it matter?"

"You're spreading lies about me."

"You're the liar. You're not worthy of Francesco's love. The mere thought of him in bed with you repulses me."

Recoiling from her hatred, I reasoned, "You have everything, Dalia. Your father is a duke, the Lord of Verona's child grows in your womb—you're even younger and prettier than me. Please allow whatever shred of dignity I still possess intact, and let me live in peace!"

"While I was suffering miserably during my initial stages of pregnancy, Francesco crept into *your* bed to make love to *you*— a fraud! You are nothing, yet he sought you out like a pig seeks its trough."

Her capacity for cruelty astonished me. "Dalia, please—"

"Shut your mouth, you low-born whore!" With that, she spat in my face.

Shocked by her vulgarity, I was about offer a scathing retort when she raised her hand slapped me. I touched my stinging cheek, then defended myself against a second blow by pushing her away from me. To my horror, she lost her balance and teetered backward.

I reached for one of her flailing arms. Dalia grasped my fingers, but she was too heavy to maintain the grip. She gasped loudly as she fell backward. The whites of her terrified eyes glowed in the flickering torchlight. There was a dull thump, then I heard the crunch of her neck snapping on the unforgiving stone steps. Her limp body continued its rolling descent with sickening thuds.

"Santa Madonna," I whispered, horrified.

I descended a few stairs but could barely make out Dalia's form in the darkness. Panicking, I bit my lip and hastily retraced my steps to the main hall. I slipped through the side door and motioned to a servant.

"Wine," I demanded.

The servant fetched me a chalice and I took a deep sip of the ruby elixir in an attempt to obliterate what I had witnessed a moment ago. Out of the corner of my eye, I saw someone approaching. I stiffened with apprehension.

"My lady?"

My body sagged with relief at the sound of Bea's voice. "Thank God it's you. Oh, Lord, forgive me."

"What's wrong? What happened?"

"I pushed her. It was an accident, I swear."

"Shhh! Calm down," she whispered, her eyes darting around the room to make sure that no one was eavesdropping.

"Oh, Bea…"

"Who did you push? Dalia?"

"Yes." I felt the blood draining from my face when I caught Dalia's maid searching for her mistress. "We have to go."

"Is she dead?"

Her focused calm unnerved me. "She fell down the stairs. I think she broke her neck!"

"Hush, my lady," Bea admonished, her eyes hard.

"It's only a matter of time before her body is discovered."

"All the more reason for you to stay and appear *innocent*." Gripping my arm, she added, "Take another hearty sip of that wine, and join *them*."

I followed her discreet gaze to a group of drunk guests who stood in a circle laughing. "But—"

"*Now*," she urged, giving me a slight push.

I took a shaky step toward the merrymakers while forcing my lips into a smile. They welcomed me into their circle. I pretended to enjoy a bawdy tale, my eyes alternately darting from Francesco to Bea.

Dalia's maid emitted a scream so loud that the main hall grew silent. She appeared in the doorway a moment later, white-faced and terrified.

"Lady Dalia is dead!"

CHAPTER 27
VERONA

The people of Verona whispered Dalia's name with regret in their eyes. The harrowing manner in which the girl died was tragic enough, but the lost baby added an extra layer of sorrow. News of Dalia being cut open in an attempt to save the infant filled me with guilt. The male child had survived for only a few hours before succumbing to death. In that brief window of time, Francesco had managed to summon a priest to hastily baptize his ninth child, thus saving him from Purgatory. Candles were lit in Dalia's honor and masses were sung for the two lost souls.

Francesco's inconsolable grief over the loss of his beloved mistress and their son became the talk of market vendors and old women.

I took all of this in with a weighted conscience. Those two deaths were *my* fault. My devastation was so great that I couldn't even face my reflection in the looking glass. As penance for my sins, I turned to fasting and self-flagellation.

"You must eat," Bea insisted one morning. Seated by my bed with a bowl of broth, she tried to convince me to open my mouth. "You cannot continue like this, my lady."

"I don't deserve food…"

"I'm going to fetch the physician."

"No."

Setting aside the bowl and spoon, she studied my reclined form. I must have looked very bad, for I glimpsed fear in her eyes. "It's been two weeks. You'll die if you keep this up. We didn't come this far to lose it all now."

"I'm bound for Hell, Bea."

"It was an accident."

"I followed Dalia to the privy with hatred and malice in my heart. I *wanted* to push her down those stairs."

"But you couldn't do it—you said so yourself. You tried to

reason with her, instead. You attempted to save her!"

"It doesn't matter. Had I stayed in the main hall with you, Dalia would be alive and so would her son."

Bea left and came back with a small bottle in her hand. "At least let me apply some linseed oil to your back."

I took off my shift, then heard her sharp intake of breath. "These welts are newly made. Did you—?"

"This morning," I replied flatly.

She gently rubbed the oil into the open flesh, her silent disapproval emanating from her like the sun's rays. "These scars may become permanent."

"I don't care."

She said nothing after that.

Alboino became my only reason for living during those dark days. My son loved the river and took delight in watching the ducks glide upon its surface. The palazzina's balcony faced the Adige, so we spent hours together quietly watching the birds. Those precious moments were a peaceful respite from my guilt.

Thanks to Bea's clever logic and comforting words, I gradually accepted the fact that my rival's death had been an unfortunate accident. In time, my inner and outer wounds healed as much as they possibly could under the circumstances. I didn't mind the outward scars. The inner scars changed me, and I became a different person. I mentally buried the old Agata alongside Dalia.

Francesco paid me a visit a few months later.

I greeted him cordially. "This is a most pleasant surprise, my lord."

Making no attempt to physically greet me, he looked me up and down. "You look well, Agata."

I immediately sensed that there was something different about him as I inclined my head in response to his words.

He continued, "How is Alboino?"

I called out to the nurse to bring out our son. "He's doing exceedingly well."

Francesco's eyes lit up when he saw Alboino. Scooping the boy up in his arms, he said, "Hello, my son. Look at you! Big and strong, like me."

"Alboino, say hello to your father," I urged.

"Papa," Alboino said. "Papa big."

Francesco chuckled. "Bravo!"

Alboino pointed to the river and I said, "He loves to sit on the balcony and stare out at the water. He counts the ducks and herons, and laughs whenever a fish jumps."

Francesco smiled at his son. "I'll teach you to fish someday, how's that?"

"He's learning to walk, too."

Francesco set Alboino down, then led him by the hand to the balcony. The little boy shuffled along with tentative steps and almost tumbled twice before being hoisted back up into his father's burly arms.

I stared at their blackened silhouettes, perfectly framed in the sunlit doorway. They gazed out at the river and Francesco pointed to the blue herons fishing along the bank. They eventually came back inside and the nurse was summoned to take Alboino.

"He'll grow into a fine man one day," Francesco commented as his son waved goodbye to him.

"*Count* Alboino," I said lightly.

Deliberately ignoring my comment, he said crisply, "I must go now. Take care of yourself."

"Surely, you have time to partake of some refreshment."

"My advisors await my return."

"I haven't yet offered you my condolences on—"

He shook his head, compelling me to shut my mouth. To my astonishment, his eyes welled up with tears.

Closing the gap between us, I placed my hand on his chest. "Let me comfort you, Francesco."

He pushed me away. "No."

Humiliated by his rejection, I inclined my head and said nothing more as he exited the palazzina.

Bea materialized in the doorway. "That was a fast visit."

I sighed tiredly "He loved her. He almost cried when I brought up her name. I'm at a loss of what to do next."

227

She thought for a moment. "Petronella has his ear."

"I know she does."

"Perhaps you should pay her a visit on the pretense of introducing the children. It would benefit you to be on good terms with the woman."

"I suppose it wouldn't hurt."

Heeding Bea's advice, I went to Petronella's home the next day accompanied by my son and his nurse.

A snub-nosed servant opened the door and I said, "Tell your mistress that the Countess Visconti is here."

A moment later I followed the girl down a corridor. We stopped before a pleasantly furnished room where Petronella greeted me with forced courtesy.

"I thought it was time for Alboino to meet his half-sister," I explained. "I hope I'm not intruding, my lady."

Petronella smiled at my son and told the servant to fetch some sweetmeats before addressing me. "The children should indeed meet."

She called for Giustina, and a lovely little girl dressed in rose silk entered the room. She played with Alboino as she would a doll. At one point, I saw her pinching his chubby cheeks.

My conversation with Petronella basically revolved around motherhood, and we exchanged medicinal curatives for various childhood ailments. I kept the visit brief and extended an invitation to my home. She said she would come in the near future, but I wasn't sure if she meant it.

Petronella led me toward the door and commented, "It's a shame what happened to Dalia."

I nodded in agreement. "She was so young…"

"Francesco is still upset about it. Dalia and I were friends, you know."

I hid my surprise. "Oh?"

"In fact, she looked up to me like an older sister."

"I'm sorry for your loss."

She offered me a tight smile, her eyes glinting in the dim light of the hallway. I felt suddenly uncomfortable under her scrutiny. Inclining my head, I took my leave.

I later learned through servant gossip that Petronella told Francesco of my pathetic attempt to win him back by currying her friendship. Needless to say, I never visited her again.

***

I hadn't received a single invitation to the Palazzo Scaligero since Dalia's death. No doubt Petronella had something to do with my social exile. Rather than let this discourage me, I focused on Alboino.

The Lord of Verona spent most of his time fighting for the glory of the Holy Roman Empire, which meant that he saw little of his son. Fighting battles no doubt kept the pain of Dalia's death at bay.

The weeks turned to months, then a year. Alboino was a cheerful boy who talked early and laughed often. On his second birthday, Francesco appeared on my doorstep with a gift for our son. The costly velvet tunic boasted silver thread around the cuffs. I was both surprised and delighted by this unexpected gesture.

I retreated to the corner of the room as the Lord of Verona got reacquainted with his son. It was good to see Francesco laughing and exuding happiness.

When the wet nurse finally collected Alboino for his nap, I approached Francesco. "It gladdens my heart to see you smile, my lord. I haven't had the pleasure of your company in a long time."

"I am rarely in Verona these days."

"You look tired."

"I *am* tired," he admitted.

"Stop fighting and stay in Verona."

"I'm doing God's will."

I didn't dare contradict him. "Alboino is a good boy and he would love to see more of his father."

"He's a fine lad, but he's still quite young. I'll take more interest in him when he's older."

"I'm relieved to hear it, my lord."

A servant entered the room bearing a tray with two chalices filled with my finest wine.

229

Francesco, who sat across from me by the hearth, lifted his vessel. "To Alboino's health."

I drank deeply to the toast.

He continued, "Alboino will train as a squire, as my other sons did. I'll make him a knight when he proves himself worthy. That's how you build character in a man."

I smiled and asked sweetly, "When will he get his title?"

"What title?"

I kept the smile plastered on my face. "You said he would have a title."

"I don't remember uttering those words," he said, setting his chalice on a nearby table.

"Well, you did," I gently countered, also placing my vessel on the table. "Don't you remember? It was the day I told you of my pregnancy and the dream of the male child. You expressed relief and joy at the thought of having another son."

"I remember you telling me of the dream and my happiness at the prospect of siring a son."

Encouraged by his acknowledgement, I continued, "You *promised* to bestow a title on Alboino."

"Promised?" he repeated, raising his eyebrow. "I cannot give to Alboino what I haven't offered my firstborn son—or any of my children, for that matter."

"My son should have a title."

"You are not a lady of noble birth to demand such a thing from your overlord," he reminded me in an icy tone.

I stood and looked down at him. "Have you forgotten that my late husband was a count? As his widow, I am a countess. Alboino is my heir."

He also stood and eyed me steadily. "Heir to what, exactly? Armando's palazzo in Venice was seized to pay off his many debts. The land he once owned in Treviso is now mine—"

"Thanks to me," I interjected, taking a step toward him and putting my face close to his. "I helped you."

"Yes, you did," he conceded. "In return, I welcomed you to Verona as a high-born lady, fed and housed you for months in my own home, and provided you with a place to live. You *are* happy here, are you not?"

"I'm content with my home and appreciate your generosity, my lord. Let me remind you that I wanted to secure my own lodgings the moment I arrived in Verona. It was *you* who insisted that I remain under your roof. I stayed in your palazzo for *your* convenience—so that you could satisfy your lust at any hour of the day or night."

"Don't flatter yourself by thinking that you were the only one warming my bed."

The combination of mockery and disdain in his eyes made me want to grab his sword and run him through with it. Furious, I balled my hands into fists. "How dare you?"

"Watch your tone and lower your voice."

Rather than heed the warning, I cried, "I trusted you!"

"Agata—"

"You're nothing more than a dishonorable liar!"

The blow I received for my outburst was so powerful that it almost knocked me to the floor. Stumbling backward, I propped myself against the wall for support as I cradled the left side of my head.

Glaring at me, he warned, "*Never* speak to me like that again. You were my *whore* for a brief period, nothing more."

"Please, Francesco, don't—"

He spat on the floor and the wad of saliva almost hit the hem of my gown. "Be careful, woman. The generosity and kindness I've bestowed on you can be easily retracted."

A sob escaped my lips as he stormed toward the door.

Before exiting the room, he looked over his shoulder and said, "Dalia was right about you."

His words hurt more than the blow he dealt me.

The moment he was gone, Bea emerged from the corridor and ran across the room to take me into her arms. "There, there, my lady, don't cry."

"He *hates* me!"

"He is a warlord, a savage."

Francesco was a warrior, yes, but a refined and educated man. I wasn't in love with the Lord of Verona, but I respected

231

him as the head of our city. Bea wasn't Veronese and therefore wouldn't understand my loyalty.

She continued, "Let me make something to help you relax."

"No, I'm fine."

Pulling away, she frowned at the red welt on the side of my face. "I can't believe that brute did this to you."

"Don't…"

"You defend him?"

"I respect him despite *this*," I said, my fingers gingerly patting the swollen flesh. "Francesco is a great man. He is Verona."

***

In the spring of 1329, the Veronese celebrated alongside their ruler when he received the title of Imperial Vicar of Mantua from the Holy Roman Emperor. Cangrande informed his trusted advisors of his intention to challenge the Gonzaga family who ruled Mantua.

A few weeks later, Ottavio hurried across the main hall waving a sheet of parchment. Spotting Ercolano in the corridor, he demanded, "Where is he?"

"In his study," the valet replied.

Ottavio ran upstairs and knocked on the door. "My lord, I have urgent news!"

"Enter," Cangrande said from within. The sight of Ottavio's flushed face made him frown. "What is it, man?"

"Treviso is within your grasp!"

Cangrande regarded him dubiously. "I'm busy, Ottavio."

"You need to see this."

He stood and snatched the parchment from his advisor's hand. As his eyes scanned the page, he said, "This is a list of nobles who have been exiled from Treviso."

Pointing to the sheet, Ottavio said, "Yes, and each one of them is willing to aid you in your military endeavors to conquer the city."

"What do they expect in return?"

"Reinstatement. Our spies in Treviso have reported great changes within the city. The ruling families are bickering

232

among themselves, causing political rifts. There have even been reports of people rioting in the streets."

Cangrande gazed out the window in deep thought.

Ottavio shifted from one foot to the other. "My lord, what would you like me to do?"

"For now, nothing," the weary warlord replied, meeting Ottavio's gaze. "I need confirmation. Send your most trusted men to Treviso. I will decide on what action to take based on their report."

"What about the preparations being made for your attack on Mantua?"

"Put them on hold for now. I need to think."

CHAPTER 28
JUNE 1329
PALAZZO DUCALE, MANTUA

Ludovico I Gonzaga, patriarch of Mantua's powerful ruling family, sat at the head of a long oak table laden with delicacies. Silver and copper bowls brimming with fresh fruits and honeyed sweetmeats gleamed in the light of numerous candles. Servants hovered discreetly in the background of the spacious chamber, ready to assist.

Arrayed in costly black velvet, the old man's rheumy eyes alighted on various family members as he thoughtfully assessed their skill, intelligence, and merit. He listened in silence as the assembled condottieri and captains—his sons and grandsons—engaged in a heated argument.

"He was recently declared the Imperial Vicar of Mantua," his second son, Guido, pointed out. "We need to act *now*."

Guido's passionate and volatile nature stood out in stark contrast to the calm demeanor displayed by Ludovico's firstborn, Filippino. "Our father met with the Lord of Verona and garnered his approval. Mantua and the Gonzaga are perfectly safe. Brother, you're being paranoid."

"And you're being naïve," Guido snapped. "Do you honestly believe a power-hungry warlord would throw away the opportunity he's been given—and by the emperor, no less? He *will* strike, and it will be sooner than you think."

Filippino shook his head. "I swear your hotheadedness will someday spark war."

Guido stared at Ludovico. "Father, please listen to reason. Cangrande is not your ally. Let me take care of this matter quickly and discreetly."

All eyes turned to their patriarch in the ensuing silence. Ludovico motioned to a servant, who immediately filled his silver chalice with diluted wine. Taking a sip, he pondered the words of his sons.

One of his nephews finally said, "If the Lord of Verona's intention was to challenge us, don't you think he would have done so by now?"

Filippino spread his hands. "Cousin, I thank you. That's *exactly* my point."

Guido sighed in frustration. "The only reason he hasn't attacked us yet is because Treviso is finally within his grasp. Our spies have reported that Trevisan exiles are rallying to Cangrande's side in droves." He stood and eyed each of his kinsmen in turn. "Trust me, if we don't take precautionary measures against this Veronese threat, the Gonzaga will fall."

Everyone began to talk at once, some shouting over the voices of others.

Ludovico raised his jeweled finger and everyone fell silent. Looking directly at Guido, he said, "Do what must be done, my son, *but*, as far as this matter is concerned, you must keep our family name as unblemished as newly fallen snow. The slightest suspicion of our involvement in Cangrande's death would invoke the emperor's wrath."

***

Nero slipped into Verona with the stealth of a cat. Clad in undyed linen tunic and black wool cloak, his nondescript appearance aided him in being unnoticed by passerby. The spy crossed the ancient Roman bridge with anxious steps. It wasn't difficult to spot her palazzina since it faced the Adige. The countess stood on the balcony with her small son—Cangrande's youngest bastard.

Nero studied the woman's delicate profile and trim figure with an appraising eye. Hopefully, he would leave the city tonight in good spirits and return to his employer with favorable news.

***

"Thank you for seeing me, Countess Visconti," said the bland-faced man after bowing with the grace of a nobleman. "My name is Nero, and I've come on behalf of my employer with a proposition for you."

Eying his shabby attire dubiously, I said, "Nero…?"

"Just *Nero*." Sensing my skepticism, he added, "Do not be fooled by my humble appearance, my lady, for I work for one of the most powerful families on the continent."

"I see."

"You were once very close to Francesco della Scala."

"Yes, *once*, but that's no longer the case." Judging by Nero's smug expression, he already knew this fact. "What does he have to do with your visit?"

"My master wants you to kill him."

I stared at him, stunned. "Get out of my house."

"We know all about you, *Contessa*. Your late husband, Count Armando Visconti, was murdered by your own hand." His eyes traveled up and down my body as a sardonic smile spread across his face. "Cangrande is a lucky man. After the count's untimely death he obtained two prizes—Armando's land in Treviso and his grieving young widow."

Bea stepped out from the behind the door where she had been quietly eavesdropping and glared at Nero.

"How dare you?" I whispered.

Bea placed her lips to my ear. "My lady, shall I summon the authorities?"

Nero looked to Bea and warned, "Your mistress will be executed for murder if you do that."

"You make wild accusations with no proof," I retorted.

"My employer's spies are *everywhere*," he countered with confidence. "Nothing escapes their notice—especially the sudden death of a noble peer."

"My husband was an old man—"

"Who was buried a few days after Cangrande and his advisor dined at his home in Venice," he interjected. "You were also seen meeting with him at a church, then at your home late at night…Shall I continue?"

I felt suddenly ill. Thankfully, Bea placed an arm around me for support.

Seeing my distress, Nero changed his tone. "Forgive me. I

didn't come here to upset you, my lady."

"No…you've come here to blackmail me!"

Unfazed by my accusation, Nero continued, "I'm offering you the means to wreak revenge on a man who has used and abandoned you. Please, hear me out—at least for the sake of your son."

"Who is your employer?"

"That doesn't matter. What *does* matter is that you will receive enough money to secure the future of your entire household. Cangrande will be dead soon enough—with or without your help—leaving your son, Alboino, a fatherless bastard. What will become of him? I doubt the Lady of Verona will take him in."

I took a moment to gather my thoughts. "There are plenty of assassins for hire these days."

"Strangers cannot be trusted."

"Kill the assassin after he commits the deed," I countered. "What's another murder when you're already bound for Hell?"

"People talk too much—including assassins. My employers are extremely cautious. Loose ends are dangerous liabilities."

"Send this evil man away," Bea advised. "You don't want to get involved in this."

Nero eyed Bea coldly. "Remember your place, woman."

"And you remember yours," Bea snapped. "You're just as much a servant as I am."

I placed my hand on her arm. "Bea, go."

"My lady—"

"Please," I insisted.

Bea tossed Nero a contemptuous look before leaving the room. Her footsteps stopped just outside the door so that she could continue eavesdropping on our exchange.

"Well?" Nero prompted. "Will you accept the offer?"

"Cangrande rescinded his promise to bestow a title upon our son. If I agree to commit this vile deed, I want to know that Alboino's future is secured. I want him to have a place in society amid the nobility."

Nodding thoughtfully, he said, "I'm sure it can be arranged."

"I have one more question: why me?"

"It's obvious, isn't it? Aside from being guilty of murdering your husband, everyone knows you've fallen out of favor with Cangrande. Of all his former mistresses, you have the most reason to seek revenge. Furthermore, you're of low birth with limited funds. Your mother is dead, your father is a drunkard, and your sister is a poor wretch—"

"Stop!" My eyes stung with unshed tears but I held them at bay. "Your employer truly does have spies everywhere."

"I wouldn't be standing before you now if they weren't sure that you would accept their generous offer."

"How am I to kill him?"

"Poison would be the most logical choice. Isn't that how you killed your husband?" A long moment of silence passed, prompting him to add, "Think of your son's future."

Those words moved me. What wouldn't a mother do for the sake of her child? The answer was simple—*nothing*.

CHAPTER 29
JULY 2, 1329
TREVISO

Cangrande rode at the head of his army. He cursed under his breath as the sweat on his brow dripped into his eyes. They departed from Verona in the coolness of dawn with a spattering of bleary-eyed citizens cheering them on. Now, he felt like a wax candle melting in the merciless heat.

Was there anything in existence that could render a warrior's hauberk immune to summer weather? Perhaps he was getting too old and too tired for these endless battles. He imagined retiring to the countryside and living in a fine villa with a comely young mistress to warm his bed at night. Maybe he could grow grapes and make wine. Teach his sons the art of war...

Cangrande smiled wryly. The fierce warrior in him would never allow for such a soft, indulgent life. Besides, he still had Treviso to conquer—and Mantua after that.

Ottavio's horse loomed beside him, ending his fanciful reverie. "How are the men?"

"Thirsty, my lord. The horses, too. We need to stop and allow the animals to drink." Pointing to a swell of land in the distance, he added, "A river runs behind that hill."

"We'll stop there."

Ottavio turned his horse around to inform the men. When they arrived at the river, the knights took turns leading their animals to the water.

"We'll continue until the sun sets, then set up camp," Cangrande said to Ottavio while eyeing the horizon. "We'll reach Treviso before nightfall tomorrow."

"Treviso will finally be yours, my lord."

"If God wills it, I will succeed in this endeavor."

"How can you not succeed? The people of Treviso believe you're going to make a move on Mantua. They're not expecting you to lay siege on their city."

"The element of surprise is definitely an advantage," Cangrande agreed. Indicating the amassed knights, he added, "I'm leaving you in charge for a bit."

"Where are you going?"

"I need to pray to the Virgin."

Ottavio watched as Cangrande delved through the shrubs and sank to his knees.

The army arrived on the outskirts of Treviso at sunset. The land Cangrande had acquired from Count Visconti allowed his army to rest without the danger of discovery. The poor serfs who worked the agricultural fields didn't care who owned the soil. Their primary concerns were fighting off starvation and warding off plague.

Cloaked in darkness, the knights circled the city of Treviso and blocked every possible exit. By the time the bells tolled to warn the people of the impending threat, it was too late.

The Lord of Verona watched the scene unfold in the light of burning torches. He kissed the crucifix around his neck while uttering a silent prayer of thanksgiving.

Ottavio stood beside his overlord. "Tempesta is no fool."

"No, he's not."

"I imagine this will all be over soon."

"I'm certain of it."

A noble exile by the name of Guecello Tempesta ruled Treviso. After having miraculously survived an assassination attempt during a wedding celebration two years ago, he had seized control of the city thanks to hired mercenaries. Those who had conspired to kill him were put to death.

Cangrande's mercy and generosity toward those who submitted to him was widely known throughout the Veneto. This knowledge, combined with a lack of allies and supplies, compelled Tempesta to surrender without bloodshed.

Victory cries resounded throughout the encampment. The Veronese had finally conquered Treviso without sacrificing the life of a single man. This great military success served as proof that God was one the side of the Ghibellines.

The Trevisan territories passed under the jurisdiction of Cangrande through a treaty signed on July 17, 1329.

The following morning, the Lord of Verona made his state entry into the city on a white horse with a ruler's staff in his hand. The Trevisans watched the public spectacle from the windows above and from the sides of the road. Those aligned with the families who had aided Cangrande cheered and waved. The rest of Treviso's citizens witnessed the scene in sullen silence. Some, with open disapproval.

Cangrande, who had dreamed of this day for years, failed to enjoy his military victory. Although he tried hard not to show it, he was in pain. A cold sweat broke out on his forehead as a severe cramp almost caused him to double over in the saddle. Was it the pheasant he ate earlier?

Ottavio urged his horse forward. "My lord, what ails you?"

"I am not well."

The entourage came to a stop before an imposing palazzo. The bishop stood at the top of the steps with outspread hands— a gesture suggesting *welcome* and *surrender*.

Cangrande practically ran up the steps. After hastily greeting the bishop, he said, "I must go inside at once before—" He stopped, his face contorting with pain. "God's teeth! Get me to the privy *now*."

The bishop motioned to a nearby servant who escorted Cangrande into the palazzo.

Ottavio said, "My apologies, Your Excellency."

The bishop's eyes followed the Veronese warlord's hasty retreat. "Is your master ill?"

"Yes."

"I shall summon my personal physician to tend to him."

Cangrande emptied his bowels in such a violent manner that he felt weak and disoriented afterward. The servants led him to one of the guest bedchambers closest to the privy and put him to bed. Feverish chills soon consumed him, causing his teeth to chatter. By the time the physician arrived, his stomach cramps

241

were unbearable.

Ottavio insisted on being present during the physical examination. His eyes traced the many battle scars his overlord had acquired during his thirty-eight years of life.

Cangrande cried out in pain when the physician dug two fingers into his lower abdomen.

"An inflammation of the stomach," the physician concluded.

"Damned pheasant," Cangrande whispered.

The physician frowned. "My lord?"

"Our midday meal consisted of pheasant and leeks," Ottavio explained. "I ate it, too, but I feel fine."

"His condition is too advanced to be the result of a recently eaten meal."

Ottavio's brow creased in thought. "There's another possibility. He drank from a stream yesterday morning. I warned him not to do it since we didn't know if it was clean."

"Contaminated water could definitely be the culprit." The physician motioned to the servant loitering by the door. "Tell the cook to prepare strong chamomile tea to ease his cramps." He then reached into his satchel and extracted a bottle. Placing it in Ottavio's hand, he said, "Black mulberry to cleanse the intestines. He should take it with—"

"My wife uses this frequently," Ottavio interjected. "I know what to do."

"Good. Feed him nothing but broth and undiluted wine for the next few days in order to fortify his blood."

The physician turned to go and Ottavio gripped the man's arm. "You must tell no one of my master's illness. We don't want to cause unnecessary alarm."

The physician nodded. "Until I know for certain what is ailing him, I have to treat his condition as I would any potential plague or pestilence in order to protect the bishop and his household. I have advised His Excellency to avoid this wing altogether." Gathering his satchel, he added, "I will say a prayer for the Lord of Verona."

Cangrande's diarrhea continued throughout the day. Although he consumed considerable quantities of chamomile

242

and black mulberry, it did little good. Growing weaker by the hour, running to the privy became an impossibility for him, so chamber pots were placed near the bed. Despite the efforts to empty them frequently, the room soon reeked of human feces.

The physician was summoned the following morning. Seeing that his patient's condition had failed to meliorate, he had the cook brew a tea of dandelion root. When it arrived, he extracted a fine powder from his satchel and added a tiny pinch to the steaming liquid.

"What's that?" Ottavio demanded, alarmed.

"A pinch of foxglove."

Ottavio removed his sword from its sheath. "Poison!"

The terrified physician placed the cup of tea on a nearest table and raised his hands in surrender. "Wait! Foxglove is only poisonous in large quantities. A pinch is harmless—I've been using it as a curative for many years."

"I want to see you swallow the same amount that you placed in that cup."

With trembling hands, the physician did as he was told.

Ottavio half-expected the man to die, but he didn't. Satisfied, he sheathed his sword. "Go ahead."

The physician brought the tea to Cangrande's lips, urging him to drink it. He then examined the contents of a chamber pot. Black stool and red blood—bad omens.

The expression on the physician's face worried Ottavio, compelling him to exit the room. The physician followed him into the corridor and closed the door to prevent Cangrande from overhearing their conversation.

"Will he die?" Ottavio demanded without preamble.

"I don't know."

"I noticed the alarm on your face when you peered into the chamber pot."

"In my experience, black stool has often been a precursor to death. I did have one person survive it, however—a young woman who enjoyed good health prior to becoming ill. The Lord of Verona is a strong man, and I'm assuming he was hearty and hale before drinking from that stream."

"Yes, he was."

"I'm doing everything within my power to heal him."

"My master wishes to be transported to the lodgings we had secured prior to visiting the bishop."

"He cannot be moved in his current condition. It's better for him to stay here."

During supper that evening, the bishop said to Ottavio, "I am aggrieved by this situation, but I don't want the mighty Cangrande to die under my roof."

"Your Excellency, I can assure you that no one would blame you if that were to happen."

"Rumors of Mastino's volatile nature suggest that he's very much like his uncle. I want to enjoy my old age in peace, my lord, with no trouble from the Scaligeri."

"I understand your concern. Hopefully, my master's health will improve by tomorrow."

The bishop crossed himself. "I pray to God that it does for everyone's sake."

On the third day, two more physicians arrived at the bishop's palazzo. Each one prescribed a different remedy for Cangrande, then monitored his condition throughout the afternoon. Finally, after a grueling day, the physicians retreated so that their patient could get some rest.

***

July 22, 1329 dawned muggy and cool. In the bluish light of that early hour, a lone figure crossed the piazza. Although she wore homespun wool in drab gray, her graceful movements betrayed a woman with a taste for finer things. She headed toward the palazzo's side entrance where deliveries were received by the bishop's servants. Nero had already bribed one of them to leave the door unlocked.

Once inside, she followed Nero's instructions precisely—up one flight, turn left, down the corridor…

She quietly slipped into the room where Cangrande convalesced. Approaching the sickbed cautiously, her eyes were glued to the man wasting away amid crumpled, foul-smelling sheets. He looked nothing like the warrior she remembered—the powerful man whose strong arms had held her in many passionate embraces.

"My lord," she whispered, gently touching his cheek.

Cangrande stirred, but his eyes remained closed.

Taking in his hollowed cheeks and ashy pallor, she placed her lips to his ear. "I have something to end your suffering."

Reaching into the hollow cleft between her breasts, she extracted a tiny ceramic amphora—the same one she had kept locked in her jewelry chest. She poured its contents into a cup of wine, then put the cup to his lips.

Cangrande was so weak that he was barely conscious. The moment his tongue came into contact with the bitter liquid, he grimaced and turned his head to the side. Undeterred, she murmured reassuring promises as she forced the poison down his gullet. When the cup was empty, she allowed his head to fall back onto the pillow.

"Goodbye, Francesco," she whispered before kissing his lips for the last time.

She fled the palazzo.

Cangrande woke up with agonizing pain in his chest and bowels. His cry provoked a string of startled servants to file into the room. Ottavio arrived shortly afterward, and was instantly dismayed by the sight of his overlord's white face. A revolting stench emanated from the bed where he had soiled himself.

In a moment of lucidity, Cangrande called for his trusted advisor to aid him in settling his affairs.

"My lord, shouldn't we wait until—"

"Basta, Ottavio. Death is coming for me today." His eyes rolled upward and he stared at the frescoed ceiling with tears in his eyes. "Sweet Madonna, receive me…I beg you."

Cangrande died a few hours later. His body was removed from Treviso at nightfall and immediately taken to Verona.

I paced the well-furnished room of the inn with my stomach tied in several knots. I hadn't eaten all day because I couldn't keep anything down. The sound of patrons laughing and chatting below evoked memories of my prostitution days in Venice, thus adding to my anxiety.

My empty belly cramped up, so I rubbed it to ease the pain.

I'm sure the pain you're feeling pales in comparison to the agony he felt after you—

My hands flew to my ears in a futile attempt to silence the nagging voice in my head. My conscience had become my tormentor.

Your son's father…how could you?

Where was Nero? He should have been here by now.

Something moved in the corner and I spun around with a startled cry. Was that Dalia's shadow in the fading light? A horrific thought crept into my head: would Francesco and Dalia rally together in death to haunt me? To drive me to the brink of madness and push me into the abyss?

No, no, no!

"Francesco," I whispered. "Is that you?"

A knock on the door yanked me back to the present.

To my immense relief, it was Nero. Throwing back the hood of his cloak, he entered the room and hastily closed the door.

"Countess," he said, inclining his head.

"What news?"

"He's dead."

I crossed myself. "God forgive me. When can I go home?"

"You'll be escorted back to Verona by one of my men tomorrow morning."

My eyes were drawn to his empty hands. "What about my payment?"

"You need not worry. You'll get it soon enough."

"When?"

"*Soon.*"

"Soon?" I repeated irritably. "I want it now. I've just killed the Lord of Verona!"

Gripping my upper arms, he led me away from the door. "My lady, *please* lower your voice!"

"I only want what was promised me!"

"Let me remind you that patience is one of the virtues listed in the Bible."

"I don't care about the Bible. What about my son, Count Alboino?"

"*Lord* Alboino," Nero corrected. "Count would be presumptuous. Does that suit you?"

"Yes, I suppose." Biting my lip, I added nervously, "I can be executed for this, Nero."

"Did anyone see you?"

"I don't think so…"

God saw you, Agata.

His eyes narrowed. "Stay calm. I'll be in Verona within the week with your payment. Everything will be fine, and you'll soon forget about this…Think of your son."

"My son," I repeated. "Yes…yes. My son will be a noble lord. A jolly lord who hosts lavish parties and he'll marry a proper lady."

He listened to my rambling then stared at me for a long time as if debating something in his head. "It's late and I should go."

"Late, yes…it's late."

I paced the room while chewing my lower lip. Nero watched me with a concerned expression on his face.

"Goodnight, my lady."

To my chagrin, his tone was cautious. Deliberate. The tone one uses to calm a rabid animal or a person who has lost their wits. I nodded, desperately clinging to whatever shred of sanity I still possessed. "Goodnight and sweet dreams…I think I'll suffer nightmares tonight."

What would Antonio think of me if he knew?

You killed Armando, Dalia and her unborn son, and now Francesco…You are a murderess bound for Hell!

I froze, my eyes darting around the room. Nero was no longer there. When did he leave? I sat down, confused, as a wave of exhaustion swept over me. A knock on the door made me jump. To my surprise, it was Bea.

"What are you doing here?" I demanded as I pulled her inside and locked the door behind her.

"I was worried," she replied. "I've had a bad feeling about this whole thing from the very beginning. I saddled Stella shortly after your departure, and rode here to make sure that you were all right."

"What about my son? I specifically left him in your care because you're the only person I trust in this world."

"He's with his nurse and he's fine. I know that you and Nero insisted on traveling here alone, but…"

"You shouldn't have come, but I'm glad you did."

"I'm relieved that you're not angry."

"Did you see Nero on your way in?"

She frowned. "No, why?"

"He was here only a moment ago."

"Did he pay you?"

"No. I'm to be escorted home tomorrow. He'll come by the following week with my payment."

"I don't trust him, my lady. Not one bit."

Overwhelmed and frustrated, I gave in to tears. Bea held me and tried to soothe me as best she could. "What if I've done this vile deed for nothing? What if they tricked me?"

"Calm yourself, my lady. There's nothing to be done about it now. Nero blackmailed you. You had no choice in the matter."

"I must confess something to you, Bea. I'm almost sure that I saw Dalia's ghost a moment ago."

My maid pulled away and eyed me warily. "You're distraught, which is natural under the circumstances. You

248

hardly slept all week, and now…"

"What?"

"Do not lose your wits, my lady."

"I'm so frightened, Bea."

"I know you are," she said while placing the palm of her hand against my cheek. "Take a deep breath and stay calm. I'm going downstairs to see if the innkeeper can whip up a draught for you. I'll return shortly."

"Be quick," I said as I watched her go.

A moment later, one of the inn's servants arrived with a tray of food. Upon my arrival earlier, I had requested that my meal be sent up to my room. My empty stomach growled at the sight of the beef stew so I ravenously devoured it.

Satiated, I sighed deeply. I was tired. Maybe Nero was right. This would eventually become a bad memory—one of many in my life. Wandering to the window, I gazed in admiration at the pink twilight sky streaked with violet clouds. Something zipped past my line of vision and, to my delight, it was a swallow. It swooped below the window, then rose high into the sky before gliding on the wind. I took it as a good omen.

I closed the shutters and headed toward the bed, but a stitch in my side made me falter in my steps. Rubbing my belly, I assumed it was only mild indigestion from eating too quickly. Suddenly, a cramp—followed by gut-wrenching pain—caused me double over.

An icy chill spread throughout my body as I recalled Nero's words: 'My employers are extremely cautious. *Loose ends are dangerous liabilities.*'

I raced to the door only to find it locked from the outside. I pounded my fists against the wood and shouted for help, but the noise downstairs swallowed the sound of my cries. I tried to remain calm. Bea would be back any minute.

You may be dead by then…

How long did I have? I plunged my forefinger down my throat to make myself vomit, but it was no use. The poison was already coursing through my veins and making me dizzy.

Alboino.

249

A crude desk stood in the corner of the room. Thankfully, there was an old sheet of parchment in the drawer. I dipped a stylus into the ink with a trembling hand. A tingling numbness spread throughout my fingers, so I banged them against the desk's surface to circulate the blood.

My brow broke into a cold sweat as I wrote: *My beloved son, I will be dead by the time you read this letter…*

I finished the brief letter with a heavy heart.

Where are you, Bea?

The stylus fell from my hand as I slid off the stool and crashed to the floor.

Antonio…

A swallow perched on the windowsill. It was the last thing I saw before everything went black.

CHAPTER 31
AUGUST 1329
MALCESINE

Bea. Was there ever a servant more loyal? A friend more faithful? I owed her my life, for it was her distrusting nature and repugnance for Nero that compelled her to purchase charcoal and keep it readily on hand.

Bea had encountered the door of my room barred from the outside when she returned with the draught. Suspecting something foul afoot, she had immediately opened the door. The sight of me sprawled on the floor had prompted her to force pulverized charcoal mixed with water down my throat. She had somehow managed to smuggle me out of the tavern and onto my horse, then to an inn outside of Treviso where I struggled between life and death for two days.

On the third day, I woke up feeling much better. We rode to Malcesine, located on the Garda Lake, then up to the highest mountain peak where a tiny hamlet protected us from the outside world. Our accommodations were crude and our rations meager, but we were safe. More importantly, we were far from Treviso.

"We should make preparations to return to Verona," I said to Bea one morning.

Her expression turned grim. "No, my lady."

I was taken aback. "I haven't seen my son in almost three weeks. I miss Alboino. We must go home."

"We cannot return to Verona."

The flat, quiet tone in which she said this scared me. "Why would you say such a thing?"

She wrung her hands nervously. "I left a letter…"

"A letter," I repeated, perplexed. "What did it say?"

"It states that you ran off with a lover and wish for Alboino to be raised with his half-brothers."

I glared at my maid. "Surely, you jest."

Bea shook her head and I lunged for her throat. I've never attacked anyone in such an aggressive manner, but my fury rendered me mad in that instant.

Restraining me at arm's length, she cried, "Calm yourself, my lady! Let me explain!"

"Traitor! I trusted you!"

"Please," she begged, warding off one of my blows.

I staggered toward the nearest wall, leaned against it, and wept. "Why would you do such a thing? Alboino was all I had left in this world."

Breathless from the struggle, she warily approached me. "Let me explain."

Realization suddenly dawned on me. "Wait…You *knew* before you left Verona that we could never return—you planned it that way."

"Yes."

The staggering magnitude of her betrayal left me feeling utterly defeated. "Why, Bea? Why would you do such a thing?"

"*Think*, my lady. Everyone knew that the Countess Visconti had fallen out of favor with the Lord of Verona. Negative rumors about you ran rampant in the city. I feared that your absence during the time of his death would incriminate you…What if you were named as a suspect in Cangrande's death? It's better for you to be seen as a morally dubious woman who abandoned her son than a murderess. At least Alboino won't be tainted by your crime. He'll be raised and well cared for alongside his siblings. I left that letter in order to protect you and your son."

"Santo Cristo," I whispered.

"Imagine if Nero had succeeded in poisoning you. What would have become of your son, then?"

Deep down, I knew she was right but it still pained me.

Bea walked to where her cloak hung on a peg. She extracted a fat pouch from the garment's inner pocket and handed it to me. It was filled with money.

"I wanted to be prepared for every possibility, so I took the liberty of selling your jewels and fine garments after you had departed for Treviso," she explained.

"Escape money," I deduced.

"Yes."

Fresh tears welled up in my eyes. "I can never go back."

"Never."

I mourned for days and Bea knew better than to disturb me.

We soon learned that Mastino, the new Lord of Verona, had already executed one of the physicians who had failed to heal his uncle. What's more, the swift act of justice had been based on mere suspicion, not fact.

This disturbing news forced me to admit that Bea had done the right thing for my son. I forgave her treachery and reconciled our friendship. I thought of Alboino daily, often consoling myself with the hope that our paths would someday cross in the future.

August slipped into September and the days of mild weather were numbered. Soon, it would get cold in the mountains and we were ill-equipped for winter.

On a cool September evening, Bea said, "Let's travel south. The warm weather and sunshine would be good for both of us."

I understood the real meaning behind her suggestion. My melancholia combined with the freezing dark days of winter may lead to the unthinkable. I admit, the thought of taking my own life had crossed my mind on more than one occasion.

She continued, "I am going to the village to get supplies. When I return, we'll pack the horse and leave tomorrow at dawn."

I ventured, "To Naples?"

She smiled hopefully. "If you wish it, my lady."

Did Antonio harbor resentment toward me? Would he reject me? *Did he still love me?*

I gave her some money and said, "We'll need to purchase another horse."

***

Bea and I discarded our female clothing, opting instead to

travel as two male merchants. I rarely spoke during the journey, keeping the hood of my cloak low over my face. It took us well over a week to reach Rome, for we prudently avoided traveling at night. Bea had struck a good bargain with the people who bought my jewels and clothing, for we had more than enough money to stay at decent inns along the way.

The further south we went, the warmer the climate. In Rome, we enjoyed sunny days and mild evenings. I found the city fascinating. The ancient Pantheon, the forum, and the colosseum were impressive testaments to a sophisticated civilization long dead. We spent three days in the Eternal City, and I used that time to summon my courage to continue on to Naples.

On the morning of our departure, Bea said, "I know you are apprehensive about seeing Signore Antonio, but there is only one way to put your mind at ease, my lady."

I nodded in response to her words. "Let's get moving."

It took another three days to reach Naples, which immediately took my breath away. We paused on the crest of a hill to enjoy the view. The city was juxtaposed against a lapis lazuli sky boasting a brilliant sun. The aquamarine bay hosted a myriad of sea vessels with Vesuvius dominating the pristine landscape. Various boats and cargo vessels glided on the water's surface, some flaunting banners and colorful sails.

Bea urged her horse to stand beside mine. "I think this would be a good place to stay for a while, don't you?"

"Yes," I replied.

"We should seek lodging, and begin our search for Signore Antonio."

"I don't know if I can do this," I confessed. "What if he's already married?"

"I will be your eyes and ears in the city, my lady."

"You must swear to be discreet."

"I always am."

We secured rooms at a respectable inn. I bought some good clean hay for our horses, along with some dried apples as a reward for the arduous journey. Next, I procured decent female garments for me and my maid.

Bea ventured out into the city on the second morning of our arrival. She didn't return until suppertime. We sat across the table from each other, picking at the stew and stale bread offered by the innkeeper.

"Please tell me that you have good news," I said after the innkeeper's daughter filled our ceramic cups with diluted wine.

Bea stared into the contents of her cup. "He is unmarried."

I clapped my hands together. "Thank the Madonna."

She continued cautiously, "He *was* betrothed to a young noblewoman for a brief period of time. Her life was cut short due to illness before they had a chance to wed."

My jealousy tasted as bitter as bile. "How long ago?"

"Almost two years. According to the apothecary who provides Signore Mauro with curatives for indigestion, Signore Antonio was devastated over the girl's demise."

My heart sank. "He must have loved her."

"Yes…but that doesn't mean he cannot love again."

"I was a fool to come here."

Bea reached across the table and took hold of my hand. "*Agata*, I am now going to speak with you as a sister and not as a servant. We have come all this way. You owe it to yourself—and to this man—to give your love a second chance."

"You're right," I conceded.

She retracted her hand and said primly, "I usually am, my lady." We both chuckled and she continued, "We should go to his villa the first thing tomorrow morning."

"Are you suggesting that I simply knock on Antonio's front door?" I asked incredulously.

"Exactly."

I found her idea a bit brazen, but it held some appeal. The sooner I discovered Antonio's feelings toward me, the quicker I could move on with my life—*for better or worse.*

I could barely sleep that night. In the morning, Bea dressed my hair and doused my skin with some cheap rosewater she had procured in the market. My new frock flaunted colorful embroidered flowers around the neckline, and the deep blue linen enhanced my eyes.

"Well?" Bea inquired, holding up a mottled looking glass.

I studied my reflection with a sigh of resignation. The girl who stared back at me seemed older and plainer than the one who wore expensive silk and jewels not so long ago. Her eyes sparkled with the wisdom gleaned from life's hardships instead of costly belladonna. Her mouth, still sensuous, held a note of bitterness. Finally, the tilt of her head belied her tenacity.

"This is all I have to offer," I said thoughtfully. "Antonio can either accept it or reject it."

Bea offered me a satisfied grin. "Spoken like a sage."

I shrugged. "I'm ready to confront my fate."

My maid accompanied me on an uphill path sparsely dotted with villas. Once we reached the top of the hill, she pointed to a spacious two-story home surrounded by trees. I continued on the path alone, then headed toward the villa's studded door. My hand shook as I took hold of the iron knocker. Taking a deep breath, I banged it several times against the sun-bleached wood.

A moment later, a servant girl opened the door. I informed her that I was an "old friend" of Antonio's and wished to see him. Luckily, he was in residence. She led me into the villa's cool frescoed interior, then told me to wait in a small room.

A giant tapestry adorned the longest wall. It depicted two lovers seated in a garden filled with bright yellow and orange flowers. Leaves and plants flaunting several shades of green and blue bordered the scene. I wandered over to the window opposite the tapestry, and admired the amazing view.

The sound of masculine footsteps turned my knees to mush. I walked away from the window and stood in the center of the room. Taking a deep breath, I braced myself.

Antonio froze in the doorway. *"Agata?"*

EPILOGUE
NAPLES
ONE YEAR LATER

I opened my eyes and squinted against the bright sunshine illuminating the spacious bedchamber. The gentle summer breeze from the open window caressed my skin. The wind carried the singsong of birds and the cries of seagulls. Inhaling the salty air, I stretched and counted my blessings for the hundredth time.

My husband, still asleep, stirred beside me in the bed. I leaned up on my elbow to study his face. The tips of his eyelashes were bleached from the sun, and the constellation of freckles across the bridge of his tanned nose charmed me.

Our villa overlooked the Naples Bay. Sea vessels and sailboats glided upon the shimmering surface of the water with Vesuvius in the distance. I never tired of the view. The base of the hill boasted a piazza with a busy market. Each morning, Neapolitan merchants whistled merry tunes while filling their stalls with fresh fish and various mollusks. One man in particular liked to sing in a robust voice as he arranged colorful fruits and vegetables into a tantalizing display to attract customers. Sometimes, I sang along with him.

Mauro had no objection to our marital union. Like Antonio, he had assumed that my presence in Naples was due to the fact that the Lord of Verona was dead. Neither one of them were aware that I had fallen out of Francesco's favor long before his death, nor did they know of Alboino's existence. Rather than correct their erroneous assumptions, I remained silent. Perhaps, one day, I would confess the truth. For now, I was content to let my past die in the north and begin a new life in the south.

Sadly, the duke died a few months after my arrival. Antonio inherited his adoptive father's villa and a substantial amount of money. In short, my timing in Naples couldn't have been more perfect.

Our infant daughter, whose jolliness proved contagious, thrived with robust health. Only three months old, Dalia was the apple of her father's eye. Antonio believed that I had chosen the name because I fancied it. In truth, it was my way of honoring *her* memory. He knew nothing about the incident, and I didn't plan on telling him.

I kept many things hidden from Antonio. There was no need to taint his bliss with my ugly past or my mortal sins. Those heavy burdens were mine to bear—*alone*.

I still refused to pray to God. He could have prevented many things from happening and helped me along the way, but He chose to forsake me. I knew that I was bound for Hell, but I didn't care. I lived in a fine home with a loving husband, a wonderful daughter, and my best friend, Bea. What more could any woman in my position ask for? I intended to suck every drop of joy I could from my earthly life and face the spiritual consequences later.

I missed my son and pined for his company every single day. Wasn't that punishment enough for my wrongdoings?

Antonio suddenly opened his brilliant blue eyes and smiled at me, breaking my reverie. I returned the gesture.

"*Buon giorno, amore mio,*" he said sleepily.

I thought my heart would burst from the love I felt for this man. *If only I could bottle this moment.*

The agate pendant dangling from the chain around his neck drew my gaze—the stone bearing my namesake. "*L'agata ti porterà gioia.* Tell me, my love, was the fortune-teller correct?"

He caressed my cheek. "More than you can imagine."

Did you enjoy this novel? The author would appreciate your review on Amazon. Thank you.

Turn the page for a sample of FORBIDDEN: A Novel Set in Medieval England.

FORBIDDEN

A NOVEL SET IN MEDIEVAL ENGLAND

C. DE MELO

ISBN-13: 978-1544065083
ISBN-10: 1544065086

To those who have fallen in battle...

To those who have fought in battle...

To the spouses and families of these brave warriors...

This book was written for you.

CHAPTER 1
KENT, ENGLAND
1127

"Whoa, girl, easy now," Lady Beatrice Fitzwilliam cooed in her horse's ear.

The white mare halted in a cloud of dust outside the imposing Romanesque cathedral. Despite her anxiety, Beatrice admired the elongated figures of Jesus, Mary, and Joseph carved into the stone lintel.

Leading the horse toward a sprawling elm tree, she dismounted and tethered the animal. The hot breath of the mare merged with her own in the cold night air, forming a delicate swirl of white vapor.

It was unwise to travel alone at night, especially in her condition, but her husband's reputation—and ultimately her family's safety—depended on this encounter. Placing both hands on her swollen belly, she took a deep breath and slowly ascended the stairs. Her heartbeat was so fierce that her temples throbbed with each step.

The heavy oak door creaked open slowly, mimicking the sound of an old woman's tired sigh. It took her eyes a moment to adjust to the dimness of the church's interior. Toward the eastern end of the building, several candles burned on the high altar.

Clutching her expensive wool cloak around her shoulders, Beatrice nuzzled her chin into the warm fur lining and walked down the long nave toward the chancel. Moonlight illuminated a small chapel, affording her a brief glimpse of a Byzantine mosaic depicting the *Ascension of Christ*. She crossed herself when she finally entered the pool of candlelight and sank to her knees before the altar. Tilting her head back, she raised her eyes to the crucified Christ figure hanging above the communion table. Blood poured from the crown of thorns on his head, and flowed onto his hollow cheeks. Christ's mouth was set in a grim line, his sad eyes reflecting the terrible suffering of humanity.

Beatrice shuddered and tore her gaze away. After a few moments she felt the heat of Edward's stare; she knew he watched silently from the shadows. She was reminded of her cat and the manner in which it stalked its prey. There was always that tense moment before it pounced and killed an unsuspecting mouse with feline precision. She imagined Edward's body coiled and rigid, his gray eyes with their sharply defined pupils narrowed into two slits, waiting...

Closing her eyes, she fought the urge to run out of the church and waited for him to show himself.

Satisfied that he had tortured Beatrice enough, Edward emerged from the darkness to stand before her in a finely cut robe of black brocade lined with costly miniver. Holy men were strongly urged to avoid such worldly luxuries, but her brother-in-law thought himself immune to monastic rules. As the second son of a powerful noble family, the strict laws of primogeniture had forced him to procure a living by means of the Church. Although he was only the Prior of Canterbury, his clothing and lifestyle were as luxuriant as the bishop's. Beatrice focused her gaze on the gold embroidery adorning the hem of his garment and wondered if Jesus had ever owned anything so fine.

"Beatrice, dear *sister*," he whispered into the silence.

Edward used the term 'sister' as a mere formality, for what he felt for her was far from fraternal. He stared down at her golden hair, which was parted in the center and fell in two long braids, before dropping his gaze to the bodice of her azure silk gown. The fullness of her young breasts, accentuated by the low neckline, caused a stirring in his loins. Despite being heavy with child, Beatrice was desirable. How he envied his older brother, Richard.

Resisting the temptation to ravage her right then and there, he cleared his throat and put out his hand. "Rise, my child."

She accepted his hand and stood, facing him. "My lord.

262

Thank you for seeing me, Edward."

He studied her face, taking in the sharp, delicate features. "How fares my brother?"

"He is the very reason why I asked to see you."

"It's cold here. My private chamber is warm and comfortable. Come."

She obediently followed him around the altar and down a narrow passageway lit by torches. They went outside through a side door that led to the cloister garden, then through another door. Nothing stirred in the quiet night as they headed toward a private wing reserved for the prior's cell.

Edward stopped. "Here we are." After opening the door, he stood aside for Beatrice to enter. When she hesitated, he placed his hand on the small of her back and gave her a slight push.

His living quarters were not only spacious, but richly furnished with exquisite tapestries, several warm fur skins, and a sturdy desk containing a pile of expensive manuscripts, inkwells, and goose quills. The high-backed chair by the desk boasted two red velvet cushions, and a stylus lay across a hornbook exposing a few Latin verses of the Paternoster. A patterned velvet curtain separated the two rooms. The luxuriant fabric was slightly pulled to one side by a golden rope, allowing a glimpse of a silk-canopied bed.

"I know it's not as grand as what you or I are accustomed to, but my father's death put an end to *that*," Edward commented derisively.

"On the contrary, my lord. Your rooms are quite grand." No expense was spared to furnish the rooms, and she wondered what the other monks thought of their prior's flagrant hypocrisy.

He walked to a table containing a silver decanter of wine and proceeded to pour the garnet liquid into two silver chalices. "Here, this will warm you."

She accepted the chalice. "Thank you."

Edward stirred the embers within the hearth, then motioned for her to sit by the small fire. "Why did you request to meet with me?"

263

Beatrice had rehearsed her speech all afternoon, but now she was at a loss for words. How could she ask for his help without her husband's knowledge?

Edward found her discomfort amusing and had to stifle the urge to smile.

"I came to ask for your help," she finally admitted.

He regarded her for a moment as he ran his index finger along the rim of his chalice. "In what way do you require my help?"

She hesitated, unsure of how to proceed. He took a long sip of wine and watched with anticipation as she, too, placed the chalice to her lips. Her full mouth was sensuous and he suddenly wanted to kiss and bite her lips. Beatrice caught his lustful stare and averted her eyes. He and Richard were so alike in appearance and stature that it was unnerving—especially their steely, gray eyes. The only difference between the two men was that Richard's hair and complexion were dark, whereas Edward was fair to the point of appearing angelic.

"Well?" he prompted.

"Richard is in trouble," she replied breathlessly.

"In *trouble*? How so?" Rather than answer the question, her face turned pale, prompting him to inquire, "Are you feeling unwell, Beatrice?"

"Forgive me, my lord. As you can see, I'm so close to my time…"

Edward sat on the edge of his seat. He was neither prepared nor inclined to help his sister-in-law give birth at such an ungodly hour. He was relieved when she took a long sip of wine and the color returned to her cheeks.

Beatrice cleared her throat and said, "Richard has enemies who wish to destroy him."

"My lady, we *all* have enemies who wish to destroy us. The richer and more powerful the noble, the greater the chance of envy and strife. The feudal lords of Europe are constantly in battle."

"It's more than that, Edward. There's talk of Richard being guilty of treason. If this kind of malicious gossip reaches the king's ears, there's no telling what can happen."

"This is indeed serious, my lady. I hope for Richard's sake that these accusations are untrue."

"Of course they're untrue! These envious and greedy lords are spreading lies."

"What can I do? I can't stop wagging tongues."

"You're powerful," she replied, leaning forward and placing a hand on his forearm.

Edward glanced down at her hand, relishing the warmth of her touch. "Go on."

She retracted her hand and blushed. "You can silence the mouths of those seeking to ruin your brother's reputation. The Bible openly condemns crooked speech and deceitfulness."

He rubbed his chin pensively. "Do you suppose Richard would help me if I were in his predicament?"

"Despite the rivalry between you two, I know he would help his own flesh and blood." In reality, she was unsure.

"Humph," he snorted, crossing his arms.

"Edward—"

He raised his hand to silence her. "You and your husband do not speak to me for months…"

"Please—"

"And now you seek me out in the middle of the night to ask for my help?"

"He's your *brother*. Please, my lord, I'm begging you. I'll do anything for the safety and well-being of my husband—even at a great risk to myself."

He looked at her pointedly. "Richard doesn't know you're here."

"No."

"He would be furious if he knew." He smiled but the gesture lacked mirth. "He would probably have you flogged." When Beatrice's eyes filled with tears, he added, "I know very well how stubborn and proud he is."

"And jealous," she added.

"Ah, yes, perhaps the most jealous man in England. You must love him a great deal to risk so much."

"I do."

Her honest proclamation of love annoyed him.

"Say that you'll help me," she pleaded.

"And keep your meeting with me a secret?"

"That, too."

Edward stared at her for a long time. "If the rumors are indeed lies, I'll dispel them. If not, be warned—I don't condone acts of treason against our monarch."

"You can rest assured that Richard is innocent. I give you my word."

"I believe you, Beatrice." He stood from his chair, indicating that their meeting was over. "Richard would be wise to tread cautiously."

Beatrice rose to her feet and pulled the hood of her cloak over her head. She looked so young and fragile in that moment that he couldn't resist touching her face.

Caressing her soft cheek, he whispered, "May the Lord watch over you."

They exchanged a brief look before she lowered her eyes and left the room. He stood in the doorway watching her retreating form until she turned the corner and was out of sight. He closed the door, refilled his chalice, and paced the floor.

A satisfied grin spread across Edward's face for he knew that Richard lurked outside. After having received Beatrice's message that morning, he had dispatched an anonymous message of his own to his brother.

The stage is set perfectly, he mused.

It had been easy to plant the seeds of doubt into the minds of a few greedy lords. Those seeds were now giving fruit as the doubts turned to suspicion, which encouraged dangerous gossip that could lead to damning accusations. The fact that Beatrice had come directly and unwittingly to the source of her woes was an extra delight he had not anticipated.

Edward caught his reflection in the polished looking glass. Was he evil for behaving so despicably? *No*, his reflection silently replied. It wasn't fair that his older brother had everything handed to him: lands, money, title, castles, and the prestige that came with being firstborn. Richard even got Beatrice, too—the only woman Edward had ever loved. The laws of primogeniture were cruel, and the resentment he fostered toward his brother resided within him like a malignancy.

***

Lord Richard Fitzwilliam, Earl of Kent, crept from behind the elm's massive trunk to witness his wife's hasty retreat. Had he not seen Beatrice with his own eyes, he would never have believed the anonymous message slipped under his door stating that his wife would betray him that night.

"Damn you to hell, Edward," Richard cursed under his breath. "And damn her, too."

A door within the cloister wall opened and he receded into the leafy shadows just as Edward walked out and stretched lazily. Richard's eyes narrowed in loathing as his vivid imagination conjured lustful images of his wife and his brother tangled in bedsheets. A low growl lay at the base of his throat as his hand involuntarily wrapped itself around the hilt of his sword.

Richard debated whether to confront his brother, but then decided against it. His experience in battle taught him that it was always better to wait for the right moment to strike.

You shall pay dearly, brother…and so shall she.

CHAPTER 2

"Push!"

"*Sweet Jesus...*"

A moment elapsed before the order came again, this time with urgency. "Push, my lady! Push *hard*!"

Beatrice's face turned crimson as she followed the old midwife's instructions and pushed with all her might. A cool, wet cloth was immediately applied to her brow by one of the servants. The stifling heat inside the bedchamber made it difficult to breathe.

"Gretta…water," Beatrice whispered to her maid.

The girl pushed back a limp strand of flaxen hair that had fallen across her mistress's cheek before going to the brown earthenware pitcher on the table. One of the older female servants added feverfew to the raging fire in the hearth. Within minutes, a heady scent permeated the room, making Beatrice nauseous. The herb was often used in aiding childbirth, but she disliked its strong scent. She prayed silently to the Virgin Mary as she gasped for air and prepared for the next push.

Gretta returned with the water and placed the cup to Beatrice's dry lips. It was cool and offered small comfort.

"I see the head, my lady! Push!" cried the ancient crone while reaching down with both hands to help the infant out. "Quick, girl, fetch me a clean cloth!"

Gretta obeyed the command as Beatrice struggled to lift herself up onto her elbows. If the baby didn't come out soon, she would surely die from exhaustion. The birth of her first son, Robert, wasn't half as difficult as this one was proving to be. Her thoughts were slowly ebbing into darkness and she began to feel drowsy.

"My lady, 'tis no time for rest!" cried the midwife.

Beatrice pushed until she could push no more, then fell back hard upon the bed. There was a brief silence, then one of the servants gasped in delight. A moment later, the infant's cry filled the room.

The brown, wrinkled face of the midwife appeared within Beatrice's line of vision. "Another boy, my lady!"

A warm little bundle wrapped in clean linen was placed in Beatrice's arms. She looked at her son for the first time and a smile lit her face. "How precious you are," she whispered before kissing his soft, pink cheek.

Unlike her other son, who had inherited her husband's dark hair, the baby's silky hair was as fair as her own. He had Richard's gray eyes, however.

"Congratulations, my lady," Gretta said, sporting an ear-to-ear grin. "He's a fine boy."

It wasn't long before all the female servants were gathered around the bed fussing over the child. The longer Beatrice gazed upon him, the more her heart swelled with love. She never wanted to let him go—not even when the wet nurse came to feed him. After reluctantly handing her son over to the buxom woman, she reclined and watched him suckle hungrily upon the woman's breast.

"A healthy appetite for such a wee babe," exclaimed the surprised wet nurse.

The woman looked at her mistress and smiled. Beatrice politely returned the gesture then closed her eyes. Spent from exhaustion, she soon fell asleep.

***

"Felicitations, my lord," Gretta said.

Richard stopped pacing and turned at the sound of Gretta's voice. "Is it over?"

"Yes. You have a fine and healthy son."

"My wife?"

"Her ladyship is resting."

"Where is the boy?"

Gretta eyed him warily. "With the wet nurse, feeding."

Richard mumbled something incoherent and waived the woman away. *A fine and healthy son…*

He sought the privacy of his bedchamber and poured himself

some wine. It wouldn't be easy to carry out his plan, and he prayed to God for courage.

***

Beatrice was awakened by the shrill cries of her newborn son. She opened her eyes to see Richard attempting to pry the infant from the wet nurse's arms. Mustering her strength, Beatrice threw off the covers and crossed the cold stone floor in her bare feet.

Taking her son from the wet nurse, she inquired, "What's wrong with you, Richard? You'll frighten the poor child."

Richard's face darkened with rage as he stared at the baby's downy blonde hair. It was the same color as Edward's. "Give him to me."

"What?"

He sighed impatiently. "I don't wish to make this more difficult than it already is. Give me the child now."

Confused, she backed away from him. "My darling, of course you can see your son. Why are you so angry?"

Eyeing her coldly, he sneered. "My son, eh?"

A cold chill settled upon her bones. Something wasn't right. "What's this all about?"

"Hand him over, Beatrice."

"I will not!"

"You'll do as you're told this instant."

Smelling the wine on his breath, she shielded the baby from him. "Not until you tell me what madness has taken possession of you."

Richard took a step forward and smacked his wife across the face. More offended than hurt, she sank to her knees, still clutching the infant to her chest. A crimson colored welt in the shape of her husband's fingers bloomed on her cheek.

"I will raise no bastards under my roof," he said icily.

"*Bastard*?" she repeated, stunned. "This is your son!"

"Liar!"

"I swear to you, this is your flesh and blood," she whispered softly. "I have *never* been unfaithful to you."

The love Richard bore for his wife was so great, it verged on hatred. He deeply resented the fact that Beatrice possessed such tremendous influence over his emotions. Even now, as she knelt on the floor clutching the infant bastard, his heart ached with longing. Her big blue eyes flooded with tears and her long, golden hair fell loosely over her shoulders. The low neckline of her dressing gown exposed the fullness of her breasts, which were heaving gently with every breath she took…

God damn the woman.

Richard averted his eyes in order to harden his resolve and resist temptation. He snatched the child out of her arms and quickly backed away.

Scrambling to her feet, she demanded, "Dear God, Richard! What do you intend to do?"

When he said nothing, she sprang to her feet and lunged at him. Beating him with her fists, she cursed him. Richard called out to his knights and two men ran in to restrain their lady by force.

Beatrice's female servants were scattered about the room, appalled, watching the scene in silence. They had witnessed many an argument between their lord and lady—especially Gretta, who was never far from her mistress's side. This outburst, however, was uglier than anything they had ever seen before. They knew their lord was a jealous and possessive man, but the last few months had been particularly grievous for his wife.

Richard held the infant at arm's length, regarding him with a look of distaste before meeting his wife's desperate stare. "As punishment for your unfaithfulness, you'll never again set eyes upon this child."

His words drew shocked reactions from everyone in the room. Accusing a noble wife of adultery before witnesses was no trivial matter.

"No!" Beatrice cried. "I'm innocent!"

The sheer agony in her voice was so great that one of her captor's winced. Her body went limp, forcing the two knights to hold Beatrice upright in order to prevent her from falling to the ground.

She knew her husband well enough to believe he would carry out this cruel punishment. Hanging her head, she wept aloud. "I beg you, Richard, don't do this!"

Richard's heart twitched slightly, but he wasn't about to let himself be manipulated. "I won't be a cuckold who houses and feeds the fruit of his wife's adultery. I do this for the affection I still bear for you, and for the sake of our son, Robert. Another man would have you beaten before divorcing you and placing you into a convent."

The thought of spending her life in a dreary convent away from her son terrified her. Despite this, she said, "Surely Lucifer or one of his demons has taken possession of your mind, husband."

Richard raised his hand as if to strike her again, then stopped. Rumors of heresy were already circulating throughout the kingdom, and the last thing he needed was to be accused of being possessed by the Devil.

"Don't ever utter such a vile thing in my presence, woman," he warned. "You're fortunate they don't burn adulteresses on the stake."

"How can you accuse your own wife of such treachery? *Look* at the baby," she implored. "Any fool can see he's yours. He even has your eyes."

Unimpressed by her words, he turned on his heel and walked toward the door.

Beatrice's mind raced frantically as she tried to find reasons to stall him. "Stop! Please…at least allow me to give him something. A gift from his mother. After all, he is innocent of sin."

Richard stared at her for a moment, contemplating her request. He nodded to the knights, who in turn slackened their hold on Beatrice. Reaching up behind her neck, she undid the clasp of the heavy gold chain she always wore. Attached to it was a large gold crucifix adorned with rubies of great value. The heirloom had been passed down from mother to daughter for generations.

"Here," she said, extending her hand toward him. "Promise

272

me that wherever you take him, he shall have this as a reminder of me." Richard said nothing. "Please," she urged, taking a step closer.

He snatched the crucifix. "I promise."

Beatrice took advantage of the knights' slackened hold and lurched forward in a desperate, futile attempt to reclaim her son.

Frustrated by her thwarted effort, she stopped crying and gave her husband a look so venomous it surprised him. "God will punish you someday for what you're doing, Richard. And if He doesn't, *I* will."

The words reverberated throughout the room and hung heavily in the air as though she had uttered a powerful curse. All eyes turned to Richard in anticipation of what he would do.

Never before had Beatrice dared to speak to him with such blatant disrespect, let alone threaten him before several witnesses. He found her words unnerving, and for the first time since their marriage, he saw something in her eyes that actually frightened him. "God has already punished me, my lady, by making me love you the way I do," he said quietly before placing the chain around the infant's neck and stalking out of the room.

CHAPTER 3
LEWES, ENGLAND

Every time the infant shifted within the crude basket, the rough burlap binding scratched his tender skin. Outside, the birth of dawn brought forth the first fragile rays of sunlight from behind the distant hills. Meanwhile, a thick fog wound its way throughout the empty courtyard of the monastery like a stealthy serpent. The church doors loomed high above the basket, and the monks attending Lauds within the sacred walls were completely oblivious to the tiny intruder outside. The infant grew restless with each passing minute, and as the hunger pangs began to gnaw at his tiny stomach, he let out a thin wail that was swallowed by the fog.

***

"Careful not to spill the water, Gwen."

Agnes McFay handed her three-year-old daughter a rough wooden bucket half filled with water, making sure it wasn't too heavy for the child to carry. The ancient well stood on a grassy knoll east of the monastery, allowing her a clear view of the horizon and spectacular sunrise. She pulled the fresh morning air into her lungs and closed her eyes for a brief moment.

"*Tom…*"

"What did you say, Mama?"

Not a day passed that Agnes didn't think of her late husband, Thomas. Pushing a lock of curly auburn hair from her eyes, she forced herself to appear cheerful. "Nothing. Go on and tell Simon I'll be along shortly."

"Yes, Mama," she said, running down the hill.

"Slow down child, lest you fall and hurt yourself!"

The little girl slowed her pace to a skip. Gwen had inherited Tom's black hair and vivid blue eyes; both were a constant reminder of the man she had loved and lost.

Destitute and with a small child to raise, Agnes was grateful when Tom's cousin, Simon, arranged for her to work alongside him at the St. John's Cluniac monastery in Lewes. Prior to her arrival six months ago, the only thing she knew about the Cluniac Order was that it was founded in Cluny. She was surprised to learn that, unlike the original Benedictine monks who believed in hard labor through agriculture, the Cluniac monks paid people to toil their land. Since their liturgical regime was one of the strictest in Europe, the monks spent several hours of their day in church. Hiring lay servants to cook, clean, and care for their needs allowed these holy men more time for education, devotion, and meditation.

Simon had worked as the monastery's kitchen knave for years. His direct supervisor was the cellarer, an educated monk named Linus who preferred to spend his time in the library. The cellarer agreed to hire Agnes under the condition that the official consent be obtained from the prior, Bartholomew.

The prior was an easygoing and compassionate man who respected his vow of chastity and avoided women, but he didn't hate the female sex. It was thanks to his balanced view of the Scriptures that Agnes and Gwen found their place at St. John's.

A raven swooped down and landed on the edge of the well, interrupting her thoughts. The service of Lauds was held at five o'clock each morning, which was followed by Prime about an hour later. The time in between was when the monks broke their fasts. She would have to hurry if she was going to help Simon prepare the morning pottage.

***

When Gwen reached the priory gates leading into the courtyard, she headed for the brick buildings behind the monastery where the kitchen was located. Hearing a strange sound, she stopped and squinted, but the remains of the morning fog made it difficult to see clearly. Her mother had told her several times to stay away from the monks and from the church, so she usually remained within the confines of the kitchen, the garden, and the dairy. She turned away and continued toward the kitchen when she heard the sound again.

Filled with curiosity, she placed the bucket on the ground

and ran toward the church. She could hear the monks chanting inside as she climbed the steps toward the basket. Something inside moved and mewled, and she imagined a furry little kitten. When she pulled back the burlap, she was surprised to see a baby.

Carefully, she dragged the basket down the stairs and through the courtyard. The church doors opened and the monks headed to the refectory for their morning meal, except for Prior Bartholomew, who walked in the opposite direction toward his chamber. She followed him into the forbidden cloister garden, then down a stone hallway before stopping at a withered door.

Gwen pounded on the faded wooden door. "Prior Bartholomew, I have something to show you!"

Bartholomew opened the door and peered down at her with a puzzled expression. "What are you doing here, Gwen? You know you're not supposed to enter the cloister garden."

She pointed to the basket. "I found a baby!"

The prior's eyes were a mixture of surprise and softness as he took the baby out of the basket and held him. The infant prattled and reached out to pull on Bartholomew's ear.

"Ho, now!" he said with a chuckle while easing the infant's hand away. "That's quite a strong grip for one so tiny." He looked to Gwen. "Where's your mother?"

"At the well."

"Where was he?"

"On the church steps. Can the baby be my brother since I don't have one?"

The prior hesitated. *What harm could come of it?* "I suppose so, at least until his mother returns."

Gwen scrunched up her little face. "Do you think she'll come back?"

"I think so."

Throughout the years a few ruined maids from the village had left the evidence of their sin on the monastery's doorstep, but the combination of maternal instinct and guilt always compelled them to return.

Just once, he wished they wouldn't...

He chastised himself for the selfish thought. The possibility of ever being a fleshly father was sacrificed forever when he swore an oath of allegiance to the Abbey of Cluny. For almost thirty years he had faithfully kept his vow of celibacy, but the strong paternal desire had always been present.

"Does the baby have a name?" Gwen inquired, cutting into his thoughts.

"I don't know."

Her little brow creased as she contemplated various names. "I want to name him Nicodemus!"

"Nicodemus?"

"Like the *farsay* in the Bible."

"Pharisee," he corrected with a smile.

Gwen's intelligence and memory never ceased to amaze him. He had told the girl the Biblical account of the Jewish Pharisee, Nicodemus, several weeks ago when he came across her playing outside by the dairy.

"Very well, our little friend will be named after a wise and faithful man. Nicodemus is a rather long name for one so small, don't you think? Perhaps Nick would be a better choice." As an afterthought, the prior added, "Nick St. John, since he was found on our steps."

The baby let out a loud cry.

"There, there, now," the prior said as he held the child and patted his back. "He's hungry."

Nick kicked his legs and, as the fabric around him shifted, something fell to the floor. Bartholomew was shocked to see a ruby and gold crucifix attached to a heavy gold chain. Gwen picked up the exquisite piece of jewelry and held it out to him.

Bartholomew took the crucifix, then studied Nick with renewed interest. Obviously, he was no son of a peasant girl to be in possession of something so valuable.

Who are you, little one?

Bewildered, he gently placed the child back in the basket. Extracting a key from the pocket of his simple habit, he unlocked the top drawer of a nearby writing desk littered with quills, and hid the crucifix inside of it.

"Come along, Gwen," he said, picking up the basket.

Simon was busily spooning pottage into wooden bowls when Agnes entered the kitchen. "Where's Gwen?" she inquired, placing the two buckets of water she was carrying on the table.

"I thought she was with you," he replied.

"I sent her in here ahead of me. What could that girl have gotten into now?"

"You know Gwen. She probably stopped to catch a butterfly or to pick flowers."

Agnes nodded as she took her place beside Simon and helped him with the pottage. Bartholomew and Gwen entered the kitchen a moment later.

"Good morning, Prior Bartholomew," Agnes said. "I'm sorry if my child is bothering you again. Gwen, what does the Bible say about obedience to one's parents?"

"Mama, I found a baby! See?"

Surprise registered on Agnes's face when she saw the basket. She picked up the child and tenderly cradled him with maternal ease. "Where did you find him?"

"Gwen found him on the stairs of the church," Bartholomew replied. "Then she brought him to me."

Simon scratched his head. "Another foolish girl from the village, no doubt."

Bartholomew decided to keep silent about the crucifix. "After the monks have broken their fasts, I need you to go into town and find a wet nurse for Nick."

Simon and Agnes asked in unison, *"Nick?"*

"Nick St. John," Gwen said proudly.

Nick cried loudly so Agnes procured a clean piece of linen and dipped it into a ceramic cup filled with warm goat's milk. Placing the sodden fabric in the infant's mouth, she watched as he suckled hungrily.

Simon looked to Agnes and said, "We can be back before Vespers if we hurry."

"Take the babe with you, but bring him back here along with the wet nurse," Bartholomew instructed.

278

Simon looked askance at the prior. "Wouldn't it be better to leave the infant in the village?"

"I think it's best if we keep Nick here at St. John's. I have my reasons. Agnes, would you mind helping to care for the child?"

"It would be a pleasure," she replied, kissing the baby's cheek.

***

The Lewes Priory was not actually in Lewes itself, but in Southover by the River Ouse. The town center of Lewes was less than a mile away, and since the day was fair they set off on foot. Accompanying them was an old mule in order to bring back the wet nurse's belongings. Gwen sat atop the mule and pretended she was riding a pony. They sang songs as they walked along the path from the lush, green valley where St. John's was located to the thriving town center.

Simon eventually came to a halt by a small, dilapidated dwelling where one of the town elders lived. Knocking on the door, he called out, "Greetings, Abraham. It's me, Simon."

A gaunt old man opened the door and peered at them. "What's all this ruckus?"

Simon reached into his leather satchel and extracted a small round of cheese wrapped in a large green leaf. "For you."

"The famous goat cheese of St. John's," the old man said as he patted Simon's shoulder in appreciation of the small gift. "What can I do for you, Simon?"

"We seek a wet nurse for the child."

Abraham's eyes slid to Agnes, then the baby.

Gwen said, "Nick is my new brother!"

Abraham grunted and frowned in thought. "Sarah Gunther. Has a child about the same age. Husband abandoned her."

Simon obtained the address, then bade Abraham farewell. It didn't take long to arrive at the neat cottage where Sarah resided. Several chickens scratched and pecked outside. As they approached, a black dog ran out from behind the cottage and barked, sending the chickens scurrying in a cloud of dust and feathers.

The commotion brought a matronly woman to the door. "Who are you and what brings you to my home?"

"We come in peace from St. John's," Simon replied. "We'd like to speak with your daughter, Sarah."

The woman exited the house followed by a plump young woman toting an infant. Simon told Sarah of their plight and their need for a wet nurse.

"You should go with them," the woman said to her daughter. "This is God's doing."

Sarah quietly agreed, then handed her son to her mother while she went about the cottage gathering her few belongings.

"My name is Anne," the woman said. "Please, come in and sit while you wait for my daughter."

Simon, Agnes, and Gwen entered the cottage and settled on wooden stools.

"This will be good for Sarah," Anne said. "Ever since my good-for-nothing son-in-law left her, all she does is cry and mope around the house." She kissed the top of her grandson's head. "I'll miss my little Jeremy."

"You can visit him whenever you wish," Simon said. "And Sarah is free to visit you whenever she wishes."

Sarah came out of an antechamber with a threadbare cloak over her shoulders and a burlap sack filled with her few earthly possessions. "I'm ready."

***

Beatrice turned her head in order to achieve a better view of the hairstyle Gretta had created with her golden locks. Her lady's maid held up a polished looking glass, anxious for a reaction.

"It pleases me," Beatrice said. "Now, please fetch the essence of rose."

Gretta obeyed and applied the sweet perfume to her mistress's temples, throat, and the tops of each breast.

"How do I look?" Beatrice asked nervously.

"A vision of loveliness, my lady."

The brocade tunic worn over her fine linen chemise was deep crimson, which flaunted the creaminess of her porcelain complexion. The low-cut neckline was trimmed with gold braid and exposed a generous amount of cleavage. Gretta fastened a black leather girdle studded with gold around Beatrice's slim waist and allowed one end to dangle down the front of her skirt, in accordance with the latest fashion. Beatrice walked to the small silver chest that housed her jewels, and selected a garnet necklace.

"Perfect," said Gretta. "You're sure to bewitch him."

"Hopefully, I'll convince him, too."

Four months had passed since the birth of her son. Richard had barely spoken to her since the terrible incident, and had avoided her bed. It was a big surprise when he summoned her to sup with him tonight. Beatrice planned to use the opportunity to win back his favor. Not a day passed that she didn't think of the beautiful gray-eyed boy.

She descended the stairs and walked toward the main hall. The torches caused eerie shadows to flicker across the walls of the fortress, which was known throughout England as *Kent Castle*. The Fitzwilliam family had lived in the mighty Norman fortress for many generations; the original structure itself dated back to the days of the Holy Roman Emperor, Charlemagne.

She shivered and longed for the comfort and warmth of her cozy bedchamber. Turning down a long corridor, she heard the fire crackling in the great hearth. Feeling the blood rush from her face due to anxiety, she quickly pinched her cheeks before entering the room.

Richard sat at the head of a table laden with delicacies. Clad in a black leather tunic with matching boots, he gave off a dark, menacing air. The elaborate silver stitching on the front of the tunic was in the form of a lion on its hind legs—the Fitzwilliam family crest. Around his muscular neck was a heavy gold chain boasting a large medallion carved into the likeness of a lion's head. Her husband normally reserved such finery for meetings with other noblemen in order to flaunt his family's noble lineage, wealth, and power. Was he attempting to send her the same message?

His black hair and goatee were both clipped and neatly

281

groomed. The heavy steel sword, which he almost always carried on his person, was propped up against the leg of the chair in which he sat.

"My lord," Beatrice said quietly.

After staring at his wife for a long moment, Richard stood. "My lady," he said, walking toward her with the stealth of a predator.

His eyes devoured her hungrily from foot to head, and Beatrice wondered who had warmed his bed these last four months. A young maid? A hired prostitute from the town? If there were other women, Gretta had neither seen nor heard anything.

He gallantly bent over her hand, his thumb gently caressing her fingers as his lips brushed against her knuckles. Beatrice wondered why he was being overly formal as he led her to the table. A silent servant stepped from the shadows to pull out a seat for her at Richard's right hand. After his lord and lady had taken their seats, the servant proceeded to pour the wine.

Beatrice avoided her husband's smoldering gaze. With a trembling hand, she reached for her chalice and took a long sip. The deep red liquid burned in her empty stomach, but it made her relax.

Richard sensed his wife's nervousness and decided to keep her in that anxious state a bit longer. Edward was plotting against him, and he had to know if his wife was in league with his brother. Up until now, Richard's jealousy and pride had kept Beatrice at a distance, but he couldn't afford any more enemies. He needed to know the truth. *Tonight.*

Beatrice finished drinking her wine and Richard motioned to the servant in the shadows. "More wine," he said, indicating her chalice.

The servant obeyed and Beatrice realized she had better eat something quickly before she lost her wits. Richard's expression was a mixture of suspicion and desire, causing her to blush.

"You look quite fetching tonight," he said. Were it not for his pride, he would have sought her bed months ago. The last words she uttered to him on that fateful day still rang in his ears, however.

She swallowed the wine with difficulty. "Thank you."

The servant stepped forward once again at Richard's urging and filled their plates. Beatrice noticed that the meal consisted of her favorite foods—stewed hare, capons stuffed with chestnuts, and poached quail eggs. Various pies and fruits were also displayed elegantly on polished silver trays.

Finally, Richard said to the servant, "Leave us." When they were alone, he continued, "You must be curious as to why I invited you to dine with me this evening."

"I am," Beatrice replied.

"I wish to propose a truce between us."

"A truce?"

"Aye, but first I need to know something." He paused. "Are you in league with Edward?"

How many times had she sworn her faithfulness to this man? "No, my lord, I have never betrayed you."

He pounded his fist on the table's surface so hard that she jumped in her seat. "I want the truth!"

Her eyelids prickled with unshed tears. "I *am* telling you the truth. You know of my whereabouts every hour of every day. When any male enters our home, you have twice as many servants spy on me. You don't afford me any opportunity to betray you."

He frowned. "Are you implying that you would do so should the opportunity arise?"

"No! I'm only pointing out that you always know where I am and what I'm doing."

"I didn't know your whereabouts when Lord Dunn's wife summoned you in the middle of the night. You simply took flight without my permission!"

"Be reasonable, husband. Lady Anabel was in labor with her first child. The poor girl was terrified and had no female relatives to assist her during the birth. How could I refuse her plea for help? Besides, I couldn't ask your permission because you were away at Court!"

"May I remind you that you spent an entire fortnight in Lord Dunn's castle? I've seen how he looks at you."

"Lady Anabel almost died during the delivery. She was so weak. God's teeth, Richard, Lord Dunn is a valuable ally and your friend."

"I sincerely doubt you spent *all* of that time at Lady Anabel's bedside."

"Actually, you're correct. I also tended to the infant and made sure the household ran smoothly while Lady Anabel convalesced."

Richard crossed his arms and glared at her. "You always have an excuse…"

Beatrice rose so suddenly that she almost knocked over her chair. "Is this why you summoned me? To interrogate me and accuse me yet again?"

Richard also stood. "I want the truth from you. My brother is plotting against me as we speak. In fact, he's been plotting for months. The last thing I need right now is a scheming, adulterous wife!"

"How can you say such a thing?"

"Do you take me for a fool? Do you think I haven't noticed the way Edward looks at you? How his lustful eyes follow you wherever you go?"

Beatrice felt a hot tear writhe its way down her cheek. "You make it sound as if I seek his attention."

"It's not only my brother—there are other men as well. I see it happen every time you and I attend Court."

"Shall I gouge out their eyes with a dagger as I pass? I don't believe the king would appreciate such behavior."

"Don't take such a tone with me, wife."

"I'm merely attempting to reason with you. I have no control over what any man does, including your brother."

"Am I to believe you had no control when you met with him in secret? Were you forced to go out in the middle of the night?"

She gasped in surprise. "How do you know about…?"

"I know *everything*," he retorted icily.

The full weight of his words crushed down upon her like a

pile of stones. Her head began to spin as the pieces of the puzzle fell into place.

"Is that why you took my son from me? Because you thought that…that Edward and I…that we..?" she trailed off, placing her hands on the table for support.

Fearing that she was about to faint, Richard took a step closer to his wife. "I received a message during the afternoon stating that you were going to betray me that night, so I followed you."

"*You*? How?"

His mouth hardened. "*How*, you ask? With the same cunning I would follow an enemy in battle. Unseen and unheard." He paused, his eyes glittering with anger. "I saw you exiting the church with my own eyes. You met with Edward *alone*, in the middle of the night, knowing how much he desires you and despises me."

"Richard—"

"What am I supposed to think, Beatrice? How can I believe that you're telling me the truth when you say you have always been a faithful wife?"

"It's true that I met with your brother in secret." At the sight of Richard's pained, yet oddly triumphant, expression, she added, "But I did it for *you*."

He grabbed hold of her shoulders, forcing her to look up at him. "Explain yourself, woman."

"I thought Edward could stop the dangerous gossip being spread about you. He's the prior of Canterbury, after all, and you're his brother. I remember the days when you two were close."

"That was a long time ago."

"Forgive me for being hopeful."

"Naïve is more like it," he snapped. "The thought of my wife crawling to my brother and begging for his help turns my stomach."

"I fear for you and for the future of our son—*sons*," she said. "If the king pays heed to these vicious rumors, it will destroy you and our family."

285

Richard laughed aloud, but the sound lacked mirth. "And you believe my brother would help prevent such a tragedy from happening?" When she didn't respond, he shook his head in disgust. "Stupid woman! Edward would be thrilled to see me fall from grace."

"Do you honestly believe that?"

"He's ready to step into my shoes and take my title, my properties—and my wife."

"He can't. There is Robert—"

"Robert is still a boy and no match for my brother's cunning. If something happened to me, Robert would not stand a chance against his uncle."

"We have allies. Don't forget that you have several men in your debt."

He balled his hands into fists. "If the king ever accused me of treason, none of our allies would help us. No one would stand against the king."

She sighed, defeated. "I was only trying to help you."

"Instead, you made matters worse for me and for yourself."

She knew he was referring to the child he believed to be a bastard. "Where is my child, Richard? *Our* child?"

Richard walked toward the fire burning in the hearth. The red light and deep shadow across his face gave his profile a sinister appearance.

"Richard," she prompted.

"The boy is safe and alive."

Beatrice sobbed in relief. "Oh, thank God…"

"I'm not the monster you believe me to be," he said defensively. "I wouldn't harm a helpless baby."

"Please, my lord, let me have my son. It's been a living hell for me not knowing where he is or how he fares," she pleaded. "I've told you the truth about my meeting with Edward."

Richard's mouth hardened as he stared at the leaping orange flames. A few days after having followed his wife to her secret rendezvous with Edward, he had been summoned to Court. Edward was also present. Knowing Beatrice would soon give birth, Edward had approached Richard and indicated another pregnant noblewoman at Court. *'Look! Lady Heddington, is as big as a house! It's rumored that her husband is a cuckold. In fact, they say Lord Heddington's nephew is the father.'* At this point Edward stared directly into Richard's eyes with a smug expression, and said, *'These days a man must be absolutely certain that the seed growing inside his wife's womb comes directly from his loins. Adultery can take place so close to home—even with a family member—right under an unsuspecting husband's nose. It's bad enough being a cuckold, but to raise a bastard...'* He trailed off, laughing. Then, with a knowing smile he inquired, *'How is Beatrice, by the way?'*

Richard could still see the mockery and insinuation in Edward's eyes. He regretted not striking his brother then and there. For days afterward, Richard conjured painful images of Edward and Beatrice intimately entwined in bed. It was a scene that played itself over and over in his head—even now.

Then a new thought occurred to him. *What if his brother's tactic was to divide and conquer?* What if the gray-eyed child was truly his and Beatrice was indeed telling the truth?

He stole a glance at Beatrice, whose gaze was also directed at the flames. She was so beautiful, so sensuous; a temptation to any man—especially to Edward, who had lusted after her since they were boys. Richard could never be sure of the infant's paternity. For Robert's sake as well as his own, the child couldn't be raised under his roof.

Suddenly, he demanded, "Did you suspect that Edward was attempting to ruin me when you went to meet with him?"

Her face paled. "No."

"No?"

"I know the relationship between you and Edward has deteriorated since…"

"*Since you chose to marry me,*" Richard said, finishing her sentence.

She looked away. It was true. She had never intended to come between a man and his brother.

"Do you regret the fact that he was not firstborn?" Richard demanded bitterly. "Your father would have arranged your

287

marriage to him instead of me if that had been the case."

Sometimes her husband's jealousy offended her deeply, but she never stopped loving him. "No, Richard. I've never regretted you being the firstborn."

"Edward loved you," he pointed out. "He still does."

"I know."

"If I ever discover that you're helping him to plot against me—"

"I would never do such a thing! Edward once loved you, too. He looked up to you as his older brother."

"I've already told you. Those days are long gone."

"I met Edward in secret because I knew how angry you'd be if you knew I was seeking his help. I had no idea he was behind anything…I didn't think him capable of such treachery. I would never betray you like that."

"Oh? How would you betray me, then?"

"How you love to twist my words, Richard. I would not betray you at all."

"The thought has never crossed your mind?"

"Never." When he cocked his eyebrow slightly, she added, "I swear on my mother's soul."

Richard stared long and hard at his wife. He was still uncertain of her marital fidelity, but he was certain that she was not plotting with Edward. His instincts would have warned him otherwise, and his spies would already have reported any suspicious behavior.

"I believe that you're not in league with Edward," he finally conceded.

"Thank the Virgin," she said, crossing herself.

"As for the other matter…I'm willing to overlook your indiscretion for the sake of our son, Robert, and my fondness for you."

"Richard, I—"

He cut her off, his face stern. "Don't push me. Many a noblewoman in your predicament has found herself out in the cold or forced to spend the rest of her days in a convent. Do I make myself clear?"

"Yes."

After a moment he stepped away from the hearth and reached for her hand. "I miss you, Beatrice," he confessed. "My bed is cold."

"As is mine, my lord," she replied dutifully.

Taking hold of her chin, he greedily plundered her mouth. Her body naturally responded to the kiss as his hand caressed her face and slid down to take gentle possession of her throat. In spite of his suspicion, he could not deny the passion he felt for this woman.

"Please let me see my son, Richard," she whispered between his kisses.

Turning his face away, he cursed under his breath and slackened his hold on her at once.

Undeterred, she prompted, "What can I do to prove to you that he's yours?"

"You ignore my threat and try my patience, Beatrice," he said before striding out of the main hall.

Filled with unsatisfied lust and rage, Richard stormed into the kitchen. His eyes fell on a flaxen-haired girl, and with a toss of his head, he indicated that she should follow him. The girl quickly wiped her hands with a cloth and rushed out of the kitchen with the eyes of the older women burning into her back.

The young scullery maid practically ran to keep up with Richard's long strides as he headed for the privacy of his study. His desire and love for Beatrice had prevented him from satisfying his lust with whores, but every man had a limit and today he had surpassed his. Opening the door, he waited for the girl to step inside before locking it behind her. She stood in the center of the room as he took in her pale skin, full mouth, and freckles. Her eyes were the color of honey and fringed with blonde lashes.

"Come here," he ordered. "How old are you?"

"Fifteen, my lord."

Without another word, he picked her up and set her down on a sturdy desk before untying the laces that kept the top of her linen shirt modestly closed. Unsure of what to do or where to look, the girl kept her eyes focused on the tapestry behind him. He pushed the shirt open, revealing a pair of plump breasts with tiny pink-nipples. She gasped when he cupped one of milky orbs with his hand.

"Have you ever been with a man?" he demanded.

The girl nodded. Had she been a virgin, would he have stopped? Instead of pondering this question, Richard's other hand slipped under the girl's skirt and he hardened with lust. Grasping her thigh, he buried his face in the warmth of her neck. Her hair smelled of smoke and freshly baked bread; comforting scents.

Beatrice's face crept into his thoughts and he froze.

"God's teeth!" he cried.

"My lord?"

He turned his face away. "Cover yourself."

As the girl slid off the desk and quickly began to lace up her shirt, Richard reached into his purse and procured a coin. "Tell no one what has happened here, do you hear me? Not a soul." The girl nodded, her eyes wide. He continued, "If anyone asks, tell them I sent you on an errand to buy cherries—or whatever bloody berries you can find at the market—for my wife. Keep the remainder as payment for your troubles."

The girl's fingers curled around the money. "Now I believe the rumors, my lord."

Richard frowned. "What rumors?"

"Forgive me, I—"

"What rumors?" he demanded impatiently.

"That you're hopelessly in love with your beautiful lady wife," she replied sheepishly.

He grimaced. "Well, for once the rumors are true." The girl wrung her hands, watching him. "What are you looking at? Go!"

She scurried off and he sighed tiredly. Beatrice had cast a spell on him—he was sure of it.

***

In the safety and comfort of her bedchamber, Beatrice poured her heart out to the only person she was allowed to

290

befriend—her lady's maid. "He threatened me, Gretta. I fear he'll soon banish me or force me into a convent if I continue badgering him."

Gretta slowly ran a comb through her mistress's hair in an attempt to soothe her. "May I speak freely?"

"Please do."

"Why not try to find the boy?" she suggested, picking the loose hair out of the ivory comb's teeth. "You're the wife of one of England's most powerful men. That alone gives you a certain amount of power as well."

Beatrice spun around in the chair and took hold of Gretta's hand. "How right you are! All this time I've been grieving over my loss rather than taking action."

Suddenly, she ran to the door to check if any of Richard's spies were lurking about. Convinced that none of his knights were eavesdropping, Beatrice whispered, "I've been living in fear of my husband rather than worrying about the well-being of my son. My mother—God rest her soul—would never have allowed my father to treat her the way that Richard treats me. Unlike me, she was a strong woman." She looked heavenward. "God, I wish I had her courage."

"You're very strong, my lady! Take this evening, for example. You left this room with your head high, even though you had no idea what to expect."

Beatrice nodded. "I must find my son, but how? Richard has every servant bribed—even you."

"Aye, 'tis true that Lord Richard asks me questions and tosses me a coin now and then, but I swear to you, my lady, that I would never tell him anything that would cause you harm. Besides, he only asks about mundane things."

"Such as?"

"Where you go when we leave the castle, who you speak to, if you correspond with anyone, and so on."

"What do you tell him?"

The girl shrugged. "I tell him the truth, my lady. That you're a good wife who never entertains the attention of other men. I tell him that you give alms to the poor and hand out bread to the beggars who come to the door, as every good Christian woman should. Lord Richard smiled when I informed him that you read from your Bible each night before retiring."

"I see, and what about the correspondence?"

"Oh, I told him that you received word from your cousin a few weeks ago and that her children are growing up fine and strong." Gretta stopped speaking and appeared uncomfortable.

"And?"

"Well, your husband left me with instructions…"

"Instructions?"

"Lord Richard is to be notified at once if any letters arrive from his brother.

"I expect you to continue obeying Lord Richard's instructions. I do, however, expect your primary loyalty to be to *me*."

"Of course, my lady. It has always been so."

"Good. I'm going to need your help and your sworn silence in order to find my son."

Someone knocked and opened the door. Only one person had the right to enter without awaiting the lady's reply—her husband. Gretta curtsied and vacated the room, leaving the couple alone. Beatrice noticed that he had a small basket of cherries in his hands.

"I got these for you," he said. "A small peace offering."

She smiled faintly. "It's been a long time since you've offered me such love tokens."

"Things were so much easier back when we were younger, were they not?" He took a deep breath and eyed her doubtfully. "Our courtship was sweet."

"Aye," she agreed, glimpsing the little boy residing within her powerful husband.

"My father's death, my brother's rivalry, the birth of my first son. All of these things change a man." He paused, his eyes sad. "I miss you, Beatrice. I miss how things were…before."

"As do I, my lord."

He placed the basket on a nearby table. "Make love to me the way you used to…like you mean it in your heart."

She took his face in her hands and gazed deeply into his eyes. "I always mean it in my heart, Richard."

They made love for the remainder of the afternoon. Afterward, Beatrice cradled him in her arms, stroking his hair. Richard was a combination of power and vulnerability. The stark contrast never ceased to amaze her, and it never fooled her into believing that he was weak—or easily manipulated.

Do you want to keep reading? FORBIDDEN is available on Amazon.

Printed in Great Britain
by Amazon